'The cloying summer weather suddenly turns to storm and
the city is flooded, spreading an unknown and deadly disease
among its now quarantined citizens . . . The real thrills are in
Brady's depictions of a rich city turning oh so quickly to riot,
robbery and rape . . . But are the rapid, awful deaths the result
of accident or something more sinister? . . . Terrifying . . .
compelling . . . an intelligent, refreshingly different take on
the thriller' *Observer*

'Gripping' *Sun*

'There are shades of *Chinatown* and *Bonfire of the Vanities* about
Brady's third thriller . . . sharp and fierce and clever, full of
horrid little details and appalled by the arrogance of
domination and the weakness of submission. Impressive'
Guardian

'A truly   ou have
ingredie   no idea

THE BLUE DEATH

Joan Brady

**SIMON &
SCHUSTER**

London · New York · Sydney · Toronto · New Delhi

A CBS COMPANY

First published in Great Britain by Simon & Schuster UK Ltd, 2012
A CBS COMPANY

This paperback edition first published, 2012

1 3 5 7 9 10 8 6 4 2

Simon & Schuster UK Ltd
1st Floor
222 Gray's Inn Road
London WC1X 8HB

www.simonandschuster.co.uk

Simon & Schuster Australia, Sydney
Simon & Schuster India, New Delhi

A CIP catalogue record for this book
is available from the British Library

Paperback ISBN: 978-0-85720-432-5
Ebook ISBN: 978-0-85720-433-2

This book is a work of fiction. Names, characters, places and incidents are
either a product of the author's imagination or are used fictitiously.
Any resemblance to actual people living or dead,
events or locales is entirely coincidental.

Typeset by M Rules
Printed and bound by CPI Group (UK) Ltd, Croydon, CR0 4YY

For Lynda
who knows how to fight

1

MISSISSIPPI RIVER: The first day in June

'David.' She didn't get up. She didn't turn.

'You expecting somebody else?'

'I'd know your step anywhere. Are you in your tux?'

'Of course.'

She sat cross-legged on the ground facing the Mississippi. Water disappeared over the horizon in front of her and off to either side: an ocean with a southerly current. 'Hello, my love.'

David Marion studied her back for a moment. Brown hair. Blonde streaks in it. Expensive.

He walked up behind her, crouched, pulled her body against his, let her nestle there a moment, then slipped his hands up under her ears. Meadowlarks make a haunting, liquid sound, unknown outside the prairies; he could hear one in the distance. As for the word carotid, it comes from the Greek for 'deep sleep'. An ancient, largely painless method: abrupt pressure on the arteries in the neck. Even her cry was muffled; she sagged forward in his arms.

Usually the earth around here is so boggy that getting to the river itself takes a pier; the earliest summer – and already the driest one — in Midwest history had changed all that. Earth throughout Illinois baked and cracked. Trees dried into blackened skeletons. Dust devils swirled along roads. He couldn't have buried her if he wanted to. The joke of it was that she'd chosen the spot herself. Nothing daunts the Mississippi, and coroners along stretches of its route get a fee per body. If the coroner at Hannibal fished her out first, he'd pronounce her dead by drowning, stick her back in the river and telephone the coroner downstream at Gilead that she was on the way. Aloysia Gonzaga, named for a saint, had prided herself on her unpredictable life. She might make it all the way to the Gulf of Mexico before anybody realized she was missing.

Only the last few yards to the river were the usual bog. He sank into mud up to his ankles, carried her out into the water until he could feel an undercurrent, held her head under until she stopped breathing, let her go.

After a drought like this, the first rain smells of vomit. Big drops began to fall as he sloshed his way back through the mud. By the time he reached his car, water bucketed out of the sky.

The weather forecast had used the word 'monsoon'. Illinois doesn't have monsoons.

2

SPRINGFIELD, ILLINOIS:
The same day, towards evening

Mayor Jimmy Zemanski twirled his half-moon glasses in front of the mirror. He put them on his nose and peered over them. Which looked better? On his nose? Off it? The question was serious. A mayor should carry his mantle easily. Victory celebrations are an ecstasy, but they don't last. The honeymoon period is over all too soon. Less than six months in, and the *Journal-Register* was whining that he hadn't completed the water utility's $20 million automated control room. What was the matter with people? How could he possibly be responsible for delays in electronic supplies?

The time had come to tell the elite of Springfield that more important changes were on the way. It was going to be a delicate job, one that called for careful handling. He'd thought hard before choosing tonight's reception. He'd laid some groundwork, recruited a couple of allies. Everybody who was anybody in town would be there, an exclusive crowd that included the Governor of the state and the President of the University of Illinois at Springfield. The *Journal-Register* would certainly cover the event. The *Chicago Tribune* just might send a journalist.

Jimmy practised what he was going to say as he combed his hair. His cowlick gave him a boyish innocence even though he was pushing fifty, and he'd been born with the sensual quality all good politicians have, an animal warmth, an ease of movement. He'd grown in stature since the election too. He was aware of that himself, pleased if a little surprised by it.

Rain battered the windows of his lakeside house. The long-term forecast had warned of severe storms throughout the summer, and the wind increased as he eased his Daimler out of the garage; it whipped leaves off trees all the way along Lake Shore Drive. His windshield wipers were struggling so hard that he had to creep through Leland Grove towards Vinegar Hill; he could hardly see the houses that got bigger and bigger until they ended at the iron gates of the Freyl property.

Springfield is the capital of Illinois, two hundred miles south of Chicago, right in the heart of the corn belt; and Freyls had ruled the town for generations. When Abraham Lincoln became President, great-great-grandfather Freyl had gone into business with Lincoln's old law partner, made money fast, started buying up property all over Illinois. He'd kept Springfield's prime site for himself; beyond the gates, a road wound nearly a quarter of a mile through woods and dense overhang, then opened out at Freyl House. Today's head of the family was Atlanta born and bred; she'd designed this Midwest mansion as though to dominate a long-forgotten South of cotton fields and mint juleps. A first floor balcony ran all around it. Two-storey-high columns rose up to a pure copper roof. Arched and many-paned windows looked out on lawns and flowers.

Cars packed the stone forecourt. Jimmy left the Daimler at the rear of the building and dashed to the cover of the veranda, his raincoat over his head. Even so, he was dripping wet when he rang the bell beside the panelled double doors.

'Good evening, Mr Mayor.' The woman who opened both doors to him wore the uniform of the Maid for You professional service. The rumble of conversation from the living room meant there had to be well over a hundred people in there already.

'Hi ... uh' – Jimmy leaned over to read her name tag before turning a smile on her – 'Billy-Jo. Where'd all this rain come from?'

She smiled back, reaching out to take his coat. 'We can certainly use it, sir.'

'Can't I put this coat somewhere myself? It's awful wet.'

She smiled again and took the coat from him.

'Jimmy!' Donna Stevenson cried, rushing out from the crowded room beyond. 'There you are!' She hugged him, kissed his cheek, hugged him again. Even on the least exciting of days, Donna looked like she'd got a finger stuck in a light socket, eyes wide, hair spiky, cheeks flushed. 'I had *such* a good time Friday.'

'Me too,' Jimmy said.

'Did you really?'

He touched her cheek. 'Let's go somewhere quiet when all this is over.'

'Let's go now, Jimmy. Right now. Right this very minute.'

He laughed. 'The dowager first.'

Donna and Jimmy had met a decade ago when he joined the Freyl law firm; she'd just got a job teaching English at the university to pay the bills while she wrote her novel. They'd both been new to town, loved it, made each other laugh, moved in together, worked on her magnum opus together – he gave it the title *Faith Like a Jackal* – talked about getting married. Helen Freyl, heir to the great fortune, stopped everything cold. That summer she'd graduated from Vassar and come home for the holidays. Jimmy took one look and acted as though he'd been hit by a truck. Donna suffered, married a broker instead, divorced him, thought about going after Jimmy again, decided she didn't really want him any more.

Now Helen had gone and married somebody else. This reception was to celebrate the marriage, and Donna found herself quite enjoying Jimmy's misery. She wasn't one to waste an opportunity either. When he'd suggested they meet at the St Nicholas Hotel last Friday, she'd agreed happily, let him buy her dinner, spent the night with him basking in his warmth as she had all those years ago – but at a comfortable distance, emotionally speaking. They hadn't talked much about the marriage. Too painful for Jimmy. Not that she thought it was a good idea herself. Nobody did.

But only old Mrs Freyl, the 'dowager' and Helen's grand-mother, hated the whole idea as much as Jimmy did, and it had become close to a blood bond between them. The groom was not suitable. Not suitable at all. Becky had despised him from the moment she first laid eyes on him; everybody knew that. Even so, this was a town where appearances mattered. The general con-sensus made it imperative to present him on society pages as a new member of the family. From now on, deference would be his due, whether he deserved it or not.

In the marble foyer of Freyl House Donna took Jimmy's arm and led him through French doors into the crowded living room.

High ceilings and deep carpets imposed a sense of calm despite the crush of people. Tall, narrow windows made the storm out-side seem like mere backdrop for brightly coloured dresses, glistening jewellery, black ties. Noise levels rose and fell amidst bursts of laughter as the two of them shook hands with young Mrs Leaplevine (who owned a stable of horses), paid obeisance to Deacon Banning of the First Presbyterian Church (where Lincoln worshipped a century and a half ago), moaned about the weather with the English MP (on a tour of British investments in the Midwest).

It took them a good ten minutes to reach the fireplace where old Mrs Freyl sat in a motorized wheelchair, a couple of people in attendance beside her, a young man at her feet. Rebecca Freyl, Becky to her friends, was at least eighty years old. Even so, a young man at her feet didn't seem incongruous; wheelchair or not, Becky had the grace and confidence that beautiful people never lose no matter how old or feeble they get.

'Hey, what's this with the chair?' Jimmy said to her. He leaned sideways to examine the contraption. It had six wheels and a control panel that belonged on a jet airplane. Becky had been walking only weeks ago when he last saw her.

She looked up at him. 'I'm tired, Jimmy.' Her Atlanta background showed in her voice, long vowels, that soft lilt. What the Southern accent didn't hint at was the iron in Becky's soul; her friends had marvelled at it for years. Who else would have the guts to throw a huge reception for a marriage everybody knew represented a slap in the face?

Jimmy bent down and kissed her cheek. 'Not easy,' he whispered in her ear.

'I'm gratified that you're here.'

'I can't say it's any real pleasure.'

'I'm all too aware of that, Jimmy.' His adoration of Helen had developed into a town joke. She turned to Donna; this time she smiled. 'You too, Donna. I'm very grateful.'

'I wish I were as brave as you,' Donna said.

'No, you don't.' Becky didn't bother to dilute the acid in her response. 'Not even God approves this dreadful union.'

Jimmy chuckled. 'Since when have you been taking note of what He thought?'

'The registry office!' Becky shot back. 'No Freyl has ever married in the registry office. I don't even know where it is.'

'It's in the—'

'I don't want to know, Jimmy. We haven't had weather like this in the history of the county. Doesn't that sound like a comment from the Almighty?'

Jimmy chuckled again. 'At least it's a new theory for global warming.'

Spring doesn't usually bother with the Midwest, but most years have a couple of days that might pass for it. This year, summer had started in March, dried up whole rivers, sucked the moisture out of the ground, turned hundreds of acres of prime Illinois farmland into something all too close to desert. Reservoirs and water tables dropped to record levels. There'd been talk of water rationing for weeks.

Less than two hours ago, skies throughout the state had opened up and started dumping all that water back to the ground at once.

'I really don't get the wheelchair,' Jimmy said as he and Donna left Becky to seek out the guests of honour.

'She took to it the day Helen told her about getting married.'

'Yeah. Sure. That's what you said. But a *wheelchair*. Jesus. Seems to me this thing's really addled her brain.'

At the St Nicholas last Friday, over dinner and in bed after that, he'd nudged Donna — gently, he'd thought — towards Becky's weaknesses. He didn't need her to tell him what a body blow this marriage had to be, but he hadn't realized how much tonight's celebration was taking out of the old woman. Mainly, though, he'd been looking for confirmation of the standard old person's fear that intellect is failing. Donna was one of Becky's inner circle; she assured him the fear was there, and he'd heaved a sigh of relief. He could work with fear, especially with a conjunction of fears.

Becky herself had taught him how. Now he even had a wheelchair thrown in. He needed Becky on his side no matter how dirty he had to fight to get her there.

'I wouldn't be surprised if this marriage finished her off,' he went on to Donna as the two of them pressed back into the crowd.

'Oh, come on, she'll eat the man alive before the year is out. What I don't get is how can Helen bear him. I mean, really. How can she?'

The room was so full of people and so noisy that Donna had to shout, and it was Helen Freyl – the bride herself – who answered the question. 'You never did know how to keep your mouth shut, Donna,' she said.

Donna swung around. 'Oh, God, Helen, I'm *so* sorry.' She flushed. She put her hand over her mouth. 'You shouldn't sneak up on people like that. Don't pay any attention to me. Where is the lucky guy anyhow?'

'How the hell would I know?'

'He's not here?'

'You jackals will just have to feed on somebody else while you wait.'

'Oh, Helen!'

'What about you, Jimmy?' Helen said, turning to him. 'Don't you want to show me you can stick a knife in too?'

Helen's tongue was as acid as her grandmother's. For Jimmy, that only added to the allure. She'd inherited her grandmother's fine-featured beauty, but her eyes were the same intense green as her father's, dark outline around the iris too. Her father had been blind. The pathos of the similarity moved Jimmy deeply. His own eyes misted over, and his mind struggled against mooncalf phrases like 'the fragile bravery of springtime bloom'. Just looking at her caused him acute physical pain.

He opened his mouth to speak, closed it again, frowned, then turned towards the buffet in the dining room without a word.

His face said it all. Donna watched his back retreat from her; he'd live the rest of his life making an ass of himself over Helen. Nobody could doubt it. That wasn't the only threat to his security of mind either. Jimmy had always had more than a streak of the con man in him, but bedding Donna just to dig into Becky's weaknesses was too crude. It hadn't fooled Donna. If he actually followed through with what she figured he had in mind, he was going to be in trouble.

She relished the prospect.

Becky Freyl's table was always special. She created the menus herself, and this time her selection included a whole loin of pork, a platter of smoked salmon, sliced Chateaubriand in a rich wine sauce. There were salads and asparagus, a vegetable pâté, strawberries, cakes, champagne.

Donna joined Jimmy as he was filling his plate. She gave him a warm smile and began filling her plate too. A crowd gathered around them as they ate. He couldn't say he was used to celebrity yet, but six months of it was enough to let him know that he wasn't going to tire of it quickly, and there wasn't anything like it to ease the pain of Helen's marriage. The other guests laughed at his jokes even though he knew they weren't as funny as all that. He made a delicate reference to Becky's wheelchair and the vagaries of an old lady's memory. They stayed with him: a promising sign. He led them step by step – another reference to Becky's frailty, a snippet of insider information – to the future he was planning for Springfield. The platters on the table began to empty.

He told them that he knew they saw the problems he faced. Who could miss them? Today's monsoon-like storms would continue to alternate with the kind of drought that the town had just experienced. All the forecasts said so. Fresh water was getting scarcer and more expensive every year. On top of that, he'd inherited a city in debt like so many cities all over the world. He'd studied environmental reports and financial balance sheets, talked to experts in town planning, city finance, water supply and global warming.

All this was true.

He said he'd come reluctantly – very reluctantly – to the conclusion that selling off public utilities to a private corporation was the only solution that would approach these problems: get money in city coffers without taking it out of people's pockets and ensure that Springfield always had an abundant water supply.

This wasn't, well, strictly true.

Worse, it was an open defiance of Becky as well as a direct U-turn on his campaign promises.

Jimmy's predecessor had been a Republican who'd proposed selling off Springfield's water utility towards the end of his term. As soon as he did, Jimmy seized his own chance. Democrat? Republican? What's the difference? Jimmy had become a Democrat for the simple reason that Becky was as staunch a Democrat as they come, and she was where the power lay. The morality of water rights interested him even less, but in Illinois, Democratic party policy opposed privatizing public utilities. So he took Becky to lunch, made her laugh, told her he'd run for mayor expressly to defeat the measure. He knew he could win if she backed him. He also knew that she'd really enjoy the challenge of designing a campaign that could beat an unbeatable Republican.

'You have little leverage, Jimmy,' she'd said to him. People had grown used to the incumbent, the face, the voice, the manner. 'You'll have to use fear.' That's when she'd taught him the techniques he intended to use on her tonight to get her support.

She'd designed his campaign to concentrate on the dangerous irresponsibility of commercial businesses: services and safety — always first out of an industry spokesman's mouth — always bottom priority on the balance sheet. She'd coupled that threat with the imminent threat of terrorist attack on public utilities. Jimmy had gloried in all of it, and the terrorist stuff had turned out to be easy; work on the control room for Springfield's water supply was almost finished despite the slurs in the *Journal-Register*.

Privatization was more problematic.

His view of it took its abrupt about-face during a long lunch with an industry representative. A week later he'd banked a substantial sum — an 'enterprise inducement' the representative had called it — in carefully laundered investments.

As for Becky, he couldn't really see her objection. Why would somebody that rich care about the price of water? Or about toeing a party line? But he knew he'd never get her to change her mind in private. She liked consistency and despite the bonds between them, she didn't like him enough to abandon it without asking questions he wasn't prepared to answer, questions that might even touch on things like 'enterprise inducements'. Presenting his change of heart to her was what he'd practised in front of the mirror before he left for this party, and he was confident that in the presence of her guests she'd give way if he presented it to her exactly as he'd rehearsed it.

'Jimmy's been invited to the White House,' Donna said as she replenished the salmon on her plate.

'Really?' said one guest. 'To discuss privatization?'

'For a reception?' asked another.

'Dinner,' said Donna.

Jimmy gave her a quizzical glance. 'Hey, Donna, isn't a reception enough? Even for a novelist?'

'Dinner? Jesus. Will you get to meet the President?'

'You mean, will *he* get to meet *me*?' Jimmy said.

The guests burst into laughter. One of the men slapped him on the back: 'That's our Jimmy.'

'I bet they seat you right beside him,' said Donna.

Jimmy winked at her, and she smiled back. The invitation was for a reception; he would be one of many hundreds. But Donna's exaggeration was the kind of joke they'd enjoyed in the early days. The only trouble with it was that Becky could skewer him with it; he was about to diffuse the threat by letting the others in on it when a silence fell over the room. All eyes were on the man who'd just come into it; he wore a bedraggled tuxedo, muddied right up to the knees.

'Jesus Christ, David,' Jimmy said. 'How the hell can you be late to your own wedding reception?'

3

SPRINGFIELD: A heartbeat later

David Marion had grown up behind the thirty-foot high walls of South Hams state prison, sent there at the age of fifteen for the murder of two men: life without the possibility of parole. The only reason he stood here in Becky's living room was that her son Hugh, Helen's father, had organized his release on the basis of a technicality.

Hugh had taught him in prison before that and taught him well, taking him from grade school all the way through a bachelor's degree; in those days, prisoners could still study under the University of Chicago's extension department. When David got out, Hugh went to work with the same zeal, fighting to civilize his protégé, make him into somebody Springfield could accept. In that, the failure had been total. Except for Helen of course. The rest of Springfield expected remorse, humility, gratitude in ex-convicts, especially in one so extraordinarily blessed as to have entrée to their circle. David showed them none. Not for Hugh's largesse nor for the tolerance it required from them. They saw hatred in his eyes. They saw contempt. They sensed something feral, predatory, held back by only the thinnest of threads.

Hugh had died three years ago. Everyone here assumed David was responsible – they'd openly accused him of it – just as they assumed he was responsible for every other suspicious death in town, every mugging, every theft. They'd also assumed Hugh's death would rid them of this ill-bred imposition on their society.

Helen's marriage had come as a terrible shock.

'Where the hell have you been?' Jimmy demanded of him now.

'Wading in the Mississippi,' David said. Hugh had gone to Harrow and Oxford. Among other things, he'd taught David grammar; along with it, David had picked up the faint English accent that Hugh Freyl had never been able to rid himself of.

'Why would you do a dumb thing like that?'

'I like big rivers.'

'I didn't think you'd show up at all,' Helen said. 'You must be starving, and this lot have eaten everything in sight.'

At just that moment, two caterers entered with fully replenished platters. Amusement softened the planes of David's face. 'You tell too many lies,' he said.

'The best food is always in the kitchen. Come with me.' She took his hand. 'You look wonderfully tousled. Was it warm?'

'Was what warm?'

'The Mississippi.'

'Very warm.'

'Did you wade far?'

'Intent on rescuing me, are you?' Black hair, black eyes, a scar that ran down the cheek and in under the chin. The eyes always had the slightly swollen look of a child awakened from sleep. A very American face despite the accent.

'You think I can?' Helen asked him. She'd never been in love before.

'Nobody else is going to try.'

'My dear friends' — she turned away from David to face the guests — 'I trust you will excuse us for a moment. We have important business to attend to.'

The room burst into an excited babble as soon as the two of them disappeared from it.

Out in the kitchen, in the midst of a flurry of caterers, Lillian Draper washed platters and bowls in a sink full of soapy water. For thirty years, Lillian had been Becky's maid and companion. She was much, much more to Helen. As far back as Helen could remember, Lillian had been the mainstay of her life. It had always been Lillian's warmth she craved, not her parents'. It was Lillian she'd run to with a scraped knee and cried out for when she woke with nightmares.

Lillian's approval was the only approval that really mattered to her. 'We've come out to get your blessing.' Helen embraced her, kissed her cheeks.

Lillian laughed. 'You got it months ago. What you all doing in here with me now?'

'Running away.'

'Think you can hide behind my skirts, huh?'

'You're not threatening to turn us out, are you? Poor David's starving.'

Lillian eyed David's sodden tux. 'Try some of that pumpkin salad afore they take it out.'

'Any good?' David asked.

'I made it myself.'

He took a plate and spooned some salad onto it. Lillian dried her hands on her apron, opened Becky's vast refrigerator, took out a Budweiser.

'Beer?' he said. Beer was the only alcohol he really liked, and he liked it in the can.

'I knew Miz Freyl wasn't going to order none, so I brought a couple from my house. A bridegroom ought to get what he wants to drink at his own wedding party.'

'That what you said to her?'

'She don't scare me.' Lillian opened the Budweiser and handed it to him.

He took it from her, then ate a bite of the pumpkin salad, nodded appreciatively. 'How's he doing?'

'How's who doing?'

David took a swig of the beer. 'I hate it when smart people act stupid.'

'Little Andy done time before.'

'That's not what I asked.'

Lillian had her own children to tend to as well as Helen. She had seven of them, and she'd fought hard for them all. Little Andy was the youngest, bright, rebellious, charming – and right now serving five years in David's *alma mater*, South Hams. South Hams had been a 'State Prison' when David entered it. It'd become a 'State Penitentiary' about halfway through his sentence. Only days after he left it, the state sold it to a private corporation. There'd been many changes, including its label; these days it was the South Hams State Correctional Facility. Little Andy had ended up in it for hacking into the university's financial records. Among other things, he'd shifted the state legislature's appropriations for combating sexually transmitted diseases among students into an account that belonged to a local whorehouse. The university was not amused.

'Oh, David' – Lillian's intake of breath was uneven – 'I really don't know how he's doing. He's always been trouble, but mostly he don't seem worried about telling me what's wrong. Kinda likes it. Figures he can shock me. This time? He won't tell me nothing.

But he don't look well. He got bags under his eyes, and his eyes is bloodshot. He's all skinny and kind of twitchy.'

'You think he's on drugs or something?' Helen asked.

'Miss Helen, I ain't sure what to think.'

David finished off the salad in a few bites. 'I could ask some questions,' he said.

'Yeah?'

'When you visiting next?'

'A week from Sunday.'

'Pick me up on your way.'

'David, you sure about that?' She took his plate from him.

'Why wouldn't I be? Nice ride in the country.' He gave her a wry glance. 'Get me away from this town for a couple of hours.'

She smiled. 'About ten o'clock? Now go on you all. Go on out to your party. Shoo, both of you.'

On their own, the elite of Springfield were just plain scared of David, but in groups – as they were tonight – they felt comfortably in control. While he and Helen were in the kitchen, plays on the name David Marion made the rounds of the party. Marion Federal Penitentiary was the harshest maximum security prison in the country, and David's prison career had begun with a brief stay there. Then there was Maid Marion of Sherwood Forest. Even better was Marion Donovan, who'd invented disposable diapers in Indiana. Or Marion Davies, Hearst's gold-digging girlfriend, especially since the Freyls were by far the richest family in this very rich capital city.

At a normal gathering, these conjunctions wouldn't cause much of a ripple. But at tonight's wedding reception they bound the guests in a Masonic brotherhood, and it was a brotherhood Jimmy knew he could exploit if he needed it. Their initial response to his project encouraged him; as soon as David and Helen's re-appearance put a stop to the mockery, he steered the group around him back to the virtues of privately owned water utilities.

They picked up themes and industry buzz words as he introduced them, got quite excited about it, started talking over one another.

'... such a sensible investment ...'

'... efficiency and cost effectiveness ...'

'... the money we'll save!'

'We need new solutions,' Jimmy was saying. 'We can't move ahead without—'

'Negotiating already, are you, Jimmy?' Becky's wheelchair wasn't altogether silent, but Jimmy had been so wrapped up in his adoring audience that he'd missed it. The alarm on his face told Becky all she needed to know.

'Negotiating?' Jimmy said. How in hell had she learned about that? Were there no secrets he could keep from her?

'He says privatization is the wave of the future,' said Donna, sensing combat ahead.

'So is crime in cyberspace,' Becky snapped.

What was it about the woman that turned grown men into naughty schoolboys? Despite himself, Jimmy lowered his eyes. 'We got some pretty complex problems here, Becky.' He launched into what he'd been rehearsing in front of the mirror. 'Sometimes senior citizens don't quite understand—'

'The problem is exceedingly simple.' Becky's interruption was sulphuric. 'You promised people one thing, and suddenly you veer off toward the opposite without so much as a warning shot.'

'He's been invited to the White House to discuss it,' one of the guests chimed in. 'He's going to have dinner with the President.'

'Fiddlesticks,' Becky said.

'Oh, God, that was a joke,' said Jimmy irritably. 'A reception is an enormous honour, enough for anybody.' But he could feel his support slipping, and he knew he had to unite the others or lose the edge he'd gained.

'Hey, David,' he said, giving his half-moon glasses a twirl, 'you got an opinion about this? Going to tell us what you think?'

David and Helen stood beside a bank of windows, rain beating down hard against the glass. David was easily the tallest man in the room; his edgy belligerence created an area of calm around her. They were deep in conversation, and the small gestures — tilt of head, movement of shoulders — revealed a physical intensity so palpable that to watch was to trespass.

'Hey, David!' Jimmy repeated with a laugh. 'I'm talking to you.'

David dragged his gaze away from Helen. He still had the beer can in his hand. 'What do I think about what?'

'Putting out bids for Springfield Power and Light.'

'That the electric company?'

'The water's what interests us at the moment.' Jimmy gave his glasses another twirl.

'You're kidding.'

'Why would I do that?'

'Well, I have to admit that I can't think of a more boring subject to have an opinion on — at least not offhand.'

'This isn't about water,' Becky said. The sulphur hadn't left her voice. 'It's about abuse of power.'

David crushed the beer can in his hand, flicked it into a waste-paper basket a few feet away and shook his head in disbelief. 'Nothing to do with me.'

Then he turned his back and walked out of the room.

4

GILEAD, ILLINOIS: The next day

Aloysia's body began its river journey just north of Hannibal, Illinois, where they have the best catfish in the state.

Europe is an upturned saucer; its rivers run down to the seas at its edges. The Mississippi scores America right down the middle, a furrow through the cheeks of a gigantic ass. Which is apt really because the river is shit-brown. Completely opaque. Midwesterners call it 'The Big Muddy', and it's a superlative place to lose a corpse even though it's so slow its surface looks like a lake. There's lots of traffic on it, commercial boats, pleasure boats, barges, towboats. When any of these makes a sharp change in direction, it throws off a huge wake that collapses back into the water and boils deep down beneath. The Mississippi is different down there; it's a maelstrom of sandbars, crags, hidden currents. The undertow that caught Aloysia managed to jet her seventy miles straight down here to Gilead in a mere twenty-four hours.

A record time for any floating object without a driving force.

5

SPRINGFIELD: Monday
after the reception

At Municipal Center West, a soulless building in glass and concrete, an executive session of the City Council was about to begin.

Six of Springfield's ten representatives — a carefully chosen majority of its aldermen and alderwomen — sat around a table with Mayor Jimmy Zemanski. Behind him, the Stars and Stripes, the white Illinois state flag and the deep blue city flag shared the wall with a projection screen that read:

The G.R.A.N.D. canal

'Where's La Gonzaga?' he asked the alderwoman beside him.

'Aloysia? God knows.' The alderwoman gave him a crooked smile.

'Allo ... Who?' An alderman asked her.

'Allo-wish-ah. Aloysius Gonzaga was a saint.' She turned to Jimmy again. 'Our saint is being "unpredictable", I bet. You're not relying on her, are you? I'm told she has a new secret lover these days.'

'Another one?'

'Um.'

'Anybody know who this time?'

'Nope.'

'What about the last one?'

'No idea.'

'Christ.' Jimmy shrugged irritably. But he didn't feel irritated. This was going to be fun, and Aloysia's presence would only distract from it. He called the meeting to order, dispensed with the preliminaries. 'You've all signed a Non-Disclosure Agreement,' he began, 'and since this is a private session, let's forget protocol. Interrupt at any time. All of us need to know just where questions arise. Our subject' – he gestured at the projection screen – 'is the G.R.A.N.D. Canal, just the "Grand" for short. I know. I know. You've heard all about it. But I bet you don't have any idea how it's being built or why it's getting built so quickly. And I bet you'd be surprised to hear that the reason you don't know is that the entire project is covered under the US National Security and Patriot Acts and the Canadian National Security Law. That's how come you had to sign those Non-Disclosure Agreements.'

Official secrets: Jimmy had them in the palm of his hand already.

'The Grand canal isn't any ordinary canal,' he went on. 'It's literally the greatest engineering project in the history of mankind. Panama? Suez? The ancient pyramids? Put them out of mind. The Grand dwarfs every one of—'

'Remind me what the initials stand for,' came the first interruption.

'The Great Recycling and Northern Development Canal,' Jimmy said. 'Even sounds impressive, doesn't it? For sixty years – *more* than sixty years – engineers have been dreaming of bringing water all the way down the east coast of Canada and deep into the United States. This dream is about to become a reality.'

A huge body of water in bright blue flashed onto Jimmy's screen, a Landsat satellite image taken at five hundred miles up. Jimmy pointed to a line – nothing natural looks so straight – that ran from one side of the water to the other, cutting off the lower half. 'What you're looking at here is the longest dyke in the world. It separates Canada's James Bay off from Hudson Bay and the Atlantic Ocean. Very soon James Bay in Quebec will be the biggest freshwater reservoir in the world.'

'It'll never work.' The protest was querulous. 'It's got to be salt water if it's off the Atlantic. We can't drink that.'

Ordinarily Jimmy wouldn't have liked the tone. But for this question? Perfect. 'The process *is* kind of magical. Dr Gonzaga promised she'd explain it, but since she hasn't arrived, I'll just have to do my best. Look at the rivers here and here and here' – he gestured at the screen – 'I can't even remember how many of them empty into James Bay, but together they amount to enormous volumes of glacier water every single day. Only fresh water comes in. The overflow gets sluiced out into the ocean through a system of locks, taking salt with it. In a surprisingly short time, you have a freshwater reservoir. It's not a new technique. It's not untried. A hundred years ago, the Dutch cut off a bay named the Zuider Zee, and the rivers pouring in made a reservoir just like the one we're making. Now the Zuider Zee is one of the Seven Wonders of the Modern World. Next to the Grand? Ladies and gentlemen, it's Lilliputian. We're making history here.'

The excitement around the table was an audible rustle.

Jimmy's next images tracked the Grand canal down through Quebec to the Canadian border: canals, locks, pipelines, dams, power plants that carry the water to the Great Lakes, flush the fresh water through them and supply American states as far east as Pennsylvania and as far west as Arizona. 'Since Illinois is at the tip of Lake Michigan, Illinois will be the first American state to benefit.' Jimmy paused, then gave them a half-puzzled, half-worried smile. 'And here's something to surprise you: Springfield will be the first city.'

The table erupted in a babble of consternation.

'I know, I know,' he said. 'We're two hundred miles inland. Why not Chicago? It's right on the lake. Or Kankakee? Or Bloomington? Look, guys, there always has to be bad news with the good news. And the bad news is the real reason why you had to sign that Non-Disclosure Agreement.' He drew his breath in sharply. 'Lake Springfield is dying.'

Lake Springfield supplied the town's water, had been purpose-built to supply it, had supplied it for nearly a century. This time the rustle around the table was fear.

'But where can we get our water from?'

'How can a lake just die?'

'What are we supposed to do? Dig wells?'

Jimmy held up his hands to quieten them. 'Water levels go down every year. They used to come back up. Not any more. Everybody in the Midwest is in trouble, but nobody's as bad off as Springfield. The simple fact is that right now we're barely coping at all. The need for this Canadian water is absolute.'

Jimmy had to hold up his hands again to quieten them. 'Yeah, sure, there are huge amounts of money involved. But guess what? It turns out that men and women with spades and shovels are faster and more reliable than machines if you can get them properly organized. I know it sounds crazy, but the progress is phenomenal. Absolutely amazing. I've seen it for myself. And the government is subsidizing it. But as I say, there are huge amounts of money involved, and there's no way we aren't going to feel the pinch ourselves. But how? Tax increases? Vast hikes in water bills?'

Jimmy knew that when questions like that came out as rhetorical, his audience belonged to him. This was how things worked when Becky Freyl kept out of it. It was how they should work. More than that: it was how they would work from now on.

'The only acceptable solution,' he said, 'is to persuade private investment to bear the brunt of the cost. We have no choice, ladies and gentlemen. We sell our publicly owned utility to a corporation that's going to pay us handsomely for it and then take over the burden of financing the Grand canal.' He paused. 'It's either that or our town dies of thirst.'

6

TAZEWELL COUNTY, ILLINOIS:
Friday of that week

Twenty-five buses, all of them white, all of them scrubbed clean — all of them with the words 'South Hams State Correctional Facility' on their sides in jazzy, friendly looking letters — travelled in a convoy along one of those straight roads that score the cornfields north of Springfield. A few miles later they stopped at a razor-wire fence with an armed guard. A sign near the gate read:

WARNING
EXTREME DANGER

Army practice range
Guard dogs
US Government Property
NO
TRESPASSING

The guard at the gate checked each of the bus drivers and waved the convoy through. The tarmac turned into an unpaved road.

The buses juddered on for half a mile, then pulled up in a stretch of cleared land and turned off their engines.

The front door of the foremost bus opened. Two men in black climbed down, bodies padded out with bulletproof vests, truncheons, ammunition belts, knee protectors. Both of them carried 12-gauge shotguns; both led police dogs.

'Inmates, move!' the biggest of them shouted.

The next person to emerge wore pyjamas in wide, horizontal black and white stripes just like the movies of olden-time chain gangs. He wore chains too, but not the kind that connected him to the next man; cuffs around both his ankles chained his legs loosely to a belt around his waist that incorporated an alarm and an electronic tag. Some forty men followed him, heads shaved, the insignia '1B' – their work detail number, first bus, B shift – printed in foot-high letters across back and chest. They formed two lines. The other guard distributed hard hats.

'March time. March!' the guard shouted

The inmates snapped into orderly rows, and the first in line began the chant: 'Left. Left. Left, right, left.' The others fell into lock step behind him.

'Hell, yes, I'm dirty . . .' the chanter went on.

'Hell, yes, I'm dirty . . .' The others echoed.

''Cause I piss dirty.'

''Cause I piss dirty.'

'Got to get my life straight . . .'

As the prisoners marched forward, the door to the next bus opened. Its guards climbed out, followed by its prisoners and its march chant.

The prisoners of Work Detail 1B continued across the open space to a set of wooden stairs that led down into a ditch as wide as a four-lane highway at the top, sides sloping downwards to a path at the bottom some twenty feet below ground level. The afternoon air was steam-bath hot, so clogged with moisture that five minutes' exposure was enough to glue clothing to backs and legs with sweat; as they descended, other prisoners struggled up the steps, filthy, soaked through, stumbling with exhaustion, harried by their own guards and their own chanter.

'Stuff our boots and mop our brow . . .'

'Stuff our boots and . . .'

'In line, inmate!'

Work Detail 1B began in the depths of the ditch. Behind them, the excavation stretched as far north as the eye could see. To the south – in front of them – the ground rose in tiers up to the surface, each tier a yard or so above and a couple of yards wider than its predecessor, each as long as a football field. Within ten minutes of the buses' arrival, the site was swarming with men – nearly a thousand of them – wielding picks, shovels, spades, pushing wheelbarrows, manoeuvring rocks out of the ground.

Work Details 18B to 22B were at work on the top ground, where the earth was easiest to dig, although today the whole area was muddy from last night's downpour. The excavation went only a metre deep, but occasional mudslides interrupted even here. Mud made the labourers slow. Their foremen – prisoners too, but skilled, privileged, wearing orange jumpsuits instead of black and white stripes – shouted at them to step it up, get moving. The guards in black were irritable, the dogs edgy.

About halfway through the shift, one convict sat down abruptly on the ground. Police dogs barked, straining at their leads.

'Up, shithead,' one of the guards called out.

The convict dropped his head into his hands.

'You make me come over there and get you up, you're gonna regret it.'

The convict didn't move.

The guard slogged over to him, poked him with the butt of the rifle.

'I ain't feeling so good,' the convict said.

'You're going to be feeling a fuck of a lot worse if you don't—'

The convict threw up, a projectile vomit that caught the guard in the crotch. The other inmates turned to laugh.

'You motherfucker.' The guard struck out with his rifle, catching the prisoner on the cheek, knocking him over. 'Come on, motherfucker. Up!' The guard kicked him. 'Up, you fuck. Get *up*!' The inmate pulled himself into a tight foetal position.

'Hey, Quack, maybe you'd better take a look.'

The inmate who clanked over was older than most of the others, slender build, a little stooped. He knelt down, checked the prisoner's pulse, felt his forehead.

'Get him back to work,' the guard said.

'I don't think that's very likely, officer.' Quack's voice was gentle, educated, respectful.

'Sure it is.'

'I'm afraid not.'

'Come on, Quack, you telling me he's not faking?'

'Clammy skin, vomiting . . . oh, and some pretty serious diarrhoea.'

'Jesus, is that what the stink is?'

His voice was so loud that several inmates swung around to look. 'Get back to work!' the guard ordered. The inmates seemed puzzled, abruptly distracted by the sick man; they moved towards him as a group. The guard fired a warning shot into the air. Other guards snapped their rifles into position. The dogs' barking was frenzied.

7

SPRINGFIELD & KNOX COUNTY, ILLINOIS: Sunday

Helen had found an old garage to convert on Van Buren Avenue just beyond the fringes of Springfield's rich west side, a rare artefact that still carried a weather-beaten sign:

Otto's of Springfield
Auto Repair & Service
at the right price!

Otto had been out of business for over thirty years now, and the area had degenerated around him. Not that Van Buren Avenue had ever had any claim to sophistication; there wasn't much of it, and it ended in the desolation of Route 54, a four-lane highway from nowhere to nowhere, with only the Irish Barrel Head Pub and the Saigon Café to keep it in business. All Otto's windows had been broken for years. Dried weeds sprouted out of its stolid 1930s roof and its tarmac forecourt.

Helen adored the seediness the way only the rich can adore what's poor and ugly. As for David, he'd grown up on Springfield's east side and saw no romance here, but he'd tried the west side for a while. Not a good idea. Van Buren Avenue provided a no-man's-land between the two ways of living.

Helen had cajoled him into supervising the reconstruction of Otto's. She hadn't had to cajole too hard. He quite liked the idea, and he wasn't without experience. He'd spent his last years at South Hams trying to escape; he'd made it once, got close a couple of other times, spent many months in solitary as punishment. Attempts to find a way had involved learning everything he could about locks, alarm systems, electricity, plumbing, prison architecture and construction; he liked techniques. When he got out, Hugh Freyl had put all that learning to use; with Hugh's backing, David became a designer and installer of security systems. He'd been good at it. Companies from Evansville in the south of Illinois to Rockford in the north hired him. That's how he'd ended up owning a house on the town's west side.

All that screeched to a halt with Hugh's death. Within days of it, the Springfield elite accused David of murder. They'd done it publicly too and hadn't stopped until he'd found them somebody else to fit up for the job. That only made them hate him more; they were still certain he was guilty, and now he'd cheated them of watching him put away for good. Nobody within two hundred miles would hire him. He lost his house, his car, his bank account, became homeless, drifted across the country, not knowing what else to do but shut out the days and nights – black stuff, China white, Georgia homeboy, Mexican Valium – and wait for something to happen. That something had been Helen, and the life of luxury she offered.

Only an idiot would turn it down.

Besides, he loved her. Not that he'd ever tell her so.

Nine days after the wedding party at Becky's, he paced back and forth in front of Otto's, waiting for Lillian, cigarette dangling from his mouth, smoke curling up into his eyes. Dumpsters were in place for demolition to begin tomorrow, scaffolds around the house-to-be.

'David!' Lillian pulled up beside him in a Toyota that Becky had given her. 'You look like one of them wild cats at the zoo. What you doing pacing like that? It's too hot. Where are them storms the forecasters keep talking about? Come on. Get in this car.' He did as she told him. 'Ain't you gonna say "Good morning"?'

He gave her an irritated glance, rolled down the window of the air-conditioned car, flicked the cigarette out into the road.

'David, I sure do appreciate you coming with me today.'

'I might not learn anything.'

'I know that.'

'If I do, you might not like it.'

'Ain't nothing I can do to help my boy when I don't know what's hurting him. How you gonna get inside? They don't allow no ex-cons in there.'

'I haven't properly introduced myself, have I?' He gave her a bow of the head. 'I do apologize. My name is Gwendolyn. Richard François Gwendolyn. I'm Canadian.'

'Oh, yeah?'

'Yeah.'

'Gwendolyn, huh? Like a girl?'

'Exactly.'

'David, them guards is gonna know who you is.'

'No they're not.'

'They ain't gonna let you near the gates.'

He shook his head. 'They're all new.'

'You can't know that.'

'It's in the papers.'

'You believe everything you read?'

'Every word.'

The sale of South Hams State Penitentiary to private enterprise had changed more than the prison's name. Private accountants had gone to work at once trimming off the fat. They'd contracted out prisoners *en masse* as a labour force and charged all running costs to a government happy to brag of 'rehabilitation' and 'work experience'. They'd got food per prisoner down to fifty cents a day, a third of the cost of feeding the dogs that guarded the grounds and accompanied inmates on work details. As for the guards, it had taken only months to break the union; the entire staff had walked out, refusing to work for the pittance the accountants offered. Standards for new staff were low, training minimal, turnover high.

Lillian started the engine, stopped it, shook her head. 'David, you got a passport or something saying you're this Gwendolyn guy?'

'Passport, driver's license, life story – even a national insurance card. Born in Peterborough, Ontario (Canadian Graduate, The University of Toronto).'

'How'd you get *that*?'

'You don't want to know.'

She shook her head again, chuckled to herself, restarted the engine. 'I never been to Canada,' she said.

'Me neither.'

'You're joshing me.'

'Nope.'

South Hams State Correctional Facility was north and west of town. Thirty-foot high, grey stone walls rose out of flat farmland that stretched away to the horizon in every direction. David hadn't been back since his release.

'What's going on here?' he said as they approached it an hour later. 'Boy scouts?'

A series of fences made a large enclosure at the base of those walls. First came a boundary fence, then a high, chain-link periphery with coiled razor wire on top, then two internal chain-link fences, also with razor wire on top. Row upon row of khaki-coloured tents big enough to sleep a hundred people clustered inside.

She snorted. 'They calls it "boot camp". Andy calls it "Tent City".'

'Yeah?'

'You build you a prison out of bricks and mortar, it gonna cost you a hundred million. One of these? Just an itty-bitty million, and you just picks it up and moves it when you want. They musta brought fifteen hundred guys down here six weeks ago. Maybe more.'

'All this for the canal?'

'Little Andy says the foremen was trained in one of them internment camps near Joliet.'

Details in the media were scanty, but anybody connected with South Hams knew that without chain gangs, the Grand canal would never get built. Leasing prisoners as labour had spread across America; they were making the country competitive again. Why farm out shoemaking, clothes manufacture, computer assembly to China and Indonesia when American prisoners could do it for less at home?

'You done wash all your clothes like I told you?' Lillian asked David.

He nodded. 'I always do what you tell me.'

'You don't got no dollar bills on you?'

'Like I say, I always do—'

'Okay, okay.' She handed him a wad of dollar bills she'd washed last night and dried in the oven.

One of the few areas that the prison's new administration had beefed up was security. The first time Lillian had come to visit Little Andy, the ion sensor that scans visitors had come up with the reading that she was carrying cocaine. They sent her away, told her she couldn't come back for forty-eight hours. When the forty-eight hours were up, the scanner said she was carrying methamphetamine. They banned her for thirty days. She'd burst into tears right there in the main control room, and somebody else's mother told her that most likely the problem was the dollar bills she was carrying; every single dollar bill in circulation has traces of drugs on it.

And few people came to South Hams State Correctional Facility without dollar bills in hand. The vending machines in the Visitation Room took only dollar bills, and only visitors could use the machines. Fifty cents a day for food kept the prisoners hungry, and the prison canteen – where inmates could buy toothpaste, candy, cigarettes – charged three times the price on the outside. No food could be brought in. Guards were forbidden to make change, and visiting hours were always over lunch.

After the thirty-day ban, Lillian's planning had been meticulous, and she'd never had trouble again. There was no trouble this time either.

Nor did the scanner pick up anything on Richard François Gwendolyn.

The Visitation Room was large. Blue and yellow plastic chairs faced each other in rows bolted to the floor. A prison guard wearing earphones walked up and down like an invigilator at a college entrance exam. David used sixteen of Lillian's one dollar bills to buy two coffees and two sandwiches.

'They're making a fortune here,' he said, handing a paper cup and a sandwich to the convict he'd come to visit. 'You don't look as healthy as I remember.'

'I'm a little tired, that's all.' He was the one they called Quack, and his freckled face showed an old man's tracery of lines, although he wasn't much over forty. 'You know, I never thought I'd see Richard François Gwendolyn again,' he said. 'It was such a surprise to get your letter — *such* a pleasure. It's been so long I can't even remember where we met.'

'University of Toronto,' said David, who had no idea whether Quack had been to Canada any more than he had.

'Aha!' said Quack. 'You mean the Hole.'

'Precisely.'

'"Introduction to Management", wasn't it?'

'That's the one.'

'Rather a dull course, I always thought.'

'Did you? I remember it fondly.'

'That's because you went into a more interesting line of business than I did.'

David had started trafficking in drugs in South Hams while Quack actually was studying a course called Introduction to Management, although not at the University of Toronto; he was a Chicago graduate, known as Brendan Kolb back then. These days he served as the prison's medic. Not that he was a real doctor either — he'd picked up medicine behind bars — but prison suited him. A prison medic has respect. Outside, he'd been just one more middle management nobody going nowhere, doing work he despised.

'This won't be the only visit, will it?' he said to David.

'Now you're going to tell me you miss me.'

'Of course I miss you. How could it be otherwise? I don't have anybody to talk to, and you're so' — Brendan searched for the word – 'so unpleasant. But I have four men in the ward recovering from something in the gut. Dunno what it is. Makes me nervous when I got four down with something I don't understand. I need to keep a careful eye on them.'

'Flu or something?'

'The medical service says gastroenteritis. I'm inclined to think food poisoning.' Medical Services Direct was a subsidiary of the St Louis-based parent corporation that owned and operated South Hams as well as dozens of other prisons in the Midwest. They consulted only by telephone; in all his years as a prison medic, Quack had encountered only two real live doctors and a handful of nurses. The subsidiary that had just taken over the catering was the one that had reduced the costs to fifty cents a day per inmate. At that price, food poisoning was the most likely explanation.

'I wish I could persuade myself it was my charms that brought you here,' Quack said, 'but I know better than that. Is there something you want me to do for you?'

'Skinny black kid.'

'There's no shortage of them in here.'

David tilted his head towards Lillian, who was sitting at the other side of the room opposite her son.

Brendan glanced over at him, then frowned. 'Oh.'

'Looks like I might need a favour.'

'He doesn't look like your type.'

'Doesn't he?'

Quack gave a sad shrug. 'I wish I'd had a mother like that.' He frowned again. 'She can't want to know. You going to tell her?'

Twenty years ago, Brendan Kolb had been a 23-year-old case of arrested development, obsessed by the desire to shock his hippy parents out of the belief that he was the world's next Lenin. Lenin said, 'Religion was the opiate of the people': Brendan became a Catholic. 'Superlative cover,' they laughed. They churned out leaflets against the 'pigsty of capitalism' and the corporate exploitation of workers; he majored in business administration for no other reason than to outrage them. Result? They bragged to their friends that he was preparing himself to 'work from within'. They marched against Barbie dolls' degradation of women; he used his college education to get a job with Barbie's manufacturer, Mattel, Inc. Result? His parents glowed with pride about his revolutionary self-sacrifice.

So one night, he turned on the gas in the fireplace in their bedroom while they slept. They never woke up. A Mattel lawyer defended him – not with much enthusiasm – but Brendan's own shock at what he'd done was so obvious and so pitiful that it kept him off Death Row. As for life imprisonment, he saw it as no more than he deserved.

Within hours of his arrival in South Hams, he was gang-raped in front of a yelping crowd. When that was over, a group of cons played poker for him. Education had a far higher value in prison than it did outside, and he was a prize worth some effort. The Shark won. Brendan became his wife, his punk, his bitch. It's a lot easier to break a man than people think. Within a couple of months, he'd lost a quarter of his body weight.

David was eighteen years old then, barely more than a boy. They were both murderers, but David had beaten his victims to death. He'd been a 15-year-old illiterate at the time; his state-appointed defender had entered a guilty plea without even interviewing his client, and he'd escaped lethal injection only because of his age. Back then the state of Illinois required schooling for convicts that young. That's how he'd met Helen's father,

Hugh, eminent Springfield lawyer, educated in England, paying what he felt was his own debt to society by teaching the likes of David to read and write. David turned out to be a star pupil, even picking up those traces of Hugh's accent. At South Hams State Prison, egghead punks like Brendan commanded high prices; straight-up eggheads-to-be like David were aristocrats.

Brendan used to envy David from across the yard. The boy seemed to shimmer with anger. A single breath of air, a single mistimed glance, a single word out of place, anything at all was going to be a match tossed in a gas tank. One day – it was one of those slow-motion terrors – Brendan saw David heading towards him. Not just towards him either: for him. Right up to him.

'You got a college education, right?' David said. Brendan just stared. The faint English accent and the absence of prison argot were far less terrifying than a gaze that didn't waver and conceded nothing. Only cops stare like that – and crazies. 'Come on. Talk to me. You got a college education or not?' Brendan gave a quick nod. 'That include algebra?' Another quick nod. 'You want out of the Shark's bed?'

To Brendan's enduring shame, he began to cry.

'You'll have to kill him.'

Once the wife of an inmate, always the wife of an inmate. That was prison law. Unless you killed your abuser with your own hands.

Brendan shook his head. 'I just can't. I just ...' He gestured helplessly at his emaciated body.

'Suppose I trade you for it,' David said.

'Trade?'

'Yes.'

'Trade what?'

'The Shark for something I want.'

'What could I have that would be of any interest to you?'

'Algebra.'

'Algebra?' Brendan almost shrieked the word. 'You want . . . *Algebra*? Why?'

David's gaze took on a harder edge. 'I don't want a wife if that's what's worrying you — especially such a scrawny one.'

Brendan hadn't believed him. He knew it wasn't true. But what choice did he have? David was younger and stronger. If he wanted the Shark's meat, he'd have it. That too was prison law.

A week or so after that meeting, the Shark was dead, and Brendan was moved to David's cell.

As soon as the guards left, David said, 'I got requirements.' Brendan had learned more than he wanted to know about sexual perversions during his time with the Shark, but he was sure there was lots more to learn.

'Um,' he said in a tiny voice.

'I like things neat.'

'Things . . .?'

'I hate disorder.'

Housework was a wife's traditional duty in prison just as it is on the outside. 'You want me to . . .' Brendan trailed off.

'Yeah. Right,' David said. 'I keep my stuff neat, and you got to keep your stuff neat.'

'What about your stuff?'

'Like I say, I keep it neat. You leave it alone.'

Brendan glanced at him, glanced away, glanced back, then said tentatively, 'It's algebra you have trouble with?'

The lesson began at once. It didn't take Brendan more than ten minutes to recognize how quick David's mind was. In ten minutes more, he'd established that David's trouble wasn't algebra at all but fractions. David had long ago trained himself not to smile, but it was clear he was delighted.

Before Brendan even knew he was going to say it, he'd blurted out, 'You killed a man just to find out you didn't know fractions?'

'You complaining?'

'No, no. Oh, no. Not me.'

'What then?'

'I don't know how to survive in this place,' Brendan said.

'I already talked to the guys that need talking to. You get trouble, you come to me.'

'Why?'

David turned that unflinching gaze on him. 'I get a kick out of it.'

'But why . . .' Brendan shook his head and sat down on the edge of the cement shelf that served as his bed. 'Why are you helping me?'

David surveyed him. 'Look at you. You're a bag of bones. I seen guys go like that. Another month and they'd be zipping you in a black bag. It was you or the Shark.' There was a pause, a shrug. 'The Shark didn't know algebra.'

David and Lillian didn't speak until they were almost halfway back to Springfield.

'You gonna tell me something or not?' she said.

David lit a cigarette, took a deep drag on it. 'South Hams is a hard place.'

'You're lying to me, David Marion.'

'I haven't said anything.'

'That's what I mean. And don't you look at me like that. Ain't nothing you can do to make me scared of you. I just talked to my boy. He lost maybe twenty-five pounds. His hands is shaking. He's scared out of his wits. He got five years to serve, and he ain't gonna make it alive.'

'Kind of little for his age.'

'They beating up on him?'

'That guy – the one I was talking to – he'll take care of it.'

'He ain't nothing but little hisself.'

'The kid does what he says, he'll start feeling better.'

They drove in silence for another few minutes. Then Lillian said, 'He's HIV positive, ain't he?'

'How would I know something like that?'

'David, I love that child. You're not supposed to love one child more than the others. I tried. I prayed 'til my knees was sore, but Little Andy, he's like my brother Joshua. There's just something about him that makes my heart turn over.'

The outskirts of Springfield are a tangle of highways that loop over each other, then straighten out as though the looping had all been just a game, town planners at play over a drunken lunch, hurriedly covering up their traces for the wife and kids at home.

'If he's sick,' David said, 'he needs a diagnosis and a medication protocol. He won't get better care in Springfield. In my day, even the Warden went to Quack.'

'"Quack"?'

'That guy.'

'He can get him medicine?'

'I said, "if he's sick". Maybe he isn't.'

'How do I pay him?'

'Don't worry about it.'

'David, I got money. I can get it to him some way or other. I don't want you paying for nothing.'

David stared out at the road ahead. 'There's a company called Ward that makes paper model skeletons for about forty dollars. Send him one of those.'

'Forty! That won't buy nothing. I'm supposed to send a skeleton to this here Quack? How come a doctor needs a skeleton?'

'Not to Quack. To the kid.'

'What is it anyhow? Some kind of voodoo or something?'

'You have objections to voodoo?'

'David, I don't got no objections to nothing. You wants a skeleton. You gots a skeleton.'

8

SPRINGFIELD: Lunchtime
the same day

'This is very inconvenient,' Becky said as Helen put a tray down on the table in the conservatory. It was a simple lunch – cold grilled chicken, potato salad, iced tea – that Lillian had prepared yesterday because of today's trip to the prison.

Becky's gardener grew vegetables in this conservatory all winter long. In summer as now, when Illinois boils, air conditioning made what should have been an oven into a cool garden, a few discreet single roses but mainly greenery, fruit trees for shade and scent: peach, apricot, blood orange, lemon.

'It's a picnic,' Helen said.

'Picnics are for children.'

'Come on, Grandma, you like picnics.'

'I hate picnics.'

'I don't know why. You sure as hell sound like a six year old. Wheel that thing over here.'

Becky's wheelchair could go up and down steps. She could raise and lower the seat. She could even speak to it to tell it what she wanted it to do, but she did that only in private. She used its sophisticated electronics to manoeuvre herself to the table and allowed Helen to help her into a dining chair.

Becky didn't really need the help. She didn't need a wheelchair either, much less one so technologically advanced. But how else was an old woman to protest such a marriage? How dare Helen present her with a fait accompli? Becky had decided guilt was the only effective card to play, but it was a hard one for her. She hated dependence. She hated weakness and passivity. She feared them, was furious at the whole world for failing to provide a dignified alternative and furious with herself for being unable to wrangle one all on her own. Worse, Helen didn't seem much concerned, which meant she suspected the ruse. That meant Becky had to redouble her efforts, hone her role. And that meant she had to use the wheelchair far more than she'd planned, and she could feel the damned thing actually making her weaker.

And that meant it was all David Marion's fault. 'Little Andy's going right down the same path as that ... that ...' She could hardly contain her fury, couldn't bring herself to speak his name. She picked up a drumstick, bit into it savagely.

Helen knew perfectly well that there was only one person who affected her grandmother this way. 'Oh, for Christ's sake, leave David out of it.'

'What on earth made that boy think he could hack into a university computer? Why would he want to?' Becky had always liked Little Andy. He had charm as well as a quick wit. She'd helped Lillian get him out of scrapes more than once, hired his lawyers, paid his bail, written letters of recommendation.

'Probably just to prove he could. Lillian keeps telling him there's nothing he can't achieve. Maybe he took her too literally.'

'You just like people who get into trouble.' Becky's voice trembled with frustration. 'You mistake bad behaviour for spirit.'

'Grandma, shut up.'

'Shut up yourself. Haven't you done enough damage already?'

Helen jumped out of her chair, ran to Becky, knelt down, put her arms around the old woman, nestled her head into the bony shoulder. 'I don't mean it, Grandma. It scares me to think I could hurt you. I wouldn't do that for the world.'

Becky stroked Helen's hair. 'I know, darling. I know.'

Helen had been sharp-tongued even as a little girl, an only child overindulged by her parents. Now that they were both dead, Becky indulged her too; this kind of bickering had become almost a ritual between them. True, David had added an alien ferocity to it, but Helen was learning the ropes of the Freyl estate. She was a business partner in all but name. She knew Becky was proud of her. She was proud of Becky too, and in general – David aside – they enjoyed each other's company more than anybody else's.

'You know what I don't like about David?' Helen went on, still nestling into Becky's shoulder. 'I go out for a walk, and everything I see reminds me of him. I sit down to work, and a part of my brain stays on him no matter how hard I scold myself. There I am, at a desk when he's off somewhere else, and I can—' She broke off, frowned, let out her breath. 'I can *feel* that voice on my skin, even though he's not within miles of me.'

'When I was a girl, we called that sex.'

'I keep trying to think his thoughts. I want to remember what it was like when he was playing around garbage cans with his friend Tony, and I probably hadn't even been born yet. Fuck the iced tea. I need a glass of wine.' Helen kissed her grandmother, got a bottle from the kitchen, opened it, poured it, handed a glass to Becky. 'You know, Grandma, sometimes I don't even want to touch him. I just want to look.'

'You're not in love with this man, Helen. You're obsessed by him.'

'Haven't you ever been in love?'

'Of course.'

'But not like this?'

'Certainly not.'

'Not even with Grandpa?'

'I was twenty-eight years old. Back then, a woman of twenty-eight had to get a move on, and I was determined to marry "up".'

Becky's family in Atlanta had been shabby genteel; the Freyls were landed American aristocracy, and the young Rebecca had been brilliant as well as beautiful, the same high cheekbones she'd passed on to her granddaughter, the same deceptive fragility, the same dimples. She'd worked her way through the University of Georgia and gone on to manage *Vogue* magazine in New York.

As she and Helen ate lunch, Helen eased Becky away from her fury at David and the wheelchair by probing for details of what it had been like to come to Springfield as a bride, an outsider who'd captured the most eligible bachelor in town. Becky confessed that she'd had to work hard for acceptance. She'd set up a card catalogue with an entry for everybody she met. She cross-referenced family members and colleagues. She kept track of jobs, hobbies, political opinions, what kind of liquor they drank, what foods they preferred. She sent gifts for birthdays and flowers for anniversaries. In two years, her dinner table was the envy of all the other wives.

It was only a start. She'd arrived in Springfield without illusions. She knew it was a provincial backwater, but she could see no reason why it should stay that way. She didn't bother with the men; tradition dictated that they concern themselves with little beyond power and liquor. She set up a women's group she called the Springfield Arts Society; its stated aim was to bring culture to a cultural wasteland. They discussed literature, history, art, how to dress, how to furnish a room. But Becky's ambitions were far greater than that. She and her Society began work in a ladylike, behind-the-scenes way to restore the Old Capitol building to the glory it had been when the town's most famous son, Abraham Lincoln, had argued cases in it, served as a representative in it, lain in state in it as an assassinated President.

Back in those days, it had been a grand structure on a charmingly small scale, a classic of American political architecture: high dome, fluted columns, wide sweep of steps, proportions straight out of ancient Athens. Town planners in search of extra office space had hoisted it up and shoved a ground floor beneath it, a hugely expensive undertaking that turned it into a clumsy caricature of what it had been. The Arts Society raised the money – state-wide campaigns in schools, shops, newspapers – and then supervised the restoration work itself. When the building shone as it once had, the Society turned their attention to a university, an art gallery, a museum, even a symphony orchestra. Over the decades, a state capital of yokels and under-the-table deals grew into a sophisticated population with a tourist industry centred around the Old Capitol and Lincoln himself.

The women had dabbled in politics right from the outset. They'd campaigned for Democratic candidates at all levels of government, knowing full well that they'd never achieve their aims without some leverage and some very persuasive lobbying. In general they'd chosen well. They'd fought hard for John F. Kennedy, and they spotted Barack Obama early, worked to make him a senator, quietly manoeuvred him into announcing his candidacy on the steps of the building that had been their first triumph half a century before.

Nobody could say either the Kennedy or the Obama election had been easy. But neither had been anywhere near as difficult as Jimmy Zemanski's.

'Jimmy Zemanski!' Becky said, turning her outrage on him as she and Helen reached this point in the conversation. They'd finished lunch. They'd finished the bottle of wine and were drinking the coffee Helen had made. 'I ought to put him over my knee and spank his bottom,' Becky ranted. 'How dare he try to privatize our water? He's a Democrat! I backed him precisely *not* to privatize. Am I supposed to be that dumb? Is that what he thinks? He didn't even have the guts to warn me first, much less consult me. He has no idea what he's getting us—'

'David!' Helen cried, jumping up from the table.

Becky turned her chair around, expecting to see her beloved granddaughter wrapped around the man, but they stood facing one another at arm's length, a physical distancing that made the bond between them look too intense to risk public exposure. The sight of it made Becky feel physically sick. 'Even Jimmy would have made you a better match,' she said bitterly.

'And a good afternoon to you too, Mrs Freyl,' David said, inclining his head in her direction.

'How can you say these things, Grandma?' Helen burst out. 'What's the matter with you?'

'I speak my mind, Helen, just as you do. I do what I can do. When I can't, I complain. Please don't smoke in here.' David was taking a pack of cigarettes out of his pocket.

Helen laughed abruptly, took the pack of cigarettes from David, lit one, drew on it. 'You're the one who's met her match in Jimmy.'

'I beg your pardon?' Becky said.

'You threaten. You rant. But it's only talk. Kid stuff. Anybody can do that to anybody.'

'I see. And what would you have me do?'

'If you're so eager for action, get the bastard. You want to slap somebody down? Slap Jimmy. You got him elected: you take him down. Leave David alone.'

'It's stupid for you to smoke,' David said as they left the house. He took the cigarette from her mouth. Not all that long ago, Helen had had surgery for a collapsed lung.

In Becky's eyes, the lung too was David's fault. They'd been rammed in a car chase. True, Becky had hired the man doing the chasing, and she'd hired him for the express purpose of 'protecting' Helen from David. The man had perhaps been a little overzealous in carrying out his duties, but David was the one driving the car with Helen in it. The impact had collapsed her lung, and he had escaped without a scratch.

Which in Becky's eyes made him responsible for the entire episode. The doctors' warnings to Helen had been severe: cigarettes were out. For good.

'Christ!' Helen said to David. 'You too! What is this? Beat Up on Helen Day?'

But she let him take the cigarette out of her mouth.

Helen loved explosions even though they terrified her; they made her feel alive. That's what David did too. They were one of the reasons she'd become a physicist: Dr Helen Freyl, MA from Vassar, PhD from Columbia University with the rare accolade of a published thesis. She'd wanted to know why things blow up, what were the preconditions, what made matter unstable, what triggered it, gunpowder, dynamite, nuclear fission, nuclear fusion. Her studies had become her insight into David, and she sensed an explosion ahead. What terrified her about this one was that David might end up dead himself because of it.

She walked with him in silence – carefully because her chest was still sore from the crash and the surgery that had followed – to where they lived, a house they'd rented just beyond the garage they were converting. Helen longed for the work to be finished. She didn't care one way or the other about the temporary house, but she knew that David hated it. It had Venetian drapes and gilded portraits. A lifetime in prison doesn't equip a person to process so many things. They lie in wait for him, rebel against him, as capricious as people.

As they approached the front door, she could feel the tension rising in him. 'Let's go for a drive,' she said. 'David?' She touched his arm.

'What?'

'Let's go somewhere.'

'I've already been somewhere.'

'You haven't driven my present yet.'

Maybe objects and David didn't go well together, but cars were different, crash or no crash. An English 1952 Riley is a real gangster car, sleek and 1930ish, exciting, dangerous. She'd given him one as a wedding present, a right-hand-drive model, still wearing its British plates.

The planes of his face relaxed. 'You got somewhere special in mind?'

'I don't care. Anywhere. Just go.'

The Riley's doors opened backwards, hinged behind front seats that still gave off a hint of leather smell. It wasn't air conditioned, but the heat of the day diminished as they headed south away from Springfield. They didn't talk, and towards evening the quiet became so intense that Helen heard a meadowlark across the cornfields just as David had heard one on the banks of the Mississippi.

She leaned over and kissed him on the cheek. 'Let's really go somewhere. I want to see Lake Michigan from the Wisconsin side. I have an ancient photograph: my great-grandfather floating in a tyre, white walrus moustache and all. He was a lawyer just like Daddy.' She was fairly sure they were heading south. Her sense of direction was poor at best, but the sun was disappearing off to her right, and they'd been driving this way since they set out – which meant Wisconsin had to be hundreds of miles in the opposite direction. 'We'll find a cottage. Cool off in the water. If Grandma can play guilt trip games with a wheelchair, we can play hookey. Log fire in the evening. Couple of cans of beer for you. Bottle of wine for me. Just the two of us.'

David was already swinging the car around. 'I can't swim.'

'Not at all?'

'Not so as you'd notice.'

'Dog paddle?' she asked.

He gave her a wry glance along with the nod. 'Not even that in more than twenty years.'

'David Marion! What about after you got out? No? Not once in the whole time? Why?'

'Shame. Pride. Maybe envy. Sloth.'

'The hardest part is just staying afloat.'

'Is it really?'

'I'll teach you the rest.'

They drove through the night, taking turns at the wheel. By the next morning, they were deep into Wisconsin and as though to justify Helen's inspiration, the very first cottage they looked at was perfect. There were trees behind it. Lake Michigan stretched out in front of it. Waves lapped gently. There was nobody for miles around.

They spent their days there doing what newlyweds are

supposed to do, neither able to let the other out of sight for more than minutes at a time, meals interrupted by scrambles to the large bed, swimming lessons cut short in shallow water and again on soft leaves beneath the trees.

9

SPRINGFIELD: Monday, a week later

'Isn't a week long enough?' Becky almost shouted her frustration down the telephone to Helen, who lay on a blanket on the front porch of the cottage, her naked body entwined around David's. 'I need you here.' Helen had called as soon as she and David set out for the lake and every day since then. 'The Springfield Arts Society needs you.'

'What for?' Helen said. 'I'm not even a member of the damned thing.'

'It was your idea.'

'What was?'

'Slapping Jimmy down. He didn't even consult me. How dare he?'

'I was just angry, Grandma.'

'You were right. I will do it. We will do it.'

'I thought the Springfield Arts Society was all about culture.'

'Day after tomorrow. Three o'clock. Donna's house.' Helen didn't reply at once. 'Helen?' Becky said. 'I mean it. I need you.'

Helen turned sideways to grin at David. 'I'll be there on one condition.'

'Granted, whatever it is.'

'I get to bring David with me.'

There was a long pause. Helen rearranged herself over him, touched his nose (broken at least once in his life) with the tip of her finger, then followed the scar that ran down his cheek and under his chin.

'The Springfield Arts Society is for women,' Becky said tartly.

'I thought it was about keeping brains active. David's brain needs keeping alive as much as mine does – not that I'm not too interested in brains at the moment. That Society of yours is getting old. About time for some new blood, don't you think?'

'I can't change the rules. You know that.'

'You can change anything you goddamned please.' Helen's hand had crossed the expanse of David's chest and reached his ribs. She smiled down at him and said into her mobile, 'Grandma, I'm not letting this man out of my sight.' She hung up before Becky could reply.

Back in Springfield, Becky looked irritably at the telephone in her hand. What could the girl mean? Why hadn't she even said 'goodbye'? David would be insolent. He would be impertinent. It was all very inconvenient, and yet Helen had been as right about Becky's power to change the Springfield Arts Society rules as about the need to slap Jimmy down. When Becky had set up the Society all those years ago and written its constitution, she'd limited membership to women her own age, either from old Springfield families or married into them as she had.

Years passed, and the group began to get stodgy. Becky suggested they draft in their daughters to liven things up. They didn't want to. Becky 'reinterpreted' the constitution she'd written, and invited their daughters herself. When mothers and daughters together resisted the inclusion of outsiders, Becky again 'reinterpreted' the constitution. A middle-aged organization needed fresh blood, just as Helen said an old one did; and Springfield's population had come to include highly respected university families.

The more Becky thought about slapping Jimmy down, the more she thought that perhaps Helen was right yet again. Perhaps the Springfield Arts Society was only the place to begin. This was a different species of activity. It was a protest. The Arts Society had never gone in for that kind of thing before. But who would be most useful?

The first person she thought of was Aloysia Gonzaga.

Aloysia was on loan from Oxford University to Springfield's branch of the University of Illinois, giving graduate lectures on hydrology and microbiology. Which is to say she knew about water. The trouble was, Becky disliked the woman. Despite the exotic name, Aloysia was English, niece of some of Hugh's friends. Becky disapproved of the English: 'a dirty people who can't manage their economy' was her tart assessment. She didn't like their accents either; they sounded 'snippity snippity' to her. The trace of one in Hugh had always distressed her, and the touch of it in David Marion was yet another reason for recoiling from him. But that was the least of Aloysia's flaws. She fell into that category of people Becky called 'monkey smart'. Aloysia was always on the lookout for weaknesses she could exploit. She built hidden agendas around them and delighted in springing them on people.

She was the one who'd warned Becky that Jimmy was negotiating with private water companies. She'd had one of those little cat-smiles as she said so. Becky knew that cat smile; she'd seen it before. It's why she'd believed the warning, and it's also why she'd been too outraged to ask for details. Now she needed the detail. All of it. Why had the Englishwoman passed this information on to somebody she knew would make Jimmy's life as difficult as possible because of it? What was there in it for her? Why had Jimmy told her so much of his plans in the first place?

She dialled the number, but all she got was an answering machine. 'You have reached Dr Gonzaga. You may leave a message if you wish, but I'm afraid you'll have to wait your turn for an answer.'

Irritating woman. She had those blonde highlights in her hair too. Becky didn't approve of women dying their hair. Except discreetly of course, as she did herself. She called Donna. Donna was in the English department, nothing to do with the sciences, but she'd volunteered to show the Englishwoman around; Donna was proud of Springfield, and she knew it well.

'Aloysia?' Donna said. 'Word is, she's gone off somewhere with her new lover.'

'Fiddlesticks. She's teaching this summer at the community college. I arranged it myself. What's her cell phone number?'

'Afraid she doesn't have a cell, Becky dear. She talks about English eccentricity a lot. She did tell the college she might not make the first week or so.'

'She didn't tell me that. Email?'

'Never answers it. I'd forget her, Becky darling.'

Donna herself became the first draftee into the protest.

She'd warned Jimmy against running for mayor in the first place. She knew him too well. The temptations were going to be more than he could withstand. Not long before Hugh Freyl died, he'd nearly got himself into trouble forging signatures on Powers of Attorney to make payments into somebody else's political fund. That could have been serious. He'd have lost his licence to practise law; he could even have ended up in prison. He'd come to Donna in a panic; she'd advised him to do nothing, and in the end nothing had come of it. She'd given Becky only the vaguest sense of what had happened for the simple reason that the signature Jimmy had forged was Hugh's.

And the last time he'd forged it, Hugh was dead.

Donna objected to the idea of admitting men to the protest, but the moment Becky hung up, she thought, 'Well, why not men?' They'd been excluded at the beginning because they wouldn't have been interested anyway. In half a century, that had changed; culture wasn't sissy stuff any more. Besides, this was politics, not culture, and men had their uses. For example, the journalist Becky could be surest of was a man called Chuck Finch: little courage but easily pushed where she wanted him to go. A male professor of something might be helpful too. Aloysia was a professor. So were several Springfield Arts Society members. But Becky was a hard-line realist: a woman professor didn't carry the weight a man did, no matter how many feminists pretended otherwise. There was the added attraction that a stray male or two would camouflage David.

The thought of new faces brought to mind another woman. This one had come to the door campaigning for Protect Marriage Illinois; Becky had too little interest in sex to see why anybody would campaign against gay marriages, but she sensed intelligence, tenacity, imagination in Kate Bagalayos. The trouble was, the woman was Filipino. Becky disapproved of Filipinos even more than she disapproved of the English. As a people, they'd allowed dictators to rob them blind: clearly a national weakness of spirit. But individuals occasionally buck a trend, and she sensed that Kate Bagalayos was one of them.

Such a pity that the woman lived on the east side of town, where Lillian lived. Nobody in the Springfield Arts Society lived there.

10

SPRINGFIELD: Ten days later, the last Thursday in June

Becky banged the gavel she'd bought well over half a century ago for her first Springfield Arts Society meeting.

'Ladies! Gentlemen!' she called out. 'I think we should begin.'

The electronic controls of her wheelchair allowed her to raise herself so that hers was the highest head around Donna's dinner table; it was an impressive dinner table, a single diagonal slice out of the heart of a very old ash. Donna's university salary wasn't too impressive, and so far her writing had come to nothing beyond a hefty manuscript that got heftier every year; without Jimmy's input, she couldn't get the final chapters to gel no matter how much work she put in. But he'd helped her through her divorce from the broker; the settlement had been very generous, and as part of it she'd kept this house in one of Springfield's most exclusive areas. Becky had advised on the refurbishment, which included this table and an antique Aubusson carpet all the way from Paris. The view from Donna's dining-room windows wasn't up to such competition. It should have been full of flowers, but the rain of the wedding reception had stopped as abruptly as it had started. After that, the ground had baked in a renewed heatwave. Even well-tended gardens like Donna's were as wilted as spinach in a frying pan.

Donna sat next to Becky at the head of the table, pen poised to take minutes. At the opposite end, David slouched beside Helen, one elbow propped up on the ash surface, the rest of him stretched away from it in a bored contempt that was a palpable force in the room. Becky had expected precisely this insolence and worried about how she'd handle it. She hadn't anticipated the effect though. In a few minutes, he'd united the dozen others so strongly against him that she knew she'd get wholehearted support for anything she wanted. The trouble was, she didn't know what that might be.

'As you know,' she said to them, 'our mayor plans to sell our water out from under us, and we have to find a way to stop him. I'm depending on you to have lots of ideas. First though, I want to introduce you to Kate Bagalayos. She's the only person here who has some hands-on experience with protest movements.'

Kate was mid-thirties, unfazed at finding herself among the elite of Springfield, black hair piled on her head in braids, a bright, quick face too wide to be pretty, skin a dark tan colour.

'Gosh, it's good of you to come,' Donna said, her frenetic enthusiasm widening her eyes so that white showed all around the iris. 'I mean, what are we going to do? Jimmy means no harm, but I know him. He loves money and meddling in things and he gets overenthusiastic. I'm afraid he's' — she glanced around at the others — 'well, I'm afraid he's trying to pull a fast one.'

She and Becky had discussed all this in detail. Donna hadn't told Becky about Jimmy's probing into an old woman's fears. She'd known exactly what he was looking for, not that he'd made any attempt to hide it from her: insinuate himself into Becky's mind, plant doubts and uncertainties that didn't exist, shake her confidence so he could manipulate her into backing him – or at least not opposing him. But Becky's circle of friends had become Donna's circle; they were the people who'd comforted her when Jimmy fell in love with Helen. Loyalty wasn't a concept Jimmy knew much about; Donna did, and his desertion of her still burned. She'd lost the man who'd become her muse and her contributing editor as well as the only man she'd ever loved; she was almost as eager as Becky herself to see him fall on his face.

But she kept losing hold of where Kate fit into the picture. 'I can't remember what Becky said you were—'

'Oh, God, Donna,' Helen interrupted with a laugh, 'she's the one who wants to ban gay marriages.'

Kate turned to Helen and nodded. 'That's me. You're Helen, right? Just got married yourself, didn't you?'

'You really care who goes to bed with what?'

'From the looks of your choice' – Kate leaned forward and scanned David – 'I don't think a single soul in the Protect Marriage Illinois campaign would object, certainly not me.'

'That doesn't answer my question.'

'I'm Catholic.'

'So?'

Kate gave her a wry smile. 'You haven't met Father Antonioni.'

Except for Kate, all these people had been at Helen and David's wedding party; they were rich people with maids and Ferraris. Sitting around a table with a Filipino from the east side was distinctly unsettling. A chunky surgeon with hands that belonged on a stevedore dismissed her with a frown.

'I'm not really clear why we shouldn't allow a few changes at Springfield Light and Power,' he said. 'My water bill is sky high.'

'I resent having to pay for water at all,' said the woman sitting next to her, tall and thin, curator of the Rebecca Freyl Museum of

Art. 'When I think how cheap it was when I first arrived here . . .' She trailed off with an irritated shrug.

'Oh, yes. I do understand.' Becky was at her most sympathetic. 'And I know Jimmy has told you privatization will improve all that. I find it interesting that he can say it to you with a straight face.' As soon as Helen had suggested slapping him down, Becky had begun intensive research. She began by telling them that much to her own surprise, she'd discovered prices soared whenever private companies took over. Infrastructure crumbled. Services deteriorated.

'Our water is *ours*!' Donna interrupted her mid-flow, unable to wait for the contribution she and Becky had decided she would make. 'That's the point. What right has he got to sell it out from under us?'

Several of the others – the very people who'd urged Jimmy on around the buffet table at Becky's – started talking all at once, a babble that quickly took on a righteous and angry edge.

'. . . a democratic society . . .'

'. . . rights of the citizen . . .'

'. . . the constitution forbids . . .'

David shifted impatiently. Becky gave him a withering glance and banged her gavel.

'You okay?' Helen whispered to him.

He gave an exasperated sigh.

'Stick it out five more minutes. Just think how happy they'll be to see us go.'

He shifted impatiently again.

'The question is,' Becky was saying, 'how do we make ourselves heard?'

'How about a rally?' said the doctor. 'We could shout slogans and march with placards. Or maybe hold one of those sleep-outs.'

'Why not a letter-writing campaign?' the curator said.

There were nods and murmurs of excited assent around the room.

'Yeah. Sure. That would work,' Donna said. 'We could write to Senators, Representatives. You know. They've got to listen to—'

David's snort of contempt silenced the table.

'You want something,' he said, 'you take it.'

Helen and David left then, and the moment they were out of the room, a clamour broke out, anger at Jimmy abruptly morphing into anger at David.

Becky let them ramble on, her crepe cheeks growing pinker and her lips tighter. It was intolerable, absolutely intolerable. She'd never agreed with David Marion before – not on any subject – and she had no intention of letting anybody see that she agreed with him now. But she'd realized the moment he said it that unless they *took* their water away from Jimmy, she had no chance of showing an ungrateful mayor who was boss in this town.

She banged her gavel. 'I think what we're all saying is that we need to act in a political fashion.' She was fairly sure this phrasing didn't reveal David as the source of the idea. 'After all, we're dealing with a politician, and what he proposes is a political act as well as a social injustice. We'll have to force him somehow. Kate, you're the only one with experience, and you haven't said a word. What do you think?'

Kate put her elbows on the table. 'Depends on what you really want.'

'We want control over our water,' Becky said.

'If he's determined, it can turn into quite a fight.'

'How do we start?'

'You're going to have to change the law. As it stands, Mayor

Zemanski has the right and the power to sell any publicly owned utility if he wants to without paying the slightest attention to anybody.'

Kate explained that Springfield had what was called a Strong Mayor System. Most American cities did. Mayors like Jimmy had almost total administrative control as well as the executive independence to do exactly what he was doing. Many American mayors had already sold off their public utilities. There'd been a few protests, notably in Stockton, California, where the residents had resisted takeover by the multinational Thames Water, once a glory of British enterprise, now a subsidiary of the German giant RWA – and as close to its continental origins as that only because the Qatari government wasn't quite quick enough on its feet in attempting a takeover.

Most other American cities had given in quietly to whatever company bid highest; in many cases, the local people hadn't even known what was happening until it was way too late.

'You have to get something on the ballot to cap his powers as mayor,' Kate went on. 'That's what they did in Stockton. And to do it, you're going to have to do what they did: persuade thousands of registered voters to sign a petition.'

'You think it could it work *here*?' Becky asked. 'In Springfield?'

Kate considered a moment. 'He's not really popular, Mrs Freyl. Lots of people voted for him only because you backed him. And protest did work in Stockton. It took years. But it worked. Not only that, it forced Thames Water into the arms of the Germans.'

Becky smiled. 'So you propose a frontal attack, do you?'

'Everything else is talk.'

11

KNOX COUNTY, ILLINOIS: The same day

Little Andy rocked back and forth on his cement bunk, curled on his side like a baby in the womb. Sitting was too painful. 'Positive?' he said.

'I'm afraid so, Andrew,' Quack said.

Little Andy glanced up at him, pulled himself into a tighter foetal position, rocked some more. Tears rolled down his cheeks. 'I want to go home.'

'I know.'

Quack sat with Little Andy in the cell Andy now shared with a toothless old man called Casper. Cement walls. Cement bunks. Rusting metal toilet. Rusting metal washbasin. High, barred window. Humidity at least ninety-five per cent. Heat just as unrelenting. There was no breeze; both their faces shone with sweat.

Hardly the Hilton, but a far better place than the cell Andy had shared with Hot Cheese, who'd claimed him for a fuck toy. A prison is a thriving complex of businesses and barter. Hot Cheese ran prostitution in South Hams, and Andy had arrived with a face made for pleasure: arched brows, big eyes and a soft mouth that dimpled into his cheeks. All this teetered on the edge of ruin now and turned him from a pretty young man into an achingly beautiful one. As one of the Everleigh sisters of the famous Chicago whorehouse said it's why she went into the trade: 'I realized I was sitting on a fortune.' That's what Hot Cheese saw in Andy, who'd remained his favourite for a full four months. Hot Cheese liked it even rougher than the Shark had liked it with Quack, and he liked watching his clients approach it the same way. Sometimes they didn't bother with Vaseline. If anybody had an interesting implement or an unexpected technique, he was eager to see it tried out.

It was going to take Andy's anus a long time to recover. The miracle was that he wasn't dead; such treatment can cause internal ruptures and wild infections. As for the psychological scars, Quack could only hope the boy was more resilient than he'd been himself.

Rescuing Andy from Hot Cheese was a rare intervention. Quack stayed clear of whatever prison businesses he could, treated the fallout, kept to the infirmary. He was a revered figure in the cell blocks; the gang bosses needed him, and they knew it. They respected his judgement, his discretion, his expertise and that's to say nothing of his ability to acquire obscure ingredients for the prison's drug trade. Their soldiers got well quickly when they went to him. So did they themselves, and because he kept as respectful a distance from prison commerce as he could, they usually gave him what he wanted when he asked for it.

Quack began Andy's rescue with a formal application to see Wolfie, the General of David's old gang, the Insiders. Wolfie had strong ties with Chicago organized crime, which made him a celebrity as well as the most powerful boss in prison. Inmates vied to sit next to him in the mess hall. They bragged about what he'd said to them. An hour after Quack's application, word came back that Wolfie would give him the rare privilege of a private interview in the yard. Dozens of inmates watched the meeting from a distance. The two men – Quack and Wolfie – walked together while Quack talked and Wolfie listened. Then Wolfie stopped, nodded, clapped Quack on the shoulder, nodded again.

The deal was done.

Everybody knew that the sicker Andy became, the more beautiful he became and that his price to clients brought in more profit than any of Hot Cheese's other bitches. But everybody also knew that inmates who broke the terms of Wolfie's deals ended up dead or castrated. Within an hour the details came through. Hot Cheese would sell Little Andy to Quack in exchange for a steady supply of freebase cocaine. A guard among Hot Cheese's clients paid in cocaine hydrochloride, the active ingredient in freebase and crack. Crack is pretty easy to mix. Freebase isn't; it takes ammonia and ethyl ether. Most of all, it takes nerve and a steady hand. Quack had the steadiest hands in the prison; he was also the only one who could be trusted to cook it up pure.

As soon as Quack and Hot Cheese had shaken hands on the deal, Wolfie arranged for Andy's transfer to the cell with Casper.

'HIV is a chronic illness, Andrew,' Quack said to Andy. 'It's no longer a death sentence.'

Little Andy kept rocking.

'We've caught it early,' Quack went on. 'That's good. The viral load is low. That's good too. Best of all, you're not drug-resistant.' Andy rocked. 'Life expectancy is getting better all the time, and there are some really powerful treatments out there.' Andy rocked. Quack studied him a moment. 'One of the advantages of being the prison medic is that I can treat my own disease.'

Andy stopped rocking. 'You too?'

Quack nodded.

'How long?'

'Nearly two decades.'

'How come you're still alive?'

'I managed to diagnose myself shortly after AZT was licensed, and I'd read that combining two retrovirals gave a patient a far better chance.'

Andy went back to his rocking.

'Andrew, I can help you only so far. I can give you the drugs you need, but if you aren't seen to be at work with me in the infirmary, they'll send you back to the canal. And quite frankly, you haven't the strength for it.'

'You were there.'

'You mean when the men got sick?'

Andy nodded.

Quack frowned, looked away, shrugged. 'It's the only day I've done that kind of work for years. But, look, the point I'm making is that they're very unlikely to send you out again if you're working with me. You're very likely to get time off your sentence for good behaviour. There's a lot to do in an infirmary. Nursing is crucial where we have such limited access to medicines and equipment. Not many people are good at nursing.'

'I won't be either.'

'David says you can do it.'

'What does he know?'

'Andrew, I could say that you must do it because you now belong to me. But that wouldn't be the truth. From here on out, nobody owns you. You're your own man. The reason you must do it is because your life depends on it. We'll begin with hygiene.'

12

SPRINGFIELD: The next day

Jimmy was a speed reader. He could scan a whole newspaper – get it pretty clearly in mind too – almost as quickly as he could turn the pages.

'Fuck!' he said, abruptly leaning forward over the *Journal-Register*. The article that stopped him was called:

A citizen's stake in Springfield

It opened with a quick run-down: Becky was the chairperson of a newly formed citizen's action group called the Coalition of Concerned Citizens of Springfield (CCCOS) – they'd borrowed both name and acronym from Stockton's successful protest – with the aim of giving townspeople the right to vote on future decisions concerning Springfield Light and Power. It went on:

Mrs Freyl calls water "our most vital resource." She says, "We can live for years without roofs over our heads. We can manage weeks without food. But without water we die in 4 days. Can we afford to let control of this God-given gift slip out of our hands?"

Mrs Freyl explained that major players in private water supply are French, German, even Russian. "These foreign conglomerates have gobbled up many of our smaller water companies. Do we in Springfield want decisions about the purity of our water taken in Moscow?"

Jimmy tossed the paper on the breakfast table. 'Shit. Shit. Shit. I thought *I* was supposed to be the one scaring people about aliens in our midst.'

Ruth Madison took the paper from him and read the first half of the article. 'Poor old Chuck is pouring out his heart for Becky.'

'Chuck Finch?'

'Um.'

'He was there?'

'What do you think?'

Ruth had been around that table at Becky's meeting; now she sat opposite Jimmy in his house out at Lake Springfield, wearing one of his favourite shirts, looking good in it too. A couple of decades ago she'd spent a summer in New York as a hopeful with Ford Models, Inc, and she was still slender and willowy, still good at draping a languid body in a provocative pose. She hadn't wanted to come home to marry the President of the First National Bank of Springfield. She certainly hadn't expected to be one of the droves of hopefuls that New York chews up and spits out every year. But then, who does?

'Doesn't even have the guts to put his name on this piece of crap.' Jimmy grabbed the paper back from her. 'Gimme some coffee.'

'Get it yourself,' she said. 'I don't think anybody would accuse Chuck of courage.'

'Why the fuck didn't you warn me about this?'

'Why would I do that?'

'Why wouldn't you?'

'And rob myself of the pleasure of seeing your face just now?'

She gave him an appraising glance. Her rich husband was a bully and a bore, as were most of the men she'd taken on to supplement his limited charms. Jimmy was an exception in his way. He had a roguish charm combined with a clear-eyed view of a lot of things if not about himself. Naked ambition added real spice. The trouble was, he was naked too, and it wasn't a becoming state for him. He needed that girdle he wore under his clothes. What did they call those things? Compression garments? Why was it that guys like him seemed to think that a single fuck was an invitation to parade their wares?

'What are you looking at me like that for?'

She couldn't hold back her laughter any longer. 'Think of it, Jimmy. Russians! First Becky has you threatening us with terrorists at the water supply. Then she slaps your wrist with *Russians*.'

'It's not funny.'

'Sure it is. Hey, come on. You didn't finish the story.' Ruth settled her chin in her hands. 'How's the rest of it go?'

He read out loud, '"Please join us," Mrs Freyl said. "We need volunteers and money. We desperately need your help to collect signatures for the ballot in two months' time. If you can spare a few minutes of . . ."' He scrunched the paper in his hands, got up, circled the table, stared out of the window at the water beyond. 'How can she do this to me?'

Another of Jimmy's troubles, Ruth thought, was that he didn't understand how many people resented his rise to power. 'How big a kickback are you figuring on?' she asked.

He swung around to face her. 'What's that supposed to mean?'

Ruth's humour used to be no more than coquettish. Recently

it had taken on a harsher edge, but it was still more sex than threat. She had large brown eyes that sloped down at the corners. God knows how many hours she spent at the gym keeping the insides of her thighs firm, but even now, even though her legs were largely hidden by the table, Jimmy had difficulty keeping his eyes away.

'I've been thinking,' she said, 'hardly anybody in the Midwest has bought into privatized utilities, and here you are on such happy terms with so many nice corporate fat cats who are all—'

'Where the fuck did you get that idea?'

'My, my, we are sensitive today, aren't we? You talk in your sleep, my sweet. I heard the word for that just the other day. Parasomething. Somnia? Is that—?'

'I talk in my sleep?' He was aghast.

She nodded. 'You do say the most fascinating things. I gather you've been discussing the real cost of the Grand canal with those fat cats. What was it you said? Three trillion? Rather more than the newspapers report, isn't it? Your friends are going to need an awful lot of customers to keep an investment like that afloat on the markets. So I think to myself, Springfield's not going to bring in all that much, but we're a leader. Where we go, people follow. The mayor auctions off the contract for our water, and the lucky winner is going to have instant entrée to hundreds of cities in . . . I don't know, ten states? Twelve? Twenty?' She stretched out, took his hand, held on to it, smiled as she pulled him to the table beside her. 'Don't be so down at the mouth, cutie-pie. I'm not going to bite. Unless you want me to, of course. You're such a smart boy, aren't you? *Such* a brilliant idea to sell a public utility. Do tell me you're bargaining for more than a mere couple of million to line Jimmy's own pockets.'

Jimmy frowned. 'Not enough?'

'How could it be? You're dangling the deal of the century in front of these guys. You must have corporations all over the world grovelling at your feet.' She tilted her head at him. 'One of these days, you must tell me how to grovel in Chinese. Sweetie, they're going to give you anything you ask. Now, pretty please, read me the rest of what Chuck has to say.' Ruth was very flexible. Still holding his hand, she crossed her legs tailor-fashion in the chair, knees wide, feet tucked beneath them, those firm thighs fully exposed. Jimmy dropped her hand and reached for them before he was even aware the thought was in his mind. 'No, no,' she said, pushing him away. 'Paper first. I want to know what it says. Jimmy! Goddamnit, get off!'

He sighed angrily and, still standing, uncrumpled the paper and spread it out with the palms of his hands. 'What the fuck do you care?'

'I get a kick out of pushing you around.'

'I read you almost all of it.'

'So read the rest.'

He sighed more angrily than before. '"Please contact our peti-tion drive coordinator Kate Baga ..."' He mouthed the name. '"Ba ... ga ... lay ... os."' He scrunched the paper up again. 'Who the *fuck* is that?'

On one of the less bedraggled streets of the poor east side of town, Kate's telephone began ringing only minutes after the paper hit the stands. Her email box started piling up. By noon, she knew there was going to be more than she could handle.

Donna Stevenson was only too happy to help.

13

SPRINGFIELD: The first Monday in July

'Teach? Me?' Helen shouted, mobile phone clutched to one ear, free hand over the other. 'Not high school kids. You've got to be kidding.'

Two pneumatic drills powered away not far from her in the fore-court of the building that in a few months would be a house for her and David. David was wielding a pickaxe, ripping out the tarmac as the drills burrowed it up. Two other workmen with sledge-hammers were inside breaking down walls. Yet another pushed a wheelbarrow back and forth, ferrying slabs of tarmac to a dumpster.

At the other end of the line, Sister Evangeline was apologetic, def-erential. She'd been head of Science and Mathematics at St Mary & Joseph Community College for thirty years, and if she hadn't been an old friend of Becky's, Helen would have cut her off well before now. 'I can hear you're busy, and I know it's very short notice.' Sister Evangeline paused, then pushed ahead. 'These boys and girls have been chosen from dozens of applicants, Helen. Most of them have had a little calculus – just not enough to make them stand out.'

'What happened to . . . Whatshername?'

'Dr Gonzaga emailed me a month ago saying she'd try very,

very hard to be back at the end of the month but wasn't sure she'd make it.' Sister Evangeline explained that her assistant had forgotten to mention the matter until this very day. She told Helen that there'd be only a session or two: Dr Gonzaga would surely be back by then. 'It's a summer term, and the students really are very bright.' She paused again, then again pressed on. 'We've assigned the class to one of the air-conditioned rooms. It's wonderfully cool in there. You'll be very comfortable.'

Living in Springfield, working with Becky, Helen had no use for her doctorate in physics. Her published thesis meant little to anybody, and the Freyl family interests weren't holding her attention as she knew they ought to. She did keep trying. Every day she forced herself to read about commodities and futures, mortgages and property development. Her mind wouldn't stay put. A stray movement of air around her or an unexplained sound behind her, and she swung around with one thought: 'David!'

This being in love was far harder than she'd imagined. She'd had no idea what it can do to a person. She'd seen stunned sows at her grandfather's farm near Lake Michigan; he'd told her that a boar's cock is something magical, and servicing leaves the sow in that state for twenty-four hours. The honeymoon period at that lake had only turned her into one of them. She needed to get back to something she'd been trained for, anything that could take her mind off beds and this man.

'Okay, Sister,' she said. 'When do I start?'

'Eleven o'clock this morning.'

'Eleven o'clock! That's only an hour off. Is there a text?'

'It'll be on your desk when you arrive.'

The college was west of Leland Grove, a large brick building with tall windows and a wide flight of steps up to an arched entryway.

There was a time when it had been the only indication that any kind of higher learning went on in Springfield. Becky herself had taught there for several years – English literature – and she'd continued to help raise funds for it ever since. Helen climbed the stairs to her second-floor classroom. The air conditioner was only a window unit, but it did cool the room, and the room itself looked out into trees that still had green leaves despite the heat that had burned so many in town. She glanced through *Calculus: Theory and Practice* while her students gathered, fresh faces, an ethnic hotchpotch, mainly boys – only a couple of girls – lots of noise, laughter. She was scared. She'd never taught kids before.

'Quiet!' she called out. They quietened at once. She hadn't expected that. 'I'm no good at names,' she went on. 'I'm not going to call roll either. If you come to class, fine. If you don't, that's your business.' She held up the text that had been lying on her desk. 'How many of you've had a look at this?' Most of the hands went up.

She tossed the book into the wastebasket beside her and looked up in surprise at the shocked titters and intakes of breath. 'Calculus isn't like that,' she said. 'You use it instinctively every time you pitch a ball or shoot a rifle. All you've got to do is think "triangle", and you're in.' She picked up a marker, turned to the whiteboard behind her and drew a right-angled triangle. 'How many of you know how to pick this thing apart?'

People with doctorates are often snobbish about teaching kids, but Helen enjoyed the hour. When it was over, her students clustered around her, anxious for more, bubbling with excitement. She only managed to extricate herself twenty minutes later, full of ideas about what came next, so preoccupied as she crossed the parking lot that she didn't even see the guy she bumped into.

'Can't you watch where you're going?' she said irritably.

'Hiya, babe.'

She looked up. 'Shit, Jimmy. What are you doing here? Aren't mayors supposed to be . . . I don't know, doing whatever mayors are supposed to do.'

'Looking for beautiful women is part of the job description.'

She rolled her eyes. 'I'm busy – and I hate being called "babe".'

'I brought you a flower.' He held out a dandelion plucked from the roadside. 'How about a cup of coffee?'

'I don't want coffee.'

'Then let me carry your books.'

'No, damnit.'

'Suppose I just walk along with you.'

She sighed. 'You've already done it. This is my car.' He leaned against the door. 'Get off.'

Ruth telling him to 'get off' had astonished him. It had hurt. Helen repeating it – no more than a couple of hours later – made him wince despite himself. He fiddled, self-conscious now, with the half-moon glasses around his neck. But he didn't move. 'Helen, I know you want me. What the hell, half the women in Springfield want to fuck the mayor. You should see my fan mail. Makes me blush sometimes. Look, I intend to be governor of this state, and I'm going to need you at my—'

'Shut up, Jimmy. I just got married.'

'That's supposed to mean something to me?'

'Get away from my car.'

'Come on. You can't really think all that much of this guy. What do you know about him other than that he's a murderer your father taught out of the kindness of his heart? I mean, look at me. Who wouldn't want me instead? I got a cute cowlick and a real bright future.'

But she only rolled her eyes again, opened her purse,

rummaged around, found an emery board and went to work on a broken nail.

'Your father wouldn't be dead if it weren't for David Marion. The guy's a loser, Helen. He'll always be a loser, and he's going to drag you down with him. Look, I know you. You only got involved with him to make me jealous, and now this fucker is using you. Anybody with eyes can see the only thing holding you—'

'Bye, Dr Freyl!' A gaggle of Helen's students ran past, waving. 'See you Thursday.'

'Looking forward to it,' she called back. 'Finished?' she said to Jimmy.

'Come to daddy, huh? All's forgiven. I promise.'

She put her emery board away. 'You going to let me go home now?'

'So he finally backs off and holds out this damned dandelion again like a votive offering.' Helen was regaling David with the encounter over dinner at the Pair-a-Dice: steak, fries, beer for him, wine for her.

'Still fiddling with those half-moon glasses, huh?' he said, tilting his beer can at her.

'If you were in prison, my darling, would you beat him to death for moving in on your woman like that?'

'Shove those glasses up his prick first.'

She burst out laughing. 'You wouldn't!'

'You going to dare me?'

'Yeah.'

'All right, you're on.'

Helen was half shocked, half enchanted. She reached over, took his hand, long fingers, broad across the palm. 'What about your day? Any excitements?'

David frowned. 'Something a little weird.'

Helen had said the Riley was a racing car back in England. 'A hundred and twenty on the open road,' she'd said. He'd tried it not far out of town, windows open, wind on his face, roar of the engine beneath him – and not a single judder. A siren behind him was inevitable. He'd looked forward to it, steeled himself for the old-time thrill of it, prepared his usual defence. Stare straight ahead. Say nothing. Don't even admit to a name.

The cop got out of his car and ambled towards him. 'Hi there, Mr Marion,' he said. 'Out for a spin in the wedding present?'

David was so taken aback that he turned to look at the cop.

The cop smiled. 'Beautiful car.' He patted the solid metal of the Riley's bonnet. 'They knew how to make them back then, didn't they? Nowadays? They just stick a tin can on an air pump and blow it until it's big enough to make a saloon. Look, there's a speed trap ahead. Just wanted to warn you. You may be a Freyl now, but it might be inconvenient, don't you think? You have a good day now.'

The cop patted the Riley again, then turned and walked back to his car.

'Cops protecting *you*?' Helen said to David.

'Seemed to be.'

'Think it's because of me?'

'The logo on the cop car,' David said. 'It was yellow. Round.' Springfield's cops wore blue, triangular logos. So did their cars.

'Sangamon County?'

He shook his head. He'd known cops' logos since he was six. The Sheriff's was badge-shaped with an eagle in it.

'Fairy godmother?' she suggested. 'It's certainly about time. Twenty years. Jesus, David. You spent twenty years in South Hams.'

The way David saw it, Helen enjoyed his role as Springfield's pariah much as she might enjoy owning an aardvark. What he couldn't for the life of him understand was why somebody like her – beautiful, rich, smart, confident – would choose to marry him. Sex, sure. She loved taking risks. She loved shocking her friends and her grandmamma. But marriage? To the man all these people kept on saying had killed her father? Or just as good as? She didn't think he'd had anything to do with it. Which left her pretty much alone. Not an easy position and not one many people could maintain for long, especially when the only person who agreed with her was Lillian. Hardly part of Helen's social circle, but then only the colour of his skin made him closer than that. What kind of life could she have in mind with him? What *could* she want from him?

He picked up a French fry and touched her nose with it. 'I wonder what it's like to be you.'

14

THE CHAIN OF ROCKS, MISSOURI: That night

The Mississippi has forty-three dams and twenty-seven locks. Aloysia's body surfaced near the last of them.

This area is known as the Rust Belt, miles and miles of abandoned factories, oil refineries, steel mills. But despite the industrial desolation, number twenty-seven is the busiest lock on the river; it's just north of St Louis, and there wouldn't be any traffic at all without a lock. Water levels were way too low. In bygone times, tectonic plates collided here and threw out layers of magma that folded in on themselves to form what's called the Chain of Rocks: a rapids at the best of times. The drought had turned it into a series of torrents that exploded in great bursts of muddy water over crags, shoals, outcroppings of stone.

Canoeists dare each other to brave it during the day, but no canoeist in his right mind would try it at night even when the water level was high. Aloysia had the rapids to herself. They tossed her from rock to rock, torrent to torrent. By dawn, she'd reached the end and was drifting south at the river's usual leisurely pace, her body not yet fished out by a single coroner along its route.

15

ST LOUIS, MISSOURI: The next day

For as long as Jimmy could remember, his hero had been quarterback and kicker George Blanda. That man had had a God-given killer instinct, just like the coach of the Oakland Raiders said. Jimmy loved football. He told people he'd been a quarterback himself, drop back in the pocket, take one look up, find his wide receiver with that, oh, so perfect spiralling pass, crowd roaring, professional career snatched out of his hands by a rebellious cartilage in his knee – all of which sounded much better than the only member of Chicago University's second team who'd never been on the field. There'd have to be some careful back-knitting for the gubernatorial race.

The bit about the knee actually was true, except that he'd wrecked it falling over a bucket of car wash when he was thirty-seven. He wore a titanium brace on it right now as he drove out of Springfield on a secondary road through soy fields. He could have headed directly south on Route 55, but the city owned a stretch of land out here. He slowed down as he approached it.

Buying the mayoralty hadn't come cheap even with Becky's help. He'd had to 'borrow' client money for it. Then he'd had to 'borrow' another, well, rather sizeable chunk to build a portfolio of good, solid investments – downtown properties, gilt-edged stocks and shares, a few hedge funds – that would gradually pay back both 'loans'. When he was a kid, he'd dreamed of being rich, and even though this borrowed wealth was only on paper, he revelled in it. The 'enterprise inducement' that he'd already received for the privatization and the 'bonus' that was to come later: these would more than cover his debts. But as Jimmy saw it, paying debts was for little people. There were serious opportunities on the market for someone like him with daring and flair. Many stocks in these troubled times showed 'interesting weaknesses'; that's how his broker put it, and he talked to his broker every day.

Just being rich wasn't the limit of Jimmy's childhood dream. The open and above-board profit from the deal would go straight towards his real ambition: he was going to give Springfield its own football team.

The National Football League is a huge, multi-billion-dollar industry, a national business, not rooted in localities like English soccer teams. A rich and powerful man can buy a team and move it wherever he wants. The St Louis Rams used to be the Los Angeles Rams, and before that they were the Cleveland Rams. Why couldn't they be the Springfield Rams? Nothing adds to a city's prestige like having an NFL team. As for the man who does the buying? He's Croesus. A team is a licence to print money. With that kind of power behind him, Jimmy wouldn't need the Beckys of the world. He could buy the governorship as though it were a candy cane for a Christmas tree.

And he knew that a first step in buying the players who would buy the governor's mansion was a spectacular new stadium for them to play in. Jimmy was going to build just that right out here in these soy fields.

He crept at five miles an hour as he passed the site. Surveyors were at work already, half a dozen of them with surveying poles and clipboards.

Beside the road, a blonde in jeans with a shirt around her waist peered through a theodolite on a red and yellow tripod. She was standing where the turn-off from the road would go. Jimmy could see it in his mind, crowds with hot dogs and pompoms, cars honking and jockeying for position, stadium rising up beyond, direction signs that would read 'The James Zemanski Memorial Stadium'. Not that he planned to be dead or anything.

He waved to the blonde as he drove past her. She waved back.

The drive to St Louis took a couple of hours. Jimmy didn't allow for more; the trip was hardly a feast for the eyes, mile after mile of cornfields all the way south along Route 55, scrappy little towns tossed here and there. Jimmy had been born back east; he didn't realize the crops looked odd until the highway began its gentle westward angle towards the Mississippi. 'Knee high by the fourth of July.' That's the old saying. He'd never paid attention to it for the simple reason that by the time he got to Springfield, modern methods had long outdated it. Corn grew much faster, shoulder height at least by this time of summer. But these fields were barely past that titanium-braced knee of his. Another old saying is that you can hear the corn grow. That one's true. Jimmy had heard it himself: a groan clearly audible beyond the rustle of the leaves, not an agonized groan, more of a sexual moan.

The way Jimmy saw it, the mirrored monolith of Follaton Tower was even sexier. Maybe the traffic crawled onto the bridge across the Mississippi, but the sight of the Follaton Tower thrusting into the skies above St Louis, dominating not just the skyline and Eero Saarinen's golden Gateway to the West but the city itself: that made everything else insignificant.

Jimmy took a long ramp down into the tower's bowels. He showed his pass, parked, took an elevator to a checkpoint; armed guards searched him, X-rayed him, exchanged parking pass for visitor's pass and waved him into a two-storey-high lobby made of brushed chrome and grey marble.

A corporation called UCAI owned this skyscraper; its logo flashed in dramatic orange and red against the muted background. UCAI was no ordinary company. It was one of the giants. Only months ago it had smashed its way into the top one hundred economies of the world, where it ranked just beneath the mighty Exxon and pushed the entire country of Kuwait down a peg. Its revenues topped $130 billion, and it had hundreds of principal companies operating in more than a hundred countries.

Jimmy took an elevator to the highest floor and a second lobby, where full-size trees in pots arched over leather chairs beneath a high glass ceiling. His appointment was for ten, and he'd been driving since seven; the fresh-faced receptionist gave him a sympathetic smile.

'Coffee, Mr Zemanski? It's two sugars, isn't it? I'll bring it in. Mr Slad is waiting for you.'

She led him to an office with a window wall that looked out over the city to the Saarinen arch, an executive throne room that called for Corbusier elegance and bold modern paintings. But the furniture here was aggressively plain. The wooden chairs belonged in a Baptist schoolroom, the desk could have come from the school's dining hall. The only decoration was a full-size, brilliantly coloured statue of Jesus on His knees before His God with His mother standing beside Him, her hand on His shoulder.

The halo over Mary's head was slightly askew. Jimmy itched to straighten it.

'Great to see you again, Mr Z,' Sebastian Slad said, getting up from the dining-hall table that served him as a desk and holding out his hand. 'I can't tell you how glad me and Francis are to be working with a man like you on this here little project.'

Sebastian was a Humpty Dumpty of a man, round, fat, bald, mouth full-lipped, mid to late thirties, enormous testicles bulging in his trousers. He and his twin brother Francis had taken control of UCAI five years ago: a 'daring palace coup', the press had called it. They'd found a corporation in trouble, mired in what would have been a ruinous scandal if they hadn't intervened.

Their predecessors had invested heavily in a new pharmaceutical that was supposed to bring in a fortune. It had hit a snag. Clinical trials caused many deaths in far-off Belarus. The Slads had no objection to the trials or the deaths – there's always collateral damage in the development of a new pharmaceutical – but the methods were absurdly crude for so powerful an organization. They'd exposed it to potentially disastrous publicity. The twins had announced shock and horror at developments that – as new heads of the corporation – they couldn't possibly have known about. They diverted attention with a daring hostile takeover of the legendary Russian-based corporation Vasiltekh, the major player in the Grand canal development.

That got UCAI marvellous publicity of precisely the right kind. *The New York Times* carried the headline:

St Louis trounces Moscow
in battle for American water

Who cares about Belarusians in a faraway country when real Russians can be beaten off our own soil?

*

The Slad twins had been born in the tiny town of Spearsville, just north of Dodge City, Kansas, father a federal marshal, mother an itinerant beautician; they'd started playing entrepreneurial games early with a lemonade stand beside the road when they were six. At twelve, when kids sometimes take on paper routes for pocket money, the Slad twins were the ones hiring them. They'd paid their way through Kansas State University giving financial advice and selling second-hand computers, then gone onto Harvard Business School. Together they'd shone there.

They were fraternal twins – physically very unalike – and Sebastian looked every inch the corn-fed boy he was. Easterners sneer at guys like that. Sebastian played it to the hilt, bumbling farm-boy speech, manners, Bible-belt fundamentalism; Francis was sophisticated, polished, highly literate. Together they made a formidable variation on good cop, bad cop. Even before they left Harvard Business School, they'd started stripping assets off little companies to build bigger ones. By their late twenties, the two of them were a force in the US business world and already in on the ground floor at UCAI, already planning the coup that would make them into heavyweights in the global market.

Jimmy shook Sebastian Slad's outstretched hand. 'Good to see you, Mr Slad. Been looking forward to it all week.' He glanced around the office. 'Your brother couldn't make it?'

'You know Francis,' Sebastian said. 'He don't like talking to people if'n he can help it. Excepting to me. And he don't like that much neither.'

'He's okay though?'

'As okay as he ever is.' Francis Slad's migraines were well known. 'Hey, look at you. You got them glasses after all, didn't you?'

Jimmy was pleased that Sebastian noticed. He'd first seen his half-moon glasses around Francis Slad's neck, and his mother had always insisted that imitation was the most sincere form of flattery. He hoped it was true; he'd had trouble connecting with Francis Slad. 'They give me a certain authority, don't you think?' he said.

'They do. They do. Take a seat, Mr Z. How'd the Council meeting go?'

Jimmy grinned. 'Like clockwork. They lapped it up, all six of them. Couldn't get enough of the Grand canal or state secrets or the money they were going to save. I never realized how dumb aldermen were.'

'How about the pretty gal?'

'"Pretty gal"? Dr Gonzaga?'

'That's the one.'

'Never showed up.'

'That the truth?'

'Stupid bitch. Didn't even email me. Who the hell does she think she is?'

Sebastian ran his fat hands over his table of a desk. 'We really got to find this gal, Mr Z.' He gave the desk a proprietary pat. 'Science ain't no job for a woman. They don't got the spine for it. So what's this flimflam I hear about concerned citizens of Springfield? Mainly the old lady, huh?'

The Slads had come to Jimmy; he hadn't sought them out, hadn't even thought of selling off utilities until they suggested it. But he'd talked to a couple of other water conglomerates just to see where the Slads stood. Nobody had even hinted at as much money as they were talking about. But then nobody else had controlling shares in the Grand canal. It was when they'd let him in on that that he'd known he could swing it with the Council. Which left Becky.

'She's a very powerful old lady,' he said.

Sebastian sighed his disapproval. 'I never did believe in women interfering in science *or* business, and here we got 'em crawling all over both.' He held up a hand. 'She's pushing for a vote on whether you privatize Springfield's water at all, right? Kind of likes a fight, don't she?'

Jimmy nodded. 'I have to hold an open Town Council meeting.'

'That's what Francis tells me. Now, Mr Z, how come you didn't come to us at once? Huh? How come we got to find out about it ourselves? That ain't the way friends are supposed to bond.'

'I can handle it.'

'Francis says why don't you arrange for a small room without air conditioning? Once they're sweating and irritable, just keep them from saying much.'

Jimmy laughed. Ideas were always attributed to Francis, but it wasn't so. The twins worked synergistically: alone they weren't all that much – neither had been scholarship material – but together they made up a single genius that just happened to come in two bodies. Touches like a small, hot room were just what Jimmy needed. He could see a route through the rest of it. Rain does its job too well. It picks up pesticides from farms, oil from roads, fibreglass from roofs. The Illinois Environmental Agency had issued a mandate requiring that cities collect and treat storm water before discharging it.

'You know, I don't think Springfield's got plans for treatment plants,' he said to Sebastian with a smile, 'much less estimates for building them. I can do a lot with that: should be enough to pin back an old lady's wings some.'

'That's the stuff, Mr Z.' Sebastian reached into a cardboard box under his desk, pulled out a thick wodge of paper bound in a manila cover and handed it over. 'Me and Francis got you a little present that just might help.'

Jimmy glanced down at it: *Springfield, Illinois: Vital Services Feasibility*

Study and Long Term Projection. The authors were the Incol Executive, a highly respected Chicago think tank. He'd used them a couple of times for corporate clients; they had strong but well-hidden internal ties to UCAI.

'Francis gave it a once-over himself, got the overall figure up to $250 million for building them facilities and the system to incorporate them. Tell your citizens they'll save $175 million over twenty years. That'll catch their attention.'

Jimmy patted the Incol report and gave a contented sigh. 'God, you people are a pleasure to deal with. I pulled some statistics together myself – couldn't get a figure anywhere near that high. How'd you do it?'

'Crumbling infrastructure. Anomalous ground formations. Unsourced industrial pollution.'

Jimmy had always thought he was pretty good at 'creative accounting', but this report was at least five hundred pages long. He opened it, glanced over a few pages. There were multiple-level equations and lengthy statistical analyses. 'It'll hold them for weeks,' he said. 'I can't tell you how grateful I am.'

Sebastian stood up and extended his hand as he had when Jimmy arrived.

Jimmy got up too, shook the hand but held on to it. 'Look, um, let me tell you something that just might be useful to you, kind of a thank-you for this report.' He'd been struggling to find a way to introduce the subject.

'What's that?'

'A man named David Marion.' Jimmy let go of the hand.

'Never heard of him.'

'He interrupted a programme of yours a while back, a very important programme. Your security department attempted to, er, regularize the situation. They failed.'

Sebastian scanned him. 'Mr Z, I ain't got the slightest idea what you're talking about. This is something that happened before me and Francis took over, right?'

'Forgive me, Mr Slad, but I'm speaking here in my official capacity as one of your legal team. I don't have to warn you about this guy. But I figure if we're going to help each other out, I ought to mention him. He's trouble.'

'A businessman? Lawyer? Banker?'

'A convicted murderer, now a part of Mrs Freyl's circle.'

Sebastian frowned, then broke into a smile. 'Hey, wait a minute,' he said then. 'He's the one married the granddaughter, ain't he? You really think he could hurt us?'

'He pries into things that don't concern him.'

'I see. I see.' Sebastian nodded. 'This nosy fellow's part of the family, right? Got an inside track? That could be worth a look-see. I sure don't want to impose or nothing, but could I ask our security guy to give you a call about it? Maybe make an appointment to see you? Would that be okay?'

Jimmy nodded. 'It'll be my pleasure,' he said.

As Jimmy eased out of the tower's bowels and back into the heavy traffic of St Louis streets, he was thinking that Sebastian Slad really was a yokel. How could anybody think David Marion had an inside track on the Freyls of all people?

But then Jimmy had been born in Massachusetts. The Midwest has a different culture, a different set of priorities, not limited to the growth of corn either. Another old saying – one he'd never heard – comes from Kansas where the Slads had grown up: 'Beware the yokel when he acts real stupid. He's lifting your wallet out of your pocket.'

16

KNOX COUNTY: A week later

'Over there, Andrew!' Quack shouted. 'Bucket!'

Little Andy scuttled, but he wasn't quick enough. A thin, grape-coloured fluid shot out from beneath the bed and splashed onto the floor. The prison infirmary held only half a dozen beds. All were full. Quack had persuaded the Warden to add another half dozen that spilled into the hallway beyond. These were full too. Each bed had a hole in the mattress to let the spurts of diarrhoea dump straight into a bucket beneath. Another dozen inmates lay on the ground outside underneath a marquee, no buckets here, only the absorbent earth.

The main thing was to get water into these men as fast as possible. By rectum? Forget it. They'd only spew it out again. Intravenous hydration? Forget that too. Clear pouches of hydration fluid did hang from makeshift scaffolds above several patients, but it wasn't feeding into veins. The last thing these men needed was massive infection, and Quack had no sterile needles. He boiled whatever the gang bosses supplied – a motley collection that included one made from the bass string of a guitar – and hydrated just beneath the skin. A couple of sites per man: abdomen, upper arms, thighs. He was expert at this — could get in several litres per man per day. Breast-like swellings arose at each site.

But he'd never known anybody to be sick like these men, had nothing to compare it to except the outbreak a month earlier. There'd been only four patients then; he himself had watched one of them collapse at the canal site. Their symptoms had been controllable enough to let him feel his way a little and confirm that forcing fluids was the only thing that seemed to help; an hour of hurried research had suggested that the antibiotic tetracycline might have an effect. It didn't. And then he'd been as taken aback at the speed of recovery as at the suddenness of onset. They'd returned to work on the canal within ten days.

Which left him without any idea why this new batch of patients were so desperately ill or what to do for them — except get water into them.

He'd spent the time between that outbreak and this one teaching Little Andy how to mitre a sheet, scrub a floor, bathe a patient in bed. Andy was a good student. Tell him once, and that was it. This new outbreak had shown that he wasn't squeamish either. Not that Quack had expected quivering delicacy in a prison whore so harshly treated that he'd be wearing diapers for weeks to come.

Quack turned back to the telephone in his hand. 'I need an ambulance, Miss Pouria, and I need it quick. Some of these men are really sick.'

'Do try to stay calm, Mr Kolb.' The voice was patient, polite: calls to Medical Services Direct were recorded to judge nurses' performance. 'We're all here to help you. I do think gastroenteritis is your most likely . . .'

Quack decided to let her talk for thirty seconds. Sometimes a wait worked, sometimes not. The trouble was, he knew that Medical Direct nurses could get fired if their average 'call handle time' exceeded something like seven minutes, and he knew that they followed elaborate computer protocols tracking symptoms through some algorithm and coming up with a verbatim speech at the end. Before these outbreaks, he'd never spoken to the same nurse twice. During them, he'd spoken only to Miss Pouria, and what she was telling him now was word for word what she'd told him throughout.

'Forgive me, Miss Pouria' – he couldn't wait any longer – 'this isn't the same as before. Two of these men are dying.'

That caught her attention. 'Dying?'

'They're deeply cyanosed, and their breathing is so shallow that—'

'Cyanosed? Blue? Are you sure?'

'I've never seen anything like it. Lips, hands – all blue. Not just pale blue. Deep blue. Bruise blue. The Latino is turning blue-grey – his whole body – right in front of my eyes.'

There was a pause. Quack knew that pause. It meant she was consulting a not-too-familiar icon on the screen in front of her. 'An ambulance will be with you as soon as possible, Mr Kolb.' Not a single change in the tone of her voice. 'I do know how difficult such patients can be, but from what you've told me, we have all the symptoms of gastroenteritis. What about temperature?'

'I have no thermometers. You know that, and you can't be serious about gastroenteritis. A couple of these guys have blood in their urine.'

'Try to be calm, Mr Kolb. The Service will arrange thermometers for you. Now perhaps a few simple instructions will help . . .'

That meant a pop-up on her screen was telling her that 'the option of a CCMD' – Call Center Medical Doctor – was 'not available'. Quack was to take faecal samples at once, temperatures every two hours, note all changes at twelve hours, twenty-four hours and forty-eight hours, take a second faecal sample after sixty hours.

'... and as before, we'd appreciate all your notes. Gastroenteritis is very common, Mr Kolb. The body usually rights itself within a few days. Fluids, a light diet, common sense.'

Quack knew he'd get no more.

'No luck?' said Little Andy, who was washing his hands for the fiftieth time in only a few hours. Quack's orders had been absolute: if he touched one patient, he needed a thorough cleansing with soap and water before he touched another.

Quack shrugged. 'Where's Monk?'

'Dunno.'

Quack had appealed to all the South Hams gang leaders, explained that they could lose men themselves for lack of nursing; they'd volunteered as many helpers as he could use. Monk was one of them, two hundred pounds of solid muscle, an albino – and a racist to the core – with swastikas tattooed on his skull, hard-working, tireless if stupid, superlative at keeping patients clean, and these patients desperately needed it.

'Go find him, will you?'

Quack went back to his measuring spoons. Baking soda, salt, sugar levelled off into a five gallon jug of water is a cheap, simple way to restore a dehydrated body's chemistry as well as its fluids. Hundreds of ordinary people die in the heat of an Illinois summer, and the South Hams prison block was old and poorly ventilated. Temperatures often rose above a hundred degrees, stayed that way day and night for weeks. This rehydrating solution was one of the first practical remedies Quack had learned as a prison medic.

That's what had succeeded the first time around with this

illness too. There'd been a quiet period before the second influx, five of them at once. Then two more, then a dozen by twos and threes. He and Andy had come to spend hours churning out his formula, a quart per man per hour. He'd had just enough equipment to get it beneath the skin of the ones who couldn't take it by mouth.

He was replenishing a bag of saline solution when the guards brought in another victim. 'Who's this?' he said. The man was a wizened ancient who hung between the two guards.

'Monk?' said one of the guards.

'No!'

Quack stared at him. He was a shrunken relic of yesterday's giant, a bag of bones, clothes glued to him, cheeks sucked in, eyeballs protruding, skin shrivelled on his hands and face. But his colour! This racist of a white man had turned into a purple dwarf so dark he was almost black. There was no bed for him. Quack eased him down on the ground under the marquee.

Monk was barely flat when he began to gasp. He clawed at his clothing, body raised up, eyes wild, tendons in his neck standing out like steel rods on a suspension bridge.

'Andrew!' Quack cried. 'Left drawer. Syringe in the small box. Now!' Little Andy came running. 'Hold him down,' Quack said, shoving the needle into Monk's arm. The clawing and gasping went on a moment longer. Monk fell back onto the ground.

'What did you do?' Little Andy said to Quack a few minutes later.

'His airways collapsed. Not an easy way to go.'

Little Andy stared at him. 'Did I just watch you kill this motherfucker?'

Quack shut Monk's eyes and nodded.

'If he's dead, how come his fucking mouth is still open?'

'Because he's so relaxed.'

Little Andy looked from Monk to Quack and back again. 'What's going on here, Quack? It's getting worse, isn't it? I thought it was . . .' He trailed off.

Quack gave a slight shrug. 'I'm very much afraid we're going to lose a couple more — maybe three — but my bet is that Monk is the last of the new cases.' Quack turned back to him, then gave another slight shrug. 'Don't listen to me, Andrew. I don't know what I'm talking about. Give me a hand with this poor guy, then get some sleep.'

'You're the guy that needs sleep.'

The network of fine wrinkles on Quack's face had come to look like a mat of spiderwebs. 'I'll manage,' he said.

'You can't go on forever like this.'

'Sure I can. I've been at it a long time now.'

One day all those years ago when Quack had been David's cellmate, David said to him, 'You need something to occupy your mind.'

'Mind? Who's got a mind?'

'You said once you wanted to be a doctor. Maybe it's time to make a move in that direction.'

Quack was still Brendan back then, still frightened of David — unsure just how far he could go — and David had that about-to-blow-up look that appeared on his face so frequently and so quickly. Quack began pleading, just as he did with Miss Pouria. 'It's too late for me. You know that.'

'Do you want to be a doctor or don't you?'

'Of course I want to be a doctor,' Brendan burst out, taken aback by his own passion. 'I've always wanted to be a doctor. I can't stop myself dreaming about it even now. I know where I want to practise: the eastern townships of Quebec, small villages – agriculture mainly. See, I'd get to know my patients that way. When I'm old and somebody brings little Maggie Pratt to me, I'll be able to put a stethoscope to her chest and say, "Ah, yes, this is the asthma that her grandfather had." Or maybe, "That murmur is the bicuspid valve she inherited from her mother."'

David was as taken aback by the outburst as Quack was. 'Let's get you a job in the prison infirmary.'

'You're kidding. What for?'

'Start your medical training. We need a contact in there.'

Prison gangs survive despite draconian measures to quash them, partly because prisoners need protection from each other as well as from the guards. Guards couldn't do both jobs even if they wanted to, and they don't want to. Somebody has to keep order. Gangs also survive because a prison's thriving economy – its drug trafficking, protection, prostitution, smuggling, gambling, liquor – requires cooperation and laws. It needs somebody to regulate the flow of goods and services, and it requires enforcement when cooperation and law fail.

David's gang – the Insiders – ran the drug and liquor trade.

'You're the perfect cover,' he said to Quack. 'You know something about medicine.'

'I don't know a damn thing.'

'Come on. What was it you just said? A "stethoscope"? A "bicuspid valve"? Sounds good enough to me.'

Quack began his medical training only days later. Even back then, it was a Herculean feat to get a real doctor into a prison; for the most part they worked – as they had entirely for the past five years – by what's known as 'telemedicine'. Broken bones went unset. HIV and AIDS went undiagnosed.

But the neglect gave Quack a free rein, not just to treat his own illness either. It was the hands-on part of treating patients that he loved. Just as with Little Andy — and for the same reasons — blood didn't bother him. Nor did vomit or shit or gangrene or ulcerated flesh or any other bodily horror. He cleaned the infirmary himself. He scrubbed the floors, laid traps for the rats and the mice, poisoned the roaches. He took the manacles off patients, delivered the linen to the laundry himself, collected it. He learned quickly that few doctors know the generic names of drugs — even for the ones they prescribe regularly — and found that he could place orders for many that David's gang were grateful to receive.

In return, David arranged for the delivery of books in anatomy, physiology, urology, cardiology, virology, even gynaecology and obstetrics (these got stolen at once). Quack studied at night. He studied during meals. He studied as he walked in the exercise yard, nodding his head like a rabbinical student at a seminary as he memorized the bones of the wrist and the cranial nerves. Nobody bothered him. Everybody gave him respect.

'He's the doc,' they said.

'He be a straight-up dawg,' they said. 'Ain't no sideways shit to him.'

Quack's voice was cadenced, unemotional, close to a chant. 'Slowly . . . lower . . . Tracy's . . . panties . . . to . . . the . . . curly . . . hairs,' he said.

'What the fuck are you talking about?' said Little Andy.

'Your skeleton, Andrew. Look at the skeleton your mother sent you.'

The pressure was off. A week had passed since Quack's call to Miss Pouria. He'd followed instructions, and he'd followed them exactly. Four of the sick men, including Monk, had died; Quack didn't know what the death certificates said, but he'd have bet anything gastroenteritis figured in there somewhere. Maybe some viral strain: 'viral' covers such a multitude of sins. The live ones remained weak and listless, but they were back in their cells if not yet ready for hard labour.

Little Andy and Quack sat in the cell that Andy shared with the toothless old inmate; Andy's injuries had healed enough so that he finally could sit, provided he settled gently into the inflated ring Quack had made for him. But the cement walls and cement bunks acted like storage heaters; temperature and humidity were more relentless than ever, a situation made even more dire with the prison's water supply on the blink. For the last twelve hours there'd been no water for the rusting metal toilet, and human shit stinks worse than any shit on earth. Anybody who'd shaved that morning, had had to shave with only sweat for a lubricant.

The cardboard skeleton Lillian had sent dangled from one of the bunks. Quack was holding out its arm, but gingerly, using only two fingers so that he wouldn't perspire on it. 'We're trying to remember the bones of the wrist, right?' he was saying. 'Scaphoid, lunate, triquetrum, pisiform, etcetera. One way to get them into your head is to match first letters to catchy phrases like *Slowly Lower Tracy's Panties* . . . ' Quack laughed at the abrupt smile. 'A couple of my books used to belong to an Australian medical student. I found lots of these scribbled in the margins.'

'They all like that?'

'Some of them are much more fun. Just wait till you get to the cranial nerves.'

'What was really wrong with those guys, Quack?'

Quack just shook his head.

'I ain't swallowing that,' Little Andy said.

'Andrew, I really don't know.'

'Not gastroenteritis though, huh?'

Quack shook his head again. 'At first I thought it could be cholera. But then—'

'Cholera! Ah, come on. That makes guys turn blue?' Andy was studying his own pink palms. 'Nah. You couldn't have thought that. That's what they get in Africa.'

'There've been outbreaks here from time to time. It's one of the reasons they put chlorine in public water supplies. Water supplies do get polluted though. The thing is, at least one of these men died of kidney failure, and cholera doesn't produce bloody urine. Not that I've ever seen a case of cholera before.' Quack took in a breath. 'I've seen guys with blue lips and fingernails, toenails: heart patients, bad bronchitis, asthma, that kind of thing. Men get so cold in winter here their hands and feet turn blue. But I've never seen whole bodies change colour like that.' He took in another breath. 'It's a pretty word: cyanosis. It comes from the Greek for blue: the blue disease – not enough oxygen in the blood.' Then in a rush: 'Medical Services Direct has never been openly obstructive before. If somebody's really sick – or sick in some unexpected way – I've always talked to a doctor about it. I thought maybe it's a little-known communicable disease, and they'd have to notify Public Health. There'd be an investigation. Not a good idea. People might find out what's going on here. I mean, can you see a call centre setting up a situation where, say, Illinois Prisoners' Rights might poke its nose in? Maybe even somebody really big like Amnesty International?'

Little Andy laughed. 'You telling me a bunch of do-gooders are going to make corporate America quake in its boots?'

'Can't you just see the headlines, Andrew? "Slave labour in American prisons"? "The Illinois Gulag"? Nobody really gives a damn about hard labour for prisoners – as long as they don't drop dead on you. Four of these did.' They'd all died before the ambulance arrived to take them away; Quack himself had shut their eyes. 'UCAI had to close down a massive pharmaceutical enterprise only a couple of years ago because it got some seriously bad headlines. Markets are jittery. Another major scandal, and even this giant's stock could collapse.'

A shrill alarm rang throughout the prison to signal the next shift of workers on the canal, and a rustle along the corridor — men pulling themselves off cement beds — added a brush-drum to the cacophony of radio, singing, clanging, crying, shouting, stamping that never died out in the cell block. Neither Quack nor Little Andy paid attention; just as Quack had promised, infirmary work meant Andy was excused from work on the canal.

'So how come guys aren't still puking and shitting?' Little Andy asked him. 'How come you knew it was going to stop when it did?'

'I didn't know.'

'How come we didn't all do it?'

'I can't answer these questions, any of them. I wish I could.'

'Come on, Quack. You got to. You have theories if not facts. You got to tell me what you think. I watched those guys die. That really scared me.'

Quack wiped his arm across the sweat on his face. 'Maybe the computer data at Medical Direct said that it would stop when it did,' he said. 'Maybe whatever it is occurred somewhere else, a small, contained outbreak. These guys were all working on the same section of the canal. Other sections seem okay. Maybe one of them got sick, and maybe there's a shithouse out there that leaks into the plumbing beneath a standpipe they drink from.'

'And some sick guy shat in it?'

'It's a possibility.'

'How come—'

'Let's give the bones of the wrist another try, huh?' Quack interrupted. 'You really are quick, aren't you? It took me ages to memorize this stuff.'

Little Andy mouthed the phrase about Tracy's panties, then began, 'Scaphoid, er, lunate . . . triquetrum—' He broke off. 'You're telling me this leaking thing happens *twice*? How'd this original sick guy get sick anyhow? Nice safari vacation in some weird country overseas? Shooting kangaroos?'

'Doesn't sound too likely, does it?'

'What then?'

Quack shook his head once more. 'The worst-case scenario—' He broke off, looked up at Little Andy, frowned, looked away. 'I know somebody wanted me on hand when the first few cases showed. Why else would the Warden send me out? I haven't done work like that in years. Medical Direct doesn't usually show even a computer-generated interest in the records I keep and no interest at all in reviewing them. But that time? They wanted full reports. This second time canal workers got sick is the only other time they'd ever paid that kind of attention. The nurse hadn't forgotten either. She said they wanted my notes "as before".'

Andy scrunched up his face, shook his head. 'I can tell that you see the connection. That's how come you figured Monk was the last new case.'

'I don't know that it's the connection. It's just that . . . New diseases crop up from time to time. New ones get created in labs. They need to be tested. Is this bug going to be any use in biological warfare? If so, what are the symptoms? What do they look like? How long do they take to subside? What's the risk to an invading army? Nothing all that serious the first time around. What happens if there's a more virulent strain of whatever it is? Might that one actually kill people? Just how might it do—'

'Lab rats?' Andy gasped. 'Us? You're kidding me.'

'I hope I am, Andrew. I truly hope so.'

17

SANGAMON COUNTY,
NORTH OF SPRINGFIELD:
The last night in July and the first
few hours of August

Weather this hot for this long makes fire. Somebody's cigarette? Or barbecue? Wood rubbing against wood in dry vegetation? Doesn't matter in the end.

Several fires had broken out during the afternoon in the wooded areas around Petersburg, just northwest of Springfield; smoke from them still made a haze across the road at midnight. A pressurized cylinder isn't safe in a fire, and both tankers were 22-wheelers carrying pressurized cylinders. At least there'd been nothing but smoke so far, and there wasn't anything but smoke at this chain-wire fence. The driver of the first tanker pulled to a stop, climbed down from his cab and ran through the smoke to open the gates. The smoke was acrid. He shut his eyes against it and felt his way to the door of a small structure beyond. He could hear the throb of machinery from inside.

Lamar Bryant was afraid of fire. He had nightmares about it. Besides, all he wanted to do was get back to his Brittany. She'd spent the last few days with her family in Peoria – arrived home only after he'd left for this job. She was blonde, a real blonde, right down to her bush. He was proud of that. Thoughts of her meant a struggle to keep his mind on the road to this place. He fumbled in his pocket for the key to the structure's door, and just the idea of putting a key in a lock made his breath come faster. His hands trembled in anticipation, and the damned smoke actually burned his eyes; the key slipped out of his hands. He shone his torch at the baked earth and squinted in search.

'Hurry it up,' called out the driver of the other tanker. He had the word 'Boss' tattooed across his knuckles, one letter per knuckle.

'I've kind of . . . well . . .'

'For fuck's sake, Bryant.'

'Got it, got it, got it.'

He unlocked the door to the structure, ran back to Boss's tanker to help him and the second man unload a stainless steel box as big as an old-fashioned jukebox. 'What *is* this thing?' he said to Boss. 'Some kind of Coke machine? Jesus, it weighs a ton. What are all these gadgets on it?'

Nobody answered him. The three of them manoeuvred the box onto a trolley and pushed it into the building. Lamar tended to his own tanker, easing it through the gates, unwinding a hose from it, pulling the hose inside. The others were already attaching the hose from their tanker to the box. Lamar craned his neck to watch, dabbing at his eyes with a Kleenex.

'Get your nose out of this,' Boss said to him.

'Jesus, you guys. Hooking up a bunch of hoses ain't exactly a state secret, is it? I mean, what could be in them tankers anyhow? Liquid gold? Pink champagne? Oil of—'

'Shut up.'

A third hose attached the gadget-laden box to a heavy container on a concrete plinth. This procedure took three hands, which made the third guy seem a masterpiece of efficient design; he had only one arm. 'What are these machines supposed to do?' Lamar went on; he stood back to survey them. 'They look . . . I don't know, maybe like some juiced-up espresso maker or some fucking thing. We going to supply the birds and bees with fresh, hot coffee? Bad idea. It'll keep them awake all night. On the other hand, I'm not so sure about that. It might be kind of pretty. All that singing in the—'

'Bryant! Shut your fucking mouth.'

While Boss went to turn on the tankers' pressure pumps, Lamar said, 'You got any idea how come we got to go out at this hour of night? Why tonight? What's so urgent about it? I mean, why couldn't we do it in the morning? Be a hell of a lot easier. We could see what we're doing.' Lamar glanced around at the cement walls. 'Not that this is a chamber fit for a lady or nothing. Probably just as ugly, day or night.'

The one-armed guy gave him an irritable glance as pressure in the pumps outside roared into action.

'I don't even know your name,' Lamar shouted over the noise. 'How the fuck can a guy work with people he doesn't even know the names of? Here's this guy with "Boss" tattooed across his right hand. Is that really his name? Nobody says so. I asked him. He says it'll do. Well, nobody's just "Boss", is he? He's got to have a name.'

The one-armed guy said nothing.

'Hey, Boss,' Lamar said as Boss reappeared, 'doesn't One Arm have a name either? He won't talk to me.'

Boss only turned to check over the couplings.

'Fuck it all,' Lamar went on, 'you have no idea how these night jobs screw up my love life. What's wrong with daytime? I could show you a much easier route. My wife was telling me about it. She knows this country, grew up near here. There are foxes and stuff in the underbrush. She keeps asking, "Lammie-love, what do you *do* on these night shifts?"'

Boss was turning slowly back to face him. 'She asks that?'

'My Brittany is full of questions.' Lamar smiled. 'It's really cute, know what I mean?'

'And what do you tell her?'

"Bout what?'

'Night shifts.'

'What am I supposed to tell her, wise guy? I tell her we help juke-boxes fuck ice-cream makers.' Lamar gave a short laugh. 'Does look kind of like that, don't it? That's what she says. Even all them gauges.'

'You told your wife what this machinery looks like?'

'What do you care what I tell her?'

Lamar Bryant got home at three in the morning. He and Brittany lived in White-tailed Deer Town, a 1960s housing estate north of Springfield and right in the flight path of planes going to Chicago. Deer Town – that's what its residents called it – was row upon row of homes, so many of them and so identical in layout that they'd once looked like wallpaper to passengers in planes flying out of Abraham Lincoln Capital Airport. Since then, trees had grown. So had hedges. Many of the houses had been torn down and replaced. Other owners had added extra storeys and extra garage space.

Lamar and Brittany's was one of the original houses, completely intact, still a single-storey, shoddy construction of plastic and wood. The whole place shook when Lamar slammed the front door behind him in his dash through the living room to the bedroom, where their one air conditioner rumbled away. He had his trousers unzipped and down as far as his knees by the time he hit the bed.

An hour later, Lamar and Brittany were deep in sleep. So were all their neighbours. There was nobody to see the man who knelt beside the window of their bedroom. Not that anybody would have been likely to see him. Lamar wasn't much of a gardener. He always said he liked weeds shoulder high; he said they looked 'natural'. A privet hedge planted by a previous owner had grown into a small forest so dense that the Bryants hardly needed curtains in the bedroom.

The kneeling man had had to cut a path to the window. He ran his hands over the elderly air conditioner that protruded from it, took a screwdriver out of the tool belt he wore around his waist and set to work.

Old-fashioned air conditioners leak water. Sometimes they leak refrigerant too. Given just the right conditions, refrigerant can be dangerous, and the first signs of trouble can easily go unnoticed in the dark: vapour streaming out from the metal box that holds the machine's compressor. The man didn't wait around to watch. He was already on his feet and running when the first thin tongue of flame peeped out. But he certainly heard the whump of the explosion. Even the seventh graders of Lincoln City Junior High – on a chartered flight to Chicago for a special morning performance of *Carmen* at the Opera House – could see the orange-red fireball that lit up the sky.

The story didn't appear in the *Journal-Register* until the day after, but it was still front-page news:

Two dead in freak fire

Home-repaired air conditioner explodes

Lamar and Brittany Bryant of White-tailed Deer Town died instantly when . . .

18

SPRINGFIELD: The first morning in August

Jimmy's campaign promise – a terrorist-proof control room for Springfield's water utility – blossomed into a reality on the night Lamar died. The first of a series of running-in periods began then. What a showcase installation this was! So fully automated that a single person could monitor it.

The single person that night was Pete Tanaka. He sat at an angled console lined with a bank of flat interactive touchscreens, all of them linked to a movable keyboard. Camera feeds to a bank of bigger screens included maps showing every distribution pipe, valve, pump station, pressure-monitoring station, water meter, even every service vehicle. GPS transmissions ensured that a touch of the finger could send out response teams to any defect, disruption, damage, threatening incident.

Pete wasn't good with humans; they veered off in such unexpected directions. But computers? He loved their glow, coloured lights, background hum, quiet crackle when the processor started up a new function. He'd studied this system, run through it many times but never been alone with it before. Now it was his until dawn. He'd spent a couple of hours feeling it out – very gently –

resizing images and zooming in on them, panning for greater detail and focus while the city of Springfield held firm around him, everything under control.

But Pete wasn't holding so firm himself. He had a bladder infection that caused what doctors call 'urgency'; when he had to take a leak, he had to do it right now. He was taking a sulphonamide for it, and sulphonamides have to be washed through the body. Lots of water in. Lots out. The problem was that the toilets for the control room weren't yet installed. The only place to pee was along a criss-cross of hallways, down a flight of stairs to the basement. He'd figured he could handle it with the mayonnaise jars his mother kept for preserving; he'd stuffed his knapsack with them, and so far tonight he'd filled only two.

At three in the morning, he discovered that the chair he sat in was as friendly as the electronics. It moved beneath him as though it were floating on air. A gentle shove: it hovered into the middle of the room. A harder shove, aim for the door at the far wall, go flying, feet off the floor, arms stuck out to provide a bumpered landing.

The jolt and crunch came as a complete shock. And yet he knew at once what had happened.

He'd set his knapsack near a corner when he arrived; he'd fetched two mayonnaise jars from it, replaced them in it. Not even so friendly a chair could fly over an obstacle like that. The stench of urine proved him right before a tentative glance inside showed the broken mayonnaise jars. And that's when the urgency hit him. It didn't even give him time to think. He hung on to his prick, made a dash for the basement, peed as fast as he could, then rushed back up the stairs.

As he reached the top of the flight, the lights went off so

suddenly that he teetered on the step and had to feel his way back along the corridors to the control room. By the time he made it through the door to his bank of computers, the only thing still powered up was the red warning signal on the angled console. As he watched, it too faded and died.

He had a torch in his backpack. The problem was finding the thing. Why is it that when you can't see, something you *know* is there isn't where you left it after all? Why does it seem that some-body's watching you? Forcing you to bumble around? Laughing at you as you pat along the skirting? When he finally found the pack, he grabbed for the torch in a panic, forgetting the broken mayon-naise jars, and leapt back with a yelp at the burn of a glass cut across his palm.

'Help!' he cried. 'Somebody help!' He held his breath and waited. Nothing. 'Help! Control room! Help!'

Nobody came. He slipped down against the wall to his haunches. His mother had taught him to count his breathing in and out if he got frightened. 'One and a two and a . . .' He clenched his fist and felt a shock of pain. Blood spurted through the fingers. 'Help! Help! Help!'

Still nobody came.

'One and a two . . .'

He took off his technician's white coat, wrapped it around his hand as both bandage and protector and probed gently amid the broken jars for his torch, found it, got to his feet, switched it on. The control room landline stood on the console. He picked up the receiver. Dead. He pulled out his mobile, dialled the utility helpline. It was engaged. He tried 911. 'Please wait for a connec-tion,' came the robot voice.

The emergency generator should have switched on automati-cally. He located the room's toolbox, balanced his torch, unscrewed a panel at the back of the console — blood dripping everywhere — found the manual override, flipped it. Still nothing. He'd just eased back on his haunches when the lights in the room flickered, and he heard the gentle bump of the computer start-up. The screens flashed. But they didn't display the utility's logo. They flashed again, trembled and went dark.

Minutes passed. Nothing happened. A yawning emptiness opened up in him. His heart hurt. They'd find out about the piss bottles. They'd say he'd deserted his post, that if he hadn't, none of this would have happened. They'd fire him. He'd never get another job, and he could see his mother crying with the shame of it.

'Please. *Please.*' He prayed directly to the computer system itself. 'Please, wake up.' Still nothing. He slumped against the console, and his mother's tears rolled down his cheeks before she had a chance to shed them.

Not long after dawn, the sprinklers were on full across the Freyl lawns. High arcs of water and a fine spray made rainbows in the morning sun. The gardener was on the far side of the house; there was nobody to see the height of the spray drop abruptly, recover, drop again. Then it paused, gurgled, choked and stopped altogether.

That gurgle and choke in the garden water supply showed itself inside the house when Lillian filled the kettle for coffee. She turned the tap off, set the kettle down, turned the tap on again. The water spat out at her. She jumped back, then glanced down at her apron. The water splattered over it was brown-grey. She brought the cloth to her nose and grimaced at the smell: dead skunks and ammonia.

She checked the basin in the downstairs bathroom. Same

thing. She checked the laundry room. Again the same. She changed her apron and went into the dining room where Becky – glasses on her nose, head bent over a pile of papers, BlackBerry resting between emails – had the TV on to catch the morning headlines.

'Miz Freyl,' Lillian said, 'I'm afraid something—'

But the news anchor beat her to it.

'Warning!' he cried from behind a black-edged yellow screen that read:

WARNING
HAZARD

'Reports have just come in,' the anchor went on, 'that water supplies to some homes on the west side of Springfield are contaminated. Springfield Light and Power has issued an emergency press release warning residents not to drink water from their taps, cook with it or brush their teeth with it. They must not even bathe in it.'

'It sure do stink,' Lillian said.

Becky glanced up, shook her head in despair. The timing couldn't be worse. The open Council meeting was on Tuesday. People would discuss Jimmy's plans to privatize Springfield's water with this awful smell lingering in their noses as well as their minds. They'd listen to a call for change.

Less than an hour later, the news programme announced that the problem had been solved and that pipework to affected homes was in the process of being flushed. The cause was unknown, it said; the present theory was an accumulation of summer algae on Lake Springfield, and there was no danger to public health.

Too little and too late. The *Journal-Register* gave Jimmy headlines better than he could have hoped for:

Springfield water stinks
Is something rotten in the state of our public utilities?

19

SPRINGFIELD: Tuesday

At a few minutes past eleven, Becky's Lexus SUV edged its way through almost solid traffic along a stretch of highway at the edge of Springfield's east side. Police were everywhere. Horns blared. People shouted. Crowds on foot threaded their way through the cars. Lillian manoeuvred the SUV towards a dilapidated building and a sign that read 'NO PARKING'.

'You can't be serious,' Becky said to her.

'They using it as a homeless-shelter,' said Lillian.

'How dare he?'

Lillian laughed. 'Usually Mr Mayor Jimmy Zemanski's sense of humour don't tickle me at all.'

'I'll have his head for this. I'll have his head.'

The public City Council meeting to discuss whether or not citizens should have a voice in selling off Springfield's public water supply had been scheduled for ten thirty in the Old Capitol building; the announcement said available venues in the New Capitol complex weren't large enough for the crowd expected. Becky dreaded the political wrangling ahead – she wasn't used to defeat – but the Old Capitol itself offered a ray of hope. President

THE BLUE DEATH 119

Lincoln practised law there; President Obama announced his candidacy there. She was the reason those two men stood on the same steps. Everybody knew that she and her Arts Society had raised the money to restore the building, and that Obama wouldn't have chosen it if she hadn't restored it. The place — those memories — might sway public opinion. At least a little.

But she and Lillian had arrived to find the streets blocked off and traffic wardens handing out leaflets:

CITY COUNCIL MEETING THIS MORNING

The Old Capitol is closed while police investigate an alleged bomb threat. Those wishing to attend the public session of the Council meeting should proceed to the Avenging Angel Shelter on Dirkson Parkway. The meeting will begin at 11:30.

Dirkson Parkway was a four-lane wasteland of used-car lots, telephone poles, cheap motels and cheaper hamburger joints. The Avenging Angel fitted right in: small, squat, ugly, with a corrugated pink siding that had looked dirty from the moment it was installed. A stretch of weed-infested and chained-off macadam made up a forecourt. Groups of the homeless, evicted for the occasion, clustered at the property's boundary while swarms of respectable-looking people elbowed each other to get into the hostel.

One of the officers knocked on the SUV's window. Lillian rolled it down.

'You can't park here, lady,' he said.

Becky leaned forward from the back seat. 'Oh, yes, we can.'

'Mrs Freyl! I didn't see you.' He took down the chain across the front yard, beckoned in the SUV, then helped Lillian unload

Becky's wheelchair into the sticky heat of the day and a clustering group of supporters.

'Darling Becky,' Donna cried, pushing her way through the crowd. 'Just look at all these people. We've had to turn droves away. Droves! There isn't anywhere near enough room, and it's all so very ugly in this place. Wait until you see inside. I mean, forget the pink siding. Inside, the plaster is peeling off.'

Becky pursed her lips. 'I suppose that dreadful Kline man is here.'

'Front row.'

'Just as I feared.'

Morris Kline was Director of Springfield Light and Power, an avid football fan and one of Jimmy's first appointments as mayor. Becky had set herself the task of bringing him into the Coalition. Her first telephone call to his secretary included an invitation to lunch. The secretary told her that he wasn't available. People like Morris Kline don't snub Rebecca Freyl. She'd called again. This time the man's secretary had had the gall to tell her that Mr Kline didn't feel it was 'appropriate to speak at this moment in time'. 'At this moment in time' was a phrase Becky particularly disliked.

Becky pursed her lips again. 'What about Aloysia?'

'No sign of her,' said Donna.

'No word either?'

'She'd have got in touch with me if she were back.'

'Thank God for small mercies.'

It's true that Aloysia's degree in hydrology made her a natural for the Coalition; after all, she was the person who'd warned Becky about Jimmy's plans. But the cat-smile that Becky knew too well had come with the warning. The first time she'd seen it had been at her own dining table. Back in May, she and Helen held a dinner party that included the Englishwoman.

Chat over iced Martinis had gone well. But when Lillian served the soup, Aloysia put the palms of her hands on the table and surveyed the company with that smile. As soon as she had everybody's attention, she turned to Helen. 'So where's this delicious husband of yours?'

Which is how Becky found out about the marriage. She'd spluttered, put down her spoon, started to get up, then sat down again. 'Husband?'

Helen reached out, took her hand. 'I kept trying to tell you, Grandma, but you just didn't want to hear.'

'I always liked a bit of rough myself,' Aloysia said dreamily.

'Lillian!' Becky had cried. 'Get my pills.'

The last thing she needed today at this Council meeting was somebody who enjoyed springing nasty surprises like that. She had enough to worry about already: Jimmy's star speaker Morris Kline, last week's stinky water, the damning headline in the *Journal-Register*. Now Jimmy's aggressive change of venue.

The shift from Old Capitol to Avenging Angel reeked of ambush, and the entryway of the shelter contributed its own smells of sweat and garbage. Donna wheeled Becky through it and into the cafeteria: long tables pushed to the sides, benches arranged in rows and crammed with people. More people perched on the tables and lined the walls. Lillian positioned Becky near the doorway – her supporters clustering around her still – to catch any breeze that might blow. The temperature outside was over a hundred and humidity at 96%. People fanned themselves with newspapers and paperback books. Not Becky. She didn't mind. She'd been brought up in Atlanta. She loved the heat.

At the end of the room, Jimmy sat with a quorum of sweat-soaked aldermen, three of them on either side of him. A lectern and a microphone stood in a cleared space in front of them. Jimmy banged his gavel, called the meeting to order, went through the ritual preliminaries and began his parade of witnesses with the Commissioner of the Department of Water Management.

The Commissioner grew passionate about crumbling city water infrastructure and soaring prices: 'We've all seen the effects of this neglect. We must act, ladies and gentlemen. Last week's "incident" of sewage in our water is only a taster of what's to come if we don't.'

City Planning explained that without private finance Springfield's citizens would have to foot the bill for compliance to new environmental laws. 'Last week's "incident" is going to cost us dear. So are the new laws. Together these will take $250 million out of your pockets.'

The Chief of the City Accounting Office waved the five hundred-page think-tank study that Sebastian Slad had given Jimmy: proof that private ownership alone could correct faults, update the system and at the same time 'put $175 million of that money right back into your pockets.'

Becky could feel the crowd waver. A few had already left. She clutched the arms of her wheelchair as Morris Kline walked to the lectern, a stiff, starched figure despite the temperature, the only person in the room who wasn't sweating.

'I'm a good soldier,' he began. 'I do what I'm told. But there are times when a soldier's duty is to disobey his orders.' A murmur of consternation went through the audience. 'Over a year ago my predecessor enacted plans to accommodate the environmental laws that concern City Planning. They're not new at all. My predecessor also streamlined existing operations and began a quiet, inexpensive expansion of facilities. Because of him, the city is already saving tax dollars. As for last week's "incident", it came during the first trial run of Mr Zemanski's new electronic system and the first time — the *very* first time — that my predecessor's system was shut down after a decade of faultless performance.'

Morris Kline left the lectern and sat down.

For a moment Jimmy was too stunned to speak. Becky could hardly believe what she'd heard.

'That's it, Morris?' Jimmy had to struggle to keep his voice even. 'This isn't quite what we . . . er, you haven't anything to add?'

Morris stood again. 'In my opinion, privatization would constitute a criminal waste of public money.'

The audience burst into applause. Becky looked around her in delight. David's insolence had created unity. All the Coalition had needed was its first scent of blood — and here it was.

Nothing could stop them now.

20

SPRINGFIELD: The following weekend

Political spats rarely interrupt Springfield society, and Jimmy was still the Freyl family lawyer.

Only the day before the meeting at the Avenging Angel, he'd been to Freyl House to discuss redrafting Becky's will; she had to make sure David couldn't get his hands on Helen's inheritance. In Becky's eyes, Jimmy's love for Helen, his animosity towards David and his anger at this disastrous marriage certainly created a bond more important than a petty disagreement about Springfield's water supply. She'd told him over a glass of iced tea that if he really wanted Helen, he was going to have to change his approach. She was the one who'd suggested that he begin with a party at his house on Saturday.

As for David, she assured him there'd be no problem. One of the prime texts for anybody involved in business in any country in the world is Sun Tzu's *Art of War*. It's the source of the expression 'Know thy enemy.' Becky had studied it herself when she took over the Freyl investments.

'I think I'm beginning to understand the man a little,' she said to Jimmy.

'So?' he said.

'Do the right thing.'

'I don't know what it is.'

'Ask him first. Before you ask us.'

Jimmy drove out early in the morning to the site where David was working on the house that he and Helen were to share. A concrete mixer churned away. A burly man with a wheelbarrow stood beside it; David shovelled cement from it into the barrow. The din from the mixer overwhelmed even the heavy beat from the radio.

'Hiya, David,' Jimmy shouted.

'What?' David shouted back. He didn't turn away from the mixer.

'Can't you turn that thing off for a minute?'

'No.'

'I wanted to ask you and Helen to dinner at my house next Saturday.'

'No.'

'I said—'

'I heard you,' David shouted.

'Can you come?'

'No.'

'Just "no"?'

David didn't respond. Jimmy stood there, not sure whether he'd gained an advantage or lost one. 'Do the right thing,' Becky had said, her mind on the ancient Chinese text about war. 'What about Helen?' Jimmy shouted at David.

'What about her?'

'You don't mind if I ask her, do you?'

'Nothing to do with me.'

*

Jimmy's house at the edge of Lake Springfield took up the entirety of what was once a modest neighbourhood. But that was years ago. A previous governor of the state had bought the tract of land, levelled it, turned it into a private park and built a monumental house there: glass, steel and rough oak. It added to Jimmy's stature; he'd bought it not long before his campaign for mayor. Spotlights lit it up from the outside.

He'd thought hard about Becky's advice on how he should behave, and he had it firmly in mind as he opened the door.

'Helen!' he said, pulling her into his arms before she could protest. 'God, you're a sight for sore eyes.' He held her out, hands on her shoulders, then let her go. 'No husband this evening? I thought he might relent just this once. I can't say I'm sorry he hasn't, but these occasions must be—'

'Leave it, Jimmy,' Helen interrupted.

'Sure, sure. I understand. And Becky!' He bent down, kissed Becky's cheek. 'Thanks for making the effort.' He laughed. 'I don't know why you aren't as worn out as I am by the Coalition's triumph at the Avenging Angel. It was so goddamned hot, I practically melted. And you seem to have more energy than ever.'

'A homeless shelter! You should be ashamed of yourself, Jimmy Zemanski.'

'Oh, I am. I am. Now come in, both of you. Allan and Ruth Madison are already here. So are the Orlandos and the Yetmans.' He laughed at the purse of Becky's lips. 'I got to have some supporters around me, Becky.' Jimmy hadn't told her that he was going to include either couple in tonight's party. Both had signed a public petition supporting the privatization plan. They were rich west siders, but neither wife had received an invitation to join the Springfield Arts Society even though both had wrangled hard for the honour. Becky didn't like them. Mrs Orlando simpered and wore shoes that were too small. The Yetmans were City Council lawyers whose money came from squeezing high rents out of run-down tenements on the east side.

Helen wheeled Becky into Jimmy's living room where the others waited. Original prints in the style of Andy Warhol covered the walls. Soft focus lighting struggled with overstuffed chairs and angular tables. Pride of place went to a football signed by George Blanda himself; it sat on a marble slab beside a chunky statuette of a player mid-dash, his head and the football somehow melded into one.

'Mrs Orlando,' Becky said.

'Oh, Mrs Freyl!' Mrs Orlando's bad knee was probably the only thing that held her back from a curtsy. Behind her, Mr Orlando bowed from the waist as best he could; he was fat and bulbous-nosed but a hedge-fund broker with a formidable reputation.

Mrs Yetman was made out of different stuff entirely. She was a handsome redhead, and she knew it. 'Nice to see you, Becky,' she said.

'Are we on first-name terms, Mrs Yetman?' Becky's voice was tart.

'Sure we are,' Mrs Yetman said. 'Don't you remember? Jimmy's just been telling me you've got some memory problems. The name's Tracy. We met lots of times at—'

'I have no trouble whatever with my memory, Mrs Yetman,' Becky interrupted. 'Ruth!' she said turning away. 'How lovely you're looking tonight.' Ruth wore a pale beige dress that showed off her willowy figure.

Jimmy opened bottles of champagne; several other couples arrived, and despite the chilly beginning, conversation tinkled on comfortably, guests in groups of three and four. Jimmy stood beside Ruth. A lightness of touch, his to hers, hers to him, made the relationship painfully clear; not that the husband seemed to mind.

Jimmy refilled glasses, then sat next to Helen. 'You and Ruth certainly get on well,' Helen said to him with a wry smile.

'I like Ruth. She tells me things. You didn't even tell me you were teaching at the college. I had to track you there to find out. That's not fair. I'm a busy man.'

Helen knew he checked on her from time to time, but when he was at his best, even an admission like that became amusing, charming, almost endearing, 'Jimmy, I didn't know myself until an hour before.'

'I teach there too.'

'You're kidding. Why? When did that start?'

'Evening classes. Adult education. A couple of months now. Adults are easier than kids. They actually want to learn. It's all, you know, what your rights are as a consumer and a citizen, make the city and the law work for you instead of against you.'

'It wasn't evening, Jimmy. It was noon.'

He laughed. 'Now you're going all technical on me.'

She gave him a puzzled glance, looked away.

'Something the matter?' he said.

'That's what David says I do.'

'Does he? How'd it go? The class I mean.'

He decided from Helen's face Becky was most likely right about his approach. 'Tact, Jimmy,' she'd said. 'You must treat Helen as though she were a client whose business you wish to secure.'

As for Helen, she was feeling rebellious – her dependence on David grated badly – but the shift in Jimmy's manner registered on her only as relief that he was a little less crude than usual tonight. She found herself talking to him with some real interest about teaching.

Dinner was old fashioned: shrimp cocktail and roast beef. As the chef brought on a dessert of baked apples, the talk turned towards water and Jimmy's plan to privatize.

Becky sat at Jimmy's right. 'I have an announcement to make,' he said, patting her hand. 'You're going to be angry.'

'Am I? Really? Haven't we put all that aside?'

'Well, Becky, sometimes things don't go exactly as we ... I'm sorry to say this has turned into a dinner party with a purpose.'

'Oh, dear, *now* what have you done?'

Jimmy poked his apple, shook his head, took in a breath. 'You know, I did try to tell you that times have changed since you were young, that things aren't as they—'

'Just spit it out, Jimmy.'

'I've negotiated a contract for Springfield.'

Becky frowned. Her lips tightened. 'A contract? What kind of contract?'

'To privatize—'

'This is a contract to sell off Springfield Light and Power?' she interrupted. 'Our water supply? You *can't* be saying that.'

Helen burst out laughing. 'You just ram your way through anything that's in your path, don't you, Jimmy?'

'Nonsense, Helen,' Becky said. 'He has no authority. He can't go around making decisions until there's been a public vote.'

The pause that followed was uncomfortable. Mr Yetman finished his last bite of apple and cleared his throat. 'I'm afraid you haven't quite understood the position.' His voice carried the authority of the City Council lawyer that he was. 'The ballot is weeks away. You see, if the Mayor waited for the vote, and if the vote were to go against him, then he wouldn't be able to negotiate a contract without presenting the details to the public for their—'

'It's hilarious,' Helen interrupted, laughing again. 'Grandma, he's trumped you. Your prized public vote is going to come after the fact. It can't affect the outcome one way or the other. Brilliant, Jimmy. Absolutely brilliant. I didn't know you had it in you. Can you really do this all on your own? Don't you even have to have the Council behind you?'

'I've scheduled a special meeting to approve it a week from Thursday,' Jimmy said.

'Becky looked around the table at the faces of people she'd known for years – people she'd ruled for years. 'You knew about this? *All* of you?' She turned to Jimmy. 'With whom is this contract?'

'Nobody Russian, Becky. That ought to please you. It's a nice local company down the road.'

'Are you talking about UCAI? No, no, Jimmy. Not even you can do that. You represent them. It's a conflict of interest. Plain and simple.'

Jimmy had to fight to keep the pleasure out of his voice. 'It will certainly be in your interest to attend the meeting, Becky. I have every confidence that the vote will go my way, but who can say? A council can be as fickle as an electorate. At any rate, we can—'

'Don't you try to tell me what to do, Jimmy Zemanski. You can't even assure me you'll redraft my will yourself. What made you seek out a shark like UCAI to play games with? They're out of your league. This can't be legal. It simply cannot be.'

'Can't it?' said Jimmy. 'Who says so? It's certainly not illegal. Ask Yetman here. Constitutional law is his specialty.'

21

SPRINGFIELD: The next morning

As soon as Becky got home from Jimmy's party, she called Morris Kline, the person who knew most about Springfield's water, the man who'd refused her invitations to lunch and the utility director who'd damned privatization as a 'criminal waste of public money'. She asked him to coffee the following morning. This time he accepted.

Lillian showed him into the room that had been Hugh Freyl's study. Technology for the blind used to dominate here. Now that Hugh was dead, no trace of him or his blindness remained. The room itself gave Becky a sense of him; she'd made it into her own study, but any personal mementoes – especially of his affliction – were just too painful. An ancient print of a samurai hung to one side of her, a small red lacquer cabinet stood on the desk in front of her. Morris sat opposite, as starched and stiff in his suit as he'd been when she first saw him at the Avenging Angel. They made small talk about the beauty of Freyl House and blistering weather outside until Lillian brought in a tray with a coffee pot, cups, brownies and little napkins.

'This morning's paper tells me you're suddenly *not* Director of the Springfield Light and Power any more,' Becky said, pouring out the coffee as Lillian left.

'I was fired.'

'I'm truly sorry to hear it.' Nobody thought Jimmy would keep him on after that surprise support of the opposition at the Council meeting. 'The *Journal-Register* also said something about your leaving for "personal reasons". Were there any? I do hope not.'

Morris shook his head. Jimmy had appointed him less than a year ago. Before that, he'd spent twenty years in Snohomish, Indiana, and risen to become director of the public utility there. The job was fine. He enjoyed it, but an unstable wife had alienated his family, then many of his friends; the acrimonious divorce that followed shook him badly. When Jimmy offered him the Springfield utility, he'd been eager to go, perhaps too eager.

'I'm unlucky in love,' he said to Becky. It was the face of a Boy Scout, but an unexpected, self-deprecating humour deepened the creases around his mouth and eyes. 'I thought I was coming here to marry a job.'

Becky nodded. 'Not many people turn down an invitation to lunch with me, especially people new to town.'

'I turned down two.'

'I found that interesting, Mr Kline.'

'The last thing I wanted was to offend you, Mrs Freyl.'

'I know that now,' she said. 'Cream? Sugar?' She watched him add both to his coffee, picked up her own cup, took a sip. 'Few people impress me either, Mr Kline. After your declaration at the Avenging Angel, I understood that you hadn't wanted to compromise what you were about to say then or your ability to continue as an independent voice afterwards.' She took another sip of coffee. 'I doubt I've ever run across anybody in public office who's both courageous and honest. The honest ones never last. How did they put up with you in Indiana?'

The creases around his mouth and eyes deepened again. 'They never tried to make a deal with UCAI.'

The humour reminded Becky of her son Hugh. So did the courage and the suffering for principles. But *good* men are so irritating. To a pragmatist like her, the Hughs and Morrises of the world were Don Quixotes on crusade, too wrapped up in the cause to hear the warning shots. She suspected that Morris had trusted people in Indiana when he shouldn't have. He'd doubtless told the truth when he should have lied. She had great faith in lies. How could society work for ten minutes without them? Or a government for five?

'Brownie?' she said, offering the platter to him. 'Lillian makes the best brownies outside Atlanta, Mr Kline. Napkin? Did Jimmy give you any reason for firing you? Beyond disloyalty, of course.'

Morris took a brownie, bit into it. 'He said that the pollution of the town's water happened on my watch. That is true, Mrs Freyl. I can't deny it. But he says it means that I failed to keep the utility up to my predecessor's standards. That is not true. I raised my predecessor's standards. The utility never functioned as economically or as efficiently as it did under my directive. I can't tell you how profoundly that contamination incident shocked me.' He looked away, then down at his brownie, then back at her. 'Twenty-five years of service to public utilities, Mrs Freyl, and there's never been a hint of a contamination incident. Never!'

He went on to explain that the reasons for the problem would emerge only after a detailed study of data log, flow rates, pressure in pipes and pumps from the control room as well as records at the treatment plant, individual pumping stations, monitored junctions, households affected. 'My team and I began gathering evidence at once, and we worked until well past midnight that first day. I arrived early the next morning—' He broke off, frowned. 'The data was gone, Mrs Freyl. Just disappeared. *All* of it: files, disks, printouts, hard drives. I called Jimmy at once.'

'It's my fault,' Jimmy had said to him. 'That terrorist-proof business. Know what I mean?' Morris had no idea what he was talking about. 'The new control room is covered by the Patriot Act,' Jimmy went on. 'You know, Non-Disclosure Agreements and all that. You and your team were supposed to sign. I just plain forgot. I'll have them ready tomorrow, then maybe a couple of days to get them cleared through the National Security Agency.'

Becky set down her cup. 'He said that?'

'He did.'

'The National Security Agency? Are you sure?'

'I'm absolutely sure. I was as taken aback as you are.'

The National Security Agency is the most secret of America's secret organizations, so much more secretive than the CIA and the FBI that the only way the rest of the world can guess the scale of its operations is by the eighteen thousand parking spaces around the biggest of its known installations, its headquarters in Fort Meade, Maryland. Just how many other installations there are spotted around the country, nobody knows. Literally nobody. This is America's Gestapo, Uncle Sam's very own Stasi, whose employees joke that the letters NSA stand for 'No Such Agency' and 'Never Say Anything'.

'What can the man be playing at?' Becky said to Morris.

'I don't understand it any more than you do, Mrs Freyl.'

While Jimmy had shuffled Non-Disclosure Agreements, Morris got on with collating samples of the contaminated water, taking them over to the lab himself. There hadn't been any need to explain how urgent the analysis was, but when he called to find out the results, the technician said they'd all been sent directly to the Mayor. Morris called Jimmy at once. Again Jimmy apologized, then told him that the lab also needed to sign Non-Disclosure Agreements.

'I found that very strange,' Morris said to Becky. 'Suppose it was sewage as the Council claimed at the public meeting. I have a duty to the public to investigate. Sewage is dangerous. It makes people sick. Because we had no lab results, we began checking hospitals. If it had been sewage, hospitals would reflect it: an increase in gastroenteritis, skin rashes, eye infections, respiratory infections. But there were fewer patients than usual. I reported my findings to Jimmy right away.'

'That's when he fired you.'

'He said he needed somebody with higher security clearance.'

Becky shook her head in wonder. 'Why on earth would you go to him with what you'd found?'

'It was my duty, Mrs Freyl.'

'Yes, yes,' she said, more tartly than she'd intended. What was a reasonable person to do with these Don Quixotes? Had they no sense at all? 'Did he mention signing the contract with UCAI?'

'I didn't know anything about it until I talked to you last night.'

Becky looked away, played with the buttons on her wheelchair, looked back. 'You know what happened to contaminate the water that day, don't you?'

'Well, er, there was so much data. I'm afraid we hadn't even begun to skim the surface.'

'But you know.'

He looked down at his brownie again. 'There were . . . anomalies that make some sense to me, but I cannot make out why power failures affected just the control room or how they caused the corruption of so much data. Perhaps Jimmy's NSA clearance makes sense – I couldn't really say – but if it does, why clear lab staff *after* they'd tested the samples, not before? How can he say there'd been sewage in the water and take no measures to ensure the public's safety? For that reason if no other, it should have been a relief to find out that sewage was unlikely. Why grow angry about it?'

'Jimmy has no scruples, Mr Kline. I wouldn't put it past him to sabotage a city's water supply just to win a vote.' The thought had occurred to her at the Avenging Angel as she listened to Jimmy's supporters. The surprise – to her – was that she hadn't thought of it earlier. 'You'll be willing to tell the public at least *some* of what you've told me?'

'They still own the facility. They have a right to know whatever I do.'

'There's the Non-Disclosure Agreement, Mr Kline.'

'Surely owners have a right to know what goes on in their business.'

Morris finished his coffee and his brownie while he and Becky discussed his speech at the Council meeting to come. 'You know,' he said as he was about to leave, 'it's such a pity Dr Gonzaga isn't back yet. I'm sure she'd have something relevant to add.'

Becky pursed her lips. 'She's the person who warned me that Jimmy planned to sell the utility.'

He nodded. 'That may well have been related to some results she'd run across.'

'Really? Contamination results? That lab work of yours is only a few days old. She warned me months ago, and I haven't heard from her since. The English are very lazy,' Becky grumbled. 'She's been gone since June. No American takes vacations that long.'

'I can't see the connection either,' Morris said, 'but I'm sure it's there. I gather she'd been doing some fieldwork shortly before she left. What she found upset her. She told me her results amounted to "incontrovertible evidence", then wouldn't say more, not even what they were evidence of – except that she might get in trouble because of them.' Becky was about to ask what kind of 'trouble', but the consternation on Morris's face stopped her. 'She said they'd already caused a break between her and Jimmy.' Morris frowned. 'I'm not adept at spotting relationships, Mrs Freyl. I hadn't known there was a connection to break.'

'Nor had I,' Becky said. 'Nor had I.'

As soon as Morris left, Becky emailed the Coalition. The subject line: 'ATTN: Emergency meeting'. More than thirty people gathered at her house the following evening to draw up plans for a demonstration that the town wouldn't forget in a hurry. Jimmy's venue for the vote on his contract with UCAI? The Old Capitol of course. The Coalition would guarantee that not even such a grand building could accommodate the crowds.

Ten days wasn't enough to pull together all they wanted, but Jimmy's weakness was his Council aldermen. Elected members on every council in America worry about winning the next time around; none of Jimmy's could fail to sense the abrupt shift that Morris Kline had brought about in the mood of the voters. The drama of the meeting at the Avenging Angel had erased the drama of water pollution in their minds. Ten days was enough to demonstrate the huge opposition to selling off Springfield's water. It was also enough to make sure that

Jimmy's behind-shut-doors contract with UCAI came off reeking of corruption.

When Morris got up and told people how he came to get fired, every member of the Mayor's Council would have to think hard before voting with him.

22

KNOX COUNTY, ILLINOIS:
The next afternoon

The Warden looked up at the man in front of him.

'Prisoner 19753. Sir!' Little Andy said, eyes straight ahead, focusing on nothing. 'You asked to see me. Sir!'

How could a man like Carl Johannsen have ended up as warden of South Hams State Correctional Facility? The prison was a shit hole. Its warden, a dollop of shit clinging to the prison's ass. Sole requirement? A high school diploma. Carl Johannsen had been Director of Consolidated Agricultural, Inc, a small Springfield company doing research into fertilizers and pesticides: two secretaries, a staff of ten, a Rolex watch and a single malt in the liquor cabinet at home. He'd inherited the business from his father, lost it to UCAI. Now this: red eyes from cheap Scotch, pouchy cheeks, too much Viagra and too little success even with its help. He sat in a captain's chair that had once commanded the QE2. That was good. His desk was highly polished. That was good too. Air conditioning throughout the Warden's quarters ensured that nobody should sweat, and yet sweat ran down his face so freely it stung his eyes. Half of it was righteous indignation; the other half, abject terror.

'You got a name, prisoner?' he shouted at Andy.

'Andrew Draper.'

'Fuck me. All I see is a nigger with a number. We got computer trouble.'

'Sir?'

'It won't work.'

'What seems to be the matter, sir?'

'How the fuck would I know? The hard drive's in the outer office. Ratty will go with you.' Ratty was the Warden's private secretary.

'You want me to . . .' Andy shrugged towards the outer office where the Warden's desktop computer stood.

'Christ Almighty, boy, fix the goddamned thing.'

It was all Andy could do to keep from laughing out loud. He'd been put in prison for hacking into university financial records and transferring federal funds to a local whorehouse. Only somebody with macaroni for a head would let him loose on the prison computer system. But then everybody said Johannsen was stupid. Everybody knew he'd never been near a prison until six months ago, fallout from one of the small companies that UCAI gobbled up before breakfast, an executive who'd probably never deigned to use a computer.

Too bad. For him anyhow. Once Andy was inside that system, the man belonged to him.

A metal table supported the computer in the outer office. Andy sat and Ratty hovered, a meek, mild, senior citizen who'd killed his own brother forty years ago. Nobody knew why. He didn't either. His nickname was easy to spot though: an upper lip that quivered in jerks like a rat sniffing out cheese for breakfast.

'I am afraid I have no grasp of these machines,' he said to Andy.

'Before your time, huh?'

Ratty nodded. 'The Warden tried to turn it on this morning. It made a beep, then the screen went black. Quite frightening really.'

Andy hadn't been all that brilliant with computers himself. He'd learned a little only because his girlfriend had dared him to hack into the university's system; the kick he'd got out of doing it came as a surprise. His present – and growing – expertise was down to Quack. He'd been deeply moved when he realized that the medic was arranging with gang bosses to bring in computer texts, much as David had done with medical books a generation before. Some of Andy's old buoyancy was making a cautious return. Maybe even a bit of hope for the future. Independent experts who specialize in computer crime are in great demand. The FBI, CIA, practically any state agency: Andy could tell them how it worked, and he didn't have all that long to serve. Good behaviour would get him out even faster. By that time, he'd be top of the game.

He sat down in front of the Warden's PC, switched it on, got as far as the beep, pressed a function key. The screen lit up in safe mode.

'Genius!' Ratty cried.

Andy flashed him a smile. 'I'm afraid it'll keep crashing unless I fix what's making it happen.'

It's way too easy to bypass username and password on a computer system as long as it's possible to press that function key. Johannsen didn't even notice it happening. He hovered nervously as Andy scanned through the machine's contents: programs, document files, email connection, Internet connection, anti-virus. It didn't take long for Andy to see why the Warden had called him and not UCAI's very efficient IT team.

'You know what I think, sir?' Andy said.

'Don't think. Just fix it.'

'Somebody's playing a joke on you. Looks to me like they've downloaded some hardcore stuff, and you'll keep crashing until—'

'Can you fix it?'

A flurry of fears and uncertainties chased themselves across the Warden's face. He fancied rape videos of very young girls, and the Slad twins' Bible-belt morality extended to all their employees, however lowly. They also rewarded employees for information about other employees: UCAI's IT team would report back. Maybe Johannsen didn't like being warden, but he'd had to manoeuvre hard to get the job; and the only reason he got it was that he was a Baptist, like the Slads. He'd professed very deep convictions. He'd appealed to the Lord's mercy; he did have four kids and a wife with cancer. Times were hard, especially for ex-executives of, well, a certain age.

The films he'd searched out would have him fired on the spot.

'Your hard drive is crawling with worms and viruses,' Andy said. It wasn't, but he'd just been studying computer bugs. Then, realizing that the Warden needed a good nigger who wouldn't tell tales on the boss man, not one uppity enough for white grammar, he burbled on. 'I'm a-feared that means your anti-virus needs updating something right awful. But don't you worry none, sir, 'cause, yes, sir, Little Andy can fix it. Little Andy can fix most anything. A couple hours maybe. They do bury this here stuff something deep.'

Databases on the Warden's computer held information on all employees, every staff member listed and photographed, date of birth, Social Security number, home address, telephone number, education, past employment history, credit rating, medical insurance information. Prison staff are inmates' main source of everything from drugs to lace panties and interdental brushes.

Occasionally they'll supply out of kindness, but fear and greed are the mainstays of business: ten dollars extorted from one to buy a carton of cigarettes from another. Every one of them would sell his immortal soul for the kind of thing that was — or could be made to be — lurking in those databases.

During his morning of fiddling, Andy added half a dozen user-names and passwords, which meant that anybody with a mobile phone could look at these records. Mobile phones were illegal in South Hams State Correctional Facility. They were in most prisons: a Texan inmate got slammed with forty years just for getting caught with one. But they're worth the risk, essential for outside business: drug dealing in Carbondale, money laundering in Chicago, riot organizing in the prison itself, threats to sentencing judges all over Illinois. Prices at South Hams ranged from fifty to five hundred dollars, depending on supply and the buyer's eagerness. Guards and chaplains brought in plastic mobiles that metal detectors missed; others arrived in soles of shoes, hollowed-out blocks of cheese, mayonnaise jars, boxes of tinned tomatoes, even in dead squirrels and by carrier pigeon.

Access via mobile to the Warden's databases meant not only that inmates could search them for nuggets that were already there; they could change the entries, add to them, cut from them, delete them entirely, create completely new ones. Imagine the potential profit — to say nothing of the unadulterated joy — in filling out a staff member's life story with 'registered sex offender' or 'arrest for possession' or 'indicted for tax evasion'.

Andy was about to acquire the status of hero of South Hams.

At noon, the Warden left for lunch, and Andy glowed with triumph. What would Lillian think of this? An email arriving on her own computer from the Warden's office? And signed by Little Andy? He could see her shake her head, try to get angry at him, then give in, pull him into her arms and say, 'How'd my boy get to be so smart?'

'Dear Mom,' he began. 'Tell David, Quack hopes that tomorrow we'll have more fine weather.' Quack had told him to say that to Lillian as soon as he got the chance.

'What for?' Andy had asked.

'Just a joke between old cellmates.'

'"Fine weather", huh?'

'You got it.'

But Andy hadn't had to wait for Lillian's visit. He was sending an email from the Warden's office itself!

'Guess where I—' But he stopped mid-sentence, suddenly realizing that he hadn't told her he was HIV positive. He'd never been volatile, not until his terrible experiences in South Hams; after that, the shifts had become abrupt and violent. This time his body went rigid in a panic of shame. His face burned. He needed her arms around him now. He needed her to tell him it would be all right now, that it wasn't his fault – none of it. He needed her to tell him that he was still a man. Why do people do things like this? How could attacking someone you love do anything to soothe your own pain?

'I know your tricks, Lillian Draper.' He banged out the words. 'I know what you think. I know the games you play. Never come see me again.'

23

SPRINGFIELD: The same afternoon

While Andy was behind bars making use of skills he'd learned in Springfield, David was in Springfield struggling to use prison skills to turn Otto's Autos into a house for him and Helen. It wasn't going well.

The problem wasn't the job itself. He'd done all that homework to find ways to escape from South Hams; after all, the best way to escape a trap is to know how it's constructed, and prisons are much like other buildings. They have electricity and plumbing. They're designed by architects and built by contractors according to standard regulations. Blueprints and building specifications were the easy part; how plans translated into cement and steel: that had taken much longer. As for the prison's security system, David imagined it as an elaborate lock, and if somebody can make a lock, there's going to be somebody else who can break it. Before life in prison, he'd been the best lock-picker on the east side.

After his release, when the question came up of what he was to do with himself, Hugh Freyl hadn't hesitated. 'Security systems testing and installation,' he'd said. Hugh's eyes and Helen's were identical, the same intense green, the same dark rim around the iris; David had found a blind man's eyes difficult at best, and he could never accustom himself to the blind man who stared at him out of her eyes.

'Yeah, sure,' David had said to him. 'So who's going to hire me for that?'

'If you have a flaw that you cannot hide, David, you must not *try* to hide it. Make a virtue of it. Who is more experienced at breaking locks than you are? Who is more experienced in breaking through unbreakable security systems?'

'I failed,' David said. His nearest success had been pure impulse, nothing to do with construction and even less to do with security systems.

'That is a level of detail that need not concern us.' Hugh's smile had been wry. 'What you will do is make a bet. You give a customer a large sum in cash that he is to store on his premises. If you cannot break in and retrieve it, he keeps the money. If you can, then the customer is vulnerable and he pays you to make him invulnerable. I know a number of people who would very much enjoy such a game – especially with an ex-convict. In fact, I doubt they'd even entertain the idea if you were not an ex-convict.'

All David had needed was the cash and a licence to practise as a journeyman electrician. Cash was no problem for Hugh. He'd also arranged the paperwork for the licence; David had never asked how, and he'd passed the written exam entirely legally. As soon as he did, a colleague of Hugh's took the bet, a computer retailer a hundred miles east in Matoon, home to the world's largest bagel and host of the annual Lender's Bagelfest. David had been shocked to find out how careless most professional security installers were, but he'd really got a kick out of defeating them. More jobs came in. They got harder. He'd studied to keep ahead.

Books with titles like *Construction Materials and Processes* and *Simplified Engineering for Architects and Contractors* stood on the desk he used at the prissy house he and Helen rented not far from Otto's Autos.

But the labour force at the construction site? How was he to handle that? For the security business, his crew had consisted of himself and a friend from his childhood. His only experience in directing workers came from the South Hams drug ring. He was an enforcer for the Insiders as well as the manager of their drug trade; his management technique boiled down to scaring his people into doing what he wanted them to. Or beating them into it.

But civilian workers? Free men with hourly pay and overtime? How could anybody control them? He found disorder physically painful, and these guys left their tools lying all over the place. Bags of cement fell over and spilled out on the ground. Newspapers, cigarette butts, empty beer cans, water bottles, sandwich wrappers, coffee cups: they were everywhere. Take that kid sprawled out on the tarmac, maybe eighteen years old, maybe twenty, a lot of muscle on him, multiple earrings, a stud in his nose. He raised himself lazily on his elbows, upended a Coke bottle in his mouth, glugged it dry, aimed it at the telephone pole on the edge of the property, missed, flicked his cigarette butt after it, missed again, then leaned back in the shade.

'Pick them up,' David said.

The kid lifted himself on his elbows again. 'What?'

'Pick up the bottle and the cigarette butt.'

'Fuck off.' The kid eased himself back down.

'Now!' David said.

'I'm taking a fifteen minute break.'

'Go pick them up.'

'Why the fuck would I do that?'

'After I cut your balls off, I'm going to shove them down your throat.'

The kid shrugged, got up, went over, picked up the bottle and the butt, looked around for somewhere to put them, tossed them into a wheelbarrow.

'In the dumpster,' David said.

'Fuck——' A glance at David's face stopped the kid short. 'Okay, okay,' he said. 'I'm doing it. I'm doing it. Just stay calm, huh?' He kept wary eyes on David as he picked up the bottle and the cigarette butt and set them carefully in the dumpster.

It wasn't the first time David had forced his workers to clean up after themselves; it was far from the first time he'd frightened one of them. But he knew what the result would be: the kid just wouldn't show up tomorrow. He'd have to find some replacement, who'd be even stupider and sloppier. As for the other three men at work, they were all taking fifteen-minute breaks too – and watching David's every move.

He could feel their eyes on him, even though his back faced them. He could take all four of them, the kid first – those earrings were a gift. Then the guy who shouted snatches of out-of-tune jingles. The other two would run shrieking. He itched to do it, could see it happening, took in a breath, let it out, then swung around. 'Get out of here. All of you,' he said to them. 'Don't come back.'

When David was in prison, he'd had a recurrent dream of running. Just running. Nobody stopping him. No walls. No guards. No prison yard. Just open streets and running. But a prison gym is all about pumping iron, not much preparation for a marathon. After he'd got out, he'd had to work months before he could run far enough and fast enough to ease the tension in him.

He forced himself to wait until his four workers disappeared off the site of Otto's Autos. Only then did he set off. The anger hadn't even started to ease when he reached the railroad tracks on North 15th Street. It was very hot, oppressively humid, steam rising up from the tar on the roads, late afternoon, a desolate area, old deserted station, tracks stretching out to the horizon ahead and behind, acres of macadam. The man slamming into him came as a complete surprise. David staggered from the blow.

'Where you think you're going?' the guy said. Despite the heat, he wore a Soviet general's winter coat, right down to the ankles. His beard was black, several inches long, unkempt. He backed away, reaching into one of the coat's deep pockets.

When the tension rips apart in a person, thought just doesn't happen. David must have charged the guy. He didn't see him reaching into his sleeve and sliding something out from there, didn't feel the hammer blow of whatever it was driving through the flesh of his arm and side. He yanked it out – a long, solid something – blood spurting after it: an iron railroad spike. The general gaped at him a moment, then turned and ran. David caught him on the tracks, a tackle that sent them both sprawling, but so much blood was pumping out of his arm and chest that the man slipped in it. So did David, lost hold of him, caught him again on the railway platform, grabbed the beard, banged the head against the brick wall of the Illinois & Midland Railroad building.

And suddenly there were cops. David didn't know how many. They pinned him to the ground. He couldn't see the guy in the Soviet uniform, just heard him whining to the cop in charge.

'He just come up after me, officer. He must be crazy or something. I didn't do nothing. Nothing at all. He just come—'

'You don't know him?' the cop interrupted.

David lurched in an abrupt attempt to escape. Blood spurted

again. More cops piled on him. Two of them? Four? The same cops? Others?

A moment of nothing, and one of the cops was sitting on David's chest. Or that's how it seemed. Close up. No, no, far away. 'You know, Mr Marion,' he was saying, 'I can't recall a specific statute about beating a Soviet general's head against the Illinois & Midland Railroad wall, so I guess you're clear on that one. But, oh my goodness me, why can't you behave yourself? Now you're going to need an anti-tetanus shot as well as . . .'

David must have passed out then, because the sting of the needle stitching his side forced him to focus on the cop even though the cop wasn't there any more. The needlework was a woman's. So was the voice.

'. . . all these sutures,' she was saying. She was middle-aged, white coat, steel-grey hair that clung to her head like a bathing cap. She paused in her needlework to check an intravenous line that fed into David's arm. 'You're too old to be running around in the sun,' she scolded. 'Not that somebody half your age should do it. People go crazy when it's as hot as this.'

Hospital smells. Hospital sounds. A badge on the woman's white coat said 'Dr Ellen Hargrove'.

'Memorial?' he asked. 'Is that where I am?'

'That's where you are,' she said. 'Emergency Room. You're lucky they didn't jail you.'

But the cop's logo: it was yellow, round, Lincoln in it. That's not the Springfield Police Department. Their logo is blue. A triangle. The Sheriff's logo is round. An eagle inside. David had seen that yellow Lincoln only once before: the cop who'd warned him against a speed trap ahead when he was doing 120 in the Riley.

24

LEADWOOD, ILLINOIS:
Two days later

Nothing about Mr Huxtable of UCAI's security department was what Jimmy expected. Certainly not this lunch. They sat at a long table in a hushed church hall, the air steam-bath heavy, only a whirring fan to stir it. No liquor. No music. Smell of oilcloth and cabbage. An almost interminable grace. Politics really does call for God; ever since his mayoralty campaign, Jimmy had spouted grace with the fervour of a new convert. But he hated cabbage. He wanted a dry Martini with a twist of lemon and the Sangamo Club's air conditioning. He started to take off his jacket.

'Please, no.' Mr Huxtable held up a hand to stop him. 'There are ladies present.'

'Mr Huxtable,' Jimmy whispered, 'this is no place to talk.'

'Perhaps a stroll after soup?' Mr Huxtable had a dish face that sloped off to one side, round glasses, a bright cherry of a mouth. The soup was as thin as he was. The bread was dry. He hadn't said as many as a hundred words to Jimmy so far, and he said no more until he'd finished his bowl and dabbed at his chin with a translucent paper napkin. 'Finished, Mr Z?'

Elderly heads turned as the two men scraped their chairs to leave.

The small white church stood in a wood on the outskirts of St Louis; Mr Huxtable and Jimmy walked away from it into the trees. The ground was baked and cracked. 'This was a stream bed only a few days ago,' Mr Huxtable said.

Jimmy took off his jacket, loosened his tie, rolled up his sleeves. 'I thought we might be meeting somebody from the NSA,' he said.

'Hmmm?'

'The, er, you know, the National Security Agency.'

'Today?'

Jimmy wasn't quite sure how to take that. 'Maybe Wet Operations?'

'Hmmm?'

'Department 4?' Jimmy wondered if it was possible for a man in Mr Huxtable's position to be unaware of what he was asking.

Department 4 of Domestic Wet Operations is known among insiders as 'Assassinations within the United States'. It's the most secret arm of the National Security Agency, the most secret of America's secret agencies and the one that takes on the nation's dirtiest jobs, and the dirtiest of these go to Department 4. An entire section of their operations concerns delicate matters of 'Quantitative Personnel Adjustment' for US-based corporations.

'I'm talking about the contract on David Marion,' Jimmy said irritably. The heat and the hot soup weren't sitting well in his stomach. His shoes were dusty. Plant spurs clung to his trousers.

'Temper, Mr Z. Temper.'

Mr Huxtable walked on, hands clasped behind his back, head bowed, studying the path in front of them. A frog jumped out, paused uncertainly in the path. He brought his heel down on it and ground it into the dirt.

'A foolish fellow, your Mr Marion,' he said abruptly. 'A Godless fellow, rooting around in search of somebody to blame Hugh Freyl's death on. I do dislike it when amateurs go blundering in affairs where they don't belong. Bulls in china shops, Mr Z. Bulls in china shops.' This sudden burst of speech came out rapid fire, very much at odds with the detachment on his face as he bent down to examine what remained of the frog. 'Senator Calder would have made a *fine* president. Many God-fearing Americans invested a great deal of money, time, ingenuity – and faith, yes, Mr Z, faith – in making him into a leader. And your fellow imagines he's found a motive for the murder of Hugh Freyl – Hugh Freyl of all people – in a remote corner of the Senator's "creative accounting". A shocking idea. Shocking. An election fund is a fluid thing, a living thing. It must be nurtured. It must be tweaked. Your ignorant fellow cares nothing for such subtleties. His threats of exposure alone caused that great man to have the stroke from which he may never recover. Bulls in china shops, Mr Z. Bulls in china shops. Such fellows are, in my humble opinion, among the most dangerous in our society. It is a matter of good business practice to cleanse the world of them.'

'Only forty-eight hours ago somebody made a pretty clumsy attempt to do the world a favour.'

'Hmmm.'

'You know about that?'

'Hmmm.'

'I do hope that's not the kind of work you lay claim to these days.'

'Most certainly not. We trust that Mr Marion is recovering well.'

Mr Huxtable crossed his hands behind his back again and walked on. For a few minutes the only sound was the soft warble of bluebirds. A pair of them flitted in and out of the trees.

'What I don't get,' Jimmy said, 'is how come David Marion is alive at all.'

'We do not like to fail, Mr Z. On the other hand, we cannot always succeed. It's the height of vanity to assume we can. At this point in time, our failure has cost us dear, but the most we can say is that the contract is under intensive administrative review.'

Jimmy was shocked. 'Jesus, the Freyls? You're holding off because of the Freyls? Do they reach even to guys like you?'

Mr Huxtable made a gurgling noise of disapproval. 'Oh, my goodness, Mr Z. Special people are, one might say, our speciality. We are monitoring the situation very closely, and we understand there has come to be some urgency in the matter. But do let me emphasize, Mr Z, that we do not like bulls in china shops. To act precipitately would be to become a bull in a china shop. You understand me, I trust?'

'Loud and clear.'

'Nor will you object if we contact you in the near future?'

'Christ, no. I'll be sitting on pins and needles. I just hope it won't be too long.' They walked on a little further. 'Anything you'd like me to do while I wait to hear from you?'

'Hear from me? Oh, no, no, you won't hear from me. Not from me personally.'

'Yeah? Who then?'

'I couldn't possibly say, but we're all the same, Mr Z. We're all faceless.'

Jimmy laughed. 'I wouldn't call you faceless.'

'You just don't know me well enough.' They strolled on a few minutes in silence. 'You had a question about Mr Morris Kline too?'

'Did I?' Jimmy said.

'Oh, I think so. Yes, Mr Z. I think so.'

25

SPRINGFIELD & CHICAGO:
The third Monday in August

'Morris!' Jimmy said, opening the front door to his lakeside house, shaking Morris's hand, retaining it a moment in both of his. 'Thanks for coming out all this way. Jesus, it's hot outside. Come in, come in. Can I get you something to drink? What'll you have? Scotch? Bourbon? I make a mean Martini.'

Morris braced himself for a difficult and embarrassing negotiation; a warm handshake and an offer of a drink was the opening he'd feared. It wasn't yet four in the afternoon. He accepted a glass of expensive mineral water and ice, followed Jimmy into his living room and sat – at Jimmy's insistence – in an original Eames chair that Jimmy had spent a year locating in Houston and paid a small fortune for.

Jimmy sat opposite him in an imitation Eames, gave his half-moon glasses a twirl, took a sip of straight Scotch in a chunky glass and began to explain the subtleties of manufacture that divided the real chair from the fake. He could see that Morris knew he was only laying ground. 'Listen, Morris,' Jimmy said then, 'I owe you an apology. You see, it was all so unexpected.'

'An apology?'

'Yeah, yeah. I do. I was wrong. I admit it. I should never have asked you for your resignation. I'd just assumed you saw this UCAI contract as the opportunity I did. When you didn't, I flew off the handle. Christ, it's not as though you have no right to your opinion. You're the guy with a right—'

'Jimmy,' Morris interrupted, 'it took you several days to fire me.'

'I'm a slow burner.' Jimmy frowned, shrugged, gave a sheepish smile. 'I'm pretty new to this mayor gig. Sometimes I . . . well, I overestimate who I am and what I'm supposed to be doing here. Look, Morris, what I'm trying to say is that I think you may have been right. I'm sitting on the fence here, and it ain't comfortable. I mean, shit, I'm not a systems analyst and I know fuck-all about utilities, but I've learned a few things that make me nervous. Morris, I want you to come back as Director of Springfield Light and Power.'

Morris set his mineral water on a shiny surface beside him, studied the ice in it, then stood up. A bribe: exactly what the handshake and the offer of a drink had led him to expect. At least it hadn't taken more than ten minutes to get to it. On Thursday morning – three days from now – Jimmy was all too likely to lose the Council vote on UCAI's contract for Springfield's water, and Morris was the reason why. Media coverage had been wide and generally against privatization; most of it touted Morris as the Coalition's star witness.

'Jimmy, I'm going to tell people just what I told them before,' Morris said. 'Selling the public's water to a private company is a crime against their rights as citizens.'

'Oh, for fuck's sake, Morris. You think I don't know that's what you intend to do? Sit down, goddamnit. Now that Hugh Freyl is dead, you're the only honest man I know. I want you to say what you think.'

'I shall.'

'The thing is, if there's solid evidence one way or the other — something definitive — I want you to know about it first. I know you'll judge it fairly. I know that if there's something wrong you'll see it and say so, even if it turns out to be your own assessment of the situation. I have to find out what really happened to contaminate the town's water a couple of weeks ago. So do you.'

'Not easy when you've denied me access to lab results and computer records.'

Morris's degree was in industrial technology; he'd gone straight from Illinois State University into senior management at the Snohomish public utility. He and Jimmy met on an airplane a few years ago, a flight from London to Chicago that spent hours on the runway at Heathrow before it left and hours more circling O'Hare before it landed. They both remembered the experience fondly: Jimmy's easy charm and legal background, a lot of liquor, Morris's intelligence and unexpected flashes of humour. Both were from poor backgrounds, and they'd grown maudlin about the opportunities that America offers to guys like them. They'd stayed in touch ever since.

'I need your help, Morris,' Jimmy said, 'but I can't release any information to you unless you come back to the utility.'

'What happened to the need for higher security clearance?'

'I'll get around it.'

'You just never stop, do you?'

'Christ! I'm not trying to bribe you,' Jimmy said. 'I'm relying on your integrity here. I'm worried.' Jimmy leaned forward, his worry abruptly palpable. 'I bet you think that contamination didn't have anything to do with sewage.'

'The hospital records make that fairly clear.'

'I bet you also think there's something fishy about the power cut taking down only the new control room.'

Morris just raised his eyebrows.

'The data *is* seriously scrambled,' Jimmy went on. 'Nobody with the usual IT techniques has a hope in hell of picking it apart, but there's this guy at the University of Illinois in Chicago with some really elaborate electronics. Quantum something. Or is it nano-something? They have a first-rate Computer Engineering department there, and he's the only guy in the US who has this stuff. He seems to be getting data out, but it doesn't make much sense. He doesn't know enough about utilities to get it to add up. That's why he needs you.'

'The National Security Agency has all the expertise you need.'

'This kid *is* NSA. Where the fuck else would anybody get this kind of equipment? And you're the expert he wants to see. Come on, Morris, sit down, please. I really do need the help of an honest man.'

When Morris had first spoken against privatization, Jimmy had been caught unprepared. It was not a mistake he would make again. He'd marginalize everything that Morris had told Becky — anomalies, withheld data, hospital records — and shroud it in patriotism and national security. But that didn't mean it wasn't possible for him to have sensed something Morris had missed. Jimmy did work a lot by gut feeling, and often he was right. It was one of the traits Morris admired in him.

Morris studied the ice cubes floating in his mineral water. People are so complex, so tangled, but there doesn't seem to be any great mystery in ice cubes, does there? They float. And yet ice is the *only* substance that does. It's dense. All other dense substances sink. How can water be so ordinary and so out of the ordinary, both at the same time?

If Jimmy was right and the Coalition was wrong, if Morris himself had misinformed the public, then he owed it to them to find out about it.

He sat down again. 'You're reappointing me as director of the utility?'

'If you'll accept, I most certainly am.'

'I'll have full access to all the information I've requested? And on Thursday, I'm to surprise everybody with what I've found?'

Jimmy sighed, nodded. 'I just don't know how to handle what this kid seems to be—' He broke off, sighed again. 'I'm not a total shit, and now I'm a little scared. Something just doesn't smell right. Morris, I don't know what to—' He broke off once more. 'Look, we have to find out what happened to that water. Catch a flight to Chicago as soon as you can. This afternoon. You can be in town by eight. See the boy genius. Study the data. We'll decide where to go from there as soon as you get back.'

'What's the young man's name?' he said.

'Dieter Flaam. All of twenty-three years old. One of those irritating kids who speaks a dozen languages and calculates faster than his computer. NSA actually built this chunk of machinery for him, and they built it in Chicago because he likes Chicago. He even has living quarters in the department.'

'What about the lab results?' Morris asked. 'I can study them on the plane.'

'They'll be waiting for you at the airport.' Jimmy finished off his Scotch and got up. 'God, it's good to have you on board again. I've missed you. Just make sure you're back in Springfield on Wednesday night, huh?'

26

SPRINGFIELD: Thursday

Coalition volunteers arrived at the Old Capitol before dawn. They set up stands around the plaza in front of Greek Revival columns and tall, carved doors. Next came hundreds of green placards, baseball caps and T-shirts that shouted:

NO TO PRIVATIZATION

or

THIS IS A DEMOCRACY

or

LET US VOTE

By eight, members of the public began to appear. By nine, there were hundreds of them: Coalition supporters, water-plant workers, sewage-plant workers, high school students, college students, clergy, ordinary townspeople. So many had taken up the placards, baseball caps, T-shirts, that they made a sea of green, which spilled out of the plaza and filled the street beyond.

Police on horseback appeared at the edges of the crowd.

A megaphone announced: 'Ladies and gentlemen! May I have your attention. Give us room. Give us room.'

A circle opened up. A giant puppet, ten feet tall, strutted out with Jimmy's cowlick and half-moon glasses. He primped the cowlick. He twirled the glasses. The crowd laughed. He drew an endlessly long baton out of his trouser pocket. He examined it. No, not a baton: a scroll. He unfurled it, and everybody could see the words:

THE PEOPLE'S RIGHT TO VOTE

He pulled out a match, flicked it. A flame shot up, and he lit the paper. The crowd roared, anger this time. The police on horseback moved in closer.

As soon as the doors to the Old Capitol opened, the crowds pushed inside, placards and all, up the sweeping north staircase and into the Representatives Hall, a high-ceilinged chamber with fluted columns and heavy chandeliers. At the far end, Jimmy Zemanski stood at the mahogany lectern where Abraham Lincoln had delivered the most important speech of his career and the opening shot in the American Civil War: 'A house divided against itself cannot stand.'

Behind Jimmy hung the portrait of George Washington, to one side, the Stars and Stripes, to the other, Springfield's own flag in blue. The city's ten aldermen and alderwomen sat at a long table in front of him. This room was the largest in the Old Capitol, but it wasn't large enough for all of the protesters. When no more could squeeze in, they crowded hallways and lobbies at the top of the stairs and below them. Jimmy himself had made arrangements for Becky. As he opened the meeting, she sat in her wheelchair, Helen by her side, Kate, Donna and a crush of Coalition members around her.

As soon as the preliminaries were over, Jimmy began.

'We can all see what's happening in the countryside around us.' He had a good voice, resonant, flexible, not too polished but fully in command. 'Baked riverbeds. The pond that used to be Lake Springfield, dead trees along the old Route 66, dead cattle in the fields beyond. We all know what the problem is: there just isn't enough water to go around, and every day there's less of it. The science makes my head spin. The political issues are mind-bending, but we *can* do something. We *can* have more water. We're your Council. You elected us to represent your interests. That's what we're going to do today: decide if we have the courage to accept UCAI's offer and embrace the world of the future.'

The audience growled.

'I hear you,' he went on. 'You don't like it. Well, I'll tell you something. I don't like it either. But I like the alternative far less. Forget the trees and cows. Think about yourselves, your children, your grandchildren. Another few years and where are you? Where are we all? If we don't act now, my friends – I mean right now – we're going to be dying of thirst ourselves. I've said this before, and I'll say it again: literally dying of thirst.'

He glanced down at the agenda in front of him, then went on. 'An issue this crucial calls for a great deal of thought and discussion. That's what we're here to do today.' He paused. 'The Chair recognizes Kate Bagalayos, the first speaker for the Coalition of Concerned Citizens of Springfield. Hand her the microphone, Walter.'

Kate rose from her seat beside Becky and took the microphone. She looked very much a foreigner in this all-too-American of places, high cheekbones, wide face, almond eyes. Her hands were trembling; the sheaf of notes she held in them trembled too. She bent her head over them.

'Water is worth money.' There was a tremor in her voice as well, and the voice was so soft that people had to cup their ears to hear. 'It's worth lots of money. In Africa they call it blue gold, and they've fought wars over it for generations. Today, the issue at home is becoming just the same as—'

She broke off as she caught a glimpse of Jimmy up at the Council table. He'd closed his eyes and was running an impatient hand over them. Her anger was so abrupt, and it took her by such surprise that her voice soared.

'What's the matter with you, Jimmy Zemanski? Why can't you see what's happening? Yeah, yeah. I know. It's bullets and tanks in Africa. Here it's only words. But it's a "water war" just the same. It's us against them, and who's to say it won't come to bullets and tanks? God gave us water because we have to have it to live. He didn't give it to UCAI for a bigger market share. He didn't give it to you or your aldermen to sell to them. Honourable members of the Council, think of Lincoln. Don't divide our house. Stay with us. Listen to us. We elected you, and we need you now. The issue is simple. Water is for life, not for profit.'

The audience gave her a standing ovation. She looked around at them, surprised all over again, a little puzzled but delighted too.

'Tell me,' Jimmy said when the room quietened. 'Did anybody else's faucet spew out some nasty stuff a couple of weeks ago? I'm not the only one, am I?'

'You probably did it yourself!' came a shout from the audience.

'Aw, come on. How come Ms Bagalayos didn't mention it? Perhaps it slipped her mind. Or – who knows? – perhaps this Coalition is sidestepping the whole issue. Now why would they do that, huh? Think maybe it's because contaminated water shows the utility isn't up to handling a commodity we have to have to live? That if we can get it at all – and that's a big "if" – it will come to us only thanks to the financial muscle of UCAI's Grand canal? That we can't possibly pay for ourselves? What kind of irresponsibility is this?'

He looked down at the agenda in front of him. 'The Chair calls Morris Kline, who's scheduled to speak in support of the Coalition. Maybe he can help us out here.'

The room fell silent. This was what they'd come to hear.

'Mr Kline?' Jimmy asked, looking around him.

Becky leaned over to Helen. 'Where's Morris gone?' she whispered.

Helen just grimaced.

'What's that supposed to mean?' Becky demanded.

'There are rumours, Grandma.'

'Rumours?'

Helen took in a breath. 'Apparently Jimmy gave him an enormous bribe to get out of town.'

'Who says so?'

'Jimmy told Ruth.'

'Ruth? Ruth Madison? Why would *he* tell *her*?'

Helen rolled her eyes. 'Grandma, he's fucking her.'

'Oh,' Becky said. 'Really? Silly woman. But Morris? Fiddlesticks.' A man with the honesty – to say nothing of the courage – to keep his opinions to himself until he could publicly defy the mayor who'd appointed him: a Don Quixote wouldn't back out now, not just for money.

The silence in the Representatives Hall was growing oppressive. 'I know you want to hear him speak,' Jimmy said then. 'Tell you what, let's move on for now. I'll rearrange the agenda until he arrives. The moment he gets here, he speaks. Okay?'

The audience rustled with discontent.

'You haven't seen him this morning?' Becky said to Helen.

Helen shook her head. 'His cell's not answering either.'

'Try it again. Kate, Donna, try to find him.'

Helen forced her way into the hallway to try his mobile again while Kate and Donna went in search through the crowds.

Three aldermen spoke. Two favoured the Coalition and were cheered. One favoured the UCAI contract and was booed. Helen, Kate and Donna returned to their seats. No sign of Morris.

When the aldermen finished, Jimmy said, 'How about Mr Kline now? He here yet? Mr Kline?'

As before, the room fell silent.

'Anyone here seen the guy?' Jimmy said.

Once more, the silence held.

'Look, I'm sorry about this folks,' he said then, 'but we got a vote to bring in. Before that, though, I want you to give Mr Sebastian Slad of UCAI a real warm welcome. Mr Slad?'

The aldermen clapped. Nobody else did. But Sebastian smiled benignly at the audience anyway. 'I know some of you don't like the idea of change much, but you all got the absolute commitment of UCAI that we'll deliver this contract—'

'Let us vote!' The interruption was spontaneous, several people at once. The rest of the audience picked it up: 'Let us vote! Let us vote!' The chant spread to the crowds outside the chamber, then echoed through the building.

Jimmy's temper was visibly fraying by the time he re-established quiet. 'Today's vote is a Council vote,' he said irritably. 'My opinion? Should this go to the people? Absolutely not. It's nothing but a gut check. Aldermen, please stand to cast your votes. "Yea" to approve. "Nay" to disprove. Ms Petrie?'

'Nay.'

The audience cheered.

'Mr Murdle?'

'Nay.'

The audience went wild.

'Mr Senich?'

Mr Senich wasn't a happy man. 'I didn't want to decide without hearing Mr Kline,' he said, 'but since he isn't here, I'm going to have to vote to endorse the contract.'

The next vote went for Jimmy too. After that, they alternated.

'Well, well,' Jimmy said when the last alderman sat down, 'divided right down the middle. That leaves the deciding vote to me.' He couldn't hold back a smile. 'The resolution to sign the UCAI contract carries, six to five.'

27

TIPTON COUNTY, TENNESSEE:
The same time

Dillon Effingham and his little brother Stonky danced and giggled along the west bank of the Mississippi River, in Tipton County, Tennessee, south of Memphis. They each had pockets full of Blow Pops, a lollipop with a hard candy exterior and bubble gum inside. Neither liked Blow Pops very much, but getting hold of so many at once was a real triumph.

The Mississippi is moody. It's unpredictable. It cuts chunks of land in its path off from where they started. Before the earthquakes of 1811–1812, the people of Tipton County went to sleep on the river's east bank. One morning they woke up on its west bank. But that's not why the county was famous. Every area has something, the biggest bagel like Matoon, the first Indian scalp like Washoga. Tipton County was the Blow Pops capital of the world. Speaker Emeritus Effingham was deeply proud of that. 'We produce a billion Blow Pops a year,' he'd say to his nephews Dillon and Stonky. 'Think of it, boys: one *billion*!' He always carried a bag of Blow Pops. He stuffed his pockets with them too. The question was, how many could a kid steal off him in one raid? The two brothers had just broken the neighbourhood record.

They'd reached the gum inside their third Blow Pop – both of them feeling queasy – when they spotted what they thought was a small whale or maybe a dolphin in the distance. Something large and white. There are no whales or dolphins in the Mississippi. They went to investigate.

This strange shape had brown hair with gold streaks in it.

'Fuck!' ten-year-old Dillon cried. 'It's a person!' He paused. 'I think.'

What would little boys do without the mobile phone? Dillon took a closer look, then threw up Blow Pops all over the corpse while eight-year-old Stonky called 911 on his mobile.

28

SPRINGFIELD, MARION & KNOX COUNTY, ILLINOIS: The same time

Quack's years of business administration at the University of Chicago had been an agonizing boredom. They hadn't borne fruit until he reached South Hams prison all those years ago and taught David how to run his drug trade as though it were a McDonald's franchise.

As he explained it – taking relish for the first time in this very American institution – McDonald's began with a modest location and a dream to bring their hamburgers to as many people in as many places as they could. There was no reason why David shouldn't do just that with drugs: reliable products at steady prices to any prisoner who could afford them. It took weeks to develop a strategy: 'a management system' Quack called it. Once they had it, David kept it operating for all of the fifteen years that remained of the eighteen he spent inside. He satisfied his customers. He moved with the changing markets. He developed new ones. He kept his profits high and his people in line, his customers as well as his subordinates.

But the freedom to employ violence had been more important

than either Quack or David realized. It was the only control mechanism David knew, and it had proved useless in turning Otto's Autos into a house. The men he'd told to go away didn't even try to come back. Potential replacements were no better: the same fearless, self-satisfied faces, the same sense of entitlement that seemed to him to border on the moronic. Lillian spotted him sitting alone on a pile of breeze blocks at the construction site, his arm in a sling; his chest bandaged, his head in his hands, cigarette balanced on the blocks beside him. The cement mixer stood silent. So did the brick splitter and the digger. She pulled her car to a stop, got out and went to sit beside him.

'Where's your crew gone to, boy?'

'They don't like me very much,' he said, not glancing up.

'Well, that don't surprise me none. You don't treat 'em right. What happened to that arm? One of them hit you with a shovel?'

'A Soviet general tried to kill me with a railway spike.'

'A Soviet general, huh? You try to kill him back?'

'I got private cops following me around. They stopped me.'

'You getting too much of the sun, child,' she said.

'Why aren't you with old Mrs Freyl?'

The day was as hot as its predecessors, as humid too; just sitting in it was enough to make a person sweat. There was no shade on the construction site. Lillian pulled out an umbrella. She'd carried one ever since the long-term forecast starting warning of storms way back in June. She opened it over them both, then sighed. 'David, I got to talk to you.'

'I'm not going anywhere.'

'I got a email from Little Andy.'

David glanced up at her then, scanned her face. 'You have to be joking.'

'From the Warden's office.'

He rarely smiled, but he hadn't heard anything so funny in years. 'How'd he manage that?'

'He's saying he don't want to see me no more.'

'You got it on you?'

Lillian opened her handbag, handed him a copy, watched him read it.

> Tell David, Quack hopes that tomorrow we'll have more fine weather. I know your tricks, Lillian Draper. I know what you think. I know the games you play. Never come see me again.

David gave it back. 'He doesn't mean it.'

She nodded. 'What'd they do to that boy in there?'

'I don't know.'

'You mean you ain't gonna tell me.'

'I can't tell you what I don't know.'

'What's that stuff about "fine weather"?'

'Search me.'

Lillian knew it meant something, but she just nodded. Men are such guarded creatures, too wary to say what they mean even when the answer can't really matter very much. 'He got raped, didn't he?'

'I don't know.'

'David, last time I seen Andy, he looked better. Put on a little weight. Smiling some. Getting a interest in things, talking about computers and stuff. But he didn't tell me nothing. This here email makes me think he's heading back right where he came from, and he don't want me to know about it.'

David shook his head. 'Not likely.'

'You willing to come out with me again?'

'I have to go anyhow.'

'"More fine weather"?'

'Something like that.' He took out a cigarette, lit it, handed it to her. She took a drag, then handed it back.

'David, can I ask you a question?'

'I'm all yours.'

'You was young and pretty when you went to prison too. How come you ain't HIV positive?'

He frowned, turned away, turned back. 'Official statistics indicate very few prisoners are, less than two per cent.'

'You believe that?'

'Some people are naturally immune.'

'Just luck?'

'You could say so.'

David Marion landed a life sentence when he was a mere fifteen years old, younger than Andy if not quite so pretty, made of tougher stuff but still recovering from internal injuries courtesy of a Springfield police 'interrogation' about the murder of two men. He hadn't confessed to the crime. He hadn't denied it either. He hadn't spoken at all, and there'd seemed to him a perverse justice in being sent to the very prison that bore his name, Marion Federal Penitentiary at Marion, Illinois.

There'd been nobody in his cell when he'd arrived. He tossed his few possessions on the floor and lay back on the narrow lower bunk of the cement-shelf beds that occupied nearly half the space. He was staring at the bottom of the top bunk when his cellmate Pama walked in. Before David had time to move, a full-fisted blow caught him on the side of the face and slammed his head against the concrete wall behind him.

'In here, bitch, you be the nigger,' Pama said. 'In here, you be my nigger. You belong to me. As soon as I gets me my dinner, I gets me some of your pretty white pussy. I bet it's nice and tight.'

He left David spitting blood into the sink.

First comes panic. Then the mind goes cold. The counsellor's office at the end of the cell block stayed open until lockdown. The counsellor himself was so wrapped up in a game called Ebony Castle on a very early computer that he only waved a hand towards the wall. David went over to the shelf holding forms that inmates could use to file complaints, authorize them to make telephone calls, receive mail. A mug sat there, a heavy glass mug with a wood handle. David pretended to study the paperwork while he slipped the mug under his shirt. Back in the cell he smashed the glass section of the mug against the concrete floor until jagged glass stuck out of it like lions' teeth.

Pama returned from his dinner, stretched, yawned and gave David a dazzling smile. Pama was a big man; he had to bend head and shoulders to ease himself back onto the lower bunk. He leaned against the concrete wall and patted the spot beside him.

'Come on over here and sit next to Pama. Talk to me.'

David glanced away.

'Come on, sugar. You ain't still mad at me, is you?'

David got up. Pama leaned towards him, but before he could unbend his body to get it out of the bunk, David thrust the jagged glass into his eyes. Blood spurted. Pama screamed. David hacked in a frenzy at eyeballs, nose, cheeks, mouth, every piece of soft flesh around the face and throat.

By the time the guards arrived, Pama was curled in a foetal position, and David stood over him with the bloodied mug.

David spent three months in isolation for that, but he'd turned Pama into a blind man. That scared people. David figured he wouldn't have to go through any more crap when he got out of solitary as long as he stayed looking crazy enough to blind the next guy in Marion who made a move on him.

He was safe.

Back in those days, Illinois law required prisons to educate the under-16s to a sixth-grade level; David's record said he was illiterate. The guards sat him down in an interrogation room with a slender man in his forties, dark haired, green eyes that didn't focus on anything.

David could hardly believe it. Another blind man. And almost the first words out of this blind man's mouth tossed him back as meat for the system's sexual predators.

'You do not belong in this facility, Mr Marion,' Hugh Freyl said to him. 'I will arrange a transfer at once.' David's reputation wouldn't have spread to another prison. Another prison meant nothing to him but another Pama.

'I ain't going nowhere.'

'This is a federal prison, and yours is not a federal offence.'

'I got to stay where I am, hear me? What the fuck does a blind cocksucker know about what *I* need?' In those days, before Hugh cleaned up David's speech, it was pure Illinois street kid.

'You were convicted of murder in a state court, Mr Marion. Do please understand that my only purpose in arranging a transfer is to make your life more bearable.' Hugh was new to prisons at the time. All Freyls made contributions to the more unfortunate of the world, and he was eager to do good. 'I understand you cannot read at all. Can this be true? Mr Marion? It is not going to help to ignore me, you know. I am not prepared to go away. How about your alphabet, Mr Marion? Do you know your letters?'

David's thoughts were racing. The next Pama wouldn't get even as far as the first Pama had. There wouldn't be any solitary this time either. Books make good shields. A schoolbook given out by an old blind guy could easily hide an inch-long blade. Jab it into the neck and you're home.

'I try reading and I get to keep the book, right?' he said to Hugh.

'Of course, Mr Marion. It belongs to you.' Hugh opened the briefcase that sat on the floor between them and felt around inside it for a moment. David watched — fascinated despite himself — while the blind fingers tremble-touched their way across the Braille titles on box files inside. Hugh pulled one out, opened it, spread an embossed manuscript in front of himself and handed a comic to David.

A comic? Way too thin, wouldn't hide anything, wouldn't protect against anything. 'Ah, fuck,' David said, turning to the guard. 'Get me out of here.'

'Not yet, Mr Marion,' said Hugh. 'You haven't even looked at it. Perhaps . . . perhaps you can see at a glance that it is too difficult.'

'Get me out of here,' David repeated.

'Too easy?'

'Get me out—'

'We are going to be together for a full forty-five minutes, Mr Marion, whether you like it or not. Let me see if I can find something more to your taste.' Hugh tried a manila folder that held a supermarket newspaper.

'Shit,' David said.

Then came *Playboy*.

'Guard!' David cried.

'What *is* it with you, Mr Marion? What do you want?' But Hugh's questions were addressed more to himself than to David. 'All right. I will try a small experiment.' He reached into his briefcase, lifted out another manila folder.

Before he had a chance to open it, David said, 'Fuck it, man, I hate Dick Tracy.'

Hugh smiled. 'Do you? How very interesting. How do you know it is Dick Tracy?'

'It was the first fucking thing you showed me.'

This time Hugh's smile was delighted. 'This *is* the folder that contains Dick Tracy, yet there is nothing to indicate that fact except a notation in Braille. Nor did I state the comic's title when I handed it to you. Your criminal record indicated intelligence, but you clearly have an exceptional brain. You can even recognize a Braille title after a single glance.'

David stared at him with loathing.

'I know how interested the more intelligent convicts are in the law. Sometimes everything else seems irrelevant.' Hugh pulled a heavy volume out from beneath the box files. 'This is the third edition of *The American System of Criminal Justice* by the great jurist George F. Cole. Do you think it might serve you a little better?'

Better? David could hardly believe it. It was perfect, more than an inch thick. It could hide a two-inch blade, maybe even more. But his pleasure snapped shut at once. No prison authority was going to let him take such a thing away. 'I hate people shitting me.'

'I have cleared all these books with all the relevant authorities, Mr Marion,' Hugh said. 'From today forward, the Cole will serve as your official reading primer. If you will accept it as such, that is. I suggest we begin with the introduction.'

David felt a shiver of anticipation. That was unexpected, and in its way it made the whole thing funny: Pama to Hugh Freyl to David: blind man to blind man to hitman.

Illinois State Correctional Institutions transferred David to South Hams State Prison, as it was called in those days, less than a month later. The attack that he'd known would come took place in the shower only hours after his release into the general population. Before the guy died, David grabbed his testicles, sawed them off and delivered them — wrapped up in pages on American justice — to the General of the Insiders, South Hams' most powerful gang.

The Insiders were impressed. They welcomed this crazy kid as their youngest member ever. David got prison tattoos to make sure everybody knew exactly who was behind him until he grew up enough to re-establish the reputation he'd left behind him at Marion.

But a crucial change had taken place in that shower. David hadn't understood the seductive power of killing before, the moment of transfiguration in teasing apart with his own hands the fabric that binds life to death — in hearing the delicate sigh that turns a healthy predator into meat ready for a butcher's block.

It's a terrible thing to look into one's soul and find a monster there. If it hadn't been for Hugh, David might never have known. How can anybody forgive a man who foists himself into a life and lays bare an inner self like that?

As for Hugh, he wasn't quick to get a glimpse of what he'd done. His life was a rich man's life, corporate law, Springfield dinner parties, a family he adored. But he puzzled over unexpected and disturbing changes in this boy, changes he couldn't pin down, a shimmer of something alien that showed itself in the voice, the choice of words, the delivery. He knew he'd provoked it himself for the simple reason that he could sense the boy hated him for it. He just couldn't figure out what his transgression had been. He began to read prisoners' stories, talk to their families, interview ex-cons, dig into old records, re-examine David's history.

Years passed before the enormity of it dawned. Hugh Freyl, gentlest of men, had allowed his own arrogance — his rich, educated man's ignorance – to turn this angry boy into a killer. He carried his guilt like Sisyphus under a stone, again and again trying to make amends. Once the kid decided to work, Hugh spent more and more time with him, hoping education would polish away such primitive urges. David flew through grade school, then through high school, then a bachelor's degree from Chicago University's extension school. Hugh encouraged him to take an interest in the world outside, to correspond with people. A couple of his friends even became visitors, and he knew that one of them got closer to David than he could ever hope to come. But that hadn't worked out well either. How could Hugh have thought it might? A break-up was inevitable. When it came, it added heavily to his sins against David, and because of it, none of the other stratagems had a chance at success.

Which left Hugh only one route to redemption. He made it his mission to get David out of prison. He bent rules for the first time in his life. He threatened people, finagled, lied, cheated. He'd never done anything like that before. In the end, David walked out a free man.

And yet the alien shimmer that had developed in the prisoner only deepened in the free man. Within a year, Hugh saw himself as Dr Frankenstein rather than Sisyphus. At last he caught sight of the monster that David had lived with for years. That moment's glimpse convinced him that what he'd created out of the best possible motives had brought only destruction – and could never bring anything else.

Death came as a release for him. He'd even thanked his killer.

29

SPRINGFIELD: After the council meeting

Becky was impressed. A vote of six to five in Jimmy's favour! She hadn't realized just how formidable an enemy the man could make.

The Coalition had been so certain of victory that they'd planned a party at the Hilton, Springfield's only skyscraper; the restaurant on its top floor looked out over the whole of town. She insisted they go ahead with it. Jimmy might have strong-armed half of his aldermen into voting his way, but he hadn't defeated them and he certainly hadn't defeated her. She'd just have to find another approach. A band played. There was laughter, dancing, liquor, good things to eat. At least their demonstrations were going to make wonderful television. Who could help being moved by such enthusiastic masses parading all in green and their spontaneous outburst of 'Let us vote'?

The party stopped for the first scheduled programme.

'Headlines in Springfield this afternoon,' began the anchor. 'At a well-attended meeting this morning, City Council members approved a contract to privatize the water utility at Springfield

Light and Power. I have Mayor Zemanski here in the studio with me right now. Mayor Zemanski, how did the vote go?'

Jimmy came on, looking sleek and pleased. 'It was close – I have to admit that – but we've awarded the contract to UCAI of St Louis. I'm proud to be in a position to be able to bring Springfield into the twenty-first century . . .'

And that was it. The news went on to motorists who'd been arrested for failing to pay parking tickets. When the anchor launched into a theft at a toy store out at the White Oaks Mall, the protesters at the Hilton burst into an uproar of protest.

'What about the radio?' somebody shouted.

'Same thing,' came the reply.

'Try another station.'

'They're all the same.'

The party broke up soon afterwards.

Back at home, Becky kept both television and radio on through dinner. The short interview with Jimmy was repeated several times. Beyond that, nothing. She went to bed early, exhausted, puzzled, hoping sleep might bring inspiration. At ten, the telephone rang.

'Becky?' It was Chuck Finch, the Coalition's tame reporter on the *Journal-Register*.

'Where have you been?' Becky said irritably. 'I want headlines tomorrow, Chuck. This is the story of a lifetime.'

'I'm on indefinite leave of absence.'

Becky pulled herself up on the pillows. '"On leave of absence"? Why? What's that mean?'

'I just wanted to let you know that you wouldn't see what you want in the paper. It isn't my fault, Becky. I did try. Really.'

'You wrote the story?'

'Felton thanked me' – Felton was Chuck's editor – 'and put it aside without even looking at it.'

Becky was too taken aback to speak.

'That's not all,' Chuck said. 'Morris Kline is dead.'

The corner of Turner and Desplaines wasn't far from Mrs O'Leary's barn, the very place her cow kicked over the gas lantern that lit Chicago's great fire in 1871. It killed hundreds of people and flattened whole swathes of the city. Nearly a century and a half later, that corner was once again dangerous at night, the area around it by now a barren semi-industrial leftover: low brick buildings and high arc lights, no place for a single person alone.

It's not far from the University of Illinois at Chicago though, and a group of their students – five of them stuffed into an ancient Volkswagen – were swinging around that corner when the car jolted. The student driving braked at once.

'We hit somebody,' she said, turning around. A hushed and worried argument followed while she focused the headlights on a shape on the road: the four others piled out of the car with her to investigate. Morris Kline's head injuries had them all retching at once.

The Chicago police told them that he'd been dead hours before the Volkswagen ran over him. Another car had smashed into him long enough ago for some of the blood around him to dry. The temperature that day had been so high that the tarmac was still hot to the touch. The flies were heavy. A car bumper and pieces from a shattered licence plate lay near the body.

As city cops consoled the students, a country cop – fifty miles northwest, not far from Duck Lake Woods – was calling in a report about the still-smouldering relic of a stolen Honda Accord that turned out to have a missing bumper and a matching plate. Nobody really knows how many cars are stolen in and around Chicago, probably double the reported figure, which comes to something like seventy-five every day; the Honda Accord tops the list of models that car thieves go for. As Chuck told Becky, the police had little hope of finding out who'd stolen this one.

A note in the dead man's pocket read: 'D Flaam, Comp Eng, 851 S Morgan, 08714413212.' It's only a short walk – if a dangerous one – from Taylor and Desplaines to South Morgan Street and the Computer Engineering department of the University.

But the department had no records of anybody by the name of Flaam, no student nor staff nor alumni. The mobile phone number was out of service.

Early the next morning, Becky sat down at her laptop to call an open meeting of the Coalition over sandwiches at noon that very day. Her email went out to all members and nearly two hundred supporters.

Lillian's family helped in the preparations, a couple of sisters, a couple of daughters, her son Hiram, and – because it was summer – a dozen of her grandchildren. They opened up the downstairs of Freyl House just as they had for the wedding reception, but this time they pressed every chair into service to make rows of seats for an audience. They set out a side table where the caterers – Coalition supporters too and eager to help with this emergency – arranged pitchers of iced tea, glasses, platters piled high with sandwiches, fruit, cookies. People began arriving just before noon. Within ten minutes they'd filled the living room, and the food was beginning to disappear. More people crowded into the dining room. Nobody had expected so many. Not even Becky. They spilled out into the entryway.

And they bristled with righteous indignation. Nothing binds a group so well. They greeted each other over one another's shoulders, slapped each other's backs, shared sandwiches, a camaraderie as strong as it had been for the Council meeting itself. They'd all spent hours on the Internet. They knew: Springfield blogs, threads, chat rooms boiled over with outrage at what had happened at that Council meeting – and what happened after it.

'Zemanski poisons the water and gags the press,' ran one.

'Sabotage at a water plant, sabotage at the Old Capitol: Heil Hitler!'

'Democracy? My ass!'

Morris Kline fared no better. A dead man has no choice but to become what the living make of him, and Springfield had rendered its verdict: Jimmy had bribed him not to appear at the Old Capitol with evidence of corruption at the heart of city government. Rumours of the amount varied widely. What didn't vary was the conviction that Morris had betrayed them and that he'd got his just deserts on a back street in Chicago.

Not long after noon, Becky manoeuvred her wheelchair into the living room to address the crowd from behind a rosewood dining table that had once belonged to Governor Adlai Stevenson. Banks of windows to either side of her looked out over sweeping lawns that were green despite the drought. At her back stood a William Morris screen, patterned flowers as delicate and yet as forceful as she was herself.

'We can't even begin to prove our mayor bribed his own utility director,' she began, 'or that either man played a role in contaminating our water. We have no evidence. But it certainly looks as though Jimmy persuaded the Council aldermen to vote in his favour even while they knew it was likely to cost them the next election. And it looks as though he went on to persuade the press to present only his view of events, not what actually happened. If nothing else, this displays a very great deal of power in the hands of one man. And I don't know about the rest of you, but I find myself thinking, "Jimmy Zemanski? He does these things by himself?"'

The crowd began talking all at once, over each other, around each other, consternation now adding to their outrage.

Becky let them chatter a moment, then she called out, 'Anybody here go to Walmart?' Several people glanced at each other and thought of Jimmy's jokes about her fragile mental state. Even Helen frowned in worry. 'Come on, children,' Becky pressed. ''Fess up. Donna?'

'I once bought a camera there,' said Donna. She was sitting in the front row. 'Becky, dear, are you all—'

'Kate?' Becky cut in.

At the back of the room, Kate shrugged. 'What choice have I got? They're cheap.' There were titters, part sympathy, mainly uncertainty and worry about Becky's wits.

'Ruth?'

Ruth Madison was draped over a sofa. She'd considered sending a copy of Becky's email to Jimmy, then decided against it. Teasing him would be more fun if the whole business came as a shock. She did love to shock him; they'd planned to meet this evening, and she was already working out her strategy. Her husband, the banker, sat beside her, his hand resting on her knee. She grimaced at Becky and shook her head. 'Vast ugly store, shaky corrugated ceiling, mountains of junk, tinkly music. Nobody would go there willingly.'

'How would you—' Becky began.

'Look, Becky,' Ruth interrupted, 'if you're not feeling so—'

'—compare them to Saudi Arabia?'

Ruth grimaced again. 'Saudi sells oil. Walmart sells sweatshop scrapings from China. No comparison.'

'Isn't it nice when people say just what you want to hear?' Becky said. 'So you'd be surprised, would you, Ruth, if I told you that Walmart is richer than all of Arabia put together?'

'I wouldn't believe a word of it.'

'It's no secret, Ruth,' Helen said irritably. 'The World Bank says so. You'll find it in *Fortune* magazine. Our own UCAI in St Louis has just managed to shove Kuwait down a—' She broke off, sucked in her breath. 'Oh, Grandma, I *see*! Jimmy isn't the power behind this. UCAI is. They turned the Council vote. They blacked out the media. Jimmy doesn't have the muscle for that kind of thing. How could we have thought he did? He's merely their puppet. And that means it's us against them, just like Kate said. And there's—' She broke off again to glance at Becky. 'Right so far?' Becky's face already glowed with pride, so Helen ploughed on. 'Jimmy is their route into Springfield. Without him, they have no spearhead. Without him, they can't take control of our water. He's got to go.'

'Impeach him!' somebody cried. The crowd took it up, just as they'd taken up 'Let us vote' in the Old Capitol. Becky had to bang her gavel again and again much as Jimmy himself had had to do.

'Judge?' she said then.

A man more ancient than she was struggled to his feet. He wore a flowered shirt. 'I hate to tell you this, but impeachment is very slow, and it doesn't necessarily mean removal from office.' The voice was quavery but everybody knew he'd served more than fifty years on the Illinois Supreme Court. 'Clinton was impeached. The alleged crimes took six years to come to light. The actual procedure of impeachment took six months. And he stayed on. Furthermore, Zemanski would have to be tried *and* convicted for high crimes and misdemeanours and, as Becky said, we have no evidence that he's done anything untoward. Nor do we have that kind of time. Nor can we be certain impeachment would achieve our aim even if we succeeded. A recall election is possible, but we'd need evidence for that too.'

The judge let his words sink in, then looked around at the audience, so glum now, so jubilant only moments ago. 'Anybody want to hear a practicable alternative?'

30

ST LOUIS: Saturday

'I always enjoy your company, Mr Mayor,' Francis Slad said, 'but what could be so urgent you have to come to my home on a Saturday?'

Francis Slad's house looked . . . Well, Jimmy had expected something radiating Christian virtue like his brother's St Louis office. How could anybody characterize this place? An orgasm of money? It stood north of the city, its foundations apparently afloat above a minor tributary of the Mississippi that burbled along beneath it, tumbled out over stones in front of it and on into the vast reaches of the river that filled the horizon. The floors belonged in a European castle, varieties of stone intricately inlaid. The furnishings were tasteful billionaire: chandeliers, embroidered silk, marble and white oak, all of it oozing cash and rarity. Nobody lived within a mile. This was protected land; no housing allowed. But as a rich lady once said, laws like that are only for the little people, not the Francis Slads of the world.

Francis was an elegant figure himself, a slender man with long fingers and a classic profile; he lounged in his chair, weight on one hip, one shoulder raised, brows knitted, a distracted air about him that Jimmy knew could switch without warning to a sarcasm that cut deep. Jimmy was amazed every time he saw the brothers together. How could these two have come from the same mother? Much less in the same birth? Sebastian dozed on a Renaissance settee, a face of well-fed contentment, fat legs spread wide, giant testicles bulging like a farmyard hog.

Jimmy felt awkward, unsure where to put his hands, embarrassed by the half-moon glasses that hung around his neck. He'd intended his imitation of Francis as flattery, but somehow he felt just clumsy: not at all what he'd expected. 'The last time Becky Freyl made trouble,' he said, shifting in his well-padded chair, 'your brother seemed distressed that I hadn't contacted you at once. This time I came as soon as I could. The Council vote didn't stop her. She's gearing up to overturn our contract.'

Francis looked up in surprise. 'You can't mean that, Mr Mayor. Your Council voted it into law.'

'I do mean it.'

'Can she do that?'

'It's a thirty-day referendum.'

'What does it entail?' Francis asked. 'Another petition? Another vote? And if she wins?'

'The contract is null and void as soon as the votes are counted on September twenty-fifth.'

'You said thirty days. The twenty-fourth is *exactly* thirty days away.'

'The papers only got filed yesterday.' Jimmy shook his head unhappily. 'I didn't hear about it until last night. Like I say, that's why I'm here.'

Francis sighed. 'Mrs Madison is your informant, I presume.'

Jimmy shifted uncomfortably. These guys were beginning to remind him of Becky. Did they know everything? An early evening of drinks and dinner together should have ended in a scramble to the bedroom before they'd finished dessert. But she'd got him talking so lyrically about the football stadium to come – and his hopes of buying the Springfield Rams to play in it – that he'd given no more than a passing thought to the firm upper thighs beneath her summer dress. Coffee came and went. Jimmy poured out brandy and talked on. But as he refilled her snifter, she brought her feet up onto the wide Eames chair, sat tailor fashion in it, knees splayed, those wonderful legs fully exposed. She wore no underwear. Jimmy didn't even remember putting his snifter down. His right hand was revelling in its goal between those thighs, his left fumbling at his trousers.

That's the moment she chose to say, 'Oh, Jimmy, I forgot. I went to an emergency Coalition meeting at Becky's. Guess what, sweetie? You haven't beaten her yet. A referendum comes next. They're going to overturn your vote.'

The thought of it made his cheeks burn. 'I got the names of dozens of professional canvassers from Chicago,' he said to Francis. 'I'll hire them and more on Monday. I can slow the Coalition down a little too.'

'How?'

Jimmy opened his briefcase and took out a sheaf of paper more than two inches thick. 'Here's volume one.'

'Of what?'

'The contract. It runs to five volumes.'

Lawyers love what Jimmy called 'swamping'. It can muddy *any* issue. 'Informed consent' does sound like a noble principle, but drowning it in reams of paper is almost too easy. Jimmy had made Ruth pay for her joke by helping him bulk out the contract with case law that went back a hundred years and stretched to nearly three thousand pages. People can't object to a contract if they haven't been given the chance to read it, which meant that the

Coalition was going to have to lug several copies around with every petition. If they didn't, Jimmy could invalidate the petition on ethical grounds.

But Francis sighed irritably. 'I'm surrounded by fools.'

'What's that supposed to mean?' Jimmy protested. 'You yourself got the Incol report up to five hundred pages.'

Francis sighed again, shook his head, turned away.

It was Sebastian who roused himself to explain.

'Mr Z, it ain't usually a real good idea to play the same trick twice. We don't figure Mrs Freyl fell for it the first time around, and she can make pretty good mileage out of it a second time. She's probably gonna have lots of fun with them professional canvassers too. And we already got enough troubles with this here weather, understand me?'

Jimmy understood all too well. There were no signs of panic in UCAI shares on world markets – not yet – but almost anything can spook investors. A referendum to overturn the contract that would open the entirety of Midwestern water to private ownership: Jimmy shuddered to think how fast the indices would plunge on that news. 'I did warn you about Becky,' he said, putting volume one back into his briefcase.

Francis wasn't impressed. 'She's after you, isn't she, Mr Mayor? You personally. She wants to bring you down, and she sees your campaign to privatize as the way to do it. She doesn't care who owns Springfield's water. This referendum is a vote of confidence in you, isn't it? Or rather, a vote of no confidence. All she cares about is who's in charge of the town itself. What it means is that if she doesn't care, nobody else does. Put her out of action.'

Jimmy wasn't sure how to respond. 'Excuse me?'

'She's old, Mr Mayor. The old are vulnerable. Now tell me about David Marion.'

This time Jimmy had no idea how to respond.

'Most men aren't interesting,' Francis went on. 'This Marion has to be. Not many people have something I want.'

Jimmy opened his mouth, shut it, watched Francis twirl his half-moon glasses. 'I can't imagine anything that guy might have that you couldn't get easily yourself. Except Helen Freyl maybe.'

'Prison is enforced childhood.' Francis spoke as though Jimmy hadn't said a word. 'That's why prisoners behave so badly behind bars. It's why they're incapable of functioning in the adult world when they get tossed back into it. But here's a man who spent his entire youth locked up, and yet negotiates his way so skilfully outside that he escapes several professional attempts to kill him. Meantime, he alienates the cream of society in an important state capital and still manages to marry into its highest echelon.'

Jimmy chuckled. 'You ought to see him at a dinner party.'

'Lost, is he?'

'Totally.'

'How?'

'He doesn't know how to fight us.'

'Really? Now that does surprise me. What else?'

'No idea how to handle his workers. They walked out on him.'

Francis gave a snort of contempt. 'What does he do with his spare time?'

'He runs.'

'I know that. Springfield has too many paths and alleyways that only children know about.'

'Does it?'

Francis glanced out at the Mississippi beyond. It's over a mile wide at that point – might as well stretch as far as an ocean, no hint of a bank on the other side. 'He doesn't swear. It's odd to spend life in prison and keep a clean mouth. Most men go the other way with a vengeance. He didn't grow up in a Christian home, so he must have stopped swearing inside. Don't you find that strange? And an English accent in an Illinois prison. That's even stranger, don't you think? You assume it's all Hugh Freyl, don't you? And yet it doesn't quite fit.'

'You knew Hugh?'

'I believe there has to have been some other English influence.'

'In an Illinois prison? You've got to be kidding.'

'I have a poor ear for accents, Mr Mayor, but I'm informed by experts that a trace of the north can be detected in his, and yet Mr Freyl never moved out of the Home Counties.'

Jimmy shrugged, looked down at his half-moon glasses, realized he was twirling them precisely as Francis was, stopped at once. His discomfort was getting serious, and he wasn't sure why. 'You seem to know more about both of them than I do. Look, you're right of course. A hefty contract won't hold the Coalition for long, but those professional canvassers can be very effective.' Jimmy leaned forward, about to get to his feet. 'If you could consider the situation and get back to—'

'Oh, please, Mr Mayor. Indulge me. Why do you hate Mr Marion?'

'I didn't say I hated him.'

'Yes you did.'

Jimmy's anger hit him so abruptly that he spat the words out before he knew he was going to say them. 'The fucker stole my girl. I want her back.'

'Ah,' said Francis, 'that's what I thought. You and I have a bond, Mr Mayor. Do you imagine that killing him is going to get her back?'

'People get over death. I'll make a good comforter. What do you mean, we "have a bond"?'

'I think he stole my girl too. You ought to pay more attention to his movements.'

'Your girl?' Jimmy had just assumed Francis was gay. 'He's cheating on *Helen*? How could he do that?'

Jimmy started googling on his iPad as soon as he was a couple of miles away. It took him nearly half an hour, but he found a small item in the British press. Why hadn't anybody here said anything? But then Jimmy knew how large a chunk UCAI owned of the Midwestern media; he'd been delighted to profit from it himself after the trauma of the Council vote, and the item was very small.

A microbiology student was complaining in an *Oxford Times* blog of five years ago:

Francis Slad is some American industrialist or something. What's he doing schmoozing with our own Aloysia Gonzaga?

31

SPRINGFIELD: The first day
in September

The opening event of the Coalition's drive was an Auction of Promises at the Illinois State Fair Grounds, and the atmosphere was jubilant. There were children and balloons, hot dogs, popcorn, candy floss; a carousel, a Ferris wheel, a rollercoaster. Picnic tables filled up with families. A pop singer ground away on an open-air stage.

The day was fiercely hot, sky cloudless, no hint of those storms forecasters had been warning about for months. Everybody came with water bottles, sun visors, umbrellas that doubled as parasols. Becky really did love the heat, even when it was as bad as this. It made her think of summers in Atlanta, when the tar melted on the roads and stayed soft into the evenings; as a little girl, she'd sat on the kerb outside her house, working her toes into the warm tar and eating chocolate ice cream. Despite her protests, the Coalition had set up a canopy just for her and a picnic table with water on it. But she hadn't expected the crowd to be so big – not this early in the campaign – or so enthusiastic. Nobody had.

'Miz Freyl, you got to drink some of that water.' Lillian said it several times. 'Old people get dehydrated easy.'

'Come on, Grandma, drink a little,' Helen urged.

Becky smiled at her. 'Ice cream, Helen. Get me ice cream. So much nicer. In a cone. That's what I really—' She stopped short. 'Not yet. Don't go yet. We're about to start.'

The auctioneer boiled over with enthusiasm; rapid-fire bidding jumped in increments of fifty dollars, then a hundred, then five hundred. The rarest item for sale was an invitation to the *Cisco Cotto Talk Show* in Chicago including after-show refreshments with Cisco himself. Other items included a children's writer who would put the name of the winner's child into her book, an architect's services for building an extension, dinner at the Sangamo Club.

Becky clocked up the sales on her BlackBerry as they happened. Tens of thousands of dollars, then a hundred thousand, then two hundred thousand. The auctioneer had pulled in almost twenty thousand more by the time the crowd began to disperse.

Becky studied the figure on the screen, then frowned in puzzlement. When she looked up, Jimmy stood in front of her.

'Hiya, Becky,' he said. 'Lot of money, huh?'

She searched his face, apprehensive now. 'There's something wrong with my cell phone, Jimmy. It's saying the wrong date.'

'Let me see.' He bent over it. 'Looks okay to me.'

'It can't be the first of September.' She glanced at her mobile.

'Sure it can.'

'Why isn't it December? Or May?'

'Tell me something, old girl, what month do you think it is?'

She studied her BlackBerry again. 'This is very strange. September? Is that what you said? September? Why not July?'

He broke into a smile. 'A little confused, aren't we?'

*

A loud clapping jolted Becky awake and into a panic. Buried alive? White coffin, head cemented in place, an insistent chuck-a-chuck-a-chuck.

But her moment of terror gave way to the realization that she was moving: an MRI scanner.

'What am I doing here?' she said to the technician as the gurney she lay on emerged from the tunnel that had been her coffin.

Lillian appeared at her side at once, dressed in a white gown. 'You had a . . . a incident.'

'A stroke?'

'Don't look like it. Miz Freyl, I done told you to drink that water. I goes to get you some of that chocolate ice cream and comes back and finds Mr Mayor Jimmy Zemanski acting——'

'Jimmy! What does he have to do with it?'

'You don't remember nothing, do you?'

'Where's Helen?'

'Dealing with the insurance.'

'Lillian, I feel terrible.'

'I know, sugar. I know. You just dehydrated. Old folks get con-fused if they don't get enough water.'

'Fiddlesticks.'

And yet Becky knew it was not just a possible cause but the probable one. Droves of people keel over every summer. The media is alive with warnings, especially to the old. It was that damned wheelchair. If it hadn't been for that, she'd have stood under Lillian's umbrella, and Lillian would have fussed until she'd drunk the water she needed. She'd come to hate that chair and everything it stood for.

The question was, how could she get rid of it and save face at the same time?

*

The sight of Becky ashen-faced, expressionless, tubes in her arm, hooked up to beeping machines with jagged lines in parade across them: that had really thrown Helen.

She dealt with the insurance in a daze. There were still butter-flies in her stomach the next morning as she hurried across the parking lot of the Catholic college west of Leland Grove. Last classes of the season: that scared her too. What did she amount to? What *could* she amount to? She had no real work. She didn't *do* anything. What would justify her existence when her pupils left her?

She didn't hear Jimmy coming up behind her, didn't have any idea he was there until he caught her arm and swung her around.

'I'm late,' she said, shaking him off.

'No you're not. You're early. I know exactly when your classes are, and you have' – he checked his watch – 'more than an hour before the first one. I, er ... I need to talk to you.' The idea that Francis Slad had planted, that David was betraying her with another woman: it made Jimmy's heart feel raw and squashed inside his chest. The sincerity in his voice was real. 'Helen, please. Let's go some place cool.'

She paused. 'Talk here or nowhere.'

'Wouldn't you prefer to get out of the heat?'

'Talk or get out of my way.'

'It's about Becky.'

The butterflies in Helen's stomach turned into an attack of out-right panic. 'What about her? She's fine. Back home.' Helen wasn't going to thank Jimmy for calling the ambulance if that's what he wanted; in less than a minute she'd have called it herself.

'How can she be "fine"?' Jimmy asked. 'She didn't know what year it was, much less what month it was or where she was or what was going on around—'

'She was dehydrated, for Christ's sake.'

'Oh, come on, she's been getting steadily worse, and you know it. She can't stand up on her own. She keeps forgetting all kinds of stuff. Yeah, sure, Becky and I squabble like a couple of alley cats on a backyard fence, but I love you, Helen — you know that — and I love her because she's part of you. I can't bear seeing her like this, especially when I know there are things that can be done. If you could just get her to take a week in St John's—'

'Shut up, Jimmy.'

'—they could—'

'Shut up!'

Everybody in Springfield over the age of sixty feared St John's. Once in for assessment, never out again: that's what they said. It wasn't true, but the threat of St John's would get most recalcitrant grandparents to cooperate. For Jimmy, it was the perfect solution. A week without Becky, and the army of professional canvassers he'd hired would collapse the referendum before it got up steam. He was sure of it. UCAI would be signed, sealed and delivered, and there wouldn't be a damn thing she could do about it.

He grabbed Helen's arm again. 'Aren't you even going to give her a chance?'

Helen shook herself loose and ran up the stairs to the college building, now boiling with anger as well as fear. She headed straight for Sister Evangeline's office and threw open the door.

Sister Evangeline looked up with a delighted smile. 'Helen!' she said. 'Come in, come in. I'm *so* glad you could make it.' Sister Evangeline had seen how much Helen enjoyed teaching — nobody could fail to notice it — and was hoping to persuade her into the fall semester.

'Where the fuck is she?' Helen demanded, dropping her books on the floor.

Sister Evangeline had worked with young offenders. Very little shocked her, certainly not Helen's language. But she'd never seen Helen so visibly upset. She rushed to the other side of her desk, put a hand on Helen's shoulder. 'What's the matter, dear? Please sit down. You don't look well at all. Do you need a doctor?'

'I hate teaching. I hate kids. I don't know why I agreed to do this in the first place.' Helen knew what she was saying was nonsense, that she didn't mean it, that she wanted to teach more than anything else right now. But she couldn't stop. 'I refuse to do another hour of it. Do you hear? Not another minute.'

'Helen, dear, it's the last day of term. Your students will be so—'

'Where *is* Aloysia Fucking Gonzaga?'

'Who?'

'"Who?" What do you mean, "Who?" The bitch whose classes I'm teaching. The bitch nobody can find. She's been gone for months. I'm the one saddled with her work. Where is she?'

This time Sister Evangeline's hand was over her mouth, her eyes open wide. 'My goodness, can you believe it? I'd forgotten all about her.'

'You'd—?' Helen was too furious to complete the sentence.

'Do sit down, Helen dear. Please don't be angry. It's all my fault. I do apologize. I'm really so very—'

'Yes, yes. Where *is* the woman?'

Sister Evangeline knitted her brows, shook her head. 'I have no idea, Helen. I was so pleased to have you here and so pleased – God forgive me – so very pleased not to have *her* that I put all thought of her aside.'

Sister Evangeline had worried that the Englishwoman would find American youngsters difficult. That's the only reason she'd looked in on one of Aloysia's classes. Aloysia was pacing back and forth in front of her pupils. She was a strong-featured woman, well built, perfectly groomed, brown hair with gold streaks in it, a slight limp – an oddly attractive limp – as though one leg were shorter than the other. She held out a paper in her hands.

'Hopeless,' she was saying to a boy with pimples and a bright red face. 'Absolutely hopeless. Are you demented? Is that brain made of rocks and dirt? What'd you say your father did? Dig ditches? My advice to you? Follow in his footsteps.'

Sister Evangeline gave Helen an unhappy shrug. 'She just crumpled up the paper and tossed it into the wastebasket.'

Helen sat down abruptly. 'Jesus, that was nasty.'

'I'm afraid none of us really took to her. We did try to make sure she was all right though. We emailed, telephoned, texted, sent plain old letters. We even went to her home. We went there twice. The second time we peeked through the letterbox. There was lots of mail piled up. She plainly hadn't come back from her vacation.' Sister Evangeline bit her lip, gave Helen a sheepish shrug of the shoulders. 'We were all so, well, relieved that we—'

'You didn't bother with the cops? Hospitals?'

Sister Evangeline pulled herself up primly. 'Surely if something were wrong, somebody would have done something.'

'Just not you, huh? Give me her address.'

Aloysia Gonzaga's house was one of the smallest in the Leland Grove area, clapboard, dead lawn in front, dead flowers in the flowerbeds. On days as hot as this, American streets are dead zones too. Not a pedestrian to be seen. Blinds in houses drawn. The only sounds were hums and whirrs from air conditioners. And the occasional dog's bark.

Helen gave the layout a quick glance and set to work.

Her wedding request to David was that he teach her how to pick a lock. He'd been an expert by the time he was ten; after that, there wasn't a secure home within miles of any foster parents willing to house him for a few months. For nearly two years after he got out of prison, he'd operated the business that Hugh had set up for him, designing and installing systems secure enough to keep him out. Helen was a diligent pupil, and she was showing progress. But as the Massachusetts Institute of Technology says, there's a Zen to the art of lock-picking. It takes years to master.

At least this was an easy Yale and an old-fashioned deadbolt, the very locks she'd been practising on. It took her more than half an hour, and the pile-up of mail was so big that she had to throw her weight against the door to open it. And the moment she squeezed past it, the classes she'd been due to teach, even her fears for Becky, dropped out of her mind. This was the first time she'd broken into a real, live house, the first time she'd caught a glimpse of the thrill that David described: the first step on forbidden territory.

The postmarks on the mail dated back to the first of June; the woman had been gone for months. Ugly furniture. Meagre belongings. Not too surprising in somebody on sabbatical. No laptop. Probably took it with her. Not much to cook with. Fridge with a few mouldy lumps and a dreadful stink. Helen shut it quickly. Bed sloppily made, but wardrobe reeking of money and fashion magazines. Same with the make-up and toiletries. Helen rifled through the papers on the desk: a couple of monographs Aloysia was working on. No hint of any of the lovers except for a supply of birth-control pills from England.

The books on the shelves were texts of microbiology, hydrology, mathematics. Helen took out *Studies in Water Flow*. She'd never liked the subject much, but the equations are pretty. She flipped through a few pages. That's when she found the postcard. The picture was one of those beautiful Mississippi riverboats that now serve as floating casinos. She turned it over to look at the message side, no salutation, no signature, just a single word in a childish script:

REMEMBER?

The shock of it made her face tingle. She put the postcard back at once, shut the book, stared at it a moment, opened it again, took out the card, slipped it into her pocket. Then she started a systematic search, every paper, every drawer, every cupboard. When she was finished, she took a towel from the kitchen and wiped every surface in the house. It was evening by the time she dialled the Springfield Police station.

'I want to report a missing person,' she said.

32

SPRINGFIELD: The same time

That single night of rest and fluids in Memorial Hospital was all it had taken to get Becky back in her own bed, propped up on pillows. She loved her bedroom. The floor was inlaid wood, plantation shutters on the windows, as little cloth as possible because of her many allergies. But photographs and books covered the walls and made the simplicity rich and warm. She could look around and see the Atlanta of her childhood, her son Hugh growing up in Springfield, the Old Capitol in stages of the reconstruction that her own Springfield Arts Society had organized and overseen.

She held a clipboard in front of her; she'd spent the last hour on ideas for cartoons ridiculing Jimmy, his five-volume contract and his army of professional canvassers. Springfield's artists supported the Coalition. They'd been wonderfully helpful with the protests against the Council vote, and many had volunteered for the campaign to overturn it – a cartoonist among them.

She was so absorbed that she heard the knock only when it came a second time. 'I'm busy, Lillian,' she said through the shut door.

'It's Mr Mayor Jimmy Zemanski and another gentleman,' Lillian called back.

'I'm in bed.'

'I told him. He says he don't mind.'

'It's not his affair to mind or not mind. What's he want?'

'Miz Freyl, he says you done sent for him. You want me to tell him you ain't seeing nobody yet?'

Becky pursed her lips. She hadn't sent for him. She was moving her legal affairs to Carrick & Kessler. Not that she'd told Jimmy. The referendum made dealing with Herndon Freyl & Zemanski seriously embarrassing, but it had only brought things to a head. A mayor must learn to delegate his professional commitments. Delays with her will had indicated an inability to do so. The first draft had demonstrated it. Her name was Rebecca Marianne Hogg Freyl, definitely not Rebecca Marilyn Freyl; there'd also been irritating punctuation errors. Which meant he couldn't juggle the demands on him. He'd apologized abjectly — for the delay as well as the errors — and yet a week had gone by with no sign of the revision.

On the other hand, the 'incident' at the Auction of Promises emphasized the need to ensure that David could not benefit from Helen's inheritance. Becky needed a signed document on record quickly, and instructing a new lawyer is a lengthy process; she could always amend the will later. She'd just decided to admit Jimmy — get the job over and done with — when he burst past Lillian and into her bedroom.

'I'm so sorry, Becky,' he said. 'I took on a new clerk last—'

'Mr Mayor, I done asked you to wait,' Lillian interrupted, following him into the room.

'Hey, Lillian, lighten up, huh?' he said. 'I'm practically a member of the family.'

'No you ain't.'

'Why are you so tough on me, old friend?' He turned to smile at her. 'You'd better get lost though. This is going to be kind of private.'

Lillian stayed where she was. 'Miz Freyl, what you want me to do?'

Lillian was a beneficiary to the tune of half a million dollars. Becky certainly didn't like the idea of her knowing that. 'No, no, you may go,' she said. 'This won't take long.' As Lillian left, she noticed Jimmy's companion. 'I assume this is the person responsible for the shoddy workmanship represented here. He's too old to be a clerk. No wonder he's having trouble. Do you wish to apologize, young man?'

Jimmy laughed. 'You have to have a witness, Becky, and you can hardly ask Lillian to do it, now can you? I thought I explained all—'

'I haven't forgotten, Jimmy.' Becky's voice was icy. 'Are you going to introduce us?' she asked. 'Or are you going to let us stare at each other like children in the park?'

Jimmy turned to the other man. 'Mrs Rebecca Freyl, this is LaFond.'

Becky took the man's hand. He was maybe fifty-five, a little plump, an easy smile, curly hair greying at the temples, a diamond ring on his little finger.

'Mr LaFond,' she said.

'It's Dr LaFond as a matter of fact,' he said. 'I've heard so much about you, Mrs Freyl.'

'Thank you for coming, Doctor. Won't you sit down?' She turned to Jimmy. 'Let's see what you've produced this time.' He handed over the pages, then sat beside LaFond. She scanned the will carefully, expecting errors but finding none. Most unlikely.

She could almost always find errors in other people's work. She thought irritably that Jimmy's success this time was another sign of God's sheer nastiness to the old. She read the draft again.

'Clean enough for you, Becky?' Jimmy said as she finished her third reading.

'Surprisingly, yes. I sign here?' Jimmy got up and leaned over the bed to point. Becky signed and the doctor signed after her. 'Thank you, Jimmy. I'm grateful to you for coming along, doctor. Lillian will show you out.' But Jimmy sat down again. 'Is there something else?' she asked.

'Becky, I'm, er, I'm a little . . .' He trailed off, frowned.

'Out with it. Out with it. I'm a busy woman.'

'I'm worried about you.'

'I beg your pardon.'

'You probably don't remember what, well . . .'

'Jimmy, you've been harping on and on about my memory, and I'm getting thoroughly sick of it.'

'After your Auction of Promises, you and I had a very strange conversation.'

Becky saw the two men exchange glances. 'My decrepitude is no affair of yours,' she said. Her tone this time was icy. 'Jimmy, I apologize if in some way I have inconvenienced you. Now if you don't mind . . .'

'Ah, come on, Becky.' Jimmy shook his head sadly. 'I love your granddaughter. You know that. I've loved her for years. Whatever else divides me and you, we're as one on the subject of David Marion. If anything I'm even more anxious than you are to prise her away from him. But I also know how much she loves you. That makes your health hugely important to me, and I can see how much that whole business upset you. It sure as hell scared me. I was the one who insisted they get you to a hospital.'

Becky picked up a pencil and tapped it on her desk. 'This has something to do with why you brought Dr LaFond instead of your ill-educated clerk?'

'You did need a witness, Becky, and we'd just finished a little business, so I thought—'

'You thought you'd kill two birds with one stone, did you? Ever efficient Jimmy. All right, Dr LaFond, I assume Jimmy has given you the details of this "strange conversation". I'm afraid he is correct in saying that I don't remember it. But as you've clearly come to some kind of diagnosis on the basis of it, I think I'm entitled to know what it is.'

LaFond put his hands together, an odd gesture a little like prayer, then clasped them. 'Symptoms like these are often hard to make sense of, Mrs Freyl,' he said. 'I wouldn't want to jump to any—'

'Fiddlesticks.'

'You're right. I do have a few thoughts about it. I'm interested that you don't remember. Not at all?'

'I woke up in an MRI machine.'

'Yes. Yes, I see.' He nodded. 'Mrs Freyl, sometimes as we get older—'

'I do not need a gentle bedside manner, doctor. If you have something to say, say it.'

'What you and Jimmy describe gives a clear picture of the early signs of dementia, and the—'

'Lillian!' Becky cried. She rang the bell beside her bed.

'—primary sign is precisely what Mr Zemanski describes: a disorientation as to time, date or place. Forgetting your lawyer's explanation of the need for witnesses is also relevant. This combination of lapses makes me certain that—'

'Lillian!' Becky cried again.

'—the only way forward is an in-patient stay in a medical assessment unit with a view—'

The bedroom door flew open. 'What's the matter, Miz Freyl?' Lillian was breathless. 'You okay?'

'Where *were* you?' Becky demanded.

'In the garage. Got here as quick as I could.'

LaFond turned to Lillian. 'This is a private medical consultation, Mrs, er . . .'

'Draper,' Jimmy supplied.

Becky's voice was Arctic now. 'Show them out, Lillian.'

Neither man moved. 'Do forgive me, Mrs Draper, but without a full, in-patient medical assessment, we cannot be certain that Mrs Freyl is not in a life-threatening situation.'

Lillian glanced at Becky, then surveyed LaFond and Jimmy. 'You trying to tell me she could be real sick?'

'I'm afraid so, Mrs Draper.'

Lillian put her hands on her hips, shook her head. 'You is full of shit, Mr Doctor *and* Mr Mayor. Now you two come with me or I call the police. Understand?'

Less than an hour later an irritable David stood in the middle of Becky's bedroom.

'So?' he said to her.

He'd been working on the construction site, trying to figure out how one man – with injuries to his side – could complete the project on his own, when a call had come in from Lillian telling him that Becky wanted to see him at once. Now. Drop everything and come. Lillian had met him at the door; she stood beside him now. His half-open shirt stuck to him. The sling that held his arm was dirty. He had a streak of cement across his forehead.

'Oh, dear.' Becky eyed him in distaste. 'You're dirty and sweaty.'

'Make it quick,' he said. 'There's nobody watching the site.'

'You don't have to be impolite too.'

'What do you want?'

Becky turned her face away from him.

'Just tell him about Jimmy, Miz Freyl,' said Lillian. Becky turned back, eyed David as she had before, faced the wall again. 'Miz Freyl, he can't do nothing less of which you talk to him.'

'I need protection,' Becky said, still facing the wall.

David was surprised. Amused too. 'Oh, yeah?'

'I fear I have annoyed some very powerful people.'

'Lots of security guys in the *Yellow Pages*.'

'Strangers are easy to buy off. Don't you dare sit in that chair.' Becky sensed movement and turned to face him. 'All that sweat and filth will ruin the upholstery.'

The chair had belonged to Becky's grandmother. She'd hated seeing Jimmy in it. Watching David throw himself down on it — especially in such an unkempt state — was pure torture. 'You want some help,' he said. 'That it?'

'You're . . .' Becky struggled to get her mouth around the word. 'You're family.'

'First I've heard about it.'

'Don't you play obtuse with me.'

'How much?'

'How much what?'

'I don't come cheap. You know that.'

When David first got out of prison, Becky had offered him a hundred thousand dollars to get out of town. He'd taken the money and stayed. When Hugh died, she'd hired him formally — he'd haggled her up to two hundred thousand — to find the killer. That time David had satisfied her terms as well as taken her money. Even so, she blamed Hugh's death on him. She had no doubt whatever that if it hadn't been for him, Hugh wouldn't have died. And she blamed herself for failing to get rid of David because it meant she had played a role in her son's death. Which only made David more bestial in her mind.

Lillian harrumphed at the both of them. 'Trouble with you two is that you is exactly alike. David, you behave yourself. Money ain't a question here, and you know it. Miz Freyl, you talk to this boy. Ain't nobody else you can trust.'

With Lillian keeping peace, he heard Becky out as she described the visit from Jimmy and LaFond.

'Nothing to do with me,' David said when she finished.

But that evening, David and Helen packed belongings into the Riley for the move into Freyl House to be on hand for Becky; Helen had had an apartment there before marrying David. He'd sworn to himself he'd never live in Becky's house, and yet he preferred it to the self-conscious prissiness of the property he and Helen had rented near the construction site at Otto's Autos.

Becky herself had designed the apartment especially for her granddaughter, a duplex in a wing of the main house, cut off for privacy but not communication. The downstairs was one huge room with a butler's kitchen in wood and stainless steel, panelled walls, books and pictures; a spiral staircase led up to a bedroom above. When Becky was a girl, what was known as a 'conversation pit' was all the rage, a dropped section of floor several feet below the rest; she'd installed one, just assuming Helen would like it. Helen didn't. But a bank of windows went down to floor level there and looked out into a wooded area as dense as a forest at the rear of Freyl House. A big desk turned it into a study.

Throughout the move from the rented house to the apartment, Helen argued that David had to hire somebody — a contractor, the architect who'd done the drawings, the engineer who'd made the calculations – to take over the reconstruction so he could concentrate on Becky. Helen was beginning to see UCAI as the machines from *Terminator*: monstrous size and illimitable power, crushing everything in its path. How could Jimmy have sold his soul to them? How many others did they own? How could she tell which ones they owned and which ones they didn't? She hadn't cried in years, but she burst into tears when she realized David planned to continue working on the house without anybody to help him, not spend much time building up protection for Becky. They ended the move in silence, didn't say a word as they carried their belongings inside.

David unpacked groceries – onions, potatoes, a tin of corned beef – while Helen arranged her books in the conversation pit. 'Hungry?' he said.

Helen didn't look up. 'Why on earth did you force her to plead for your help?'

'Your grandmother?'

'Who else?'

'I enjoyed it.' He was amused all over again.

'Why?'

'She's too fond of pushing people around.'

Helen had always been mercurial, but she hadn't had temper tantrums since her father died. She'd already had one this morning at the Catholic college because of Jimmy. Then she'd burst into tears in the car coming here. Now she found herself abruptly in the full swing of a second tantrum. 'How can you *say* that?' she shouted at David. He gave her a curious glance. 'What's that supposed to mean?' Her voice shot up a level. 'Christ, you don't love anybody. In all this time, you've never said a single word about love. Not one!'

'Why are you shouting?'

The calm of his voice made her angrier still. 'I have a right to know.'

'Know what?'

'Why did you force her to her knees?'

David considered a moment. 'If I'd thought of it, I would have. She could use the exercise. I don't see the point of shouting about it.'

When Helen had done her shouting in the past, people ran out of the room or shouted back. How was she to cope with somebody who just got on with corned beef hash? David had worked for several years as a prison cook. The menu had hardly been exciting, and his interest in food remained slight; she couldn't even scramble an egg. She watched his back as he heated a frying pan, then she flounced into the conversation pit, sat down at her desk and pretended to read.

'Glass of wine?' he said to her a few minutes later.

She looked up in surprise, about to say she knew he'd rather have beer, stopped herself. Of course he'd rather have beer. He didn't really like any other alcohol. Well, she thought huffily, it was about time he learned something about how to be a Freyl. 'Sure,' she said. 'Sure, why not?'

'Glasses?'

'Top left.'

He got out a couple of tumblers, poured the wine, brought her a glass and sat on the edge of the desk. She gave him an irritated glance, but he stayed where he was. Ten minutes later, he got up to tend to the hash, came back, sat on her desk for another ten minutes before he had to tend to the hash again. By this time her glass was empty. So was his. He poured another for both of them.

'Getting me drunk, are you?' she said irritably.

'It's worth a try.'

'Not really.'

It was past sunset by this time and already pitch-black outside. The wooded area beyond the windows was too dense for light from the moon or from the town to penetrate. He leaned over Helen and pointed into the dark. 'See that bird out there?'

'Bird? What bird?'

'That bird. See it?'

'Christ, David, it's too damn dark to see anything out there. You can't see a bird out there. Nobody can.'

'*I* can.'

'Really.' She turned resolutely back to her book.

'I used to watch you like that,' he said. 'Other guys watched starlings and pigeons. I watched you.'

She pretended not to hear.

'The first time . . .' He paused, started again. 'You were wearing ribbons in your hair. It was your birthday party and—'

'Jesus, David, you were in prison.'

He only nodded. 'Summer. Lots of flowers in bloom. Lots of kids playing. Punch and hot dogs in a tent. Huge pile of presents. You pulled a little boy's hair, scratched a little girl, ate all the icing off your cake and threw up.'

'I didn't!' she said despite herself.

'The next summer you fell off your horse and dislocated your kneecap. That was very painful, but you didn't cry. I was proud of you.'

'Daddy told you all this?'

He nodded again.

'You must have been bored out of your wits,' she said.

He looked away, looked back. 'I hated it when you went east to school. He'd sometimes tell me about your letters, but they were so cut-and-dried I couldn't figure out what was going on in your life. You barely even mentioned that you'd been elected to give the valedictory speech at your graduation. I was proud of you for that too.'

'David Marion, are you flirting with me?'

'I used to be good at flirting. Long time ago.'

'How the fuck can you flirt with me *and* humiliate my family?'

He got up and went to tend the hash once more. 'I don't think your grandmother had any idea it would go this far.'

'Oh, Jesus, David. Call the police. You can't handle this. Nobody can. Call the cops. Call the FBI. Call somebody.'

'And tell them what? A concerned friend worries that an old woman might be in need of medical help?'

'Well, what the fuck can an ex-con like you do?'

'Work out a security system. Look up some people I know. This house is a joke. Any fool can break in. She needs to get out of that wheelchair. She's an easier target if she can't move on her own.'

Helen stared at him in fury, then all at once collapsed into laughter. 'David, they can kill her, but she'll never get out of that chair. How's she going to rule me without it?'

'It's part of the deal.' He turned to look at her, the spatula in his hand, and she could see a childlike triumph on his face. 'She walks or she looks somewhere else for security.'

Corned beef hash can be pretty good if you're not too picky an eater. The bottle of wine turned into two, then three. By midnight he was stretched out on the floor; she was sitting cross-legged beside him when there was a sudden small movement in the dark forest beyond the windows.

'David, there *is* a bird out there.'

He raised himself up on an elbow. 'Told you so.'

'How come prisoners watch pigeons and starlings? They're such dull birds.'

'They won't leave you.'

'What's that supposed to mean?'

'All the others fly away to sunny winters in Florida. Not pigeons and starlings. They're always there.'

She reached out to touch him, withdrew quickly, saw from his face that he'd noticed the gesture.

'Goddamnit,' she said irritably, 'Why can't I hate you? Why are you *always* on my mind?'

His face softened.

'Oh, Christ,' she said, 'you're not going to make me apologize, are you?'

'What for?'

'Getting mad.'

'Why would I do a thing like that?' He took her hand, kissed the inside of her wrist, then pulled her down on top of him.

Helen woke abruptly with the first rays of dawn and reached out for David. He wasn't there. Not a surprise. He was rarely beside her when she woke. People in prison tend to go one of two ways: learn to sleep through anything or lose the capacity to sleep for more than short stretches at a time. A couple of hours was David's maximum.

And yet this time, she bolted out of bed in a panic and began a frantic search. Calculus text? No. Purse? No. Grocery bags? God, how stupid. Her hands trembled as she reached into the pocket of the jeans she'd been wearing and pulled out the postcard she'd found at Aloysia's house. She stared at the photograph of the Mississippi sidewheeler for a moment, then gingerly turned the card over to see the single-word message on the other side:

REMEMBER?

The thing is, her father had been so obsessed with David that he'd discussed the case at breakfast, dinner, on the long walks they'd taken together. By the time she was ten, she was as fascinated as he was, thought of David as her secret brother, begged for more details. Hugh had shown her some of David's homework then, and she'd made the puzzled comment that her own script was already more sophisticated than his, even though he was eight years older. She'd read his homework often after that; she'd watched that script grow up. Every stage of its progress was familiar.

She was pretty sure 'Remember?' dated from the time he was about twenty.

33

KNOX COUNTY, ILLINOIS: Labor Day

Black Jesus suffered from a condition called vitiligo. Areas of his face and arms had lost pigmentation; they made pink patches on his brown skin. Streaks in his eyelashes were dead white. Right now the eyes beneath them jiggled up and down, side to side in their sockets as fast as scintillating icons on the Web. 'King the crown. Hold me down,' he croaked. 'Click away. Hold me down.' But he didn't need holding down. He sagged between two guards – knees dragging, sweat running – as they struggled him into Quack's infirmary to die.

This wasn't another outbreak of the prison's mysterious illness. This is what the weather can do when it really puts its back into the job.

During the first few days in September, Springfield's thermometers edged towards a hundred and twenty, humidity hovered around ninety per cent, no air moved – not so much as a whiff of a breeze. Earthquakes? Hurricanes? Volcanos? They're small fry in the armoury. Heat is the big killer, and it was killing all over Illinois: a thousand people so far and thirty thousand head of cattle. Most of the dead people were old or sick; Becky had been one of the luckier ones, just a lack of water, quickly replenished. Heatstroke is what killed the young and healthy. The media went wild over three high school athletes who keeled over in the middle of Springfield vs. Bloomington track events and a couple of soldiers on punishment detail at Sparta, not far from Carbondale.

But nobody reported what was going on at the canal site. Nobody got within a mile of it. Armed guards, razor wire and those signs reading:

WARNING
EXTREME DANGER

Army practice range
Guard dogs
US Government Property
NO
TRESPASSING

kept eyes away from the first man who'd dropped to his knees like a stunned beast at a Chicago meat market. He died in Quack's infirmary. That was yesterday. Right this very moment Black Jesus was getting ready to follow him into the prison cemetery, where dead men with no families ended up.

When the body's internal temperature climbs as far as forty-one degrees Celsius, the internal organs start to cook. Cooling down as fast as possible is the only emergency treatment known, and there's no seriously effective method for it that isn't expensive. Patients in the infirmary were naked. Inmates with spray bottles walked among them, moistening the bare skin again and again, a cold water film that a bank of fans evaporated within minutes. Andy went from bed to bed with rehydrating solution. Quack himself tended to subcutaneous lines for the sickest.

Maybe fans and water sprays were primitive but they were what Quack had asked for; more modern equipment really was out of the question, and the fans had arrived only days ago. The hospital-sterile subcutaneous equipment came at the same time. So did many of the beds. There was morphine in the infirmary medicine cabinet as well as supplies of drugs for many of the ailments that Quack had been unable to treat for years. He had thermometers, bedpans and an unbroken sphygmomanometer for blood pressure.

This bounty constituted the fallout of a week-old miracle that had him pinching himself just to be sure it was real.

Back in June, hats and water breaks every half hour had been enough to keep the work on the canal going at an acceptable speed even though the heat was already breaking records. That's when there'd been a first outbreak of the mysterious 'gastro-enteritis'. Nobody except Quack paid much attention to it, but the whole prison knew about the July outbreak. How could they *not* know? Four men died.

The heat got worse too, and a rebellious grumbling began in the prison population: riot on the horizon. Prison riots are bad enough when there isn't a production target to be reached. They bring out journalists, and UCAI would crucify the Warden if media people started chattering about thousands of shackled men labouring like chain gangs from the 1930s or slaves before the Civil War.

That wouldn't be the extent of it either. Once rioters started talking to media people, they'd blabber about those outbreaks of 'gastroenteritis'. The Warden could refer to Medical Services Direct; he could sing their praises and the sophistication of telemedicine; he could even reveal copies of the death certificates, all of which reflected gastroenteritis. But the outbreaks were hardly far in the past. Why had nobody alerted the health authorities about a whole spate of cases with *very* unusual symptoms? Especially when four prisoners died?

With the support of Medical Services Direct, the Warden declared an emergency cut in work hours on the canal and arranged authorization to ship convicts into Knox County from UCAI prisons in Alabama, Mississippi, Louisiana. The Tent City around the prison ballooned in size until it almost obscured the high stone walls; canal progress stayed on schedule, and tensions eased.

But August had come in even hotter, more humid, air barely moving at all. Fights developed over anything and everything. The cell blocks simmered with resentment. So did the mess hall, the prison yard and the acres of Tent City. Talk of a riot began to sound like more than just talk; the Warden summoned Wolfie, General of David's old gang, the Insiders.

After the Warden, the General was the most powerful person in South Hams. The call for a riot would come from him. He was also a lucky General, and as Napoleon once said, lucky generals are the best kind. Only the day before his interview with the Warden, Quack had approached him with Little Andy's work on the Warden's computer: usernames and passwords that revealed the Warden's rape films, little girls in pigtails and Sunday school dresses. The timing couldn't have been better. The General was fighting to re-establish the McDonald's-style drug trade that had flourished under David's management and fallen to pieces when he was released. So far, he'd failed.

But when he entered the Warden's office with Little Andy's information, he had a deal all worked out. Within a week, it was operational. Every day a supply of pharmacopoeia-grade opiates and hypnotics made its way into the general population via Quack's infirmary. Under strict controls of course. For use only after work hours. Quack's part of the deal was that bounty of equipment and supplies to treat his heatstroke victims as well as medication for several dozen patients who hadn't been able to get the treatment they needed.

Even the Warden was a happy man. As the hottest Labor Day on record drew to a close, he knew he could stop worrying about canal progress. He could stop worrying about a riot and a media take on those strange outbreaks earlier in the summer. He could even stop worrying about the films he'd downloaded and that gave him such solace.

At long last, South Hams State Correctional Facility was a calm and contented place despite its busy infirmary and its dead prisoners.

34

SPRINGFIELD: The first half
of September

September should have cooled things some. It didn't. Death tolls throughout Illinois kept on rising, livestock keeling over, crops failing, farmers going broke. Outside their houses, the citizens of Springfield moved slowly, deliberately as equatorial peoples do.

Despite David's insistence that he could keep up with the construction at Otto's Autos *and* arrange Becky's protection, he didn't raise a single objection when Helen hired a crew of fencers to close off the site. Nor did he object when she suggested they build the electrical enclosure he'd designed around Freyl House. The work went slowly because of the heat, but she could tell he was relieved that Lillian took charge of the men and had no difficulty managing them. Unlike the men who'd worked for him, they seemed to keep their tools in order, clean up their litter, tidy the site: all of this without being told. And then he clearly enjoyed being free to install and test CCTV cameras and motion sensors – a complex, demanding job – although the heat slowed him too. As for the men he interviewed who appeared from nowhere, who were not at all the kind of people that people like the Freyls employed but who set up camps at the corners of the property: Helen and Lillian stayed well away. Becky simply assumed they didn't exist.

The one thing that the heat didn't affect was the groundswell of support for her referendum. Jimmy's professional canvassers were objects of fun. He himself was a joke. So were his five-volume contract and his attempt to put Becky into St John's. David suggested she make the most of that. 'Best protection available,' he said. 'Anything happens to you, you make him the first one they'll look at.' As soon as school opened, Becky's many years of devotion to Springfield education added a swarm of kids to the campaign. The first week of high school saw students exploring the democratic process at work in the referendum itself. Junior high schools concentrated on citizens' rights and public ownership of natural resources. Groups of grade-school children accompanied campaigners and dragged copies of Jimmy's vast contract in little wagons with parasols attached.

Even Jimmy's hard-bitten supporters laughed at that – and were sometimes persuaded to contribute to the cause.

The effect of all this civic activity wasn't limited to Springfield either. Water stocks were market leaders in New York, London, Tokyo, and the financial media watched the town carefully. Stories and editorials around the country were amused, supportive; the children with their wagons and parasols appeared on front pages from coast to coast. Every day UCAI stock slipped a little further. Only the growth in the booming prison industry prevented a dramatic fall.

The Slad twins left St Louis on a whirlwind trip to top-secret conferences with some of the most powerful water companies in the world, the Russian RKS, Vivendi in Paris, the German giant RWA, Suez, Ferrovial and a consortium of Koreans just pulling into the big time. They scheduled Thames Water and Severn Trent in London for the end of September, planning to stay in England for Michaelmas, celebration of the warrior archangel Michael who defeated Lucifer in the battle for the heavens.

They didn't plan to come back until well after the referendum had its say.

35

SANGAMON COUNTY, NORTH
OF SPRINGFIELD: Wednesday

At midnight, long, jagged streaks of lightning lit up the country-side for miles around. The thunder was loud enough to split eardrums. The first rain in months came in huge plops that kicked up dust from the ground like scatters of buckshot. A whoosh of wind, then water just dumped out of the sky. Earth can't absorb it that fast. Within minutes, ground everywhere was ankle-deep in streams. By now the wind howled; an hour later, the hail began.

Here at last was a storm to justify the long-range forecast. Hailstones clattered against the aluminium tankers standing out-side a small brick building enclosed in a chain-wire fence. Inside the building, three men stood waiting while a couple of pressur-ized pipes from the first of the tankers began to empty their load into a gauge-covered stainless-steel box that they'd connected to a heavy metal structure on a concrete plinth. One of the hoses began to tremble.

'Turn them off!' cried Boss.

Not that 'Boss' was necessarily his name. People don't usually tattoo their own names on their knuckles, but it's what Lamar

Bryant had called him before getting himself and his pretty Brittany burned to a crisp by an ancient air conditioner. The man with one arm — he'd been along with Lamar that night too — was already fighting his way out the door and into wind strong enough to rip the coat off his back. Lamar's replacement stood staring from the hose that still trembled to the strange assembly that Brittany Bryant had imagined as a sex act between a jukebox and an ice-cream maker. He was very young, barely more than a boy, scantily bearded to hide severe acne.

'Get away from there!' Boss called out to him.

Before the boy could bring himself to react, a jet-stream spray shot out from the trembling hose, caught his hard hat and knocked it off with such force that it smashed into the ceiling and ricocheted off a far wall. He staggered from the impact and fell to his knees. The one-armed man must have managed to close the valves on the tankers outside just then because the pressure shut off; the jet stream eased into the gentle arc of a drinking fountain.

'You okay?' Boss said to Lamar's replacement.

'What was that?'

'Pinhole leak.'

A tiny hole in a pressurized hose can release fluid at close to the muzzle velocity of a gun. At that speed, a thin stream of liquid becomes a hypodermic needle, goes straight through clothing, through the skin and drives into the muscle tissue itself. Sometimes gangrene and amputation result; that's how the one-armed man had ended up with only one arm.

Lamar's replacement stared at his hat with a dazed expression on his face. 'It's broke.'

Boss paid no attention. He was examining the gauges on the stainless-steel box. He wasn't sure how far the dials had shifted, only that they weren't where they had been. 'Fuck it,' he said as soon as the one-armed man reappeared, dripping with rain and breathing heavily from his dash. 'I got no idea how to recalibrate this thing. Do you?'

The one-armed man studied the gauges himself, shook his head. 'Can't make that much difference, can it?'

Boss studied the dials a moment longer, then shrugged. 'What the fuck do I care if it does? Turn the pressure back on.'

36

SPRINGFIELD: Thursday

'Miss Helen! You upstairs? Miss Helen!'

It was four in the morning. Helen had taken a double dose of Becky's sleeping pills; she'd slept through those claps of thunder even though they'd shaken the windows. She'd slept through the wind shaking the whole house, the rain bucketing down, even the hailstones that hit the copper roof like an avalanche.

'Come on, girl.' Lillian had hold of her shoulders, shaking hard. 'We ain't got much time.'

'David?' Helen was still asleep.

'Miss Helen Freyl. You wake up.' Lillian shook harder. 'You hear me? Wake up!'

'Where's David?'

'Well, he ain't laying here now, is he? Wake up!' Lillian was already threading Helen's arms into a sweatshirt as she used to do when Helen was no more than three years old.

'What's . . .' Helen stumbled as she tried to get into underwear. 'I want David. Where is—?' She was abruptly awake, abruptly terrified out of her sleep just as she'd been a week ago and for the same reasons. 'Where *is* he?' The postcard: why hadn't she destroyed it? Was it still in her pocket? Could she have dropped it somewhere? In the street? No, no. Wouldn't matter if she had. No address. No salutation. No signature. Nobody could make anything out of it but her, and she wouldn't have made anything of it herself if she hadn't found it at Aloysia's house. She'd overlooked something else. That had to be what'd happened, and the police had found it, whatever it was. 'Oh, my God' – she clutched Lillian's arm – 'have they arrested him already? What's the charge?'

'Shush up, girl. He's waiting outside.' Lillian knelt down, slipped one boot on Helen's foot while Helen fumbled with the other. As Lillian opened the outside door, she took hold of Helen's arm. 'Hang on, sugar. It's bad out there.'

Everything whipped, the rain so hard that Helen could hardly breathe, the wind so strong and the water covering the parking lot outside so gusty that she could stay upright only by clinging to Lillian. They sloshed together towards a mud-spattered truck. Lillian bundled her in it beside David at the wheel.

'Have they issued a warrant?' Helen demanded of him as Lillian crawled up beside her. He didn't glance at her, just let the hand-brake off. The racket of the downpour on the truck's roof was so loud that it was hard to hear anything else. 'Oh, sweet Jesus,' she went on in a moan. 'Why did you steal this truck? It's an Isuzu. Even I could spot it.'

'Trusting, isn't she?' David said to Lillian.

'Fuck it all, David—' What Helen saw in the headlights stopped her mid-sentence.

The road from her apartment curved around to the sweep of lawns and flowerbeds in front of Freyl House. But the truck's headlights scanned through a break in the downpour, and she gasped at the sight. No sweeping lawns. Not any more. No Gerber daisies. Not even a stately sunflower.

The famous Freyl gardens were a lake.

'Where's Grandma?' Her voice shook. 'I want Grandma.'

'We got her safe before we come for you,' Lillian said.

David eased the truck into the water and began a slow crossing to the private road on the other side and the public street beyond that.

The ground around Springfield is flat; its height doesn't vary more than a few feet, lower in the west, higher in the east. Donna Stevenson's house was a little east of the Freyl property.

She woke just after dawn and a dream of Niagara Falls; she stretched out in her bed, luxuriated in the sound a moment, then bolted for the window. The wind shook the floor beneath her. The rain battered so heavily against the glass that she couldn't see anything outside. Absolutely nothing. Not so far as the tree in front of her own house.

It was the smell that got her to start down the stairs. She knew at once what it was. Sewage. Broken mains. People in Kansas and Missouri had broken mains in a storm a year or so ago. That storm had made headlines all over, so severe that they'd even coined a new name for it. She strained to remember it, panicked because she couldn't, panicked again as she got halfway down the stairs and could see her front door.

Dirty water hid the floor of the hallway that led to it as well as the antique Aubusson carpet that Becky had helped her order from Paris — maybe an inch deep, maybe two — an even, semi-reflective, brown-tan surface, nothing visible beneath. She ran back upstairs for her mobile: 'No service'. She tried the landline. It was dead.

At least she didn't have to worry about her novel. She always took a hard copy to her bedroom so she could spend the first hour of the morning on it. She shut the door against the smell, curled up on the bed with her pages, tried to concentrate, failed, ended up on the stairs with a washcloth over her nose to keep out the smell while she watched water creep up over the legs of the sofa that her father called 'the Lincoln sofa' because family legend said Abraham Lincoln had once sat on it.

Only a few blocks further east, Allan and Ruth Madison were better prepared. *Much* better prepared. Allan Madison, President of the First National Bank of Springfield, was a figure of weight in the town, if something of a pedant at home. He clucked over pictures out of alignment, read *Consumer Reports* cover to cover, listened to *Weather Radio All Hazards* every day and insulated himself, his wife Ruth and his house against every threat he could think of.

Unlike Donna, he remembered the name they'd given to the storm in June of 2011. First they'd called it an 'inland hurricane', then they'd upgraded it to a 'derecho'. The word means straight in Spanish; it's a thunderstorm as widespread, long-lived and violent as a hurricane, but where hurricanes swirl in a circle with a hole in the middle, a derecho cuts across countryside as straight as a road through Kansas. They'd shown weather maps with red and green areas; they'd said that this derecho showed 'a bow-echo on radar, an inflow notch and a bookend vortex'. Allan had no idea how to interpret those phrases but he had no trouble understanding winds of close to a hundred miles an hour, and he could guess all too easily what an 'eye wall' thirty miles across might mean. He'd gone out at once and bought flood pumps that could get rid of seven thousand gallons of water an hour.

When he'd heard the forecast last night, he and Ruth had set up the pumps and barricaded the doors with sandbags. He'd woken at midnight to thunder and gone back to sleep, pleased with his foresight. Nor was he alarmed at water still bucketing out of the sky in the morning. In the bathroom, he turned the tap. It gurgled. Then it spat. Then it spewed out sewage. The toilet struggled to fill its tank with more filthy water. That did not please him, but his prescience had covered the eventuality; he'd stocked the attic with cases of bottled water.

'Ruth!' he called out, knowing she'd have discovered the dirty water too and gone straight to the attic.

'Cold coffee this morning.' She stood in the bathroom doorway, but she had to shout over the roar of the wind.

'Oh?'

'No electricity.'

That did not please him either. But he'd bought a camping stove, containers of gas, batteries in all sizes. He and Ruth listened to the news while they drank the only pot of hot coffee in the entire neighbourhood.

'. . . not just a derecho but a *super*-derecho.' The newscaster's voice was strained, excited, tired, scared. 'We have winds of more than a hundred miles an hour. Flash floods all over the west side of Springfield. Sewage mains broken. That means the west side's water supply is contaminated again. Listen to me, folks. DO NOT DRINK the water unless you can boil it. Not easy when you don't have electricity. The city is rushing out supplies of purification tablets, but until we get them to you, drink *only* bottled water or Coke.'

Despite his irritation at the inconvenience, Allan gave Ruth a satisfied glance. 'What a good banker God is,' he said.

'Really?' Nothing bored her more than bankers.

'Most of the bank's investments are on the east side. You

know, I think we own more than seventy per cent of Springfield's low-cost housing.'

At ten in the morning, the storm stopped. Just like that. Wind and rain just shut off as though somebody had flicked a switch on a movie set.

Donna looked out of her bedroom window. The even, semi-reflective, brown-tan surface that hid her ground floor, hid all the ground outside. Houses floated in it as calm and placid as plastic ducks in a baby's bath. Hedges and bushes cut out irregular shapes in the water and tree branches floated peacefully. She watched a full-sized oil can drift past, then a couple of spare tyres and a bathtub. A dog paddled across.

Down in her living room, the water had reached the knees of the Lincoln sofa; from it, she gauged the street at a depth of six inches. When she was a Girl Scout, she'd received one of the few river-fishing merit badges in the county; she figured she could handle a puddle like that. She pulled on some boots, sloshed through her house and out to the garage. She'd had a struggle with her conscience before giving way to her passion for a Hummer; the water barely reached the hubcaps of her 4-wheel-drive beloved. She started the engine, turned on the radio.

The newscaster reported the warnings that the Madisons had heard a couple of hours earlier, and then went on, 'The Sangamon River, the Sugar, the Spring, the Horse: they've all burst their banks. The streets are extremely dangerous, especially on the west side. Surface water may look calm, but you can't see the undercurrents. Undertows can sweep you away before you know it. DO NOT GO OUT OF YOUR HOUSE.'

Donna put the Hummer in gear, eased it into the street and began to ford her way south towards Schnucks, Springfield's most elegant supermarket. The route was slow and painful; the Hummer slid off course if she tried to go as fast as five miles an hour. Trees were down. Some leaned against lamp-posts. Wiggins Avenue was impassable. So was Cherry Road. But Willemore was the real shock. She'd always liked Willemore, even thought of moving there. It wasn't even a street any more. It was a rapids. Tan-brown water boiled down it; chunks of wood, boxes, planks of flooring, tangles of wire, newspapers, twigs bobbed in it as they swept past her. She headed towards the Shop 'n Save on Wabash instead, not a patch on Schnucks, but it was further east, higher up. Water levels dropped as she approached. By the time she got there, sun glistened off puddles in an entirely visible parking lot.

And the parking lot was packed. The store inside was even more packed. The soft drinks aisle was so solid with people that she couldn't even see the shelves, and when she got to them, all that was left was twenty yards of emptiness and a single quart of Pepsi. She was oddly pleased; she'd rather liked Pepsi when she was a child. All the fresh milk was gone. So were the fruit juices.

'What are we supposed to drink?' she demanded of the check-out.

'Got any cash on you?'

'Why?'

'Lot of businesses setting up in the parking lot.'

'Already?'

The check-out gave her a crooked smile. 'Springfield's a town of enterprising people.'

Outside, the day was heating up. Steam rose from the damp tarmac. A row of cars waited at the edge of the parking lot with open doors, seats filled with bottles of water and soft drinks.

'How much?' Donna asked a bald man sitting in a station wagon.

'Coke's ten bucks a quart. Water's five.'

She laughed. 'You can't mean that, can you?'

'You don't like it, go somewhere else.'

Next to him was a woman with a price of ten bucks for Evian. Donna finally found a kid willing to part with Pepsi for six. She bought two more quarts, feeling bullied and idiotic as she handed over the money. By the time she got back home, there'd been no rain for nearly three hours, and the water level had dropped enough so that tufts of the carpet were just beginning to reappear. She got out the bottle of Pepsi, swallowed some of it, filled the bottle up with bourbon, and sat on the stairs to drink it as she watched the water recede.

During the afternoon, ground emerged all over a sodden and debris-strewn west side.

The copper roof at the Freyl property still gave off its warm verdigris glow, and the walls still stood firm, but the gardens were a city dump: a landscape of car tyres, plastic bags of rubbish spilling out garbage, an orange plastic chair from some far-flung neighbour, a dead sheep with flies swarming over it and vultures circling above.

The chaos was just as bad inside. Mud covered the floors and soaked up curtains and drapes. Doors hung part-way off hinges, chairs and tables on their sides, sodden books, papers, magazines strewn everywhere.

'Jesus, what a stench,' Helen said, her hand over her nose.

'The sewers done bust open,' said Lillian.

David had made two long, slow journeys to the Hilton, first Becky and all her pills, then Helen. The Hilton wasn't just the tallest building in Springfield; it had its own generator and a commercial supply of bottled water. The Executive Suite he'd taken them to was sleek and clean-lined, blanched cedar and slate in dappled earth colours; several bedrooms, two reception rooms, dining room, kitchen. Neither woman had any idea how he'd managed to claim such a prize at such an hour without any notice, especially when half of a besieged Springfield was clamouring for hotel rooms; a terrified assistant manager explained to Helen that she'd 'relocated' a party of holidaymakers after a five-minute discussion with him.

Becky had suppressed a smile at that, even though being carried out of her own house in David's arms was a trauma she'd never forgive him. Or forgive Helen. Or Lillian. He'd told her that her removal came under the terms of his contract to protect her; and while she was in the process of losing the edge in this negotiation, Lillian was getting her dressed just as she had with Helen. It was all inexcusable. And yet Becky slept better in the Hilton's Executive Suite than she had in years. When she woke, the only missing amenity was her wheelchair. That's why she'd had breakfast in bed. That's why she'd stayed in bed all morning, had lunch there too, had her nap as usual, then propped herself up on pillows to watch the news from bed while Helen and David went to pick up Lillian and assess the damage at Freyl House.

But nobody could have expected devastation on such a scale. Not even Becky's wheelchair had escaped. It should have been safe upstairs, but it lay across a window sill in her study, a broken and filthy wreck, picked up by the flood waters, tossed halfway through the double-glazed pane.

'*You* did that!' Helen said to David.

He only shrugged.

She started to laugh, but the laugh turned at once into a sob. 'Oh, God, we can't fix this.'

'We gonna make it all okay.' Lillian put a comforting arm around her shoulders. 'Just you wait, sugar. Just you wait.'

And that spirit pretty much prevailed throughout the town despite the private enterprise that boomed in the Shop 'n Save parking lot.

When the first fleet of water trucks arrived towards evening, the rich of Springfield gathered in orderly English queues with buckets and empty wine bottles. People chattered and laughed like kids at camp. As dark fell, there was spontaneous singing, a street party, a band, dancing.

But twenty-four hours without air conditioning, running water, a shower or a bath is simply not acceptable. By morning, the party spirit was dead. People got out of bed grim-faced and irritable.

They certainly hadn't expected to find squad cars blocking access to still-flooded streets, where officials in fluorescent jackets and high boots waded knee-deep, looking determined but seeming to go nowhere and find nothing. In no longer flooded streets firefighters and volunteer firefighters clustered around huge pipes, pumping out water from basements. Trucks manoeuvred their way to deliver eight hundred gallon containers to crossroads and supermarket parking lots. Nobody could miss the UCAI logos on both trucks and containers; people weren't impressed. Nor were they impressed by the UCAI logos on the tankers that followed, filling the containers with water. They grumbled that the multinational was making use of a disaster to advertise itself, but then they were ready to grumble about anything and everything. They were openly hostile to the Red Cross, which came next to set up tables beside the containers, unload packets of water-purifying tablets and signs that explained how to use them.

Loudspeakers perched on top of cars fresh from Becky's campaign blared out Jimmy's message, not the Coalition's. 'We'll get through this,' he was saying. 'I promise you that. We're filling water containers as fast as we can. Please drink *only* this water. Please purify it with the tablets *before* you drink it. Do not use the water from your faucets, not to brush your teeth or bathe in or cook with it. Don't use flood water for any purpose, and do not let your kids play in it. This is serious, folks. We don't want anybody to get sick.'

The directions for purifying tablets were hard to follow. Water wasn't redelivered at once. Waiting in long lines like Third-World peasants for water – for *water*, for Christ's sake – didn't sit easily. By noon, people were driving their cars to containers and working in relays to fill up every bottle, bucket, kitchen utensil they owned. The eight hundred gallon containers were empty almost as soon as they were filled. Supplies of purifying tablets ran out at once. People jostled each other. Scuffles broke out.

At two o'clock, Jimmy introduced a rationing system and a police guard to enforce it.

At the same time, supermarkets all over town imposed their own rationing systems for bottled water, and these systems called for a police guard too. Since there was no electricity, supplies like charcoal for barbecues, kindling, container gas, batteries, also had to be rationed and quickly needed a police guard as well. Lines were long and slow. Tempers frayed easily.

Cops moved black marketeers out of supermarket parking lots, but they clustered nearby, and the atmosphere was quite different; car boots overflowed with supplies from the east side and from neighbouring towns. Trade was lively. Haggling the rule. Waits were short. At three o'clock Coke soared to twenty dollars a bottle. By five it had dropped to its supermarket price. By eight, it was back up to ten.

Poor families from the east side could make a month's wages in a couple of hours. Late that night, the city got an injunction banning all outdoor trading within a quarter of a mile of supermarkets.

37

SPRINGFIELD: Saturday

Saint Thomas says one of the joys of the blessed is hanging over the bar of heaven to watch the damned suffer in hell. Allan and Ruth Madison were the blessed of Springfield. The waters never touched them. All they had to do was lie back and enjoy the fruits of Allan's clever anticipation of the crisis.

To be sure, their freezer full of food was thawing, but he'd stocked the basement and the attic with enough canned goods for weeks. He'd never liked air conditioning anyway, and the lack of it bothered Ruth less than it did many people; their indoor swimming pool provided a huge supply of water for cooling off in as well as keeping clean. Not even sleep was difficult; a sheet dampened in the pool and spread over bare skin made for a reasonably comfortable night provided the lounge chairs they slept on lay in the path of open doors to catch whatever air was moving.

The Madisons slept so well that neither one woke when the intruders stepped over them. It was the sudden blast of music — an ear-splitting heavy beat — that jolted Allan to his feet, and what confronted him was as unsettling as Donna's first glimpse of her flooded house. He stood there gaping, too stunned to speak.

The room flickered in light from torches the intruders carried. His eye picked out a potato-faced man in a Viking helmet and a T-shirt that said 'You suck', another guy in a balaclava wearing a purple satin tablecloth with a fringe, a naked woman in green full-body paint with three big dogs that strained at chains around their necks and began howling at the music. A dozen others danced to it, heads and bodies jerking side to side, back to front, up and down, all of them howling with the dogs. As Allan watched, half of them — and the dogs — jumped into the pool and began splashing.

He pulled his damp sheet around him like a toga. 'Hey!' he cried. 'What the hell do you think you're doing?' But the music was so loud that nobody heard him.

Ruth pulled her own damp sheet around her, got up from her lounge chair, went over to the portable sound blaster and turned it off. The howling, dancing, splashing, went on for a minute, then petered out slowly; the intruders turned one by one, more baffled than angry, to face the sheeted Madisons.

'It's ghosts,' one of them whispered.

'Ghosts?' another whispered.

'Ghosts!' a third shrieked.

A chant arose. 'Ghosts! Ghosts! Ghosts! Get 'em. Get 'em. Get 'em.'

They rushed towards the Madisons.

Several scrambled over each other to get at Allan. They shoved him down on the ground. They hoisted him up on their shoulders. They threw him into the pool and themselves in after him, pushed him back and forth between them in the water, dunked him, yanked him up gasping and choking, dunked him again.

Others hovered around Ruth, encircling her, poking fingers at the sheet as though to find out just what might lie beneath it. She pulled it tighter. One of them — a man with missing teeth and orange hair in puffs — jerked at it, then ripped it off her. 'Ooooooooh, ain't this naked ghostie something?' he said. He stuck his tongue out as far as it would go down his chin. She shrank away. He pulled his tongue in, stuck it out again, in, out, in, out. He grabbed at her with both hands. 'Ooooooh, this sure do feel like—'

'Your eyes is shit,' interrupted the green-painted woman in disgust. 'She's a old bitch. I bet you can't even do her. I bet . . . Okay, okay, lemme help you. Hey, old lady, stop fighting so hard. Come on! Stop it! I'm telling you— Now you're home, Archangel. Hit her! Hit her! Hit her!'

Half an hour later, the intruders were gone. Ruth's bloodied hands could barely hold her mobile as she punched in 911, and Allan floated face down, dead in his own swimming pool.

38

SPRINGFIELD: Sunday

Local hospitals were used to dealing with dehydration and heat-stroke in people too poor to afford more than a fan. Now the numbers swelled by the hour with the wealthy who were too unfamiliar with the risks to recognize symptoms. Cases due to sewage came in even faster: the gastroenteritis, skin rashes, eye and respiratory infections that Morris Kline had told Becky were nowhere to be found after the first contamination episode.

This is why medical staff were already busy when the first cases of some alien sickness appeared not long after dawn: a couple of small children rushed to St Margaret's Hospital by their nanny in their mother's Mercedes-Benz. The Emergency Room doctor diagnosed gastroenteritis and hospitalized the children, but the cases were much more severe than any of the others he'd seen. Half a dozen more cases like them appeared before lunch. The symptoms were extreme enough for one of the ER doctors to consult the hospital director. The Director had spent several years with Médecins sans Frontières in Africa. To her, this sounded too much like what she'd seen there; she put in a call to Jimmy.

'Jimmy, I think we got a problem,' she said. She'd known him for twenty years, and she was fully aware that suspicions like hers were political dynamite; she spoke softly, circumspectly, a little surprised that he let her go on without comment.

'Sit on it,' he said as soon as she finished.

'Perhaps I haven't made myself clear. What I'm trying to say—'

'Yeah, sure,' he interrupted. 'A cholera epidemic is just what we need to calm a social group of rich people who get hysterical if there are spots on the bathroom basin. Like I say, sit on it.'

'I have to notify public health, Jimmy. It's the law.'

'You examine these patients yourself?'

'Good Lord, Jimmy, don't you think I can trust my own ER—'

'So you're just guessing cholera,' he interrupted again. 'You've got to grow — what did you call it? — a "culture" to be sure. How long is that going to take?'

'Jimmy, I have a responsibility—'

'How long?'

The Director sighed. 'Couple of days. Maybe three.'

'Then you have to figure out what's in this culture, don't you? What it means?'

'We ought to be able to identify it at once.'

'Oh.' Jimmy was taken aback. 'Well, in that case, er ... That gives us maybe three days, right? Before the law insists you report? We'll have water running again in half that time, maybe even less.'

She was abruptly excited; there was no water in her house either. 'God, that's wonderful. No kidding? When?'

'For Christ's sake, Maureen,' Jimmy said irritably, 'we have black markets operating all over this fucking town. We got respectable people socking each other on the street. There's a pack of weirdos roaming the town. They killed Allan Madison right in his own swimming pool. They raped his wife.'

There was a pause. 'The news didn't say anything about a rape or a murder.'

'What you want to do? Provoke more panic? We have to put a lid on this situation, at least until the National Guard shows. Or FEMA. Bastards. The Governor tried to get both in here as soon as I could see how bad that flood was.' FEMA was the Federal Emergency Management Agency, charged with coordinating a response to disasters that are too much for local authorities to handle. But it was a cumbersome arm of Homeland Security, a lot of red tape including a formal request to the President himself. As for the National Guard, they were on a training exercise in some far-flung reach of the Canadian tundra. 'We're talking an explosive population here,' Jimmy went on, 'and until noon today we're on our own.'

She sighed again. 'What do you want me to say?'

'Nothing. Not a word. I'll do it when the time is right.'

'My friends,' Jimmy's next announcement went, 'I have some good news at last. We expect power to be restored by this afternoon. Once we have power, you can purify your own water by boiling it. Just hang in there, guys. The end's clearly in sight.'

But the UCAI water containers in the parking lot at Schnuck's supermarket stayed empty for more than an hour. The lines waiting grew longer, the people more frustrated. Donna waited with them, as hot, thirsty, irritable as the rest of them. But the best supermarket in town, even without a black market to ease the pressure, needed no more than a lone policeman on duty to keep order.

Until the rats, that is. It was just a pair of them at first. They bolted across the macadam like twin suicide bombers heading straight towards the line of people. A dozen more followed, bringing a stench with them, acrid, dank, faecal. As they reached the queue, people pulled back as fast as they could, falling over each other to get away, pushing, shoving, elbowing, throwing whatever was to hand: the containers they'd brought with them for water, their shoes, their mobile phones, their newly bought groceries.

Then more rats came – and more – until they were a solid carpet of living flesh that boiled across the parking lot. They screeched. They squealed. They leapt at the legs and feet of anybody who couldn't get out of their way quick enough.

And then they were gone.

But the people went right on screaming and throwing everything they could lay their hands on. They overwhelmed the policeman before he had a chance to call for backup, then rushed into the supermarket itself. Donna knelt beside him on the ground.

'I'm okay. I'm okay,' he said. 'What's got into these guys anyhow?'

Donna shrugged.

He frowned. 'Mr Bridgeman hit me.'

'Mr Bridgeman?' she asked.

'We discussed my mortgage only yesterday. And that woman with the red hair: she's my kid's teacher.' He started to get up, staggered.

'You'd better lie down again,' Donna said. She folded her raincoat beneath his head. 'I'd be happy to testify that Mr Bridgeman hit you.'

'Jesus, no!' the cop said, his face terrified. 'I'll never get a mortgage. Just forget it, huh? Please?'

She helped him call for backup. As sirens became audible a few minutes later, people began pouring out of the store again with boxes of whatever had been closest at hand: armloads of groceries, toiletries, detergents, soft drinks. Some pushed trolleys full of the stuff. One pushed a pram full of Jack Daniel's. Another trailed a sky-wheeler suitcase overflowing with frozen peas, ice cream, chicken dinners. Yet another, a child's wagon full of tins and jars.

Donna caught hold of a man whose jacket she knew was Armani. 'Why are you doing this?'

He turned a happy smile on her. 'Because it's free. Everybody's doing it.'

She stopped another man, a very old man, laden down with DVDs. 'I don't have any water in the house,' he said. Tears began to flow down his face. 'I don't have any water in my house,' he repeated.

A little boy burst into tears too, his arms full of Popsicles. 'They won't be no Popsicles here tomorrow.'

A dozen police entered the store to find people crawling up on counters, pushing over displays, grabbing everything they could reach. Smashed jars of peanut butter and jam on the floor glued together heaps of Cheerios, newspapers, spaghetti. There were pools of gin, milk, broken glass. A man rode a bicycle up and down through the mess. Grown men skidded through it as though they were on skateboards. Strangers laughed, hugged each other, swigged bourbon from stolen bottles.

The atmosphere was so joyous that the cops too pocketed bottles of liquor before trying to restore order.

About the same time, looting started out at White Oaks Mall. Downtown too, where a skirmish broke out between two groups of looters. A bunch of west side rich kids stormed the east side. They broke into houses where water was still flowing. They turned on all the taps, threw buckets of water over furniture and each other, danced in spray from hoses; east side families cowered out of their way, pleaded for them to leave, then finally got angry too. They threatened with shotguns and pistols. They attacked with brooms and shovels.

As the afternoon wore on, it became clear that Jimmy's promise of electricity was not going to materialize, and skirmishes flared up all over the downtown area. They coalesced into a crowd of hundreds of people in front of the Old Capitol where Becky's protest had taken place. A fundamentalist preacher with a megaphone shouted that Judgement Day had come at last. The press was there in force, and Americans all over the country watched a disordered mass of people, fighting among themselves at first, begin to form a single-purpose mob in order to confront the phalanx of cops — white helmets with visors for faces, police batons, guns — that formed a line all the way across East Washington Street, one man deep, then two men, then three with trash cans piled up and squad cars strategically placed to block people in.

A breakaway group of teenage boys corralled a weak flank of cops; they clapped and chanted in a circle around them, 'Hoo, hoo, hoo, hoo, hoo, hoo'. Another group of people broke away to systematically smash police car windows and turn over the cars themselves. Children ran between the cops' legs to light fires under the trees that decorate that area of town. The rest of the crowd threw bottles, eggs, crystal glassware, anything they could get hold of.

None of them even noticed the first shots, and when they did become aware they were being shot at, they panicked. The police seemed to panic too, firing tear gas and rubber bullets — hard blocks of plastic that hurt badly when they hit — into unarmed people, women and children as well as men and teenagers. People started running in all directions: cops, kids, protesters, even the fundamentalist with his megaphone. Dozens were injured.

A police helicopter flew above and kept repeating, 'Everybody needs to leave immediately.'

When it was over, a surreal quiet fell over the area around the Old Capitol. Store windows and street lights were smashed, awnings torn down, garbage cans overturned and contents strewn, benches ripped out of the pavement, trees scarred and blackened, columns daubed with paint. Trash littered the streets.

The fading daylight turned dusty yellow, a colour as surreal as the landscape itself.

39

SPRINGFIELD: Monday

At midnight, a parade of evenly spaced headlights entered Springfield along Route 55 from the north.

By the time the parade reached Clear Lake Avenue, cameras and mobile phones were capturing footage of armoured vehicles all in white and armoured people carriers all in white too, some with tarpaulin down and some with tarpaulin up to reveal a white grid of scaffolding with dark shapes beyond like circus beasts on their way to the big top.

The convoy made its way across South Grand and turned into Macarthur, then disappeared beyond the gates of Camp Lincoln, home of the Illinois National Guard. All night long, cyberspace frothed with this fresh excitement. Everybody knew they'd seen the US Army out in force. A couple of hours later, the National Guard field troops at last returned from their training exercise in the Rockies. Everybody knew about them too. And yet when patrols fanned across Springfield before dawn, people couldn't take in what was happening to them. It had the feel of a clip from an animated movie. The armoured cars had square edges, clumsy, klutzy, like poorly made toys. The guns looked like toys too, huge, outlandish, ridiculous. The soldiers carrying them were avatars out of a virtual world: wraparound sunglasses with blue helmets on top, noses poking out beneath. True, there wasn't anybody who hadn't seen scenes like these on TV. But they belonged in Afghanistan, Iraq, Haiti, faraway places where people spoke funny languages, wore funny clothes, stepped warily through bombed-out buildings. But in Springfield? It couldn't be.

People who'd burned Jimmy in effigy yesterday waited uneasily for word from him. It came before breakfast. The camera honed in on a tired, rumpled mayor dressed in dirty jeans, shirtsleeves rolled up, a smear of oil across his cheek. Beside him a group of firefighters and volunteers as dirty as he was were pumping out a basement on Willemore.

'We've got a long road ahead of us,' he began. 'All these memories, all these years of development just stripped away. All these things we loved——' His voice broke and in an attempt to cover it, he waved his hand at the wreckage of what had once been one of Springfield's most desirable houses in one of its most desirable streets and gave a helpless shrug. 'Look, we're all scared. It's stupid not to be. Nobody can control a freak storm like the one that hit us. The one thing we *can* control is ourselves, and we just plain didn't do it. That's how come we have soldiers all over the place.'

He explained that those armoured cars were Mine Resistant Ambush Protected vehicles designed for Iraq and Afghanistan. The guns were the newest M16s, capable of shooting nine hundred rounds a minute. The soldiers were combat troops. 'We will survive this thing – of course we will – but we have to have order if we're going to survive it with some dignity. That's what they're here for. Do your damnedest to be polite. They're here to help with the donkey work as well as the babysitting, and they'll go away as soon as we show them we can behave ourselves.' He glanced again at the bedraggled house on Willemore. 'Now I got to help get this basement clean.'

He turned his back on the cameras and joined in with a couple of firefighters hoisting a pump into position.

Know how the mercury in a meat thermometer climbs abruptly when you stick it in a hot leg of lamb? Within an hour, Jimmy's popularity – close to nil after the riots – took an upward jolt in every online poll. Could it be Springfield's despised mayor was turning into Springfield's everyman?

An hour later, Sergeant Olivia Dulcan, in command of one of those armoured cars, spotted three people splayed out beneath a tree. 'What the fuck do they think they're doing out here?' she demanded of her driver. 'Wake them up. It's fucking stupid to be that drunk this early in the morning.'

The driver got out, approached the three, examined them quickly. 'You'd better notify burial detail,' he yelled back.

About noon, the Director at St Margaret's Hospital called the Illinois Department of Public Health.

She didn't tell them she'd called Jimmy less than twenty-four hours before, but she told them, as she'd told him, that she'd had experience with Médecins sans Frontières in Africa, and that now she had more than a dozen patients suffering with some illness that looked a lot like cholera. She knew that deep blue-purple colour of the skin. In cholera patients the dehydration can reach a point where the blood literally congeals in the veins. She'd seen it only in black-skinned people of course – it showed only in mouths, genitalia, palms, fingernails, toenails, soles of feet – but some of these people, these white people, were turning blue all over. And there was something else. Some had bloody urine; their kidneys were failing. That doesn't happen with cholera. Yet the first two cases to appear – the two children – had died of kidney failure so quickly and so unexpectedly that they'd lain dead in their beds for half an hour before a nurse noticed them.

Almost as soon as the Director of St Margaret's finished her call, both Memorial Hospital and St John's contacted Public Health too. Between them they had over a hundred cases and eight dead.

By mid-afternoon, there were twenty-three dead. The first notice of the real potential of Springfield's disaster reached the White House as the President was sitting down to dinner with two prime ministers and an emperor:

```
Number of dead approximately 35.
Transmission: likely waterborne,
possibly airborne. Diagnosis
unknown. Incubation period
unknown. Treatment unknown.
Quarantine imperative.

Terrorist link probable.
```

40

SPRINGFIELD: Tuesday,
the day of the Referendum

Within an hour, an executive order extended Springfield's state of emergency to a full quarantine under the Official Secrets Act, the Patriot Act and Homeland Security.

All public and commercial transport halted at once. Abraham Lincoln Capital Airport became a military flight base. So did the half dozen heliports in the town. Soldiers with rifles barred civilian personnel from the Amtrak train station on Washington Street. Government technicians jammed radio signals in a cordon around the city and blocked landline communications to and from any area code beyond city limits; the Army and the National Guard began setting up a double perimeter, two road blocks across every major and minor route in or out of Springfield.

During the morning, the news to the citizens of the city itself came via loudspeakers atop a fleet of army trucks airlifted to Springfield from all over the Midwest.

'As of 1900 hours today, a military curfew is in effect. Anyone found on the streets between 1900 hours and 0800 hours will be subject to immediate arrest. All public meetings are cancelled.

All schools are shut. Any public gathering of more than five people will be dispersed. Please be aware that floodwaters can carry infection. To ensure that nobody spreads infection, we request that you do not leave town. This is your duty as responsible Americans, and you will be subject to arrest if you try. If you are feeling sick in any way yourself, please call 911 or go to your nearest hospital.'

Leaflets followed, repeating the message. So did the single local radio station permitted to broadcast. All other radio stations gave out only static. So did TV screens. Mobile phones went dead in the middle of conversations. Internet connections failed in the middle of downloads.

There was no mention of epidemic. There was no mention of terrorists. Nor was there any mention of the cordon around the town or that anyone attempting to leave was going to end up in a military detention camp. All these directives had come straight from the White House, and the reasoning had been the same as Jimmy's: the last thing this town needed was panic. It needed control, diagnosis, medical attention, containment. Every hour increased the military presence on the streets.

How could the irony have been harsher?

This was the very day Springfield had scheduled to demonstrate its democratic right to quash UCAI's hostile takeover of the water that its citizens had owned for a century and a half, ever since their ancestors laid the first pipes. Voters should have been rushing to the polls to have their say, but the polls were shut by military order. Combat troops guarded them. Whatever the town's residents had thought of themselves last night, this morning they were a captive people, a conquered people, imprisoned in their homes, listening to military boots tramp along their sidewalks, watching military vehicles patrolling streets that once belonged to them, knowing soldiers could enter and search their houses at will, stop and search them personally when they went out for supplies or water, arrest them at any time without charge.

Their one hope seemed to be Jimmy Zemanski, the man they'd been calling Springfield's Hitler only days before.

Armies didn't mean just regular soldiers either. Most people in Springfield thought of the armed forces as Uncle Sam's tax-funded boys and girls. Not so. Despite a high unemployment rate and aggressive recruitment campaigns throughout the country, Uncle Sam couldn't find enough young people willing to join: pay too low, conditions too uncomfortable, risks too great, prospects too poor.

This meant mercenaries.

There were dozens of private security firms in operation. America had been using them for years; they'd fought in every war, helped keep every peace. They had every power a US soldier had too; they could carry combat weapons, operate combat vehicles and artillery, enforce military orders on civilians. But they got triple the pay, weren't subject to military law, claimed nearly half the US military budget – and were never at a loss for volunteers. A handful of these companies arrived in Springfield to reinforce government troops. Task forces from them marked out territories around the Capitol buildings, the banks, the rich of the town: DynCorp, American Security Group, Kroll, an Israeli company with the astonishing name of Instinctive Shooting International. Every mercenary and every mercenary vehicle displayed a logo. Blackwater, responsible for the murders of dozens of Iraqi civilians, was the most famous one: a black bear claw in red cross-hairs. The biggest and newest on the scene was Janus Secure: a one-headed, two-faced hawk in full flight, one beak to the east, the other to the west: goes anywhere, eyes everywhere.

Even without logos, everybody could tell the mercenaries from the regular soldiers. They were testosterone machines – no women allowed – all in ammo vests or Flak jackets with ammo pouches, all with guns strapped to their legs as well as automatic weapons in their hands. Most wore T-shirts that showed off the bulging muscles of their arms, and all had the commanding walk as well as the iron-pumped bodies of professional wrestlers.

Or of prison gladiators like David.

From the top floor of the Hilton, David couldn't see them, but he could see the lights from road blocks across several of the major routes into Springfield.

'So you just might pass for one of those guys,' Helen was saying to him. 'This is a stupid idea.'

'What do you care?' David said. He kept his cigarette in his mouth as he spoke.

'Why the fuck won't you listen to me?' She stroked his back. 'All that matters is a turned-around collar. Nobody stops a man of God.'

'I hate that.'

'It would work and you know it.'

'Nobody's going to stop me.'

She stroked his back again. 'It really suits you, you know, that turned-around collar. You remind me of one of those fire and brimstone Methodists in old movies. Now listen to Mommy: "Preachers don't steal cars."'

David put his cigarette down and pulled her around to face him. 'Cars are convenient.'

'Preachers go by bus.'

'I hate buses too.'

But she was abruptly angry. 'What's that supposed to mean?' she shouted at him. 'You accuse *me* of having tantrums. You accuse *me* of being irrational. What do you call this? If this isn't irrational, I don't know what it is. You think you can play me, and you're wrong. I know you.'

'Why are you angry?' He was truly puzzled.

'Nothing stops you, does it? You go right ahead, ploughing through whatever's in front of you. David the invincible. David the conquering hero. Don't you ever think of anybody else?'

So far as he could see, this second argument was no more rational than its predecessor. These people outside prison – lazy workmen, complacent aristocrats, irritable wives – often made him long for the easily decipherable order of South Hams.

'Why are you angry?' he repeated.

She started to slap his face, burst into tears instead, ran out of the room and slammed the door behind her. She didn't emerge until just before eleven.

'Ready to go?' she said, her mood wholly changed again. Courage on display now. Love. He knew it because he could feel her hands tremble on his arm as she went with him to the fire escape above the laundry. She stood there tense, fearful; she watched him drop to the alleyway below and wait in the Hilton's shadow for her all-clear.

David knew these alleys at the backs of downtown buildings; he knew how they connected to each other and to the alleys where householders in residential districts put out their garbage. Alleys don't change. Those residential alleys had been his childhood territory, his beat. He could only guess at the number of times he and his friend Tony had dashed through the ones that divided the backyards on the west side: two little east side boys laden down under televisions, radios, fan heaters, men's wallets, women's purses (no computers back then) – half their minds on the cash to come and half on the game of evading cops in pursuit who hadn't chased them often enough for their liking. And hadn't ever caught them.

They'd both got done for shoplifting, dealing and stealing car radios. But theft from houses? Never.

The old routes were as viable tonight as they'd ever been. They brought David out to the badlands at the edge of town, mile upon mile of commercial fringe that looked in the dark like the ruins of a civilization bombed out of existence, well away from the street patrols in the town. Behind this fringe lay fields of crops flattened by the derecho. The wooded country beyond them took him to the abandoned washrooms of Broadwell Tavern at the decaying stagecoach stop of Clayville Rural Life Center, ten miles west of Springfield.

41

KNOX COUNTY: Wednesday

Nobody would ever find the Honda that killed Morris Kline in Chicago simply because it was one of so many Hondas that are stolen there every day. But not just Chicago. Hondas are the most commonly stolen car all over America. What half-decent thief doesn't keep an old Honda key? So a master key isn't easy to find, so what? The key to almost any other Honda will do: a little jiggling and sawing, and it'll start the engine as well as open the door.

David stole a Honda in Pleasant Plaines, drove to Galesburg and spent a couple of hours at a shopping mall there, splitting his time between the best men's stores and the charity shops that perched their tattered wares in the windows of fancier shops gone bust. By noon he was approaching the thirty-foot high walls of South Hams State Correctional Facility. The last time he'd been here, the Tent City at their base had looked huge to him, a dozen tents big enough to sleep a hundred men. Now it was more than double the size. Maybe triple. Its inner enclosure of razor-wire fencing and the outer enclosure separated from it by some three metres made a barrier long enough and impenetrable enough to guard Auschwitz. A group of guards, dogs straining at leashes, were patrolling inside as David drove past. One of them glanced over at him, smiled, waved.

Or so it seemed. Prison guards don't wave at strangers.

Inside the prison, David handed over his Canadian passport as he had when he'd visited with Lillian. The response then had been the familiar mix of contempt and disgust. This time the guard took the passport and stared at it dreamily for a moment.

'Mr Gwendolyn, huh?' he said. 'I had a girl called Gwendolyn once. Most beautiful girl I ever saw. Oldest of the six most beautiful girls in Wichita Falls, Texas. We're all from Texas – shipped in by the truckload.' He sighed. 'I miss Texas.' David followed another Texan into the Visitation Room.

'Well, if it isn't Richard François Gwendolyn,' Quack said, sitting down in a yellow and blue plastic chair opposite David. Quite a few families had gathered today, but the usual smell of raw desperation was hardly present at all, and there was little sign of the standard forced brightness. A third Texan watched benevolently as a couple of children ran up and down the aisles.

Kids on the loose was strictly against the rules.

David handed a sandwich to Quack, who took it and bit into it greedily.

'Am I dead or something?' David asked. 'Even the guards are high.'

Quack stopped chewing and wiped his hand across his mouth. 'What about, "How are you, old friend? I'm so sorry I haven't been to visit recently."'

'I'm feeding you. Isn't that enough? What *is* going on here?'

'Well, Richard . . . You don't mind if I call you Richard, do you? We find we have a very, very efficient, er, McDonald's franchise at work here. I think you've been surpassed, my friend.'

'That how come you wanted to see me?'

David and Quack had been cellmates and business partners for many years. They'd developed a shorthand, a way of speaking to carry on the prison's drug trade even if they were monitored. Mostly they played it by ear – they got a real kick out of the game – but there were a couple of code phrases for emergencies. Which is to say it wasn't Andy's email to Lillian that had prompted David to arrange this meeting but the email's opening line, 'Tomorrow there'll be more fine weather.'

Quack used the same elliptical approach to explain Little Andy's foray into the Warden's computer, the rape and snuff films he'd found there and the Insider General's stroke of genius that was bringing David's old drug trade to an apotheosis that nobody could have imagined. And, true, now the guards were as drugged-up and friendly as the prisoners were drugged-up and calm.

David was amused, but he hadn't expected the abrupt sense of foreignness; he no longer understood the way things worked here. Only last night he'd been thinking, well, fondly of the familiarity of this place, where he knew the rules, where things made sense. It was a shock to see that life here had changed profoundly since he'd left, that he was no longer an insider in a sense far more general than his old gang's name, that South Hams had become practically as alien as Springfield's west side.

'Media blackouts don't work any more,' Quack was saying. If there'd been a transition, David had missed it. 'I don't know why people think they do. Or how they possibly could work. Officials can issue all the statements they want about calling out the army to stop looting and riots. But blogs, cell phones, Twitter: everybody knows that's crap. *Everybody* knows there's some kind of sickness. What's funny – not so very funny, I guess – is that a disease is exactly what I wanted to talk to you about when I informed you of the, er, weather conditions. And now I'm afraid——' He broke off, took in a breath. 'Look, old friend, I know this sounds nuts. I think this is an entirely *new* disease, and I think they tried it out on us first.'

There weren't many people David had ever trusted. Of those few, everyone except Quack had betrayed him, and at the moment he wasn't feeling sure of Quack. 'It doesn't just *sound* nuts,' he said irritably.

'Yeah, yeah. I know. Quite right.' A glance found the Texan guard kneeling with the children, running a hand up the little girl's leg. 'Look, nobody's ever accused me of a vivid imagination,' Quack went on, 'but back in early summer I saw a new disease right here: fever, vomiting, diarrhoea, dehydration severe enough to coagulate blood in the veins. Kidney failure too. Nothing fit. I'm sure it wasn't food poisoning or anything like that. It wasn't cholera. No antibiotic touched it, and yet it hit guys, killed some and then stopped. Not like flu or the measles either. No petering out through the community. It appeared, infected these men, did its damage. Then bang. Finish. Almost as though it had only one life cycle. I couldn't get any answers from the Medical Services Direct people. "Gastroenteritis," they said. "Gastroenteritis"? You have got to be joking.'

'What's "Medical Services Direct"?'

'They're the guys that took over telemedicine when South Hams went private. Real business acumen there. Never have to see a patient. Never have to touch one. Their predecessors occasionally had to produce a doctor and not all that rarely, a nurse. These guys have it all worked out. Doctors come under "not an option". See what I'm saying?' Quack's voice was urgent. 'First experiment on prisoners. Then toss the stuff at the civilian population.'

'You talking terrorists or something?'

'The media are screaming terrorists. Worst attack since the Twin Towers, they say. Me? I have no idea. None. But I'm going to give you a number, a username, a password and the name of a database. Download it and keep it. I need you to do this for me. I have to know that I'm not the only person who knows about it. And don't tell me it's not your problem. And I need another sandwich, damnit. Come on, you don't have to believe me. Just feed me. Huh?'

More washed dollar bills went into the vending machine. Quack wolfed down this second sandwich as eagerly as he had the first. 'Now why don't you tell me why you're here.'

'We've just been talking about it.'

'You could have come about that weeks ago. Instead you wait until you've got road blocks in the way. What's worrying you? Tell me. I want to know.'

David glanced down at his shoes, glanced up. 'Workmen,' he said.

If it had been anybody else, Quack would have laughed. 'What about workmen?' he said.

David described the construction site at Otto's Autos in Springfield where he'd failed so badly to manage his crew. 'I thought maybe you could give me some business administration advice. Otherwise, I'm going to have to turn the project over to a construction company.'

'That would be bad.'

'Yes.'

'You enjoy the work, don't you?'

'I like taking one pattern and turning it into another. I just don't like people much.'

Not far from Quack and David, a father in work clothes sat opposite his multiply pierced son, ears, nose, eyebrows, all pierced and ringed, crude piercings, crude rings, all prison gear, an advertisement for HIV infection. Tears ran down the older man's face; the two hadn't exchanged a word in all this time, not even a glance.

Quack frowned. 'The problem isn't people, Richard. It's men. You're overly fond of scaring them, beating them up, killing them. They can sense it. And they have no trouble sensing that you're good at it.' Quack frowned again. 'The solution is simple. Hire women.'

David wasn't easily taken aback. 'What for?'

'They're no fun to beat up. Not for you. Too easy. Besides, you really like women. Women might not have the muscle power, but they have greater endurance than men. There are lots of carpenters, electricians, all kinds of trades. They're patient and they tend to be neater and cheaper. What about your own construction company? Maybe insist on a rota so one woman – on full pay – looks after the others' children during working hours. Of course, not all of them will have children. You'll get a fair share of lesbians.'

David nodded. 'They'd probably be strongest. Best for construction.'

'Now why don't you tell me why you're really here?'

David got up without a word, fetched a third sandwich from the vending machine, sat down again, handed over the sandwich. 'I want you to tell me what's wrong with somebody,' he said.

Quack stared at him. 'You're here for a *medical* opinion?'

'You going to hear me out or what?'

'Is this guy in hiding?'

'What difference does it make?'

Quack nodded. 'Okay. He's somebody you know?'

'Yes.'

'Think it could be related to this new disease?'

David looked abruptly away. 'You're the doctor. Not me.'

'Yes, yes. Of course. I'm so sorry. There's diarrhoea?'

'How am I supposed to know something like that?'

'Fever?'

'No.'

'What about nausea? Vomiting?'

'Yes.'

Quack studied his friend. He'd learned a lot about David in their years as cellmates; he'd even learned to anticipate some of the mercurial changes of temperament, but he'd never known David to show an interest – much less concern – about anybody's health.

'How about . . . irritability?' Quack suggested, watching David carefully.

'Rollercoaster. One end of the spectrum to the other.'

Quack paused, then took the plunge. 'I'll lay you a bet Helen is pregnant,' he said gently. 'There might be odd cravings too. Marinated artichokes. Raw carrots. Chocolate prunes. That kind of thing.'

David didn't speak.

'She does know you're here, doesn't she?' Quack asked.

'She washed the dollar bills so you could have all these sandwiches.'

Quack smiled. 'Thank her for me, will you? And keep her away from the water. You too. It's waterborne, this new disease. I'm sure of it. I don't know much about it, but I'm certain it's waterborne, and I feel fairly sure it has a single life cycle.' He took the last bite of his sandwich, savoured it. 'I was very devout when I got sent to prison,' he said then. David nodded. The sight of Quack on his knees had been a constant irritant for most of the first decade they'd been cellmates. 'I loved God,' Quack went on. 'I loved His anger and His wisdom and especially His sense of justice. I lost my faith in here.'

'That doesn't surprise me.' David remembered his relief when the kneeling had stopped.

'Oh, it wasn't what you think. It wasn't violence or sex or HIV, and it wasn't bearing witness to lots of other guys going through the same thing. I figured I deserved that — all of it, even the witnessing — for the sin I'd committed against God's justice. "Honour thy mother and father." "Thou shalt not kill." Doesn't quite fit gassing your parents, does it? No, no, it's *your* fault. You're the person responsible.'

There was a pause. 'That does surprise me.'

'Those medical books you helped me get? I studied so hard that I had nightmares about vomiting up human parts and human diseases. I'd had no idea there were so many in either category. I began to see it as a battle: me against disease. At last I was going to glorify God in His justice. Eight years, three months, twelve days of studying those books, watching the sick who came to me, worrying over them day and night, straining to help them with everything I had in my—'

Quack broke off, put down his sandwich wrapper, picked it up again, crumpled it in his hands. 'I realized God didn't care which side won. Me or the bacterium. It's all the same to Him.'

42

BOSTON, MASSACHUSETTS:
Later that day

Freyl money certainly simplified things. David had bought everything he needed in Galesburg before he visited Quack. The Honda may have been stolen, but he drove it straight to the Hilton at O'Hare. An hour later, he emerged into the airport itself – showered, shaved, formally dressed – to blend not all that badly with rich businessmen in a first-class lounge, where he spent another hour surfing the Net.

Quack had told him how feverish the reports about Springfield were, but he hadn't said anything about how strongly divided people were between the Scaremongers and the Deniers, as the opposing sides called each other.

The Scaremongers were the hot and bothered lot that Quack had described. Terrorism was a given. But which terrorists? Al-Qaeda? Neo-Nazis? Islamic Jihad? A crazy loner? Scuffles broke out in bars. Lynch mobs formed in Alabama and Mississippi. 'Inside information' told them that the bioweapon inflicted on Springfield was cholera. Or mutant swine flu. Or a new hospital bug gone mad. Or the Andromeda Strain. The living had to step over the dead in the streets. The whole US was in danger. We were all going to die.

The Deniers were calm, rational, dismissive. Springfield had suffered a terrible storm, terrible floods, contaminated water, no electricity. Rioting was par for the course. So was looting. The medical complications of exposure to raw sewage are often under-estimated. They can be varied, widespread, dangerous. But rarely lethal. The only deaths so far had been a couple of old people trampled during the rioting, an unrelated case of food poisoning and two children swept away in the flood. As for the army, it was there to help, and qualified volunteers – especially medical personnel – would be welcome to join in.

Subject to the army's discretion of course.

The balance of the argument was painfully clear. The wild-haired hysteria of the Scaremongers ensured that the Deniers and the official media remained comfortably in the ascendant.

It's true that Freyl money simplified things for David, but it made him feel all the more alien. He didn't belong in South Hams any more – that was clear – but he didn't belong in a first-class lounge either. He'd have felt less of an impostor if he'd stolen the money to get into it. Besides, O'Hare Airport is where Hugh Freyl had gone blind. He'd just been sitting there and gone blind. Nobody ever found out why. David had been through the place several times; it made him uneasy every time. Frantic bustle and total aimlessness, vast empty spaces and sporadic knots of people: it looked too much like the furniture inside his own head. A couple of hours later he landed in Boston's Logan Airport, which was more of the same. A chauffeur greeted him – very deferential – ushered him to a limo and began a tortured trip into a city at night.

David didn't care for cities any more than airports. He'd seen London. He'd seen New York. He'd seen others too after he got out of prison, but only New York and London on Freyl money. Now Boston of course. As for Springfield, he knew it like the back of his hand — except that he was never sure what the back of his hand looked like. Boston seemed a mishmash of leftovers from the rest, warmed up in a microwave. More water though. And bridges that looked like iron scaffolds for teepees.

> So this is good old Boston,
> The home of the bean and the cod,
> Where the Lowells talk only to the Cabots.
> And the Cabots talk only to God.

So?

So he was a Freyl, and abruptly — wholly without warning — that was a pleasure. Not just a pleasure either. Much, much more.

The chauffeur's deference at the airport had irritated him. He'd resisted it, scorned it, another of the great unwashed bowing and scraping to a social rank for ever out of reach, this guy so eager that he didn't know an impostor when he saw one. But there are revelations and revelations. David's first had come when he realized Hugh Freyl really was going to have him transferred from Marion Federal Penitentiary to South Hams State Prison. This second?

It had started this afternoon with Quack when David had felt an outsider at South Hams. And now, Boston's night lights through the limo's tinted windows — a split-second pattern identical to the floodlights of South Hams' yard at night — showed him how the chauffeur's bowing and scraping fit into a new scheme of things.

He'd arrived in South Hams planning to beat a man to death,

saw off his balls and deliver them to a gang leader. The choice
that Hugh had forced on him was stark: do something as dramatic as that or face what Quack and Andy and thousands of
others faced. David had been mad as hell all his life, ever since he
could remember, but a killer? No. The deaths that sent him to
prison had been pure fury: cornered by two guys in an oil pit
beneath a car, no idea how the blood and brains that got splattered
turned out to be theirs, not his. All he'd intended with his South
Hams plan was to make other prisoners keep their distance. And
yet the moment he made the decision to kill, he sensed that he'd
mastered the language of prison. This was a society he could control.

He'd carried out his plan and not been surprised to find grown
men bowing and scraping to a mere boy because of it. He'd
enjoyed the deference, grown used to it, killed to maintain the
power it brought him. He rose fast in the prison hierarchy until he
sat at the right hand of the Insiders' General — a social rank well
beyond the aspirations of the vast majority of prisoners — and
knew he was the heir apparent.

Yet not until now, not until this ride in a Boston limo, did he
realize that Freyl money was buying for him outside bars what
killing had bought for him behind them. Money was his ticket
into another way of life, another society whose language he could
master, another he could control.

Two revelations: both of them down to Hugh Freyl.

It was nearly nine, very dark except for Boston's night brilliance,
when the chauffeur pulled up at a kerb in the middle of
Commonwealth Avenue. Trees behind, a tree in front of an old
building made of carved stone, a flight of steps up to an arched
door. A man in a better suit than David's Galesburg purchase led

him into the main dining floor – a suite of rooms, large tables, well spaced, every one filled with diners – to an old elevator with sliding metal doors, along a wood-panelled corridor and into a room. The lighting was softer here, three walls book-lined, the fourth a Chinese cityscape in brocade, the space easily big enough for eight, but easily intimate enough for two. The woman who rose to greet David was a redhead, hair close-cropped, short upper lip, almond eyes, no make-up, dressed for business, not pleasure.

'Why are your suits always new when I see you?' she asked. She wasn't flirting with him. She was just curious. Nor was humour her strong point. 'I don't like this one.'

'I rented the last one,' he said.

'You know, I half thought you were going to kiss me.'

'I thought so too.'

'Why didn't you?' Again, just curiosity.

'You scare me.'

'What an excellent basis for dialogue.'

This was Christina Haggarty, CEO of Galleas International. She was just about the Slad twins' age – younger than David – and like them she was already a legend in the financial world: an icy clarity of mind and a royal contempt for received wisdom. David had met her in New York when he was looking for somebody to pin Hugh's murder on. Their discussion had concerned Hugh's involvement with UCAI and Galleas; the Freyl firm still dealt with both.

In those days, Galleas International was little known to the public; financial reporters hinted at connections with crime lords and unsavoury dictators. Now, the corporation appeared regularly in the media while remaining the most secretive of the vast multinationals. Not even its total sales were known although pundits claimed it wielded an economy as big as Exxon's, which is to say it was smaller than UCAI and Kuwait, but bigger than New Zealand and Mitsubishi. This formidable competitor had forced UCAI out of the uranium game only a year or so before, and economists liked to tell their students that the two were officially at war. Not just metaphor either. Both maintained international private security firms, large, full-scale mercenary armies just like the ones helping to occupy Springfield. There'd been rumours of skirmishes, death tolls, civilian casualties: those uranium mines, oil pipelines in the Middle East, water sources and distribution routes. These days rumours also hinted at a hostile takeover, sometimes with Galleas as aggressor, sometimes as victim.

'So what's going on in that town of yours?' Christina asked David as the attendant in the elegant suit seated her.

'Lot of damage. That much water makes a mess. Rats everywhere. Army too.'

'What about your plague?'

'You tell me.'

'No bodies in the streets?'

'If they're there, I haven't seen any.'

'Terrorists?'

'I haven't seen any of those either.'

The attendant pulled out a chair and seated David too.

'What does Mrs Freyl want in exchange for her information?' Christina asked then. She never agreed to meetings without a detailed brief.

'Springfield.'

'The town itself?'

'Nothing less.'

Becky had explained to David that Galleas was a minority shareholder in the Grand canal and that from what she'd read Christina intended to be not just a major player in the water game but *the* major player. David hadn't needed her to tell him that the crisis in Springfield, especially combined with the loss of the referendum, had cemented UCAI's position and was quickly cementing Jimmy's. Becky and Galleas were already allied in spirit. All she needed was a formal acknowledgement.

'Ambassador David Marion, eh?' Christina said.

'Something like that.'

'I hope you come bearing gifts.'

'We have a start. Not strong, but a start.'

Back before the Council vote, when it looked as though Morris Kline was the key to ousting Jimmy, Becky had served Morris coffee and brownies in her study so she could record their conversation. David had a digital copy with him: Kline's evidence of a cover-up of the contamination episode in the town, something that called for far more power than a mayor could wield. There was also bribery of council aldermen to swing the vote in favour of privatization and gagging the press to hide the massive public reaction against it. As David handed the recording over to Christina, he told her that Becky thought there had to be a way to tie UCAI into all of it.

A sommelier arrived with champagne and a ceremonial opening of the bottle. Two attendants arrived with bread in several baskets.

Christina tasted the wine, approved it but shook her head at David. 'UCAI and the Mayor could be linked at the hip, and they'd happily set him up for the fall if that's what they need.'

'The old lady talks about trade agreements.'

'NAFTA?'

'Among others.'

The first David had heard of the acronym was when Becky briefed him for this meeting. She'd said that the letters stand for the North American Free Trade Agreement, set up to regulate just such international deals as the shipment of Canadian water to the United States. If a NAFTA tribunal were to find UCAI guilty of an illegal act like the sabotage that Becky was certain she could prove, the Slads would lose their right to the water from Canada's James Bay. Galleas would be able to take over.

'Forget it, Mr Marion,' Christina said. 'NAFTA's rules are squishy enough to take on any shape UCAI might like them to. We have to have something dirty, something public and shameful, something to make Sebastian and Francis Slad hobble away in disgrace along with UCAI. Unless the corporation's executive branch goes down, we've lost. I'm not denying that there's potential in Mrs Freyl's information, but on its own it's not anywhere near—' She broke off, studied David a minute. 'You do know that Aloysia Gonzaga has a role to play in all this.'

David took a swig of champagne. 'If you're trying to tell me something, just spit it out.'

'The Slads think you know where she is.'

'Why would I know a thing like that?'

'They have a record of the marriage, Mr Marion.'

Hugh Freyl liked women as much as David did, and the upright principles he'd betrayed to get David released were tied to the law, not to sex. Aloysia may have been the daughter of a schoolmaster who'd become a friend, but he'd known where he wanted this to go as soon as he met her at Lambert-St Louis Airport on her first trip to the Midwest.

'Mississippi sidewheelers,' she'd whispered into his ear even before saying 'Hello'. All this happened a quarter of a century ago.

'Sidewheelers? What about them?'

'I read that they've become gambling boats,' she said. 'They paddle down the Mississippi. I want to gamble on one.'

'I believe they are all moored now, Aloysia. Not even engines to drive the paddles. No gaming tables either, only slot machines and smoke. Although—' He broke off. 'There was a piece in the *Post-Dispatch* about a new venture that just might—'

'I'm going to play roulette,' she interrupted.

She'd embraced him then, kissed him on the mouth.

Hugh's wife Rose had died the year before, an icy road, a moment's distraction, her car head-on into a tree. Grief isn't orderly. Emptiness, yes. Aimlessness, yes. All that's at least half expected. But the crazed preoccupation with sex had come as a shock.

The casino boat was called *Maverick*, and it was a floating slice of wedding cake right out of the movie; it even had red velvet plush and serious gamblers. But Aloysia lost again and again. Within an hour, she was as depressed and disappointed as she'd been excited when she set out. Hugh turned her attention to *Maverick*'s famous restaurant. As they ate, he talked to her about David, knowing how very sexy talk of murderers can be. There really wasn't any need for it; by the time they reached coffee, even the waiter could smell sex on her.

'I want to play again,' she said.

'Not roulette.'

'Everything on red.'

'Aloysia, you will only lose. Why not a room upstairs instead?'

'Here's the deal. If I win, you fix it so I can bed this exciting murderer of yours as well as you.'

'You would have to marry him to do that.'

'Would I?'

'I am afraid so.'

She considered a moment, then said dreamily, 'Aloysia Gonzaga, patron saint of plagues and wife of a murderer. I like it. Promise me you agree. Promise?' She put a hand on his thigh.

'So you got lucky,' David said to Hugh during their next prison lesson. 'How come you're telling me about it?' David had just turned eighteen. Prison sex is power and release. Pleasure doesn't come into it. For most inmates, a woman is Nirvana.

'She won, David.'

Hugh had taken the talk as foreplay. He wasn't wrong, but by morning, she was already pressing him to fulfil his promise. She kept the pressure up, so hard – so insistently – that he said he'd tell David about it if for no other reason than to keep her quiet. She made him swear he would.

'You play a game of roulette to get laid and I'm the bait?' David said.

Hugh was puzzled rather than shamed. 'I seem to have lost all sense of proportion.'

'What about conjugal visits?'

'You cannot be taking the idea seriously.'

'If you can get her in here, I want her.'

'She walks with a limp. One leg is shorter than the other.'

'So?'

'David, this is not a good idea. She made it disagreeably clear that she enjoyed pressuring me into this.'

'Conjugal visits or not?'

How could Hugh hold back from David the only thing that gave him solace himself? Besides, maybe a wife on the outside would calm that explosive temperament. 'I believe they now allow one every other month.'

'When?'

'When what?'

'How soon can you get her here?'

Hugh made the arrangements and served as witness to the prison chaplain's blessings. There were two conjugal visits before Aloysia returned to England. A correspondence carried on for months, growing more desultory on her side – more desperate on his – until she stopped responding at all. He wrote again and again, trying to rekindle her interest, amuse her, shame her, anything to get her back for another visit.

He even exchanged a month's supply of crack to get one of the guards to seek out a postcard of a Mississippi sidewheeler for him. He'd written the single word 'Remember?' on it, sent it to her in an envelope.

He'd received no answer.

Christina rang a bell beside her that brought attendants with a platter of shellfish and a small bottle of white Bordeaux; the sommelier poured it out with what David considered an irritating reverence. He wasn't a picky eater, didn't pay much attention to the taste of the fish, but the wine: for some reason it pleased him.

'I presume your new wife doesn't know about your old one,' Christina said, setting down her fork.

Prisoners learn to eat fast. David's plate was empty. 'No,' he said.

'Or the boy?'

'What boy?'

'You have a son.'

'Not me.'

'I gather Dr Gonzaga managed to confirm paternity.'

'Unlikely.'

'The prison probably has your DNA on file.' Christina studied him a minute. 'I don't suppose she's going to show up now and complicate matters, is she?'

'No.'

'Good, good. Excellent. She's important to the Slads. I'm sorry to say I don't know why. What I do know is that they want you alive until they have some idea what happened to her. Or perhaps to some of her work. Hence the suspension of the contract on you.'

'They don't happen to operate a little local security company of some kind, do they?'

Christina smiled. 'You've noticed.'

'Yellow logo? Round? A Lincoln's head inside it.'

'That's the one. Sangamon Security.'

David told her that one of them had warned him against a speed trap when he was pushing the Riley to its impressive 120 miles an hour and that a couple of them had intervened to keep him from getting arrested for a fight on the railroad tracks – even deposited him at a hospital to get patched up.

'It's quite touching, don't you think?' she said. 'They want to make certain nothing bad happens to you. I gather that the Messrs Slad are fairly certain you're hiding Dr Gonzaga. They don't know you very well, do they?'

David didn't ask Christina how she'd come by her information. He'd learned for himself, back when he'd been looking for Hugh Freyl's murderer, that the many Cold War secret services, CIA, KGB, MI6, had put themselves at the disposal of large corporations as soon as international amity made their personnel redundant by the thousands. After all, what were the spies of the world to do with their specialized training when governments needed so much less of it? And corporations were falling all over themselves to acquire it?

The sommelier appeared with fresh glasses and a bottle wrapped in a napkin. 'Mr Marion,' Christina said then, 'I need something solid, something well beyond Mr Zemanski. I need to get the men at the top not just the corporation: the Slads personally. Their worries about Dr Gonzaga tell me she's deeply involved. Perhaps somebody she knows? Some professional contacts she has? Perhaps something in England? Work she's done? Come back when you've got something I can use.'

'Suppose I can't find anything?'

'That would be foolish.'

David nodded and tasted the new wine.

'You look puzzled, Mr Marion,' Christina said.

'This one doesn't have a nasty wine taste either.' She laughed. A rack of lamb accompanied the wine. A second bottle came with cheeses and fruit, then cognac in snifters. It was midnight before he and Christina were ready to leave. 'What about the papers?' he asked her.

'You didn't give us much time,' she said, 'but I'm sure you'll manage. Anything else, you let me know.' She handed him an envelope, which he slipped into his breast pocket.

43

TIPTON COUNTY, TENNESSEE:
Thursday morning

Marina Rodriguez was the first female undertaker to practise in the Blow Pops capital of the world. She was a much-loved figure in the community – they even forgave her for marrying a Mexican – but the summer had been slow; she'd welcomed the floater that Dillon Effingham and his little brother Stonky found on the banks of the Mississippi.

Ordinarily, the coroner of Tipton County would have collected the body-finding fee – set and regulated by the state of Tennessee – chucked the body back in the river and phoned a coroner further south in expectation of the agreed (if not statutory) fifty-dollar acknowledgement of a professional courtesy rendered. But Marina's Uncle Bill was the coroner of Tipton County; she'd roasted him a whole pig for his fiftieth birthday. She'd invited everybody he loved, the best birthday he'd ever had, and he was deeply grateful.

Uncle Bill turned the floater – and its burial fee – over to her as a thank-you.

The law says unknown dead people are to be held for thirty

days to give relatives a chance to find them and claim them. That's why the body had still been lying in Marina's storeroom when the Springfield Police Department issued a Missing Persons Alert for Aloysia Gonzaga. The Illinois alerts pages carried photographs. They gave details: age, mid-forties; height, approximately five foot eight; eyes, brown; hair, brown with gold highlights; teeth, professionally perfect; distinguishing characteristics, one leg shorter than the other.

Marina hadn't noted the eye colour because the eyes were long gone by the time she got the body, and there was no way to make out features on the face to match a photograph on the Net. But she'd taken note of what she could, the height, teeth, one short leg, the hair. She'd liked those gold highlights, even on a corpse; she'd put them in her own hair at once. Which is to say she had all she needed to identify the dead woman, and yet it was hardly any wonder that she didn't. There are well over a hundred thousand active Missing Persons cases in America. Of these, something like fifteen thousand will never be heard from again. Besides, Missing Persons alerts tend to stay in the state where they're issued, and Marina was in Tennessee, two states south of Illinois. On the other side of the Mississippi as well.

As for the thirty days, that was up not long after the storms hit Springfield. They hadn't touched Tennessee; like everybody else in Tipton County, Marina read about them, felt relieved not to be involved and went back to work. She was meticulous in her job. She'd begun that thirtieth day doing the paperwork for the county's indigent burial programme; she accompanied the floater to an open field not far from where Blow Pops first went on sale, conducted a simple ceremony, watched the coffin lowered into the ground beneath a numbered stake.

But the media shut-down in Springfield, the military

occupation and the terrifying rumours: the entire world was glued to news in any and all formats. Marina was only one of billions who'd spent days trawling the Net for something, anything that would give her a peep into what was really going on.

She happened across Aloysia Gonzaga listed as one of the 'Missing Persons in Illinois' just by chance.

44

SPRINGFIELD: Thursday noon

At eight in the morning, the Greyhound bus from Chicago deposited David near the town of Sherman, Illinois, just north of Springfield. He walked for an hour along the old Route 55 before he reached the road block for the outer perimeter around town.

Four soldiers guarded it. One, a blonde — hair in a tight bun at the back of her head — sat behind a desk under an open tent. Soldiers on either side of her held M16s in their arms. Another soldier watched from an army truck in front of the cordon that cut off the road. The scaremongering rumours of Springfield's disease showed their power here. Money poured in, but people who might otherwise have volunteered to help, found they had commitments elsewhere. Barely a handful of volunteers waited at the road block, most of them from the Salvation Army.

David fitted right in.

'Padre?' the desk soldier said to him. He wore the turned-around collar that Helen insisted he take with him. His clothes were baggy and worn, courtesy of Galesburg's charity shops. He hadn't slept since he left a day and a half ago, and the weariness showed.

'I understand that Springfield is in need of spiritual aid,' he said.

'You go in there, you ain't coming out,' said the soldier.

'I do not wish to come out. I wish to go in.'

'Got any documentation on you?'

David handed her the contents of the envelope Christina had given him in Boston. He'd studied it as best he could on the bus. It said he was Jeremiah Michaeljohn, born in Devon, England, a man of God with a Master of Theology from Oklahoma Baptist University; his present post was Director of Bright Hope, Nagaland.

'Nagaland?' said the soldier. 'Where's that?'

David had never heard of it. For all he knew, some Galleas technician had made it up on the spot. 'West Africa,' he said, 'off the Ivory Coast.' He didn't know where the Ivory Coast was either.

'What do you do there?'

David's papers did tell him that. 'I train poor people in Piggery.'

'You ... Jesus. I got to pat you down. Search that bag.' David handed over a bag as worn as his clothes. It contained a Bible, some underwear, two shirts, another pair of trousers and a somewhat less-worn black suit for official duties.

Half a mile further on, at a road block on the inner perimeter, he repeated his story.

The smell hit him first. It wasn't that he didn't know what was causing it, but a mere thirty-six hours was enough to make him forget how intense it was – and it was worse now.

In a single night, the flood had created a whole year's worth of garbage.

Garbage spilled out over front yards, higher-than-the-head heaps of it for block after block, whole housefuls sodden and smeared with mud: stoves, washing machines, air conditioning units; mattresses, sofas, lamps, chests of drawers; windows and window frames; plasterboard ripped off with wallpaper still intact. Nothing reeks like hundreds of broken refrigerators that have spent days in the sun. Human shit may be the worst smelling shit there is, and the pressure of the flood had turned toilets into geysers that belched it out; but the stench of rotting meat overwhelmed it. Flies and wasps hovered and buzzed in swarms. People moved slowly, grown-ups and children both, adding item after item to the gigantic heaps, handkerchiefs or masks across their noses and mouths to keep out the smell.

Everything had to go, and the clean-up had barely begun. On the luckiest streets, construction trucks with vast jaws — bucket excavators, shovel excavators — tore into the heaps of detritus to deposit mouthful after mouthful into massive container trucks that ferried their loads to long-deserted landfill sites reopened for the emergency.

As for the military, nobody was attempting to make its presence look like anything other than occupation. Soldiers were everywhere. Foot patrols threaded their way through the streets with automatic weapons in their arms, and masks to keep out the smell beneath their wraparound sunglasses. Vehicle patrols drove carefully along roads that could abruptly turn into no more than slabs of tarmac ripped out of the ground by the force of water alone. Nobody in uniform took up a shovel to help. Why should they? The quarantine meant that there was no media to watch them doing good deeds. Residents grumbled among themselves, but they were too disoriented, too tired, too scared to do anything beyond grumble.

As David approached the centre of town, private security firms began to dominate, each one easily identified by its logo as well as the guns strapped to their legs. Janus Secure stood in formation around Springfield's New Capitol, built more than a hundred years ago, tallest Capitol building in America, far taller than Becky's beloved Old Capitol, more beautiful too, more wedding cake even than a Mississippi sidewheeler, wings out to either side, square of columns rising to circle of columns, then to tier of arched windows, then to zinc and stained-glass cupola. A bronze Lincoln stood in front – unhappy, skinny Abe in a rumpled vest and a coat that hung badly – looking down on four mercenaries, one stationed at each corner of his pedestal. Blackwater troops surrounded the Illinois State Supreme Court and the Illinois General Assembly. DyneCorp guarded the premises of Herndon Freyl & Zemanski, the most prominent law firm in town. Banks, brokers, businesses, as well as other major law firms: mercenaries were on guard wherever the army wasn't.

The streets were cleaner around here. Most of the detritus was gone. But the roar of machinery was deafening. On some streets, flood water gushed out of the sides of buildings like torrents through spillways in a dam; on others, huge mobile pumps sucked water out through blue hoses as thick as a man's chest.

David listened for ambulances, his mind on what he'd read online at O'Hare, as well as what Christina and Quack had told him. He didn't hear any. It didn't occur to him that they'd been silenced during the night when military intelligence realized that their increasing frequency carried its own message.

According to the World Health Organization, there are specific steps to be taken in an epidemic:

1. *Isolate patients*
2. *Clean all surfaces touched by patients and burn all clothing*
3. *Increase garbage collection and institute hygienic disposal mechanisms for all bedding*

4. Conduct a massive public education campaign to acquaint people with the signs and symptoms of the disease and instruct them in home care

The first three steps were just plain impossible in a flood-devastated town like Springfield. As for education, how can you educate people about a disease when you don't have any idea what it is? A group of army epidemiologists taking samples at Memorial Hospital decided to name it Springfield Fever, if for no other reason than to give themselves as well as the government and the military a sense that progress was being made.

But there's always so much confusion when disasters like this hit. The military took a careful count of hospital mortuaries; the number of deaths shot up to two hundred.

The four functioning hospitals in Springfield – fifteen hundred beds among them – coped with the early cases, but the numbers mounted up so quickly that the army had to fly in military cots from all over the Midwest. The hospitals began to look like refugee camps in Africa or concentration camps in the Balkans: military cots squeezing between regular hospital beds, lining the corridors, crowding into staff meeting rooms, public visiting rooms, the main lobby, even the basement.

The public? They had their hands full with garbage and the basic necessities of life, which had become as time-consuming as they are in a Third World village.

Besides, ever since Jimmy's first speech in front of the devastated house on Willemore, he'd been warning people that if hospitals seemed crowded, it was their own fault. They weren't being careful enough about exposure to sewage, and they *must* be more vigilant. He didn't just scold though. Every day, sometimes two or three times a day, he spoke on the single radio station and the single TV station: tips about how to kill the rats that grew bolder by the hour, how to disinfect household items that the flood hadn't destroyed, how to understand the ration books the army distributed, how to use them to collect food from the heavily guarded supermarkets. He sounded confident, on top of things; again and again he assured residents that 'this too will pass', that things were already getting better. And things did seem to be looking up. The army restored power so that Springfield could boil its own water and cook its food. There'd been no rioting since Sunday. Very little looting too.

Which meant the army might leave soon.

But when inflatable hospitals started going up, Jimmy had to rethink his strategy. An inflatable hospital is a technological marvel, fully functioning in just over a day, with its own electricity, air conditioning, fresh water, elaborate waste-disposal system, hospital equipment, nurses' station, consulting rooms and hundreds of army cots for patients. But inflatable hospitals looks like giant fungal growths; they're bulbous, enormous white tents with their roofs resting on scaffolds of inflatable tubes. When these sprouted up around town, nobody could pretend that exposure to sewage explained them.

Late Thursday evening, Jimmy knew he had to tell his people the truth. At least some of it.

'My friends,' he began, 'it looks like we have a new situation.'

45

SPRINGFIELD: Friday and Saturday

Jimmy's speech sent Springfield to bed that night trembling with fears that only fucking and liquor can ease – and only briefly at that. Donna couldn't face anybody. She swallowed Valium and bourbon, slept fitfully, jolted awake every hour or so with childish nightmares of pursuit and entrapment.

She prayed for dawn.

But when dawn finally came, it filled her with dread. She dragged herself out of her sheets, dressed and stared from her window as she had every day she'd lived here. She still couldn't quite believe the desolation she saw, and yet her neighbourhood was the luckiest in Springfield: it was the very first to have its garbage cleared. Front yards that had looked like landfill sites were now uneven stretches of dried mud, broken shrubs, broken driveways, dead trees, all of it blended together beneath a fine powder of grey-brown dust.

Odd to feel grateful for a desolation like this, but the stench of rotting meat was gone; the lingering smell of shit and methane was beginning to fade. And then hers wasn't just a good neighbourhood. To her surprise, it turned out to be a neighbourly one,

one capable of actual solidarity. People formed teams. The strongest did the heavy work; they'd shovelled mud and debris out of most of the houses, and were already rebuilding swept-away walls and broken window frames. The less able waited in line for rations, collected supplies and water, prepared meals, looked after children. A retired doctor turned his large house into an infirmary, organized an ambulance service, chose a team to tend the sick.

But there'd been so much fear even before Jimmy's speech. People had known. They'd known. They'd learned the signs. A fever. An upset stomach. The runs. Nausea. Unable to keep food down. Every sniffle was cause for nervousness. A stomach ache inspired fear. But the colour blue! Usually blue is such a benign, peaceful colour – sky, sea – and yet it had taken on a terror like nothing else. You start turning blue, and you're dead within the hour. That's what people said. Maybe scientists were calling the disease Springfield Fever; the citizens of Springfield didn't know anything about that. All they were sure of was that whatever it was, it was a killer and it came in blue.

The retired doctor's ambulance service was too often in use with new victims. Shortly after he opened his infirmary, it was full. When his first patient died, shock vied with an abrupt awareness that his house was probably a better place to die in than the hospitals. Just thinking about it was enough to bring on all those symptoms.

Donna was about to turn away from the window and get something to eat when she saw the first patrol of the morning. If soldiers with automatic weapons and wraparound sunglasses had seemed an unwanted and alien force in town before, their new garb made them into a sci-fi horror. Their heads were harnessed into full-face, black biomasks with a voice membrane and exhalation valve:

neoprene pig snouts and blank insect eyes. They looked like men from Mars.

Soldiers afraid to breathe the very air? The air the rest of them had no choice but to breathe?

Donna's shock at the sight of biomasks on soldiers was so visceral, so fierce that she ran to the car without a thought in her head, no breakfast, no mobile on her, no money either. She just had to get out of there. She'd drive east. Lots of people on the east side were sick – so many had been working on the west side during the night of the flood – but green things still grew there. Trees still looked like trees, yards like yards, houses like houses. It looked normal.

But she'd barely turned the corner when she saw a new set of sci-fi invaders pulling up at the far end of the street in front of the doctor's house-infirmary. Their truck was yellow, the colour of epidemic. A sign on the outside of it carried the black arcs-in-a-triangle sign and the words:

**Warning
Biohazard**

As she drew nearer, three creatures got out in full biohazard masks that made the neoprene pig snouts look almost homely: shiny hoods in the same yellow as their vehicles with bubbles of glass over their faces. Their uniforms were white, the Communicable Diseases Center's costume: here came the ghosts that Allan Madison's killers had feared.

Just looking made Donna's stomach feel odd. Her own fault. She'd had an awful lot of Valium and bourbon last night. Her head felt hot. No wonder; the day was well into the eighties. It would pass. Of course it would. She started towards the Fair

Grounds where Becky had held her Auction of Promises. Why? No reason. None at all. Except that she'd heard there was an inflatable hospital there, and an inflatable hospital in such a place was so incongruous it might take her mind off the cramps she could feel just starting. She could see the white plastic structures long before she reached them; they'd commandeered the entire grounds where the auctioneer had brought in so much money. Only a few days ago there'd been so much excitement and gaiety here, so much hope for the future.

As she approached the Ferris wheel, she finally admitted to herself that she'd driven here because she knew she had no choice. She pulled the car off on a verge, locked the door and headed towards a tent beneath the wheel, in between the merry-go-round and the Tilt-a-Whirl: 'Admissions', the sign said. She'd almost reached it when a jolt of agony from somewhere deep inside her threw her to her knees, doubled her up on the ground. The pain was so great that she was barely aware of soldiers manoeuvring her inside.

'Name?' somebody said to her.

She couldn't straighten herself up enough to focus on who it was. Another jolt of pain shook her so violently that she cried out loud, fainted even as her body's contents exploded from every orifice. There was a brief moment of clarity as she was being lifted onto an army cot that was one in an endless line of cots. Consciousness was fitful after that.

It never occurred to her that the inflatable hospital ward she lay in wasn't beneath the Ferris wheel but in the race track where she and Becky had placed bets every year, that the intravenous scaffold hovering above her and the hydration fluid dribbling into her came from a storeroom in the batting cage — a mechanical pitcher that fired baseballs at fair-goers — or that the adventure playground's miniature train (she'd pined to ride it, never dared say so, certain that Becky would brand her puerile) now carried supplies from the batting cage to her.

By Saturday morning, a disorderly line began to form outside the Ferris-wheel tent where she'd been assessed at once and admitted. By noon, the line was long, men, women, children all too ill to weep or wail, too ill to do anything but wait. Some died there, just waiting. By Saturday noon, Donna was dead too.

Since she hadn't been able to get out her name and had no identification on her, her death certificate read 'Unknown Female'. They zipped her into a body bag – the town had run out of coffins days ago – and took her out to the old ticket office that abutted the race track and now served as the Fair Grounds' morgue. Dead bodies are supposed to just lie there, nice and quiet, but Donna didn't. Rigor mortis jutted out her legs as though she were a kick-boxer in mid-attack. She wasn't the only one either. Corpses often refuse to behave. Body bags can look more like they're filled with half-broken furniture than with limp humans. Given such disorder, who would notice three extra bodies deposited there Sunday night? Who would have the stomach to look inside them if they did?

By the time identification of their bodies came around, the best coroners could do was to note that with these three, the cause of death was unknown – but not Springfield Fever – that one of them was painfully young and scantily bearded to hide his severe acne, that another had only one arm and that the third had 'Boss' tattooed across the knuckles of his right hand.

46

CHAMPAIGN-URBANA:
Sunday morning

Professor Richard Stands loved his morning bath. In hot water and bubbles, he was a free man. Nobody could get at him. This morning he was contemplating the pleasures of the day ahead of him.

It's the detective work that makes microbiology fun. Prof Richard Stands may have been pushing eighty, but he'd felt like the young Sherlock Holmes on a new case when samples of Springfield Fever arrived at Champaign-Urbana's Department of Microbiology late yesterday afternoon. The department tolerated such an old man partly because he'd won the Marjorie Stephenson Prize for his study of protozoan metabolism but mainly because he was a popular science expert on TV. That brought in funding. Also he still carried the title of Head of Department, and he'd be damned if he'd let that go. How would he fill his time if he retired? Besides, he loved labs.

Not that Champaign-Urbana had been singled out to work on the Fever case. Springfield was so shrouded in military secrecy that the Communicable Diseases Center in Georgia wasn't officially notified until Jimmy's speech late on Thursday. On Saturday morning samples went out to labs all over the country. Neither Prof Stands – nor any of the other recipients of samples – had real grounds to believe this sample was related to an epidemic in Springfield or anywhere else. Nobody said so. But every technician assumed it was because identifying it was 'top priority', because all of them had to sign Non-Disclosure Agreements before accepting the work and because they'd been 'requested' to begin work this very morning, a Sunday.

The hunt to identify a bug isn't unlike the hunt for a terrorist. Investigators convene, draw up plans, assign tasks. But microbiology is law enforcement's poor relation. Terrorists are profiled on international databases. Not so bad bugs. Most of their genomes haven't been sequenced anywhere; the ones that have, aren't centrally computerized. Flushing them out is very labour intensive, yet nobody has the money or the manpower for the job.

But what dwarfs even these shortcomings is the sheer number of suspects. Microbiologists guess – they *guess* – that they have information on about one per cent of the bugs that share the earth with us. But it could be ten per cent. Or a tenth of a per cent. Or a hundredth. The vast majority of bugs seem to be friendly or indifferent. The rest? The world's genetic tree has a mere five kingdoms. There's animals. There's plants. There's a kingdom that doesn't properly contain bugs. In the remaining two, we have so many potential enemies that we can make only more wild guesses at numbers.

Army epidemiologists had already identified the sample from Springfield as a member of the kingdom Protozoa and of a species called *cryptosporidium parvum*. Such a good name for a terrorist suspect: *crypto* means 'hidden' or 'secret'; *sporidium* tells of the four devil's tails that emerge from it as though they were a pack of witch's familiars. That does leave, er, *parvum*, which means 'little, small, petty, puny'. It *is* small. No denying it, no bigger than half the size of a red blood cell, and its big brothers — other crypto-sporidia — are a hundred times bigger. But 'petty'? 'Puny'? It's a slap across the bug's face. The bug doesn't like it.

This is a nasty beast.

47

SPRINGFIELD: The first
ten days of October

'I need money,' David said to Becky on Monday evening.

'Why?' she demanded. 'This place is costing me a fortune already.'

'You complaining?'

She ruffled her shoulders irritably. She had no idea that Donna was dead, but she was all too aware that her friends had had to face the terrors of an unknown disease on top of the destruction of a flood. Most of them were still waiting for excavators to clear away the mountains of garbage, and all of them were queuing like Third World poor people for water and then for food, subject to the humiliation of an all-powerful invading army. Not Becky.

Because of David, she and Helen hadn't had any contact with the flood waters or any of the sick. Because of him, they'd enjoyed the Hilton's glass aerie of bleached cedar, gently warm slate, dapple of earth colours and daily maid service, not a whiff of anything but the smell-less smell of air conditioning. Food appeared magically, supplied by the Janus Secure troops that guarded the building and controlled the black markets. Water was rationed but safe and delivered to the room. The only people who'd fallen ill at the hotel were cleaning staff who'd been working second shifts in the Capitol area and all over the west side on the night of the flood. Neither Becky nor Helen had even noticed that they'd gone.

But security was David's business. He'd noticed and carefully vetted every replacement who served the Freyl Executive Suite. He'd been brooding over what Quack had told him about the disease too: not airborne, seems to be going wild but instead stops short after about ten days, as though the bug has only a single life cycle in it. After less than twenty-four hours of wearing biomasks, the troops abandoned them. Which would seem to indicate that the epidemiologists in yellow had realized what Quack knew already: water was the carrier, not air. This very morning, the news announced that the death rate seemed to be declining. And that just might indicate that Quack's additional theory was true too: a pathogen limited to a single life cycle.

David stood with his back to the plate-glass window that looked out over the whole of Springfield as lights went on across the town. 'I never can figure out why places like this have such bad security systems,' he said to Becky. 'You're going to be vulnerable here when UCAI realizes you still threaten their profit margin.'

Becky pursed her lips. 'Why would I do that? How could I?'

'No idea. I just know you've planned something. I don't have to know what it is, but it might help if you told me why.'

She kept her lips pursed. It was all so puzzling. This hated man had become the only person outside of Lillian she could trust with her life, and to her extreme annoyance she realized even her hatred was softening. 'You say Galleas needs something solid,' she said to him. 'I understand that. They want criminal activity directly attributable to the Slad twins. Something they can't possibly pin on Jimmy or some underling at UCAI. The question is how we get it.' She watched David's eyes watching her. There was a childlike quality to the unrelenting gaze. Could it be innocence she was looking at? A cold-blooded murderer? Innocent of what? 'I can't imagine anybody knows better than you,' she went on, 'that finding an opponent's weakness isn't always easy. You watch. You wait. You listen. If nothing shows up, you have to rattle cages. If you're lucky, something interesting falls out. We need to buy Galleas time to make a move. If we don't – maybe even if we do – UCAI will take over soon after the army leaves. I don't see how we can help except by rattling somebody.'

David nodded. 'I've hired a crew of forty,' he said. 'I'll get your house ready as soon as I can.'

'*Forty?* You! You failed to maintain a crew of five for your own project. How could you possibly expect to handle forty?'

David nodded again. 'A photographer spent today at your house, and she'll be with us throughout the clean-up to record what we do for the insurance. The first twenty labourers begin work in the morning, and I want to pay them in cash at four in the afternoon when the second shift begins. I'll pay the second shift at midnight. For this I need money.'

'I will wait no longer than ten days,' Becky said. 'I have to get moving on this.'

'Two weeks would be stretching it.'

'Why do I listen to you at all?' Her voice as tart as of old. 'Ten days from now is Thursday. I institute my programme then from Freyl House if you can control this crew of yours well enough to make it habitable, which I sincerely doubt. If not, I will take my risks here. It's all so ridiculous. A crew of forty! Fiddlesticks. Even if there were some truth in such a fanciful tale, you have to have clean water to clean a house. How are you going to get it?

There isn't any. How are you going to get materials? There aren't any.'

David's gaze eased a little. A revelation is a revelation: whatever can be achieved in prison with killing, can be achieved on the outside with money. The language doesn't even need translation.

'Bribery, extortion, intimidation, theft, blackmail.' He paused, then added, 'Just the usual cage-rattling.'

On the morning David had got back to Springfield, he, Lillian and Helen had composed a poster and printed off hundreds of copies.

Women Workers Wanted

Laborers, Painters, Carpenters, Plumbers, Electricians

UNION RATES PLUS 10%

Women only need apply

We also require a state-certified child-care provider for our employees' children

Lillian had spent the afternoon putting these posters up on the east side, where many women were out of work at the best of times, more of them now because west-side employers no longer had functional houses to clean or businesses to clerk. David had taken on Springfield's singles bars, lesbian bars, all-women hotels, gyms. Helen called members of the Springfield Arts Society, and they spread the word to the Springfield branches of women's associations, local and national. She also persuaded the single functioning radio and TV station that the story would bring out a World War II spirit of cooperation, camaraderie, hope for the future: battalions of women doing traditional men's jobs like the Women's Land Army in England and America's counterpart, a pin-up of a shipyard worker called Rosie the Riveter.

In any normal time, an all-female construction company like David's would cause sex-equality grumbles right at the beginning. But this was hardly a normal time. Fear of disease. Fear of terrorists. Fear of what else the weather might have to throw at the town. What these people needed was inspiration. They also needed all the information they could get on how to deal with the after-effects of the flood. Most of all, they needed cash in hand. The black markets were still thriving, albeit a little more discreetly – many of them under the watchful eye of private security firms who supplied them, insisted on extortionate prices for a quart of milk, took three-quarters of the profit. But nobody wanted to shut them down. There was plenty of food, but without the black markets and the mercenaries, not enough manpower to distribute it.

Springfield's single functioning TV station covered the first day's work on Becky's house. The opening shots showed David's team arriving, twenty women, all in boots and rubber gloves, hair cropped or tied back under a scarf or a cap, a motley mixture of races and ages, chattering and smiling. Before any work started, the mud had to go. Tools in use were shovels, hoes and wheelbarrows. Lillian directed operations. David stayed in the background.

He'd known even as he made it that his proposal of two weeks wasn't really enough time to clean up the mess that the flood had made of Freyl House. Becky's insistence on ten days was out of the question, but he'd taken it as a dare. He kept hiring. He rotated his teams twenty-four hours a day every day, just like the prison inmates on the Grand canal.

During the first few days of the Freyl clean-up, Springfield Fever lost its grip on the town. The death rate plummeted. Makeshift wards in hospitals emptied. Military camp beds disappeared. On the fifth day after David began work on Becky's house – at precisely three o'clock in the afternoon – the water was declared safe and the quarantine was lifted.

Liberation!

The news came over radio and television. Loudspeakers blared it from the tops of trucks. Horns honked all over town. People ran out of their houses and hugged the first person they met. Spontaneous parties erupted in the streets, singing, dancing, music, crying, hollering. Within hours, TV crews started arriving from all over the country. Radio too. The next day they arrived from all over the globe. Neither the country nor the world seemed able to get enough of this town and these Americans who'd suffered through a terrorist attack as frightening as the Twin Towers. Hardly any street was without a camera crew recording the damage. Reporters vied for interviews with residents. Anyone who'd been through the quarantine was a hero. Movie stars posed in front of garbage dumps and ruined houses.

Jimmy organized a celebration parade with marching bands and the floats that usually came out only for Lincoln's birthday. People appeared from neighbouring towns to distribute popcorn, balloons, cotton candy for the kids, to barbecue great racks of spare ribs for the residents and pass around booze by the gallon. To hell with austerity. After a climatic disaster, a plague and a full-scale military occupation, Springfield was free.

But nobody could forget that these were a people who'd lost

children, parents, spouses, friends. Lots of them. The final death toll neared a thousand. Those were the stories the world really craved, just as they had after the Twin Towers. Anybody who wept for the cameras hit big time. Many residents got rich with tearful stories of a hard-working father's first realization that he'd fallen victim, of shy little Benny's last moments in an inflatable hospital and of poor blind Jennifer, who'd returned home after the quarantine lifted to find her entire family gone. The President of the United States himself gave a prayer for the dead on the steps of the Old Capitol. Hollywood studios sent crews to work up film scripts.

Daily life was abruptly easier. Supplies flooded onto supermarket shelves and volunteers flooded in to help, crews from colleges and universities, from political parties, religious organizations of every variety, Rotarians, Elks, Kiwanis, national women's groups, even the Camp Fire Girls. As for David's construction company, its workforce increased as fast as he could interview candidates, and there were dozens of them. Quack's lessons in business administration went into high gear again just as they had during the early days of the drug trade in South Hams State Correctional Facility.

Becky played no part in any of this. She refused all interviews despite offers from America's most prestigious talk shows. She had work to do. The Hilton hosted meetings of the Springfield Arts Society, the Coalition of Concerned Citizens of Springfield and the League of Women Voters. And on the morning of the tenth day after David began work on the house, she left the Hilton.

Lillian drove her through Springfield in a new Porsche. The floods had washed the Lexus away, and Becky had decided that now she actually *needed* a four-wheel drive. She wasn't wrong, even though Lillian had worked out a route to bypass the most badly damaged streets. The trouble is, television can only hint at what it's really like on the ground weeks after a flood. Block after block of the town's once-beautiful houses were no more than shamed and filthy relics isolated in acres of dried and cracked mud. It wasn't possible to avoid neighbourhoods where garbage hadn't been cleared, and not even the Porsche's advanced air conditioning could entirely kill the stench.

Becky sat tense throughout the trip, horrified by what had happened to her town, profoundly fearful of what she'd find at the end of her journey. She was somewhat reassured to find the iron gates outside the Freyl property locked, guarded, electrified. A sign warned of guard dogs and trip wires. Lillian drove slowly down the quarter of a mile of Freyl woods that led to the house itself; the road was rough. Becky held her breath as the trees gave way and she rounded the bend for her first view.

And if she'd been anyone but Rebecca Freyl, she'd have burst into tears. It wasn't perfect, but it bore no resemblance to the terrifying wreck she'd left. Its two-storey-high columns looked as noble and as pristine as ever. The pure copper roof still gave off a warmth that no other material can match. One team from 'Lillian's crew' – as the TV programme had titled David's workforce – were painting the arched and many-paned windows. Another team were laying turf for the famous Freyl lawns.

Nobody had enjoyed this crisis or its aftermath like Jimmy. He'd been king in the wartime of the flood with army troops at his command. He'd liaised regularly with the Governor. He'd stood on the steps of the Old Capitol and introduced the President of the United States to his people. He'd spoken daily on radio and television, become an icon for Springfield; and in the days that followed the army's withdrawal, his approval ratings soared right alongside

UCAI's stock and Springfield's spirits. The university proposed to give him an honorary doctorate. If this kept up, maybe by the middle of November, he'd be ready to announce dates for work to begin on the James Zemanski Memorial Stadium.

The last thing this man of the moment expected was the summons that landed on his desk:

IN THE CIRCUIT COURT OF THE _Seventh_ JUDICIAL CIRCUIT
Sangamon COUNTY, ILLINOIS

Plaintiff

COALITION OF CONCERNED CITIZENS OF
SPRINGFIELD and LEAGUE OF WOMEN
VOTERS OF SANGAMON COUNTY

v.

Defendant

CITY OF SPRINGFIELD, CITY OF
SPRINGFIELD COUNCIL

and

UCAI, INC
(Party of Interest)

YOU ARE HEREBY SUMMONED to appear on _November 15_ ...

48

SPRINGFIELD: Friday

Jimmy paced back and forth across his study at home, clutching the telephone to his ear; it was barely eight o'clock in the morning, and he hadn't slept since he'd received Becky's summons. 'What the hell are we supposed to do about this goddamned thing?' he cried.

'Why, Mr Mayor,' said Sebastian Slad, 'you sound all a-flutter.'

'I tried to contact you. You know that. I drove to St Louis at once. You refused to see me. A phone is hardly the appropriate place to discuss something like this.'

'Hey, come on now, Mr Z, ain't no cause to be uncivil. We got a summons too. Don't know what good seeing yours would do us.'

'With all due respect, Mr Slad, I'm not sure you realize just how serious this is.'

'Don't I? Funny. Thought I did. Maybe not though. You go right ahead and tell me all about it.'

Jimmy shut his eyes. '"Privatization in and of itself creates a significant change in the environmental status of the water department."' Even to himself he sounded like an automaton; his pacing took on a mechanical beat. 'Changes like this require an environmental impact report. Look, Mr Slad, the Council vote to accept UCAI's purchase of Springfield's water utility can be construed as a self-declared exemption from the report, and that can be construed as an abuse of discretion. And that is exactly what the citizens of Stockton did a while back.' Stockton was the California town that Becky and her Coalition had used as a template for their campaign; Ruth had told Jimmy all about it. 'The bastards won.'

There was a pause. 'Go on.'

'"Go on" where? Can't you see how serious this is?'

'Yep. Yep, I can, but you ain't told me nothing I don't know already.'

'Why isn't your brother in on this conference? We need all the brains we can get.'

'He got kind of a busy agenda today.'

This was not as it had been. Up until now, Jimmy had been pleasingly aware that the Slads had cancelled meetings to accommodate his schedule. His calls went through to their private number on a priority basis. That's the kind of deference he'd expected when he'd arrived at Follaton Tower with the summons. He'd left Springfield within minutes of receiving it, driven as fast as he dared, made it to St Louis in record time.

But security wouldn't even let him near the elevators to the Slads' floor. They told him to take a seat in the main lobby, that somebody would be down to see him. He'd watched the seconds tick by for half an hour, and the 'somebody' turned out to be the secretary's secretary. The *secretary's* secretary, for Christ's sake. A mousy little thing with no-colour hair in a Dutchboy bob. She told him to call the CEOs' secretary tomorrow. He was furious. He swore at her. She turned on her heel and left him standing there like an idiot, staring after her.

He called at half past seven the next morning; the Slads' private secretary told him that the twins were extremely busy. Neither twin would be free to see him for at least a week, but she could squeeze him in this morning on the telephone if he could hold a few minutes. For nearly another half hour he listened to beeps every second.

'One thing you can help me out with, Mr Z,' Sebastian went on, 'is how come a high-powered New York attorney for Galleas International got mixed up in these here cornfields of ours.'

Jimmy's face went prickly. 'A Galleas lawyer?'

'Who-all was you thinking done the ground work for a summons like that?'

This time Jimmy felt faint; he had to sit down. 'How in the name of Christ did Galleas figure a way to muscle in?'

'I'd like the answer to that one myself.'

'What do they know that we don't? What *could* they know?'

'You get me them answers, Mr Mayor, and we can talk. Now I got me a important meeting downstairs in ... oh, me, oh, my, it began five minutes ago.'

'*This* is an important meeting,' Jimmy protested.

'Not to me it ain't.'

'UCAI works fast,' Becky said, looking at Helen over the morning's *Journal-Register*, not even trying to hide the glee in her voice.

They sat at the breakfast table in Freyl House. The room was plainer than it had been when they'd last had breakfast there. The chairs belonged in the conservatory; all upholstered furniture had gone to a specialist firm in Chicago. The television stand was bereft of a television, and the pictures were still with the restorers in St Louis. But the table itself had been scrubbed, disinfected and deodorized; it looked exactly as it had before the flood. The silver coffee pot was as highly polished as ever.

'Have you rattled a cage already?' Helen asked. 'Let me see.'

Becky held the up the paper:

Terrorists Threaten Entire
Midwest Water Supply

'Doesn't look like a rattling cage to me.' Helen went back to her poached egg.

'You just don't know a rattled cage when you see one. The think tank they quote is the Incol Executive.'

'Never heard of them.'

'Oh, Helen, how can you be so dense? I told you all about them. At that first Council meeting, Jimmy based his whole case on one of their math-packed treatises.'

Helen put down her spoon. 'Are Incol the ones . . .'

'With secret ties to UCAI,' Becky finished for her. 'They most certainly are.'

The story reported that just last night the Incol Executive had issued an abstract of its report on their findings in Springfield. The full report would become public only when it was 'finalized' and 'cleared by the Department of Homeland Security'.

'That *does* make it sound like a rush job,' Helen said. 'How long have they had now? A week? Just collating the statistics could take months.'

'It claims that chance alone made Springfield the first major city to suffer floods on this scale,' Becky said. 'It says *no* town in the Midwest has a sewage system capable of dealing with such a situation. They are just as pessimistic about water purity. "Crumbling infrastructure in public utilities throughout the Midwest, poorly trained and underpaid staff, years of financial mismanagement, failure to make use of scientific advances and to take into account the extreme unpredictability of climate change. Even without the threat of terrorism these elements render public utilities incapable of insuring a clean water supply."'

'Nobody is safe without private water?' Helen gave a laugh, half incredulity, half that annoying academic contempt. 'You've got to give them credit for sheer gall.'

Beyond the tall windows of the breakfast room, Lillian's crew were pounding down the final strips of turf. There were no flowers in the flowerbeds, but the famous Freyl lawns were as green and lush as they'd ever been.

Becky glanced out at them, then went on reading out loud. '"Terrorism threatens our society at the level of its most basic needs, and the pitiful state of our public utilities gives terrorists a helping hand to kill Americans right in their own homes."' She took a bite of toast. 'UCAI stock shot up ten points this morning – the moment the markets got wind of this report.'

Helen reached out for the paper. 'What about Jimmy's terrorist-proof control room?'

'Not even mentioned.'

'And the summons itself?'

'I assume the primary aim was to push it off the front page. They succeeded.'

'Second page?'

Becky shook her head. 'The war on terror takes up the second and the third. But the fourth page makes it perfectly clear that UCAI and Jimmy can't touch Springfield until the case is settled. And it's hardly as though anybody can try intimidation. Not with hundreds of plaintiffs.'

'Think we could get hold of this report? Not just the abstract, but the report itself? They've made mistakes, Grandma. I know it. They got it out too fast.'

'Could you spot them?'

'I could try.'

'I will get it for you, Helen.'

'Sounds like it's got "Top Secret" plastered all over it.'

'Leave that to me.'

Helen read the front pages for herself. According to the Incol Executive, tests of the water, carried out by their scientific team, showed traces of arsenic and pesticides as well as 'unidentified' bacterial agents in the town's water. 'I don't suppose they can say the bacterial agent is Springfield Fever until somebody figures out what it is, but pesticides and arsenic? I sure as hell didn't know anything about that.'

Becky shook her head. 'It's meaningless.' She'd done a lot of reading about water over the past few months. 'There can't be a single water supply in the entire Western World that doesn't have "traces" of pesticides and arsenic in it.' She couldn't help adding, 'You're the family scientist, Helen. You should know that. It's like being shocked to find out that butter contains fat. More coffee?'

Helen gave her grandmother an irritated glance. 'For people who don't have your insider knowledge, Grandma, this is very shocking stuff. It's going to scare them. It scares me.' Helen glanced at the article again, bit her lip, then burst out laughing.

Becky pursed her lips. 'What's funny about it?'

'Don't you see, Grandma? You wanted your town back, and one way or another, you're going to get it. UCAI doesn't need Jimmy any more. What with epidemics, terrorists and floods on their side, what use is a mayor whose main ambition in life is to own a football team?'

'He's still Mayor, Helen. They can't take over without him.'

'Why don't they just kill him? Wouldn't that be simplest?'

'It's the city and the Council we're suing, not the Mayor.'

'If Jimmy were out of the picture, would you withdraw?'

Becky thought a moment. 'I'm not certain how much choice I'll be given in the matter.'

'A.L.O.—— What?' The desk cop was tired even though it wasn't the end of his shift. A very long day. Not that the days had been anything but long for weeks. Floods, riots, epidemics, armies. And garbage everywhere. Then wild celebrations, a visit from the President himself, endless funerals. And drunks all over the place as well as garbage. Media people too.

Everybody in town was exhausted. Even the telephone sounded tired. It crackled and squeaked.

'A.L.O.Y.S.I.A.,' Marina Rodriguez said. 'You deaf or something? That's the third time I've spelled it for you.'

'How do you pronounce it?'

'Who cares? All I know is that I buried her after some kids found her on the banks of the Mississippi in Tipton County, Tennessee. Last name Gonzaga.'

'A Hispanic, huh?'

'Missing Persons says she's English.'

'Sounds Hispanic to me. How long she been dead for?'

'She disappeared four months ago. It kind of fits. Hard to tell with a body in the water that long.'

'Four months! Lady, you got any idea how many people got lost just since the flood? We got a heap of files here. Who'd have thought so many people could go missing all at once?' He sighed wearily. 'Dozens right from Springfield. What makes you think I could use another from Tennessee?'

'Like I said' – Marina's voice was stony – 'she's on the Illinois Missing Persons website as missing from Springfield.' Marina had tried to get through when she first recognized the similarities between the woman she'd buried and the listing on the site, but that was during the time when Springfield was incommunicado. She'd had to put the file aside. By the time she could have got through, her personal life was all-consuming: husband on leave from Afghanistan, storm of sex and exhilaration. She'd just plain forgotten Aloysia until she ran across the file in a sheaf of other papers.

'The coroner took a DNA sample?' the Springfield cop asked.

'Of course he did.'

The cop sighed again. 'Get him to send it on. We'll see what we can do.'

'Shouldn't you notify her family?'

'Yeah, right. 'Course we will. Now if you'll excuse—'

'Is she somehow less important than your other cases?' Marina interrupted. 'You got something against a person with a Hispanic name? Like me for example? Rodriguez? Gonzales? What do people like us matter? She worked at the university. You have to talk to them too.'

'Yeah, yeah. Sure. But look, lady—'

'You're going to do fuck-all, aren't you? I will deliver the DNA sample and the coroner's full report personally, and I will make sure the information reaches a detective. Her family needs to know. So do her colleagues.'

'You don't even know if it's her yet.'

'*And* I will file a complaint against you for racial slurs against Hispanics.'

The cop sighed once more. 'That'll really make my day.'

Marina slammed down the phone so hard that it broke.

49

LONDON, ILLINOIS: That evening

London didn't live up to the grandeur of its name. It didn't even live up to its nickname.

People called it the 'Lily of Knox County' because it had started out life famous for its painted ladies. There were forests and lumberjacks in the prairies a century and a half ago; that explained the painted ladies. Unregulated felling put an end to the trees. The lumberjacks left. The painted ladies went out of business, and London turned into just another prairie town, announcing itself as they all did: two rusting gas stations and an active one, a few houses, a clutch of tumbledown motels separated by empty lots and a supermarket. Main Street was a row of parked cars along the highway and a row of arc lights. Not that they did much lighting. The brightest thing in town at night was a ten-foot-tall neon woodsman; he lifted his axe and swung it down in half a dozen jerks to announce the Lumberjack Bar and Grill.

Inside, the lights were low, the mirrors grimy, the bar battered, the bartender plump, young, a gold front tooth glinting through his smile as he watched David approach.

'Johannsen?' David said to him.

The bartender nodded his head towards a booth off to one side. 'What are you drinking, friend?'

'Budweiser. What's he drinking?'

'Oban.'

'What's that?'

'Most expensive Scotch I could find. A single malt. He said to put it on your tab. He's already had three, and he wasn't all that steady when he came in.'

David nodded. 'Better make this one a double.'

'You don't want none yourself?'

'Not me.'

David carried his beer and the Oban to the booth. The man who sat there was gazing at the drink in front of him. 'You Johannsen?' David asked.

The Warden of South Hams State Correctional Facility looked up at him, then back at his drink. 'I'd know you anywhere,' he said. He hadn't been warden in David's time. He'd been living in Springfield then, but when Hugh Freyl got David released, there'd been publicity.

David set the Oban down on the table and slid into the booth.

The Warden swallowed back the remains of the glass in front of him, and pulled this new glass closer. 'Compliments of Mrs Freyl, right?' he said.

'Right.'

'I'll have another after it. And maybe another after that.'

'You live nearby?'

'What the fuck is it to you?'

'Just worried about you getting home.' London was only fifteen miles from the prison.

Johannson gave him an irritable glance. 'There wasn't anything my wife wanted more than to be a member of that fucking Arts

Society of Rebecca Freyl's. Fuck it all, man, I was Director of Consolidated Agricultural, Incorporated. Two secretaries and a staff of ten. And my wife isn't good enough for that fucking society? She's a nice lady, my wife. Not getting in damned near killed her. Gave her cancer instead. So now old Mrs Freyl wants a favour from *me*? For the price of a couple of drinks? I don't think I'll grant it. Whatever it is.'

'That doesn't sound friendly.' David's voice was mild.

'I don't feel friendly.'

'You might regret it later.'

'Look, Marion, I don't talk to ex-cons, much less haggle with them. Or was that a threat? I don't listen to threats from them either.'

'But here you are, sitting and drinking with me just like we're old pals.'

'What is this? Blackmail or something?'

David raised his eyebrows, and a flurry of fear skittered across the Warden's brow. 'I been hearing this rumour,' David said, 'about little girls' pictures on a prison computer. Ring any bells? No? Sure about that? Oh, yeah, then there's this other rumour about pharmaceutical-grade narcotics getting into South Hams as regular as clockwork.'

Prison grapevines are notorious; some ex-cons stay part of the network, and even though the Warden had allowed himself to sample some of the products that Wolfie had for sale as a result of their deal, he hadn't taken enough to dampen the stabs of anxiety that hit him every time he thought about possible consequences.

'What does she want from me?' he asked.

'Mrs Freyl knows nothing about your drug supplies or your taste in entertainment,' David said. This was the truth. He hadn't told her about either. 'But she has a nephew in the Heights.' This was *not* the truth. The Heights was a UCAI correctional facility in Missouri, and no member of the Freyl family had been in prison there or anywhere else in America. Or in any other country. All David had told Becky was that he needed her to set up an informal meeting with the Warden; she knew better than to ask questions when she sensed she'd be better off not knowing the answers.

'A Freyl?' The Warden's tension burst into laughter. 'In the Heights? You're shitting me.'

'No.'

'What's his name?'

'I'm sure you'll appreciate that she wants to keep that confidential. She's afraid he has HIV.'

'They've all got HIV.'

'She needs to speak to somebody with access to his medical records at source.'

'Oh, yeah, why?'

'Her reasons are also confidential,' David said. 'All UCAI prisons use Medical Services Direct, right?'

'Why the fuck ask me? You sound as though you know it already.'

David took a swig of his beer and leaned back in the booth. 'Personally, I like the idea of a prison full of happy customers. I'd be the last man to try to upset your supply line. And I couldn't care less about how you amuse yourself on the Internet. But I need a favour from you for Mrs Freyl. She'll pay you well for it, and I'll do everything I can to protect your secrets.'

The Warden's wife loved him. Truly loved him. She used to spend hours at the farmers' market choosing the best melon for his breakfast and the finest catfish for his dinner. Now she was dying in a hospice, and he was alone. But at least — for the moment — there was Oban. He swallowed David's offering in a single gulp and held out the empty glass. David got up and collected a replacement.

'What's the favour?' the Warden asked as David slid into the booth with another double Scotch.

'A meeting with the appropriate contact at Medical Services Direct.'

'What's it worth to her?'

'Ten thousand.'

The Warden laughed. 'You're fucking me.'

'The offer is serious.'

'Why?'

'She's rich.'

The Warden shook his head. 'You're telling me this rich bitch is going to pay me ten thousand just to get somebody at Medical Services Direct who'll talk to her? What is she? My fairy godmother? Why should I believe a dumb story like that? It's nuts. What does she really want?'

'What do you care?'

'You're saying it's about this kid's medical record?'

'That's right.'

'There'd better be money in it for this person too.'

'There is.'

The Warden pushed his glass a little further away from him, pulled it back, then shook his head again. 'Just how dumb does she think I am? A nephew's medical records? Whatever she wants, I very much doubt that ten thousand is enough to cover the risk.'

'How about twenty thousand?'

The Warden thought a moment. 'You ever been to Cairo?'

'Used to drive through it regularly.'

'Not *Kay*-ro, you dope.' *Kay*-ro is how Hoosiers pronounce the name of the town Cairo, south of Springfield on Route 57. Illinois has an Athens, a Geneva, a Genoa as well as a London and a Cairo. 'My wife wanted to see the Sphinx more than anything else in the world. We got the plane tickets, all that stuff. Twice we did that. Both times I cancelled the day before we were supposed to leave.' He pushed his glass away from him and pulled it back as he had before. 'Egyptians speak Arab or some goddamned thing. I don't like it when I have to keep guessing at what people mean. See, I'm having a hell of a time guessing at what Mrs Freyl wants, and all twenty thousand tells me is that it's even riskier than I been figuring.'

'Thirty thousand,' David said. 'Top offer.'

The Warden swallowed back the rest of his Oban. 'Ever been to Gary, Indiana? No? Well, you have a real treat in store.'

50

GARY, INDIANA: The next morning

'Is that Marion?'

He couldn't see her. 'You're the nurse? Where are you?'

'I'm on the other side of the mesh guard. Don't come any closer. You think I'm stupid or something? You're not seeing my face. Let's have the money.'

'Talk first. Money later.'

'That's not the arrangement.'

'It is now.'

David knew voices like hers. Bully and bravado in a thin veneer over cowardice. The woman behind the screen went by the name of Jane Doe; the Warden had emphasized that Jane wasn't her real name any more than Doe was. He'd also said that she could be in serious trouble for talking to an outsider like David. But since David had already talked to the Warden, she'd be in the same trouble whether she talked or not. She was right about not being stupid. If she hadn't recognized the peril she was in either way, she'd have fought to get the money first — and told him nothing.

'You bother to look at the warehouse?' she asked David.

'How come the sign on it doesn't mention Medical Services Direct?'

'Why should it? Medical Services Direct is just another offshoot of Premier, Inc. We only acquired the prison contracts last spring. Most of our business is private.'

'Premier is medical insurance?'

'One of the biggest in the Midwest.'

On his way into Gary, David had circled what looked like a non-functioning warehouse surrounded by a huge parking lot and a chain-link fence. A tiny sign on the fence read:

Not a public building.

Premier, Inc

'How do you get into that warehouse anyhow?' he asked her.

'An electronic badge and a phone system that uses passwords.'

'No people?'

'People cost money.'

Gary, Indiana, hardly seemed like the place for a medical service of any kind. It stank. Not like Springfield, not spoiled meat, shit and garbage but rotten eggs, sulphur, raw coal tars and a stew of other toxic chemicals thrown off from blast furnaces, steel mills, oil refineries. Half a century ago Gary had produced two-thirds of the world's steel supply, mile after mile of industry along its shoreline. In those days, the stench killed people; it inflamed the lungs, weakened the heart, paralysed the nerves. A quarter of a century later, when Asia promised a better profit margin, US steel moved out. The foundries have been silent and empty ever since, great rusted relics of a bygone age; Gary itself became that rare phenomenon, a major metropolitan ghost town.

But not even time could get rid of the stench. On his way in,

David had smelled Gary before he'd seen it. And its once-booming centre was as dead and redolent as the foundries. His eyes were smarting and his stomach uneasy as he parked on a deserted and litter-strewn street, walked through an abandoned shopping mall, doors open, windows broken, nothing on display but filth and debris. At its height, Gary was the murder capital of America; all its official buildings were armoured against attack. Jane Doe had agreed to meet him in the wreckage of a post office, where she could hide her face behind an iron-mesh screen that once protected postal clerks.

'Tell me how Medical Services Direct works,' he said to her. He lit a cigarette from the butt in his mouth; tobacco seemed to help the nausea some if not much.

'I thought you wanted to ask about some patient in the Heights.'

'What's a nurse do in that building? Just talk on the phone?'

'I am not a *nurse*.' Her sarcasm was heavy. 'I'm an "agent in production", and I sit in a "production area". I do not use a phone. It's an "aspect", and we never touch it.'

'You don't like your job much, do you?'

'Everything I do – *everything* – is computerized, set by computer or monitored by computer, how long I talk, what I say, if and when I consult a doctor, even my bathroom breaks.' She'd started speaking more quickly. 'A beep in my headset, and the stopwatch on the screen in front of me starts a countdown: more than seven minutes and twenty seconds with a single patient and I lose my job. A "transfer box" pops onto my screen: name and location of patient, patient's medical history, call history, medications. I enter the chief complaint, and a symptom-based algorithm in the form of "yes" and "no" questions walks me through the consultation in "member service language—"'

'What's that?'

'You're slowing me down. I only have half an hour. I thought you just wanted to know——'

'What's "member service language",' he pressed.

A shaft of sunlight entered the far side of the post office through a gauze of cobwebs. 'It's a verbatim speech I read out to get the patient's history as quickly as possible.' By now she was speaking so quickly herself that he had to lean closer to catch what she said. 'If the condition sounds really bad I click "yes" on the category "911" to get an ambulance. If it doesn't sound quite as bad as all that I "send a message" by email as "clinically urgent – response time within four hours". That is, I *can* do it, if there isn't a pop-up box advising me that the option of a doctor is not available and to reassess the patient for an alternate plan.'

'That might be a prescription?'

'Sure. Why not?'

'Nurses can't write prescriptions.'

'Of course they can't.' The sarcasm was heavy again. 'I make "alternate plan proposals" that magically appear as correctly processed prescriptions at the patient's local drugstore. With the prisons, it's a little trickier. What's this got to do with an HIV case?'

'How do I know that he's not getting some cheap drug instead of what he really needs?'

'You think American pharmaceuticals are made in America? You nuts or something? The profits aren't high enough. US drugs come from all over the place: India, Venezuela, Egypt, China. Especially China. The pay is so low that there's barely a wink when workers skim off drugs for private sale. It's the only way they can eat. Lots of that skimming comes here too – much cheaper than legit drugs. Our couriers collect regular shipments from the airport.'

'They go straight out to the prisons?'

'Now how'd you guess that?'

The Warden had explained to David that his 'arrangement' with Wolfie to supply drugs went via this Jane Doe and that he didn't know her real name either. He'd assured her that David wholly approved the arrangement, was interested only in unrelated medical matters and would pay well for the information.

'Now tell me what happened at South Hams in June and July,' David said.

'You said this kid was at the Heights.'

'There was an outbreak of "gastroenteritis" that wasn't really gastroenteritis.'

She paused. 'I have no idea what you're talking about.'

'Sure you do.'

This time the pause was long; he could feel her weighing options. 'That's what you're here for?'

'Yes.'

'I *really* hate this job.' At least it was anger rather than sarcasm this time. 'But after you do it for a while you get a feel for the software. "Member service language" has its own style. You learn what should come up, what won't. Protocols involving South Hams in June and July were way out of line. Right in the "transfer box" — you know, the patient's location and stuff — a pop-up stated that the option of a doctor wasn't available. The option of an ambulance wasn't either. That's never happened before. Never. Then came up the protocol for "gastroenteritis" as the chief complaint before I'd had a chance to type in anything, then home-care instructions that made no sense at all: "take faecal samples every four hours". I've never run across such an instruction before either. That is—' She stopped short.

'"That is" what?' he prompted.

'Premier holds a group insurance policy for almost everybody in a town called Cawkerville. Very tiny place. Family business of some kind, way out in the Illinois cornfields. And back in early spring, I took a call from there. That's the only other time the "gastroenteritis" protocol popped up before I'd entered the chief complaint. But that time, a pop-up box said a doctor was on the way.'

'What about ambulances?'

'For Cawkerville? Nope. "Option not available." Can I have the money now?'

He tossed the envelope on the counter, turned to leave, then turned back.

'Tell me something. Who owns Premier?'

'One of those vast conglomerates. St Louis, I think.'

'UCAI?'

'That's the one.'

51

CAWKERVILLE, ILLINOIS:
That afternoon

The drive should have taken only four hours, but David had to stop so often to throw up by the side of the road that it was twilight when he hit Cawkerville. Springfield Fever? He didn't know, felt too sick to care.

He saw the sign for the town – he was sure of that much – but the town itself was hazy around the edges. He pulled over, pressed his fingers over his eyes in an attempt to make them focus. What they seemed to see when he opened them again was a grizzled face and long white hair underneath a flamingo-pink baseball cap.

'Howdy, stranger, you look mighty peaked to me.'

'Oh, for Christ's sake, George' – an old woman's quaver – 'cut the hillbilly crap. Let's just get this guy inside.'

David couldn't have resisted the two old people even if he'd wanted to. They manoeuvred him out of the car, across a dusty street, through a door and onto a flat surface. The sleep mechanism is breakable. David's had broken within a few months of his life sentence and it hadn't got any better outside, except for the occasional fluke. Two hours was about his maximum; twilight had barely turned into night when the old man's hand was beneath his head and a mug of something hot was at his lips.

And then it was magically somewhere around noon. The light through the window showed that. It also showed he was lying beneath the fronds of a brilliant green palm tree painted on the ceiling. A tangle of painted vines in blue, green, purple, shared the walls with butterflies, birds and flowers on stalks. A path of crocodile scales in yellow and red wove through all this – the ceiling too – and across the floor.

The old man stood over him. 'You're better today,' he said.

'No "hillbilly crap"?' David asked. He was as comfortable as a cat in front of a fire after Sunday lunch, stomach, eyes, head – everything – in a state of bliss.

'Wasn't sure you'd remember arriving. Been to Gary, huh? Bad place.'

'How'd you know?'

'You got a map in your car. Gary used to make my mother sick like that. Maybe not quite so bad as you. You *really* got to stay away from pollution, know that?'

'I like the treatment.'

'Just a little home brew. You been out near enough to two days, boy. Gave us plenty of time to establish you weren't a fed.'

David tried to focus on the old man. The flamingo-pink cap said 'Grandpa' on it. 'Where'd you get that idea?'

'You hungry? You probably don't know, do you? Take it from me, you're hungry. Can you stand? Almost, huh? Steady now. Here we go.'

The old man supported him into another room as brilliantly painted as the one he'd left; an entire menagerie paraded around the walls, across the floor and up again towards the fronds of a purple-coloured palm tree on the ceiling. 'This is Grandma,' he said, nodding at an old woman with hair as long and as white as his.

'Oh, for Christ's sake, George, my name's Margaret. I hate being called "Grandma". You're David. Hello, David. You're still pretty high from the looks of you, but you need food even so.'

David slept again.

When he woke it was evening, and he felt more rested than he had in years. He wore a long nightgown; his clothes had been tossed haphazardly at a chair painted with zodiacal signs. He could hear laughing and talking in the other room; he dressed and went to join them. Four people sat around the table, another man and woman as old as Margaret and George. Both wore brightly coloured clothes and beads.

'Sit down, David,' Margaret said. 'Meet Popeye and Olive.' Popeye got up and shook David's hand. Olive embraced him. She must have been very pretty a long time ago. 'God knows why they want to be known by such stupid names,' Margaret went on. 'That's Polly and Cerise over there.' She pointed at two old women, cuddled in each other's arms and dead to the world. 'They've been in love for near onto fifty years.'

'What are you people?' David asked. 'Some kind of retirement home?'

All four laughed uproariously, but when they calmed down, Margaret frowned and said, 'You know, he's right. Jesus. Fuck it all. Christ. That's *just* what we are. Our kids grew up. They're long gone now, and we're all as old as God. We just never got around to leaving. Or to growing up.'

'You got around to the farming though,' David said.

'Seemed natural.'

Smells had dominated everything in David's life for days, and it was the smell that had given them away: hay, grass, pine; flowers, citrus, metal; musty, musky, earthy; like skunk if it's old. Each kind of marijuana has its own smell, and there was variety in the air. As the director of the Insiders' drug trade, David was used to evaluating the various weeds as well as the various narcotics and chemical brews that float on the market either briefly or for good. But he'd never paid a great deal of attention to how any of it came into being – had no idea what the plants looked like.

George glanced up at the fronds above him. 'This here's Purple Haze. Seen from a bug's view of course. In the other room, it's Power Skunk.'

'Not palm trees after all,' David said.

'Nope.'

'How *do* you manage? You're right out in the open.'

The words came straight out of a 1960s soundtrack. 'Hey, dude, you got to get your mind in the groove. We're in the business of love and freedom.' But the 1960s argot dropped away just as the hillbilly had. 'When morphine won't kill the pain, we can. Lot of sick people out there. We got customers with muscular dystrophy, cancer, rheumatoid arthritis. Then, sure, maybe their kids want to get high. Maybe college people need escape from the jungle, and maybe the profits from marijuana just don't seem high enough to interest the CIA. At least not so far. But times are getting tough. Which is why we worried you might be a fed. Anyhow, I'm going to be kind of sorry if Illinois legalizes the stuff. What I don't get is why a guy like you is sniffing around.'

Margaret served a meal of beans and chilli, and David explained that he was following an erratic trail of outbreaks of a poorly explained gastroenteritis that seemed to resemble Springfield Fever. He didn't mention UCAI or how he'd found out about the outbreaks in Cawkerville, nor did he go into South Hams' troubles. There was a pause when he finished.

'You spent a long time inside,' George said then.

David nodded. 'There was some publicity when I got out.'

'Never see the papers. But prison tattoos are pretty obvious. Prison-pumped bodies too. And all them scars. But you ain't telling us the truth.'

'Not all of it.'

'How come?'

'I can't.'

'Then I got nothing to say to you.'

'Oh, for Christ's sake, George,' Margaret said. 'He's on the level. I know that. Popeye and Olive know it. You know it too. You're the one talked to his wife, and we all know there's something funny going on.'

Today's old people of Cawkerville were the young and wild of 1960s San Francisco. A bunch of them had settled here to do what hippies did: live free, love free and stay high. Most were college educated and middle class; the one secret they'd kept from each other and from themselves was that their commune couldn't have survived without money from their parents.

But they'd found they enjoyed raising and tending the plants, harvesting and trimming flowers and leaves; and they'd acquired a reputation. For fifty years, the local cops had turned a blind eye in exchange for some of the produce and, as George said, the CIA didn't seem interested. Meantime, all that free living and loving produced a crop of kids who grew up to become accountants and bankers, leaving some thirty old people behind, and there's nothing like old age to give a person an appreciation of modern medicine. Diabetes, emphysema, osteoporosis: it had come as a shock to find out that cannabis wouldn't take care of all the body's problems. People their age should have been entitled to Medicare, but none of these people had ever held a job or paid tax. None had even bothered with anything as bourgeois as a Social Security number, which meant they had no access to government programmes, medical or otherwise. More and more of their budget was going on doctors and hospitals.

Then one day, an insurance salesman appeared. A man in a suit. Nobody in Cawkerville trusted the men in suits that their parents had been and that their children had become, but this one offered them a Group Insurance Plan with Premier, Inc, and it came with a year's free trial. They thought, what the hell? What's there to lose? What impressed them most, even while they mocked themselves for it, was that Premier was linked to the highly reputable corporation UCAI of St Louis.

The coverage was straight from an aging pot-head's dream. Premier gave every member of the commune a thorough physical. They prescribed diuretics for Popeye's high blood pressure and insulin for Margaret's diabetes; they arranged surgery for a clot in George's left leg. The nursing staff at the call centre were helpful and encouraging. They often put Cawkerville residents straight through to a doctor, who urged them to call if anything seemed wrong and explained that Premier could help with many practical problems if they concerned health. That's why we didn't think twice about calling them when the water went funny,' Olive said. 'We realized we shouldn't drink it, but some of us already had. We were sure it was going to make us sick.'

'When was that?' David asked.

'Maybe eighteen months ago.'

'Two years,' said Popeye.

George dismissed the other two with a contemptuous wave of the hand. 'At *least* four years.'

'For Christ's sake, George,' Margaret said, 'you spend too much time high to get any kind of timing right.'

'Anyhow,' Olive went on irritably, 'they sent a nurse right over to check us all out, and they brought supplies of bottled water. Nobody did get sick or anything, but she seemed really concerned. And the second time—'

'It happened twice?' David interrupted.

'Oh, yes. The second time — that was early this year — several of us got really sick, very, very sick, and three—' Olive broke off abruptly, stifled a sob, tried to pull herself together, couldn't.

'Diarrhoea, vomiting, prostration, coughing,' George said. 'Jesus, old people are disgusting enough without all that, and those three . . . Premier sent out a doctor and loads of equipment. Ran lots of tests. Doctor said it was gastroenteritis or stomach flu or some goddamned thing. Nothing to do with the water. We aren't exactly hygienic – as he pointed out – so most likely it was a wildcat bug that our lifestyle let in. But they took really good care of us. It's just that those three . . . They spewed out their guts and—'

'They turned *blue*,' Olive interrupted. 'I've had some wild trips in my life, but this was *real*. They turned this ugly blue colour, and then they died. And then . . .'

'"And then" what?' David prompted.

Olive only shook her head; George took up the tale. 'We were sent compensation for the dead guys. Now we know we're pretty remote when it comes to the ways of the world, but that seemed a little weird even to us. We do see ourselves as sisters and brothers, but it's hardly the way authorities of any kind see us. We started thinking that no insurance company is that nice, and then somebody suggested it was a pay-off—'

'Not just *somebody*,' Popeye interrupted. 'It was Aloysia.'

David was sure he couldn't have heard the name right. 'Who?' he said.

'Aloysia. English bird. Forgot her last name—'

'Gonzaga?' David said.

'That's the one,' George said. 'Know her, do you? Smart lady and a new customer but a good one and she—'

'Oh, for Christ's sake, George, she hasn't shown up in months.' Margaret turned to David. 'She just happened to come for a supply when the bad bout began. She took one look at us and seemed mad as hell. We knew she was medical in some kind of way, not sure what, but we needed all the help we could get. She took lots of samples. Oh, Christ, though, she didn't think much of the Premier doctor.'

'They met?' David asked.

'She told him he was an idiot. She told him the symptoms couldn't be whatever he said they were. Plainly the water was what was making us sick, and she sure as fuck was going to do something about it. Then I took her out to the well house and she collected some more samples. That's when she said, "Compensation? You can't be that silly. They're paying you not to make a fuss." I mean, fuck it all, how could *we* make a fuss? We don't exist. When I told her that, all she said was "Precisely."'

Aloysia hadn't said anything about any of this to David. Not that she'd had that much of a chance. But Quack certainly had. 'Waterborne,' he'd said of the outbreaks in Springfield as well as South Hams. He'd also said whatever it was couldn't be gastro-enteritis. And a 'well house' might sound like where the non-sick kept themselves, but David knew it was where their water came from. That's why Aloysia would have wanted to see it.

'Can you show me the well house?' he asked Margaret.

⋆

The Cawkerville well house was a small structure at the edge of town that could have served for public toilets or an electrical utility of some kind. There was a fence around it, but no sign on the door.

'Any idea where the water comes from?' David asked Margaret.

'Mahomet Aquifer – the biggest underground reservoir in the Midwest. It's a major reason why we settled here.'

'Where'd she take the samples?'

Margaret took him inside the structure. If David had known about the description that got Brittany and Lamar Bryant burned to a crisp by their air conditioner, he couldn't have characterized what he saw better: a clunky, crude mechanism very like a cast-off industrial ice-cream maker or an espresso machine from Starbucks sat in a puddle of rust on a concrete plinth.

'What is it?' David asked.

'It's a pump.'

'A pump?'

'You got to pump the water up out of the ground, child. What did you have in mind? Us old folk reeling in buckets on a rope?'

52

CHAMPAIGN-URBANA: Tuesday

For some bugs there are well-worked-up systems to match speci-
mens to known strains. *Cryptosporidium parvum* the species that
Springfield Fever belonged to – isn't one of them.

To see one in a sample, you smear faeces over a glass slide, stain
and examine under a microscope. What shows under high mag-
nification is a scatter of perfect little spheres. They're called
oocysts, and each is a heavily armoured egg containing dark internal structures that promise life. The armour works too. It protects
cryptosporidium even from chlorine in a water-treatment plant; not
that outbreaks of the disease it causes are as uncommon as they
ought to be. You'd also see 'ghosts' on your slide – 'ghosts' is actually the term microbiologists use – similar in size to the armoured
blobs but without any structures inside. Just empty armour? The
sign of a resolving infection? Nobody's sure.

But if you can't identify your bug quickly, you have to start
serious investigations; and this was clearly an unusual strain.
There'd been blood in some of the Springfield samples sent to the
lab, and some patients had died of kidney failure: not *cryptosporidium
parvum*'s style. To this day, scientists verify a bug's credentials with

a system that dates back to 1882 and a German called Koch who first identified the tuberculosis bug. Grow the sample in a culture, inject it into an animal, see if it produces the symptoms, extract it, grow it again in a culture and match the second growth to the first. But *cryptosporidium parvum* is notoriously difficult to grow. Not even Prof Richard Stands, Champaign-Urbana's eminent microbiologist and television personality, could get his sample to do anything but lie there. Nor could any of the other labs.

He set to work on the other avenue open to him: extracting chunks of DNA from the sample, sequencing them, trying to match them to a computer database, much as the CIA might try to match a terrorist to the DNA in a blood sample left at the scene of a bombing. But the human genome is known; matching techniques are advanced, and there's a good chance of identification. Not so with *cryptosporidium*. Only bits of its DNA are on record, and matching techniques are primitive: chances of spotting the suspect on the vast databases are poor at best. Even so, his spirits were high. So were his team's.

The thing about challenges like this unidentified Springfield bug is that they don't come around all that often, and they cause a real stir when they do. Whichever lab got the answer first reaped the glory and banked the funding. Labs spied on each other. They sniped at each other in the press. They withheld data. They shaded what they had towards their own research. From the beginning Prof Stands had suffered nightmares about hotshot kids in California or Zurich getting there before he did.

And yet this morning as he lay in his bath, he felt an abrupt sense of familiarity with this bug. They'd met before. They shared a history.

There were all those 'ghosts'. Yet another theory about 'ghosts' is that they indicate a dying strain. Lots of researchers had commented that there were far more of them in the Springfield Fever samples than they'd ever seen. And then the *parvum* in *cryptosporidium parvum* really does mean small; the standard bug is very tiny, a single-celled parasite that utility plants have to use special filters to keep out. But this bug was tinier even than that. Lots of researchers had commented that Springfield's filters weren't small enough to have caught it. Nobody's were. This last piece of information explained the secrecy around research into the bug. If nobody's filters were small enough to keep it out, it was the perfect tool for bioterrorism. Which had everybody scared rigid.

That's when Prof Stands knew. Why hadn't he thought of it before? He leapt out of his bath just like Archimedes back in ancient Greece. He ran dripping to his study.

But this was no Eureka moment. Age plays such nasty tricks.

By the time he had pencil to paper, the insight was gone.

53

SPRINGFIELD & ST LOUIS:
Wednesday

When it comes to identification, corpses without names have more in common with bugs than with terrorists, especially in the chaotic aftermath of a catastrophe like Springfield's. Unknown homeless people died. Drifters from God knows where died. Runaways died. Even respectable people like Donna Stevenson died without papers on them, and victims of the Fever were so profoundly dehydrated that they weren't physically recognizable.

But Donna's neighbours had reported her missing, and the time of her disappearance tallied with the death of an 'Unknown Female' in one of the body bags. Her height, hair colour, eye colour all matched. The police found her Hummer parked not far from the Ferris wheel and the admissions tent she'd stumbled into, and the Hummer's keys were in her clothing on the same ring as her house keys. Her friends and her family were satisfied; nobody saw the need for DNA confirmation.

Aloysia Gonzaga might have presented a far more serious challenge if it hadn't been for Marina Rodriguez and her Uncle Bill the coroner. But there is real empowerment in standing up for the rights of a person nobody else gives a damn about, and Marina still wore Aloysia's highlights in her hair. There was sisterhood too, and Marina's back was up. As she saw it, Springfield cops weren't interested in what happened to people named Gonzaga, especially when people named Rodriguez were inquiring.

'I represent the coroner of Tipton County, Tennessee,' she announced to the Springfield policewoman at reception in the station.

'Yeah?'

'And I insist on seeing a detective.'

'What about?'

'Look, lady, I'm already filing a complaint against the Springfield Police Department for prejudice against Hispanics. Push me a single inch and I'll add a complaint on the grounds of injury to a citizen of Tennessee due to maladministration in the state of Illinois.'

Five minutes later, she sat opposite a detective. He looked very young. 'Are you sure you're a detective?' she asked.

'Yes, ma'am. Nearly six months now. Please tell me what the trouble is. I do hope they haven't kept you waiting.'

She was so ready to do battle that his sheer niceness only annoyed her. 'You reported her missing, and you don't care. A couple of kids called the coroner in Tipton County, Tennessee, and *he* cares. I buried her, and *I* care. We want her formally identified. We want to make sure her family knows she's been found.'

The coroner's official report included both a DNA sample and an X-ray of Aloysia's teeth clearly showing the 'professionally perfect' job that had been done on them. Marina hadn't stopped there. She'd searched out Aloysia on a national database called NameUs; she'd ticked boxes on the website that cross-checked sex, race, teeth, tattoos, hair colour and practically everything else. NameUs had come up with Aloysia Gonzaga.

Marina slapped a printout down on the detective's desk.

The burial of Springfield's dead was the focus of a national grief and fear just like the aftermath of the Trade Center bombings. Each corpse took on the iconic state of a martyr, and unidentified victims always give the heart a special wrench. There was human interest in a Tennessee mortician insisting on the proper identification of a floater several months old, but it just didn't have the headline appeal of the epidemic.

The media and the nation heard about Aloysia and Donna on the same day: two more victims of Springfield's tragedy, whose families were at long last free to grieve.

'The Lord sure do look after His own,' Sebastian Slad said to his twin, handing him the *St Louis Post-Dispatch* with a respectful glance at the full-size statue of Jesus in his office at the top of the Follaton Tower. The weather was bright and clear, the single McDonald's arch — Eero Saarinen's celebration of St Louis as the Gateway to the West — catching the sun in the distance.

Francis scanned Aloysia's obituary. 'Marion's kept her in Springfield all this time? You have to be joking.'

'Well, now Francis, if'n the paper says she was staying round there somewhere, who am I to argue? The Internet says it too. The TV says it. I'm just a simple country boy. All them powerful journalists is plenty good enough to convince me.'

'I don't like it.'

'Ah, come on, if anybody'd put two and two together, there ain't nothing that woulda kept 'em quiet.' Sebastian shook his head at his twin's worried face. 'So we had a little accident, the lid's—'

'A little accident?'

'—back on the toy box, 'cause there ain't nobody left to say nothing. Francis, it don't make no difference where she's been. She's home with papa now.'

Francis scanned the article again. It mentioned Aloysia's work as a microbiologist at Oxford University as well as her position on the staff at the University of Illinois. 'I don't like it,' he repeated. 'No. No, I really don't like it.'

54

Springfield: The same day

Becky and Helen had invited themselves to coffee at Ruth Madison's on the morning the news of Aloysia and Donna hit the public. There'd been so many shocks during this shocking time that neither quite registered this last one beyond simple relief that Aloysia wasn't a part of their lives any more. But Donna? There's just so much death a person can handle, and they'd lost so many friends to the disease, half a dozen of them from the Arts Society alone. Helen wouldn't have shed tears for Donna in any case; they'd never much liked each other. For Becky, it was going to be harder. Donna's admiration had been real. So had Becky's fondness for her.

As for Ruth, she was a sympathy call, and there'd been way too many of those as well. Freyls and Madisons had traded dinners and drinks for years, done good works for the Arts Society together, banked together, gossiped together, sniped behind each other's backs. Similar bonds held in many of the other sympathy calls, but Becky and Helen had put this one off again and again. A shared tragedy is one thing. There's a sense of community even in harrowed faces and emotional storms; people have some grasp of what others are suffering. But a raped widow who'd watched her husband murdered in front of her own eyes? What kind of sympathy makes sense for that?

Becky walked slowly up to Ruth's door, on her feet at last and leaning on Helen's arm more for reassurance than for support, no sign of a wheelchair, not even a cane. The relief was enormous. She'd hated the cripple's life, just couldn't see a dignified way out of it. When David had refused to protect her unless she got stronger, she'd felt real triumph. Forced against her will into exactly what she wanted? Perfect. But she did hold onto Helen a bit harder when Ruth opened the door, looking all too much the part, eyes and cheeks still swollen from her ordeal, bruising going yellow, hair untidy, clothes rumpled, fingers unmanicured. She brought out some Nescafé, a kettle of water and three mugs that didn't look entirely clean. Springfield society does not serve coffee this way, no matter what the circumstances; even so, Helen and Becky launched into half an hour of condolences, sympathies, offers of help that had come close to ritual in a town that reeled every day with funerals and mourning.

'I was so glad to hear that your children are with you, Ruth,' Becky said, steering the visit towards a wind-up. Ruth's son was twenty-two, her daughter twenty; both had set off to college in the east just a week before the flood. 'This is certainly no time to be alone.'

'Dear Christ, Becky,' Ruth said. 'What's happened to gossip in this town? Little Julia shouted at me that the whole thing was my fault, and noble Mark just slammed out the door. They were gone within twenty-four hours of arriving.' She stared down into her mug of Nescafé. 'Fuck 'em both. I never liked either of them. They took after Allan, and I can't tell you how glad I am that he's dead. If I'd realized how much pleasure I get out of it now, I'd have done it myself years ago.'

She got up and crossed the room to a portrait of herself that hung over the fireplace, gazed at it – some twenty years younger but not that much more beautiful despite bruises, swelling, unkempt clothes – then turned back to Helen and Becky. 'Remember the old song "Do your balls hang low? Can you swing them to and fro?" Anyhow, before I married him, I thought it was a joke. Yeah, sure, I married him for his money, not his charms, and I resolved early not to give up a penny of it.'

Helen murmured reassurances; like everybody else in town, she'd learned how violent emotions can be when experiences are too much for the mind to take in. Becky glanced down at her watch. 'Oh, dear, it is getting—'

'Don't go yet,' Ruth interrupted. She went back and sat again. 'Look, I do need your help. I want to go to law school.'

'You *what*?' Helen said.

Nobody thought Ruth was stupid. She was lazy, ready to trade on her looks, irritatingly coquettish, possibly nymphomaniac – and very smart. But *law school*? The woman had to be at least forty-five whether she looked it or not. She'd probably be pushing fifty before she could practise.

Becky only nodded. 'Such a brave way to grieve, Ruth. I don't mean for Allan. I mean for yourself. We badly need people who can help other women who've been—'

'Forget it, Becky,' Ruth interrupted. 'Not rape. I'm tired of women's innards. Getting raped myself quite put me off the sub-ject.' She picked up her Nescafé, stared into it as she had before, put it down again. 'All those parties with lawyers and bankers. Years of them. Years! I always loved hearing the lawyers talk: courts, precedents, cross, closings. But all the time I'm thinking to myself, "I could do this." I mean, it's simple at heart. Forget the rules unless you can find one you can club your opponent over the head with. Reserve emotion for use only when you need it. Manipulate everybody in range. I qualify on all grounds.' She gave Becky and Helen a wry smile. 'It's the one thing I can think of that'll get me out of this rut, make me clean myself up, maybe even care a little about something. Trouble is, I have no idea how to get a foot in the door. Who to see. Where to go. How to prepare.'

'Wouldn't Jimmy be more helpful?' Becky asked.

Ruth nodded. 'Sure he would, but I don't want to put myself in the position of owing him.' She laughed then. 'Don't worry, ladies, I don't intend to take something from you for nothing. One of many lessons Jimmy taught me is that information is the only commodity more valuable than money. Two small incidents. One before the flood. One shortly after it.'

Ruth had arrived to spend a lunch hour with Jimmy out at his lakeside house on the day before the Council vote to sell off Springfield's water to UCAI. She did enjoy her beddings with him. He entertained her, and sometimes he put himself out to give her pleasure. This particular noon, he'd really tried.

As they lay sweating in his black satin sheets, she pulled herself up on one elbow, reached across to him, stroked his belly. 'Okay, dear Mayor, what is it you want that you're willing to work so hard for?'

He looked up at her. 'I wish I loved you, Ruth.'

'Sure you do. I wish I loved somebody. Almost anybody. You're lucky to love Helen, even if she eludes you. Look, my crumpet, I have to get out to the mall and back to the house before five.' She got up and began to dress.

He reached out for her, pulled her back. 'It's a little strange.'

'Strange? Really? That's not like you.'

'Can you start a rumour for me?'

'Why not? What's it about?'

'Tell people I bought off Morris Kline.'

'The utility director? He's the guy that's going to destroy you at the Old Capitol tomorrow, isn't he? Sure. Why not? But I have to admit it doesn't sound very promising to me. All he has to do is show up and deny it.'

'He's not going to show up, Ruth.'

Jimmy ran a hand up her thigh as he explained that he'd re-hired Morris as Director of Springfield Light and Power and sent him off to Chicago to help with the recovery of data that had been lost during the town's first water-contamination incident. There was this boy genius Dieter Flaam at the university there with some really elaborate electronics who seemed to be recovering the lost data and needed Morris's help to collate it.

'Dieter Flaam, huh?' she said. She did sense something not just 'a little strange' but something dangerous, and there's nothing like danger to add spice to sex. She sat back down on the bed. 'Does this kid even exist?'

'Don't know. Don't think so.'

'Isn't it going to be a little difficult when Kline gets to Chicago and this somebody isn't to be found? Why doesn't he fly back at once and tell the meeting you sent him off on a wild-goose chase to keep him away?'

Jimmy smiled up at her. 'Can't you just do this for me?'

'Jimmy, I have to know. Is this Kline guy going to show up at the Council meeting or isn't he? If he shows up I'm going to look like a total idiot. I hate looking like an idiot.'

'I might let you look like an idiot, Ruth' – he spread her legs and bent his head into her lap – 'but I have no intention whatever of looking like one myself. Believe me. It's not going to happen.'

'Dieter Flaam,' Becky said. 'That's the name Morris had on him when the police found him dead.'

'Yes,' said Ruth.

'Do you think Jimmy *knew* Morris was going to Chicago to die?'

Ruth thought a moment. 'Jimmy's very good at pretending to himself he doesn't know things he does know. But, looking back on it, I think maybe he was getting scared. He was very . . . attentive to me after that. I don't mean just the next few minutes, but I saw him more afterwards than I ever had before.'

'What could he have been afraid of?'

'No idea.'

'And the second incident?' Becky asked.

'The day after the rape.'

'Right after the attack on you? Right after Allan's murder?'

Jimmy had come to visit Ruth at Memorial even though the town was in turmoil. She was too full of morphine to be more than dimly aware of him at first.

'God, you look good to me, Ruth,' he said. 'Ridiculous, isn't it? Here you are really looking like some battlefield casualty, but I was so afraid you might die that I . . .'

She must have dozed off then, but she couldn't have been asleep for more than a few minutes because he was sitting beside her when she woke, staring into space. They were alone in the room together, and he was speaking in a very low voice as though he didn't want to wake her. Something he'd said had caught her attention even through the morphine haze, and she struggled to listen, aware that he wouldn't be saying anything at all if he thought she could hear.

'. . . got this call from the Director at St Margaret's Hospital. Maureen. Remember her? Of course not. Why would you? I don't think you've ever met her. She's got all fat and sloppy, not like you. Pity the way some women let themselves go. I've known her for — I don't know — twenty years or so.' He paused, took in a breath, let it out. 'She'd seen some cases in Africa or somewhere and thought she recognized cholera, wanted to run to the Department of Health at once. I couldn't let her do that, could I? I mean, look at what happened to my beautiful Ruth. Weirdos on the loose. Respectable people looting and clashing with cops. All we need is a story threatening a cholera epidemic. I told her to sit on it, and thank God she did.'

He paused, glanced again at Ruth. Her eyes were still closed.

'Besides,' he said, 'all we can do is pray that this thing doesn't get out of hand. They didn't warn me, Ruth. They didn't tell me what they expected to happen, and then some accident *did* happen. I couldn't quite get just what the accident was, except that it was bad and that they . . . Oh, fuck it, what difference does it make? All they'll talk about now is God's will. Meantime, it's certainly not going to help to scare people more than they're scared already.'

He got up, leaned over to kiss Ruth's forehead, straightened, stared at her for a moment, kissed her forehead again. 'I can't help wondering when Maureen will figure out that it isn't cholera. Just don't die on me, huh?'

55

SPRINGFIELD: Thursday morning

'Don't start shouting now,' David said to Helen. At first her out-bursts had puzzled him, then annoyed him, then, well, then they'd come to seem just plain funny; and he wasn't used to find-ing himself close to laughter.

A week ago, the very day that David's construction crews got Freyl House in condition for Becky to move in, Helen went reluctantly, resentfully to the family doctor. He'd confirmed Quack's diagnosis of pregnancy. The shouting only increased. Helen was scared of this baby to come. So was David. Parenthood. Seesaw of emotions. Biological fulfilment and at the same time a visceral step towards the edge: no longer the centre of God's universe. They'd talked about termination. She'd shouted that it was her body and she'd do the deciding; he was only too happy to let her do it. And yet neither had seri-ously considered the possibility. Neither knew why they hadn't. Which was even more disconcerting. The one real distraction? Finding something – anything – that Christina Haggarty could use to defeat the Slads before anybody could get to Becky. Or to David. Not that Helen knew anything about their contract on David's life, although he was edgily aware that the announcement of Aloysia's death increased the danger for all of them.

They were living again in Helen's apartment in Freyl House, where Becky's beloved conversation pit had spent a couple of days as a pond. Helen's desk hadn't survived. Nor had her letters from her father, and that hit her hard. The table she and David sat at really belonged in Becky's guest suite. The remains of a makeshift breakfast and unfinished cups of coffee shared it with laptops, books, printers, scanners.

And a pile of printouts.

'You know as well as I do,' David went on, 'that nobody cares if unimportant people get sick. Poor people. Old people. Institutionalized people.'

'"Poor people"?' Sarcasm replaced Helen's shout. '"Nobody cares"? Oh, shit, now you're turning political on me.'

He lit a cigarette, took a drag. 'Suppose you wanted to put pressure on rich people. I figure you might try your methods out first on people nobody cares about.'

Helen gave him an angry grimace, clattered the plates together as she picked them up, then put them down abruptly and sat down herself. 'Jimmy. That's what you're talking about, isn't it? How come he knew *weeks* ago that Springfield Fever isn't cholera? The entire nation's expertise took several days ruling it out, and they still have no idea what it really is.'

'Suppose Cawkerville was a trial run, a bunch of old hippies making happy with their weeds. Who cares? Hardly anybody could be as cut off as they are either. Nobody's even going to know. A second set of tests on prisoners. The hippies get sick in the spring. Inmates at South Hams get sick in the early summer. Late summer and Springfield's west side—'

'No, no, David,' she interrupted. 'It doesn't make sense. There's clearly a pattern here, but what's the *point?*'

'There's a connection between Cawkerville and Springfield that might mean something.' He pushed the coffee cups aside, pulled his laptop over and turned it to face her. 'You're looking at the Mahomet Aquifer.'

David hadn't thought about what an aquifer might be beyond the old hippy's description of it as the source of Cawkerville's underground water, but somebody who runs a prison drug ring – or a McDonald's franchise – takes a methodical approach to detail. He'd spent many hours on the Net, checking out the telemedicine centre in Gary, the various UCAI-connected insurers that used it, UCAI prisons; he'd found little he didn't know already and moved onto the hippies themselves, their children, the art of growing marijuana. Aquifers and underground water were just items on the list.

Everybody knows that wells are holes in the ground with water at the bottom of them. He'd just assumed the water got there from underground lakes and streams that functioned much like lakes and streams on the surface, much like lines from a poem he'd studied for his high school English course: 'Where Alph the sacred river ran in caverns measureless to man down to a sunless sea.'

All wrong.

Start digging a hole at the beach. The dry sand gets damp, then wet, then saturated. When the hole is deep enough, clear water begins to seep in. A well in the prairies turns out to work like that except that the sand can be clay or almost any other gravelly material, and the water that makes it wet comes from rain, melted snow, riverbeds, prehistoric glaciers, water that's been sinking into the ground for thousands of years. The gravelly material is the crucial part, and most areas on earth have a layer of it. The layer can be widespread or localized, shallow or deep, close to the surface or inaccessible. The biggest accessible layer in America is the Ogallala that spreads out in a thin sheet under eight Western states. The Mahomet is smaller, but it produces a hundred million gallons of water every day for fifteen counties of Illinois.

Cawkerville lay right at the southern edge of it.

David pointed to a line on the map that started at Cawkerville and stretched to Springfield. 'That's a water pipe,' he said. Most people don't really know where their water comes from, and residents of Springfield tended to assume theirs came exclusively from Lake Springfield even though the utility's website also listed the South Fork Sangamon River. They were proud of their lake; they'd built it themselves back in 1935 and owned it ever since.

'The Mahomet Aquifer turns out to be another source,' David said. 'About ten years ago, a couple of your father's friends came up with the money-making idea that the west side needed purer water. A lot of city, state and federal cash disappeared under a table, and a Springfield company called Capital Water Plus got rich building this pipeline from the aquifer to the Capitol complex and a good chunk of the west side. The first pumping station is off a spur that serves Cawkerville. Another spur looks to me close to where crews were working on the canal in June and July. A couple of pumping stations just north of here supply Springfield itself.'

Helen studied the pipeline. 'UCAI set up Capital Water Plus?'

'UCAI didn't even exist back then.'

'Do they own it now?'

'It doesn't exist now.'

She studied the pipeline, shook her head. 'I don't see what difference it makes.'

'No?'

'No.'

David picked a piece of tobacco off his tongue. 'We have a call centre that just happens to supply medical services to both South Hams and Cawkerville. We have the timeline of outbreaks of an unexplained disease that connects South Hams, Cawkerville and Springfield. We have the Mayor of Springfield's knowledge that the Fever wasn't cholera well before any of the doctors knew, and we have his mention of some kind of an accident. We also know that Springfield Fever is waterborne and now we find a water pipeline that connects Cawkerville, South Hams and Springfield.'

This time Helen nodded. 'We need a lot more connective tissue, don't we?'

'You get anywhere with the report?'

Becky had called Helen into her study a few days before.

'He does well,' Becky said, staring fixedly out at the lawn. Shrubs were going into the borders right at that moment. A few flowers too.

'Who?'

'I won't say it again.'

'I have no idea what you're ... David? You're talking about David?'

Becky looked down at her desk, then up. 'I've received an email attachment for you. It's very long.'

'Who's it from? What's he got to do with it?'

'I believe it's from Galleas International.'

'The Incol Report? Is this industrial espionage at work? What's David got to do with it?'

Becky had no intention of telling her granddaughter that Galleas had delivered the report not to her but to David and that this was another transaction she'd arranged with him and carefully avoided involving herself in. 'Helen, are you interested in this message or aren't you?'

The long message was indeed a copy of the original Incol Report, kept from the public except for an abstract that made headlines a week ago:

Terrorists Threaten Entire
Midwest Water Supply

The think tank's secret links to UCAI were enough to make any-body suspicious, but it was the speed of the thing's appearance that had really got Helen interested in it. She printed out the whole report, spent many hours with searches of the Word docu-ment as well as the hard copy, which sat now beside the dirty dishes, Post-its in yellow, green, blue, red, sticking out along its top edge. She pushed David's laptop out of the way, set the report in its place and opened to the first yellow Post-it.

'What do you think of this?'

A quick glance showed an equation with multiple layers and lots of letters; David was fast and accurate with accounts and elec-tronic circuits, but anything beyond the most basic algebra made him queasy. 'I hate that stuff.'

'That's what they're counting on, David.'

He sighed irritably, pulled out a fresh pack of cigarettes, lit one.

'Equations like this *look* so terrifying,' she went on, 'that they don't have to mean anything. Suppose a drug company wants to scam Medicare out of millions of dollars? Get an Ivy League uni-versity to write a scary-looking equation. Nobody will raise a question. How to make the public believe depression is financial recovery? Same trick — except you use statistics.' She pointed to a 'd' midway down the equation and off to the right-hand side of it. 'This represents water contamination from broken supply pipes, and a lot of their argument hinges on it.' She gave a short laugh. 'You have to jump in and out of footnotes and back and forth between references to see how they arrive at a value for it. And guess what? It comes down to private water's *estimates* of public utility efficiency. No facts at all. Just "estimates".'

David took the page from her. 'This "d" here?'

'That's the one. The Incol Executive hosted a weekend for water companies in Jamaica. They polled the "consultants" who attended.'

'It doesn't say who they are?'

'Not anywhere in the report. I found details of the conference on the Executive's website, including everybody who attended. All of them were executives, and nobody outside the private sector was involved.'

'No scientists?'

'No scientists.'

'Show me,' he said.

Helen led him through the yellow Post-its to a brief footnote that identified 'd' as estimates of 'consultants' at a conference in Jamaica a few years ago.

He leaned back. 'What a big bad world there is outside prison.'

'There's nothing wrong with the actual formula,' she said. 'Mathematically, it's fine. Who's to know that the crucial element in making practical sense of it is down to unqualified people who have a financial stake in making the figure as large as possible? Besides, why should anybody doubt a think tank? Life's too short. Why not just settle for whatever the experts hand out?'

He read the footnote again. 'What about the blue markers?'

Those dealt with the west side and the Capitol area, where

Springfield contamination was at its worst; there was a great deal of detail on water flow, pipe capacity and potential threats from inadequate infrastructure. 'It fits in with your aquifer,' she said, 'at least by default. There's no mention of the Mahomet. No mention of Cawkerville either, not in connection with water supply or pollution of any kind.'

'South Hams?'

'Not so much as a footnote. Oh, but David, it gets so much weirder than that.' She started in on the green Post-its. 'They discuss an "unidentified bacterial agent" as though nobody knew that it caused something called Springfield Fever. Remember Legionnaire's Disease? People were calling it Legionnaire's Disease long before they knew what caused it. And then there are only a dozen references to this "unidentified bacterial agent". A mere dozen references to what's got to be the most serious epidemic in modern American history, and "unidentified bacterial agent" seems to be the only phrase they use. And yet everybody seems to be saying that it's a *cryptosporidium*, not a bacterium at all.'

'Is there a difference?'

'Biologically? I didn't know – had to check. *Cryptosporidium* seems to have no more in common with a bacterium than you have with a holly bush. Completely different kingdoms. But it gets better.' She flipped through the report to a red Post-it. '"The threat of epidemic cannot be ruled out,"' she read. '"Long-term epidemiological studies will require intensive analysis at a later stage."'

He took the report from her, read over the sentence, looked up at her, frowned. 'They wrote this report *before* the epidemic. When the worst that loomed was "threat of an epidemic".'

'That's the way I figure it. If Grandma's summons had captured front pages all over the world – and with the media eye on Springfield, it couldn't help doing that – UCAI stock would have plummeted. Think of the money they'd lose! They let on about the report long before they were ready simply because they *had* to keep her summons out of the headlines. Terrorists at our throats is the only thing that would do the job.'

He set the report down, lit another cigarette, shook his head. 'Still not enough. Nobody can prove the report is a template for what UCAI advisers thought might happen. Nobody could even begin to prove an unknown "accident" turned it into something far worse. At most, we might tarnish the Incol Executive's reputation with what they'd dismiss as an unauthorized draft. Even if somehow or other UCAI began to look dirty, some minor executive would take the fall for it.'

Helen's shoulders slumped a little. 'Nothing to touch the guys at the top.'

'Not even near.'

She pulled her coffee over, took a sip, then almost dropped the cup as she put it down. 'David! Maybe we're not looking at this from the right angle. Maybe we should be thinking Nixon, not crime busters.'

'Nixon?'

'Richard Milhous Nixon. "I'm not a crook" Nixon. Brought down by Watergate. It's the cover-up that brought him down. That's what he said himself, "It's not the crime that gets you, it's the cover-up."'

David leaned over and stroked her cheek. 'Know something? You're much smarter when you're not shouting.'

56

SPRINGFIELD: The same day
lunchtime

'I'm guessing there won't be a kickback now,' Ruth said to Jimmy. 'What do you think?'

He looked up from his naval orange crème brulée (with candied orange peel and bittersweet hazelnut fudge). 'What *are* you talking about?'

She smiled at him. 'You know, Jimmy, maybe we should have reserved a private room upstairs. So much better for intimate conversation. Oh, yes, I remember. I'm supposed to call it a "bonus", aren't I? Banker's kickbacks are called bonuses. That's what makes them legal. But Jimmy, dearest, a mayor's kickback is just a kickback.'

They were having lunch at the country club, where the tables were large and well spaced, the chairs upholstered and comfortable. This was Ruth's first appearance in public, and with Becky's commitment to get her into law school, she'd decided to enjoy it. The 'raped widow' was a town celebrity. Springfield's finest got up to give her hugs and kisses and tell her how brave she was. The club's only drawback was its floor-to-ceiling windows that looked out over the golf course. The golf course reminded her of Allan, and the thought of him wiggling his bottom the way golfers do would be quite enough to put her off her food. She'd laid claim to the seat facing away from it.

But she was under no illusions as to what this lunch was really about; it had nothing to do with cheering up a friend who's had a hard time. Jimmy wanted to parade the most dramatic of the surviving victims to remind people of his heroic leadership during the crisis. Becky's summons had hit him harder than Becky herself could have hoped, and he badly needed some favourable press.

Life in town was returning to normal. People were beginning to reassess what had happened to them. They hadn't forgotten Jimmy the hero who helped firefighters pump out basements and whose voice had offered hope in the darkest moments. But Jimmy was also the guy who'd promised them water and electricity knowing there wasn't any, who'd promised them things were looking up when Springfield Fever was spreading everywhere, who couldn't get food distributed without mercenaries charging extortionate prices for a quart of milk. He was Jimmy the bumbler whose inefficiency had forced them to wait hours for water, buckets in hand like Third World peasants, and Jimmy the dictator who'd given the order to fire rubber bullets into crowds of citizens.

Jokes about his half-moon glasses weren't anywhere near enough. Resentments like this need a serious outlet, and nothing could have been better than Becky's summons. Few residents knew what an 'environmental impact study' was but the *Chicago Tribune* quoted Becky's legal team – on loan from Galleas International – as saying that the study was a statutory requirement in transferring a public utility into private hands, and he hadn't carried it out. Cyberspace hummed with cries for revenge. More and more people were joining the Coalition of Concerned Citizens.

The abstract from the Incol Executive report? So it said private water was safer than utility water. Well, maybe it was and maybe it wasn't. The town was divided on the point; a report like that makes quite an impression on anybody who doesn't go through it with the care that Helen had, to say nothing of her expertise. But the town wasn't divided on UCAI. If private water was safer, why *that* company? There were lots of contenders out there. Maybe there were better deals on offer. Maybe there weren't. Either way, it was their democratic right to choose, most assuredly not Jimmy's. Who'd he think he was anyhow?

'Don't tease me, Ruth,' he said, setting down his dessert spoon and sliding his hand over hers. 'I'm feeling delicate. You know, this beat-up look really becomes you. Maybe I should try it myself. What do you think?'

She laughed. 'Tell you what, we'll call a kickback a bonus, just to cheer you up.'

He squeezed her hand. 'How about "enterprise inducement"?'

'Oh, silly me. That is what you said it was, wasn't it? I just plain forgot. And you're really going to need the money, aren't you? God, it's heart-rending when such a good idea stumbles. First mayor in the Midwest to go private. I suppose an epidemic was just a delightfully unexpected sparkler on the cake, wasn't it? God does favour a winning hand.' She tilted her head to one side. 'Just like Allan. Which is why I think brother Frank would have refused you even a much smaller loan.'

Jimmy withdrew his hand. 'Hey, this is beginning to hurt.'

'You see, Frank is every bit as boring as Allan, Jimmy, but he's not any stupider.' Frank Madison had succeeded his murdered brother as President of First National. 'With Herndon Freyl & Zemanski hobbling around on its financial knees, he's certainly not—'

'Enough, Ruth.'

'—going to fork over a couple of million. What made you think he would? In fact, I think it was Frank—' she broke off. 'Or could it have been Allan himself? They're both so dull it's hard to remember which one is which. Anyhow, they told me that some savings-and-loan golf buddy said he'd refused to refinance your law offices. Amazing really. I'm sure Hugh owned the building, which means you must have mortgaged it. Campaign funds maybe? I wonder if Becky knows about that. I mean, she still holds the title. I'm not even sure what class of a criminal that makes you.' She studied him. 'Can't be an ordinary old thief. Not our Jimmy.'

'I don't know how to talk to you when you're like this,' he said.

'Well, poppet, I'd advise you to learn. I'm still a fan, Jimmy. There aren't many of us left either.'

'You'd knife me in the back if it amused you.'

'Maybe I already have, my cherub. On the other hand, why would I need to? You've done such a good job yourself.'

Jimmy pushed out his chair to get up.

'Leaving so soon?' Ruth glanced around at the other tables. 'Do you think that's wise? I might break down and cry. Think what that would do to your reputation.'

He sat down at once.

'Jimmy, I am fond of you, you know. It's just that you're so goddamned cocky, I can't help—' She broke off, patted his hand. 'You really are going through a tough time, aren't you?'

A tough time? Speak of understatement. His head was spinning. It was all so sudden. The voters who'd finally learned to trust him were now hating him all over again, and buying their support for the mayoralty in the first place hadn't come cheap even with Becky's help. He'd had to 'borrow' client money for it.

Then he'd had to 'borrow' more with the firm as surety to build a portfolio of high yield investments so he could pay back the client 'loan'. He was nearly there when Wall Street plunged. Half of what he held disappeared at once. The other half was in a hedge fund that capsized during the flood and the military occupation. He had no idea what'd happened until just a week ago, and it left him scrabbling to cover his tracks before the IRS picked up the scent. And oh, dear, the scrabbling was leaving its own trail of bank statements and contracts that charted otherwise impenetrably complex transfers of assets, cash, inventory as well as capital borrowed from more client accounts that had been abruptly renamed 'loans' to be repaid to, well, to Jimmy. Which is to say, there was evidence of God knows what all kinds of fraud.

He needed every penny of that UCAI kickback just to pay off the client accounts. The question now was how to manoeuvre the privatization's open-and-above-board profit away from Springfield's own football stadium and towards the rest of the mess.

As a thoroughly depressed Jimmy was driving Ruth home, he got a call from Donna's sister on his mobile. She told him she had to leave on the afternoon plane to Chicago and would stop en route to drop off a package marked for him. She arrived at his house not long after he did and handed over a package big enough to hold a year's subscription of *The New Yorker*. On the top it said:

For J. Zemanski in the event of my death.

'Good Christ,' he said. 'It's huge. What is it?'

'That novel she was working on, I imagine,' the sister said.

'Why send it to me? Why not to Becky?'

'She loved you, Jimmy.'

Nothing seemed less appealing than Donna's endless novel, but he could hardly afford to affront the relative of a Springfield Fever victim. 'I know,' he said. 'I know. I loved her too. Look, I'm really grateful to you for bringing this over. How about some coffee? Maybe a chocolate cookie?'

He set the package beside the fake Eames chair, served the sister more coffee than he'd intended – she was a woman who liked to talk – before he managed to get her out of the house and start in on some serious drinking. He downed a third of a bottle of Scotch, watched daylight fade, watched the moon rise, ate a can of baked beans and had just started in on what remained of the chocolate-chip cookies when he suddenly realized that the handwriting on that package wasn't Donna's.

He hoisted it up on a coffee table, unwrapped it, opened the box inside. A covering letter lay atop an A4 envelope and a mass of paper:

I hope you will never read this note. If by some absurd chance you do, I trust you will do the right thing by my legacy to the world in appreciation of the gossip in the envelope.
Aloysia Gonzaga

The envelope read simply 'David Marion'. Jimmy ripped it open. Inside was a clutch of pages held together at the upper left-hand corner with those connectors that British solicitors use, like tiny shoelaces with long aglets. And the first sheet almost made him drop the glass in his hand. It also made him think of that same Nixon aphorism that Helen had quoted to David: 'It's not the crime that gets you. It's the cover-up.'

That first document was an original copy of the marriage certificate for Aloysia Hermione Olivier Gonzaga and David

Marion. The witness: Hugh Freyl. The officiator the prison chaplain at South Hams State Penitentiary.

Jimmy's hands were shaking with anticipation as he set the marriage certificate aside; he felt as though his life had just been snatched out of the jaws of the devil. The second document was a letter from a ten-year-old Helen. A note of its author and its date arrival appeared at the top in Hugh Freyl's own handwriting. This one Jimmy recognized at once. He'd forged it often enough:

> How could you help marry off
> my David to that funny woman?
> I hate you for that.
> I hate you.
> I hate you.

Then came a sheaf of letters from David to Aloysia that made painful reading even for Jimmy; the desperation was so raw. Apparently she'd visited David only once after the wedding.

The last entries were a birth certificate for 'Aloysius David Gonzaga' with David listed as the father, the child's death certificate at the age of 'one week' and a letter from Hugh, saying both he and Helen sent their deepest sympathies for Aloysia's loss.

The large 'David Marion' envelope included a small envelope that said:

> Keys to my house in Leland Grove

Jimmy poured himself another Scotch. Bigamy is a Class 4 felony in Illinois, punishable by four years in prison. Since Helen knew about this prison marriage – and how could she deny so passionate a letter in her own hand? – she too was guilty. Most importantly though, bigamy would violate the conditions of David's release. He'd be put away for the rest of his life, and without Hugh Freyl, he'd never get out. Nothing like that would happen to Helen of course, but the stigma would be hard to erase from people's minds, especially since according to Illinois law it would remain a permanent part of her official record.

Jimmy had known in his bones that David Marion was Aloysia's killer. He just hadn't had any idea why. The only question now was how to use this material to best advantage and still protect his future wife's reputation.

The night ahead was a rollercoaster.

First came some very tense telephone calls. Jimmy had to strike bargains. He had to pull in favours. At about three in the morning he set off on an errand into town, and for more than one solid hour, he was scared out of his wits. There was *so* much at stake.

On the drive back, he was euphoric. He'd done it! He'd actually pulled it off. But it's only a twenty-minute drive to his lakeside house, and by the time he got home, he was so tightly wound he couldn't go to bed. He went over detail after detail of every minute of that hour, as terrified as he'd been during it, pacing back and forth until there were shooting pains in his bad knee. When he couldn't spot a hitch, he was euphoric again. He lay down on the Eames instead of his satin sheets, feet up on the matching stool – tipped back, an Eames makes a recliner as comfortable as an opium dream – but still he couldn't rest. He got up, paced some more, reviewed that hour again.

Not a single hitch. Not one.

57

SPRINGFIELD: Eight o'clock
Friday morning

'Mr Marion?' The voice was female, frightened. David didn't recognize it. He and two women were digging trenches for the drainage pipes at Otto's Autos.

'Who is this?' he asked.

'I work on the Vinegar Hill site.' That one was a big job, a house almost as large as Becky's, just as badly damaged too. 'Your wife is trapped under some scaffolding, and we just—'

'I'll be right there.'

'Wait! Wait! Not this site. Not one of ours at all. Eastdale Avenue.'

'Number?'

Eastdale Avenue was not only on the east side; it was industrial. There was no reason for Helen to be there. None.

David screeched out of the Otto's Autos in one of the company's new vans. 'Lillian's Crew' it said on the side.

By the time he reached Eastdale Avenue, he'd run every red light en route. The site wasn't large. The scaffolding around the structure looked intact as he slammed to a halt and got out. He paused a moment then. Nobody running out to meet him. No ambulance. From inside the structure, a radio blasted, and the site was as messy as Otto's Autos used to be while his staff was still male. He picked up a piece of wood the size of a baseball bat and went inside through the open door.

The entry was a large hallway, divided off from the rest of the space by studs for walls-to-be, and so crammed with bags of cement, plasterboard, doors, wheelbarrows full of bricks that two people couldn't walk down it side by side. Tools lay everywhere. Ahead of him a couple of guys were more or less occupied at laying bricks to hold a door frame in place. One of them was so heavily tattooed that there was no skin visible.

The tattooed guy looked up at David. 'You motherfucker,' he said. 'You knew that bottle of water was mine, and you went right ahead and drank it anyhow. Now you come in here *looking* for me?'

Whoever said a trap has to make sense?

The door slammed shut behind David. Tattoo grabbed a circular saw attached to an extension cord, pulled the guard back, fired it up, got the blade spinning and started for him. There was nothing to do but back away and jab at Tattoo with the stick, but the hallway was so cluttered that secure footing wasn't possible and Tattoo kept coming, revving up the saw. David lunged with his stick and clipped the hand holding the blade guard. The guard slipped; the blade jammed and juddered helplessly: 'Click, click, click.'

David wasn't aware of anybody behind him. There wasn't any pain, no sense that he'd been hit. He just felt suddenly drunk. Not about to throw up or anything, just hazy, groggy.

Then came sleep.

58

CHAMPAIGN-URBANA:
Same day, same time

Prof Richard Stands luxuriated in his morning bath, remembering when he was King of America. That was his entire first week in school. Five years old, and chosen by God Himself. Monday? Pure magic. Everybody in his class *and* his teacher, Miss Penfold, swore to serve him for ever.

King Richard was kindly, but he demanded obeisance from his classmates. By Friday – in the playground near the swings – one little girl had had enough.

'King Richard?' she said with a sneer. 'There ain't no King Richard.'

'*I* am Richard Stands, the boy just under God.'

She looked him up and down. 'You're stupid.'

At home, his mother was so doubled up with laughter that she could barely get the words out. 'Dicky darling, it's "I pledge allegiance to the flag of the United States of America and to the republic for *which it stands*" not "for *Richard Stands*".'

Three-quarters of a century later, Professor Richard Stands – all of eighty years old – leapt out of the bath for the second time in under a week, and ran to his study. And it was 'Eureka!' now.

He'd kept detailed notes of his entire scientific life because his memory had always been a weak point; he'd trained himself so well that his right hand kept taking notes even when his mind had disengaged. Twenty years ago he'd been visiting Oxford in England in what had turned into a publicity tour after winning his prize. King again: Prof Richard Stands, famous for his study of protozoan metabolism, winner of microbiology's coveted Marjorie Stephenson Prize, inspecting British labs before giving a lecture to the Royal Society that evening. He wasn't used to being fêted. It was thrilling, ennobling, terrifying, all at the same time.

How could he keep his mind on his guide? He certainly couldn't hide his preoccupation, and his guide grew as impatient as the little girl in the playground. '*I* have a patent on a protozoan,' she was saying. Clearly a very self-centred woman – all too like that little girl – hair so expensive, teeth too white.

'Oh?' he'd said, catching his reflection in a shiny microscope.

'Would you like to see it?'

'The patent?'

'The *bug*.'

'Of course. Of course.'

What had yanked him out of his morning bath was the edge of a memory of the slides she'd shown him: a bug that just might – just might – be related to the one he and his team were studying in search of Springfield Fever.

It took him less than twenty minutes to dig out his notes; his hands trembled as he opened to his sketch of his guide's protozoan: clearly a *cryptosporidium parvum* – and an unusually tiny one. The notes went on to explain that she was Dr Aloysia Gonzaga and that she'd been researching this minute and as yet unidentified variety of the very bug he'd been sent to study. He wasn't sure at first why he'd suspected that she shouldn't be showing him her sample — something in her manner? — but she was so annoyed at this new King Richard that she couldn't help herself.

Cryptosporidium: the most important waterborne pathogen in the developed world. Since its armour keeps it safe from the chlorine that kills most bugs and since processing-plant filters can and do fail to catch it, outbreaks aren't uncommon. People become ill in varying ways, and there are deaths among the weak. Aloysia had hijacked the toxin-producing genes of another bug, *E. coli* 0157, and inserted them into the *cryptosporidium* genome. *E. coli* 0157 kills much more easily. It can destroy the kidneys and cause the intestines to haemorrhage. It can't get past chlorine itself, but *cryptosporidium*'s armour would get it through. Most importantly, it was so very tiny — well under a micron in diameter — that it would simply float past water utility filters. It and its *E. coli* 0157 payload could take out whole swathes of a population.

A couple of details like this, and Prof Stands knew Aloysia shouldn't be talking to him at all. Poisoning an enemy's water supply is a holy grail in biological warfare, and he had no clearance for work on biological weaponry. But back then nobody was stitching bits of one bug's DNA into another bug's genome, which made her seem more nut job than a dangerous innovative researcher. But nut jobs sometimes come up with interesting ideas. His notes continued, although they became sketchier.

Injecting the *E. coli* 0157 toxin caused a flaw that made delivery complex. The bug couldn't function without a protein that had to be kept separate until the delivery itself, rather like detonator and explosive. There was an important upside though. The disease wouldn't spread beyond the first generation. An invading army would remain safe from its effects; the second generation were almost entirely 'ghosts': those empty *cryptosporidium* shells that had kept Prof Stands awake for weeks.

Aloysia had even designed a delivery system for introducing her weapon into a city's water supply. He couldn't piece it together in any detail, although she'd plainly adapted industrial equipment to deliver the bug. He had sketched her drawing, but his sketch was the sketch of a man with his mind on his speech to come. He turned it upside down. Then right side up. It looked a little like an old-fashioned jukebox from his teenage years, curved pipes, push-button dials, gauges – exactly what it had seemed like to Lamar Bryant's wife Brittany, who'd paid for the observation with her life and her husband's. An industrial whatsit? Prof Stands couldn't think of the name, but he'd seen machines like it that were used to deliver specific amounts of gases. On this one, the gauges might set the mixture, and then the tubes would deliver specified amounts of bug and protein from a carrier into a city's pumping station. The carrier would probably have to be a specialized truck of some kind.

Beside the sketch he'd written what looked like 'pressurized tanker', but he couldn't be sure. Certainly a pressurized tanker, a couple of hoses and a very simple industrial whatsit would do the job. Aha, manifold! That was the whatsit's name. The assembly wouldn't need more than two or three men to handle it either, maybe a couple of hoses to get from the carrier to the manifold, which could probably be hooked up directly to the pump. A small contribution of protein, and the bugs weren't energized enough to cause anything at all. Increasing amounts of protein caused increasing illness. A huge amount? Springfield Fever.

He'd need Aloysia's patent registration before he could declare victory, but he had no doubt. He'd won. He'd cracked it. The victory was his. And it wasn't even nine o'clock in the morning.

There *was* one thing that seemed a total mystery. What terrorist group would perpetuate such an atrocity on such a scale and with such success — and yet fail to lay claim to it? Could somebody have intended something else? And made a mistake? A miscalculation with the manifold that resulted in pressure changes in the delivery system?

Of course, there could have been some kind of accident. But the why and the how of such an attack was hardly his problem.

59

SPRINGFIELD: Same morning

Jimmy hadn't slept, and even the idea of breakfast made him queasy, but he'd showered, shaved, put on clean clothes. He was ready to go at nine-thirty – right on schedule – when he received the call he'd had to bargain hardest for. He left at once and drove to the Springfield Police station.

'I want to report a murder,' he said to the desk sergeant.

Then came a bit of plain old luck.

The desk sergeant showed him in to Detective Inspector Sullivan. Irish cop. Freckles and one of those soft Dublin faces: the right kind of Irish cop. Maybe you could *see* both hands on the table but somehow one was picking twenty-dollar bills out of your pocket even so. They'd played poker together for years. It takes two to cheat effectively in the game – it's called 'collusion' even in poker – and they made a brilliant team. Their discussion took less than half an hour.

The rest of the morning was harder to get through. Much harder. Mayor James Zemanski fizzed with anxiety, barely able to keep his mind on congratulations to an ancient citizen on her hundredth birthday, press worries over garbage, telephone calls to bereaved families, the ruffled feathers of a couple of aldermen who were always at each other's throats. An aide had written his lunchtime speech to the Rotary Club; he put on his half-moon glasses to read it, began, then tossed the speech aside, released some of the morning's tension in the form of passion for the Rotarians' worldwide Youth Exchange Program – not that he gave a damn about it – and it got him a standing ovation.

On the way back from the Rotarians to his office, Sullivan came through on Jimmy's mobile.

'You know what's really funny?' Sullivan said. 'We were bringing Marion into custody right while you were—'

'You *what*?' Jimmy interrupted, voice incredulous but heart soaring.

'We were bringing the bastard in, my friend. Right at that very moment.'

'He killed somebody *else*?'

'Naw. Pity about that. Just assault and reckless driving. But even before you came in, I knew we'd get him on something sooner or later. I knew it. The call came—'

'Jesus,' Jimmy interrupted again, 'assault certainly sounds like him but . . . Anybody hurt?'

'A few cuts and bruises.'

'Marion just . . . put his hands behind his back and surrendered?'

'You might say that.'

Jimmy took in a breath, let it out. 'What about the house? You find anything there?'

'You're fucking right we did.'

At the police station, Jimmy had turned over the package addressed 'For J. Zemanski in the event of my death' and the envelope marked 'David Marion'. He'd explained that the great mass of material had been academic manuscript, which the police were welcome to if they wanted it. Sullivan dismissed it with a shrug. Like Jimmy, what he cared about was the 'David Marion' envelope. Not that Jimmy had turned over *all* its contents. He'd decided Aloysia's covering letter was relevant as well as a selection of the angriest letters from David to her. Put together, they looked – so Jimmy and Sullivan agreed – as though she might well be afraid David was going to kill her, was entrusting the letters with Jimmy as evidence for the simple reason that everybody in Springfield, including Aloysia, knew how much he loved Helen and hated David Marion.

Jimmy went on to tell Sullivan about last June when David had arrived late at his own wedding party, sodden and mud-covered, and said that he'd just come from the Mississippi. Floaters are common enough for policemen to get a feel of how long it takes a corpse to travel down river. The three months before Aloysia turned up in Tennessee wasn't a bad fit if he'd drowned her somewhere near, say, Hannibal, just west of Springfield, on the day of the wedding party.

'It isn't enough evidence to book him on,' Jimmy had said to Sullivan. 'I know that. But look, it occurs to me that the Gonzagas only got in from England a day or so ago. A lot of unhappy paperwork. A lot of grieving. Donna's sister said they haven't been able to bring themselves to go out to Aloysia's house yet, much less start an inventory. You just might find something there.'

He certainly hadn't given Sullivan the small envelope labelled 'The key to my house in Leland Grove' or the key itself. The woman had known that Jimmy was the only person she could rely on to carry out her plans if she died, and he'd fulfilled her final wishes. Sullivan's boys found the results of his terrifying predawn errand at her house: the remainder of the 'David Marion' file, the gentler, more loving letters he'd written her, the marriage certificate, the birth certificate for the child with David listed as the father and the child's death certificate. Clear evidence of bigamy. But better – oh, far better – these documents constituted a painfully clear motive for murder. Even a dumb prosecutor could land a guilty verdict.

Kill wife Number One to secure marriage to rich wife Number Two as well as escape an otherwise inescapable life sentence. Who wouldn't kill for that?

And, oh, dear God, did the people of Springfield want to see David Marion back behind bars for good.

Jimmy's role was pure glory. He was not only the informant in the case but the star witness. He was also the one who'd put the facts together and to whom the victim had left her legacy as well as her proof. He'd have no choice but to be prominent in both the investigation and the trial, and he could maximize that part of it to the hilt. The exposure would bring in new clients and with them new client accounts from which he could 'borrow'. It would tell Springfield that the hero of dark times was their hero still. It would revive the town saint, Hugh Freyl, and everybody was certain Hugh had been David's victim too. If Jimmy worked that part of it right, he could even bring Becky back on board, and *that* would really turn the momentum in his favour.

A bit of careful manoeuvring, and he might yet set foot in the governor's mansion with Helen at his side.

Jimmy had almost forgotten the joy of winning – pure oxygen mixed with ecstasy.

All afternoon, he kept having to repress smiles as he signed by-laws passed by his Council, chaired a planning committee meeting and cut a ribbon to open a new runway at Abraham Lincoln

Capital Airport. He didn't even have time to go home before dinner at the Sangamo Club with representatives of a reluctant Chinese investor; by the time coffee arrived, his ebullience and optimism won the Chinese over to a restoration programme that mayors rarely dream of.

He didn't start back home until well past eleven, still flying high on adrenalin. Only as the garage doors closed behind him did the exhaustion hit. He could barely stay upright as he got out of the car and into the house.

'Fuck!' he said as he caught a whiff of the air inside.

The firm he'd hired last week to clean for him didn't seem able to get it through their thick skulls that he didn't want *anybody* smoking in his house. He dithered a moment. Thirty-six hours without sleep, too much liquor and an emotional rollercoaster like he'd never known: he was so tired his stomach was turning over. The smoke almost made him gag. He switched on the lights, stormed into the living room to open the windows over the lake.

And stopped dead.

David Marion lay dozing in the original Eames where he himself had been lying only that morning. The prison-pumped, arrogant body was unmistakable even with the face turned away. And he had his feet actually on the footstool, the original one where only Jimmy's feet were allowed to rest. Nobody else would do that. Cigarette butts nearly filled a Murano glass bowl worth a small fortune. Nobody else would do that either. A waft of cigarette smoke curled up from the hidden face, and Jimmy's terror was so abrupt – it hit him right beneath the ribs – that his eyes went out of focus.

'You!' he cried.

60

SPRINGFIELD: The early hours
of Saturday

David didn't move, didn't even roll his head to look at Jimmy.
'Don't shout like that. I have a *very* bad headache. You set me up,
Mr Mayor. That wasn't nice.'

'Oh, fuck, what are you going to do?' The words stumbled out
of Jimmy's mouth. 'You're here to kill me, aren't you? Please don't
kill me. I don't want to die, David. Please.'

'When I started going through Aloysia's papers' – David spoke
as though he hadn't heard Jimmy – 'I couldn't see why you'd
kept—'

'Come on, David, talk to me. You're scaring me shitless.'

'I don't look all that dangerous, do I? That childish letter of
Helen's, angry because her daddy had married me off to Aloysia:
why keep it? And yet here it is. Right out in the open. Or rather,
hidden in that new safe of yours. Didn't anybody ever tell you
that the first place an electrician looks for a hidden safe—?'

'Oh, God,' Jimmy moaned.

'—is behind the wall outlets in the bedroom? And lo! Yours
was right there. A straightforward plan would have been best, Mr

Mayor. Trap the beast, kill it, capture the princess and her fortune. Maybe not even need UCAI's money? Ten million under the table, wasn't it? You *really* think they'd have paid you off?' Jimmy sagged against the wall, hardly breathing, not daring to ask how David knew the amount. 'The first puzzle is that you didn't kill me, so it was ... Are you still standing? Sit down, sit down.' David waved a weary hand towards the fake Eames. 'It makes me tired to know you're on your feet. Aloysia's easy. She wanted to make as much trouble as possible for as many people as possible. Especially me, but the Freyls too, as well as a number of others. Gave you ideas, didn't she? If I'd died in some back street, nobody would ever know what a hero you were for getting rid of me. So you get me beat up, land me in the slammer, plant Aloysia's dirt to keep me there for good. But you're a businessman. Businessmen need insurance. My present thinking is that here's where Helen's letter comes in. If Plan A doesn't work, old Mrs Freyl will pay through the nose to suppress evidence that Helen knowingly entered into a bigamous marriage.'

'Goddamn you!' Jimmy's voice trembled with a righteous outrage that overrode his fear as well as his exhaustion. 'I kept Helen's letter to protect her. She was only a little girl when she wrote that. Just a child. I'd never do anything to hurt her. *Never!*'

'Yeah.' David nodded. 'Yeah, that does make sense. Nobody else will believe you, but I think I do.'

Jimmy was so surprised at this response that he sat down abruptly and blurted out, 'Why aren't you in jail?'

'You know, I think I've fallen in love with corporate power. I was out of custody ten minutes after a telephone call that old Mrs Freyl would describe as "interesting". A new experience for me. A serious thrill. Not that big business buys everything. It didn't buy me into your house tonight.'

A couple of years installing security systems makes even an ex-con part of a fraternity that gossips about clients just as doctors do about patients. While Jimmy was walking into the Sangamo Club, David was having a drink with a ferret – a small, nervous, nerdy man – who headed AU Security in Springfield. AU Security cost an arm and a leg but ensured a ten-minute response time to any break-in. The trouble with systems like that is that they're sensitive. They lock down easily, and way too many owners forget the secret pass codes they've set to bypass the lockdown. Maybe they demand the security, but they sure as hell get mad at the money and inconvenience involved in resetting the system. Most firms – AU Security included – leave a loophole, an internal password that bypasses all that. A drink, a ferret's commiseration at the ambush carried out on a fellow professional, and here David sat in Jimmy's living room without the necessity of an overtly illegal act.

David figured the method showed serious progress in his education as a rich man. He was beginning to see that the rich don't *have* to break laws. He eased his feet off the Eames footstool and gradually pulled himself upright in the chair.

That's when Jimmy first caught sight of the face. Christ Almighty, could that patchwork of stitches really be David Marion? Jimmy swallowed, fought against the vomit in his mouth. Forehead, chin – as though ripped off and basted back into place – and cheeks so swollen that if it hadn't been for the body and the voice, Jimmy wouldn't have recognized him at all. Frankenstein's monster? He was a beauty next to this. And that's not even taking account of one eye blackened shut and the other barely more than a slit.

Jimmy could only mumble the words. 'I didn't know they'd hurt you. That wasn't part of the deal. I swear to you . . .' He trailed off, too shocked at that face to continue.

His instructions had been simple: 'Get the guy arrested for assault. Maybe mess his face up a little.' He knew that getting David into custody for something else was the only way of pressing murder and bigamy charges without immediate Freyl obstruction. Freyl influence could buy a lot, especially in this town, but it couldn't buy off a murder charge against a convicted felon already in custody. So, well, what had bought it off? Federal muscle? The NSA? That was the only possibility. But why would the feds intervene for David Marion of all people? Or . . . Could it be? The feds under UCAI's guidance? The security guy the Slads had sent Jimmy to see – that nasty church lunch with old ladies and no Martinis – he certainly had ties to the NSA. Had they switched sides, teamed up with David against Jimmy instead of Jimmy against David? Could that be what David meant by being in love with 'corporate power'? And how he knew the amount of the kickback? But why would UCAI help David? They had a contract out on the man's life. And they'd employed the NSA to carry it out.

Jimmy watched in fascinated horror as this creature he'd created slowly and painfully lifted a briefcase onto the footstool and removed a wodge of paper – easily recognizable as the bulk of Aloysia's enclosures – and started through the pages.

'Who could have expected a gift like this?' the David creature asked, mouth twisting a little, cigarette dangling, smoke curling up. 'I can't tell you how pleased . . . No, not "pleased". I can't think of a word that describes it. Thought maybe I was hallucinating. I *was* looking for something from Aloysia – she had to be your source for the bigamy charge – but I certainly didn't expect *this*.' He ran a loving hand over the pages. 'Anyhow, most of it's technical. I can't catch more than a gist of what she's saying, but scattered throughout, there are a number of letters, notes, clips from a diary, printed-out emails. They do make a picture. The boring part – the technical stuff – seems to be a sketchy outline of some brew she'd cooked up a couple of decades ago that killed a bunch of rats. She was certain that British secret services would fall all over themselves to get at it. The first person she sent her research to simply lost it. The second held onto it for a year, then said the delivery system was too complex for practical use. There was a third – she clearly didn't have the right contacts – and she ended up only with the reputation of a nuisance. After that, she couldn't get a look-in. She fought with colleagues, accused them of stealing her ideas, started in on crack, abandoned it with the help of a local hash dealer in Keble College.'

David took out another cigarette, lit it from the one in his mouth. 'What she really wanted to lay out for future generations began five years ago at a party in London' – David opened to a page about a third of the way through the wodge of paper – 'where she ran across an American called Francis Slad.'

'So *that's* where he met her.'

Jimmy remembered his surprise when Francis told him that David had stolen his girl – Francis Slad? A *girl*? – and then his shock when he'd searched his iPad and found a microbiology student gossiping those five years ago in an *Oxford Times* blog:

Francis Slad is some American industrialist or something. What's he doing schmoozing with our own Aloysia Gonzaga?

Part of what had taken Jimmy aback was that a couple of his non-Council-approved sessions with Aloysia had been enough to let him in on her gift for sex as well as some of her less attractive personality traits. In bed – or anywhere else – she had a truly professional talent with men. He'd taken her home one night to make a meal of her, worn himself out, fallen into a stupor, got up for a glass of water towards morning – and found her going through his desk. She'd been completely unrepentant. Just shrugged, said she'd seen what she needed to see and walked out. He'd been very cautious in his dealings with her after that.

David's slit of an eye shut for a moment – Jimmy watched it transfixed – then opened again. 'The twin brothers hadn't yet made the strategic move in their great takeover of UCAI. They were jetting around Europe gathering up allies for it. The fat one had his wife along, but Francis? Hard to tell. I'd have said his taste ran to boys, but he and Aloysia hit it off at this London party, spent time together, smoked everything they could get their hands on. They met in Oxford a couple of weeks later for more of the same. He stayed at her house, talked about her work, commiserated with her attempts to get it recognized, promised to pull some strings for her. She was used to promises that came to nothing, didn't really expect these to and when she didn't hear from Francis Slad, she just tacked him onto her ever-growing hate list. Then Springfield offered her a two-year sabbatical—'

'She made a lot of contacts fucking Hugh Freyl.'

David nodded again. 'Somebody at the university suggested Cawkerville for supplies of any plants she wanted to smoke. That was back in January. In March, at just about the time UCAI was initiating secret talks with you – so many discussions about how to pressure the Midwest into privatizing – Cawkerville hosted the first outbreak of Springfield Fever.'

Jimmy jolted partway out of the fake Eames, fell heavily back into it; the chair squealed in protest. 'You're kidding me. That was real? I didn't believe a word of it. Don't believe a word of it now. She said—'

'"I have incontrovertible evidence",' David interrupted, reading from the sheet in front of him, '"that UCAI has stolen my patent. I can now only assume that Springfield's plans to privatize bodes ill for the future of the town's water supply."' David ran his hand again over the pages in front of him. 'I really didn't expect to find a treasure like this. She'd taken samples at Cawkerville. Their water supply was swarming with the microscopic whatever that she'd created, patented and tried to flog to the British secret services: Springfield Fever.'

Jimmy glanced at the mess that had been David's face, winced despite himself, leaned back in the fake Eames so he didn't have to look at it. 'She emailed me about that too. You can't believe anything she says. Nobody could. She had a truly weird imagination.'

'Her notes record interviews with Cawkerville people who told her that they ran a regular supply to Francis Slad. Apparently they were quite proud of the contact. Protective of it too, mentioned it only because she was so concerned about their health.'

Jimmy shook his head. 'That's the dumbest part of all. She kills her rats in a nice little lab in far-off Oxford. If UCAI is experimenting on Cawkerville – and making plans for Springfield – they're going to need their own supply. For all I know, they'll need truckloads of it. Somebody's got to manufacture it. Come on. Gimme a break. Who are they going to get to do that? Some outfit in Peoria? You have to have special licenses for that kind of work.'

'In America, yes,' David said.

'My point exactly.'

'Ever been to Gary, Indiana?'

David sketched for Jimmy what Jane Doe had explained to him from behind a mesh screen. As she'd told him, US pharmaceuticals tended to be made where profits were highest and wages lowest: India, Venezuela, Egypt, Pakistan. Workers skimmed off drugs for sale to customers on the Net and to private contractors like Medical Services Direct. They also ran small, unregulated labs to do jobs for special customers. Manufacturing Aloysia's patented *cryptosporidium* was just another order to fill, and importing it was just another shipment. Medical Direct's courier picked it up at Gary International Airport along with supplies for South Hams and the rest of UCAI's prisons.

When David stopped talking, Jimmy stared at him a moment, then got up. He sat down. Got up again, bolted to the downstairs toilet – black porcelain, heated slate floor, cost a fortune – and threw up, leaned on his haunches, then threw up again. David seemed to be dozing as before when he managed to stagger back to the living room. Jimmy had been very little when he saw Lon Chaney in the old black and white movie of *Frankenstein*; he'd had nightmares for weeks about that shambling wreck.

It took him a while to control his voice. 'They told me it wasn't cholera,' he said at last.

'I know.'

'They said just to sit on it.'

'I know,' David repeated.

'They'd thought, just a little outbreak of something. Very mild. Stomach flu. Gastroenteritis. Nobody'd ever know. The pipeline from the aquifer – the pumping stations too – they don't show up on utility maps. All it'd take was a little electrical blip in the control room, and nobody could ever trace the entry point. They hadn't counted on the flood. Funny thing is, they didn't need an outbreak, but they'd already done whatever they'd done. It was too late.'

'That's what they said? Something "very mild"?'

'Just enough to scare people. That was the idea, but I never got any impression – I swear to you – that it would be so—'

'What about the "accident"?' David interrupted.

'"Accident"? Oh, that. Those twins ... There was talk of some hose that sprung a leak or something. It didn't make much sense to me, but then I didn't really want to dwell on how they were going about it. I've never been sure what gastroenteritis—' He broke off, took in a breath, and the words ripped out of him. 'You *are* going to kill me, aren't you?'

David sighed. 'You know what the real pity is? I told Helen that if I beat you to death, I'd shove those glasses up your prick first. I'd enjoy that. It breaks my heart to tell you that neither is an option for a man of means like me. If I hadn't found all these glorious papers of Aloysia's, I might have had to exert a little gentlemanly force, but this material ...' David took in a breath of appreciation. 'It's far more than I'd figured I'd get by sticking your hand in the kitchen grinder — far more than I needed. Kill you though? No. I've brokered a deal, and I never go back on a deal.'

'A deal?'

David replaced Aloysia's pages in his briefcase, snapped it shut, took hold of it and pulled himself painfully out of the Eames. 'Quite frankly, I don't see how anybody could swallow the idea of you masterminding as ruthless and daring a plan as poisoning a town to scare it into privatizing its water, much less having the guts to carry—'

'I had nothing to do with this. Nothing!"

'Doesn't matter. There'll be plenty on your iPad to build a case around you. Aloysia's emails to you certainly look like proof that you knew about the "incontrovertible evidence" *and* her Cawkerville investigations. The stupidest thing you did was to forward the information to the Slads. It upset them. They don't like being upset, and then they couldn't find the woman to mitigate the damage she might do. That was another upset. A bad one.

Since you knew all this stuff, they had to keep you on board until she showed up. They had to keep me around too, just in case I was hiding her somewhere. Now that she's dead, they have no use for either of us.' David paused. 'Or rather they have no use for you. Fortunately, I found a way to make myself valuable to them.'

'I swear to Christ, I had nothing—' Jimmy broke off, tears rolling down his cheeks. 'You've got to believe me. I wouldn't do anything like that. I *couldn't*.'

David was also learning that rich men don't have to take responsibility for what they do. 'I'm just looking into this for a colleague, Mr Mayor,' he said, patting the briefcase. 'I'm afraid nobody cares whether I believe you or not.'

61

SPRINGFIELD: A few minutes later

It was David, briefcase in hand, who opened the door to two policemen. He nodded towards the living room as he left.

The two cops found Jimmy slumped in the fake Eames, tears still rolling down his cheeks.

'Mr Zemanski?'

Jimmy looked up. 'Greg?' he said in astonishment. Tall, gawky Greg owed him. Getting the kid off a charge of rape — rape of an underage boy at that — hadn't been easy. Jimmy even managed to get the record erased, and now Greg had reached the level of Detective Sergeant. The work had been a personal favour; Greg's uncle was Commissioner and an important client of Jimmy's. Of course, he was one of the clients whose account had helped swell Jimmy's election fund, but neither he nor his nephew knew anything about that.

'How the hell did you get in here?' Jimmy went on.

'Door was open.'

'Well, fuck it all, however you got in, you have no idea how glad I am to see you, but why in the name of Christ didn't you take David Marion? He was right *here*. You know he killed Aloysia Gonzaga because she was going to expose him, and she—'

'Mr James Zemanski,' Greg interrupted, 'I have a warrant for your arrest for—'

'What!' Jimmy cried, only half hearing the words.

'—the murder of Morris Kline.'

'For the murder of—? What is this? Some kind of joke? You're out of your fucking mind. Where's your uncle? Call your uncle.'

'You have the right to remain silent . . .'

David's revelations had shaken Jimmy to the core, but now that David was gone, the idea that Jimmy himself could be charged with responsibility for the Springfield epidemic was too ludicrous to be terrifying. It would never play in court. Morris Kline? Well, yes, it just could – except for its ramifications. UCAI's security guy Huxtable had given the orders for Morris's Chicago trip as well as the rumour that the poor bastard had taken a bribe. Maybe Jimmy couldn't prove that. Besides, the more he thought about it, the more he thought Huxtable had to be NSA and the NSA survives everything. Jimmy couldn't kid himself into believing he'd ever see Aloysia's 'legacy' again, but Aloysia's patent, her emails to him, the very fact that he'd forwarded them to the Slads: together they could lay bare something that would shake the world. UCAI would sink in shit. No way were the big boys of government going to let that happen.

So what was *really* going on in this arrest?

Greg's hands on Jimmy's shoulder – steadying him to be cuffed – abruptly brought back a childhood Sunday school lesson. The verses appear in Leviticus, a difficult book, a lawyer's book. First there's something about a laying on of hands, just like Greg's, that transforms the innocent into the bearer of all transgressions – Jimmy strained to remember the words – 'and the goat Azazel shall take upon him all the sins', and something, something, we shall 'kill the goat' and 'dip our fingers in his blood'.

There's just so much a person can take. The pain in Jimmy's head began as a flash of that goat's blood. He'd never felt a pain like it, fire and ice that exploded into a pounding agony behind his left eye. The room around him tilted sideways. Eames chairs, Murano bowl with David's cigarettes: all slithered towards his peripheral vision. The final words of Greg's Miranda caution came out as an animal's yammering.

Jimmy tried to say he really *was* the innocent in all this, but his words too came out as nothing but yammering. And yet nothing seemed unreal, not the pain, not the yammering, not even finding himself suspended somewhere near the ceiling while he watched the cops support him out of the house. They were gentle – he appreciated it too – but his right foot dragged behind him like the club end of a tree trunk. It didn't even seem unreal to remain suspended at ceiling height during the entire time it took them to transport him to the squad car, drive him to the police station, put him into a cell there. For the next four hours, he lay in a foetal position in a police cell while the James Zemanski he'd known for forty-nine years dissolved into the iron cot beneath him.

Towards dawn, the charges against him escalated abruptly: bioterrorism and the murder of eight hundred and twenty-three citizens of Springfield, Illinois. Early morning newscasts announced the charges; they added a discussion of rumours flying about that Mayor Zemanski had suffered a cerebrovascular 'incident' during his rendition to Guantanamo Bay for safeguarding until his trial.

62

ST LOUIS: Late November

Aloysia Gonzaga? The coroner's official ruling was 'Accidental Death'.

As for the Marriage certificate that proved David's bigamy – if nothing else – somehow it got lost in the shuffle of papers from the active file on David Marion to safekeeping in the evidence room. Since it wasn't available for forensic examination, it could just as well have been a fake. If anybody had followed up the case – nobody did – they'd have found a copy of the marriage in the Knox County Recorder's Office, but why would anybody try? All that was left as evidence against this member of the Freyl family were letters from a lovelorn prisoner and a birth certificate naming that prisoner as the father of a child who'd died.

Nor was any trace ever found of the papers David took away from Jimmy's house. Not that anybody had any reason whatever to look for them. And yet those papers did exactly what Jimmy thought they would: they shook the world, even if only a select few were aware of it at the time.

As Jimmy himself was on his way to Guantanamo, fevered negotiations were going on in high places. The announcement of the result came in late November. Christina Haggarty held a press conference in the Follaton Tower with Francis and Sebastian Slad at her side. Behind them, a huge screen held the simple initials: IPWAC.

'Ladies and gentlemen,' she said to the cameras, 'the events in Springfield, Illinois, make a terrifying and tragic episode in United States history. Nothing can repair the damage done to the people of that city or the scar left behind on the American soul. If any good has come out of this terrible evil, it is that at long last we have learned our lesson. It's a simple enough lesson. Water is our greatest resource, and it is profoundly vulnerable. We *must* protect it.'

A murmur of assent went up from the gathering of reporters.

'But protection brings us up against a dilemma: the old way of doing things versus the harsh necessities of the modern world. Not until the Twin Towers did we grasp how imminent the threat of terrorism is. Not until Springfield have we . . .' She paused, shut her eyes, took in a breath. 'Nearly a thousand people had to pay with their lives to make us understand that bioterrorism is as great a threat as bombs, artillery, airplanes. We are just going to have to give up some of our ancient rights to ensure our survival here and now.'

The flash of cameras was almost continual. 'So how do we go about protecting ourselves? Not an easy answer. It took years of negotiation to establish an International Monetary Fund to protect our financial system and an International Atomic Energy Agency to protect our nuclear resources. They not only do their job supremely well, they serve us as a template. We at Galleas International and our new partners at UCAI have joined with the US government, the Canadian government, the European Union and a dozen of our most valued major enterprises to form an entirely new world entity: The International Protection of Water Consortium.'

She gestured at the screen behind her and the logo IPWAC. 'Hereafter, no citizen of the countries in which this regulatory agency operates will have to fear the inadequate regulation that our old-fashioned, inadequately protected, publicly owned systems failed so sadly to deliver in Springfield. As of today, all public utilities will begin dismantlement.'

She bowed her head. 'Now I come to James Zemanski. At nine-thirty yesterday evening, this man died of the massive stroke he'd suffered en route to Guantanamo Bay.'

Pandemonium broke out in the lobby of Follaton Tower. Nobody had heard this news, and it ensured headlines on front pages for an announcement that otherwise might have languished in financial sections. Security guards needed a five full minutes to restore order. Only then did Christina go on.

'The loss of any human life – even his – is sad. But in his case what's saddest of all is that we'll never know *why* he did what he did. We'll never know *how* he did it either. We can only guess and fear. Terrorism comes in all forms and sometimes – as in the case of James Zemanski – in the person of somebody we thought we knew. Somebody we trusted. That really hurts. We *trusted* him.' She paused again, took in another breath, then looked directly at the cameras.

'The International Protection of Water Consortium is not only the best way we can protect ourselves, it is the *only* way. We can't afford another Zemanski. Ladies and gentlemen, we simply cannot afford it.'

63

SPRINGFIELD: March

When Louis XIII was born, cannon resounded throughout Paris. When an heir to Spain is born, there's a salvo of twenty-one guns. But fireworks celebrated America's Lincoln on his bicentennial, and they were Becky's choice for the first male Freyl in sixty years.

The ice storm was God's contribution. Ice storms belong in Canada. Illinois doesn't have them any more than it has last summer's droughts and floods. A sandwich of cold air with a filling of warm air means that snow starts as regular snow, melts, then *super*-cools: too damned cold even to freeze. Everything it touches gets an even coat of ice all around, not frost, ice as clear as plate glass and gloriously beautiful. Dangerous too: a quarter of an inch adds five hundred pounds of weight. Branches on massive trees snap like twigs. Electricity pylons crash to the ground.

But the famous Freyl lawns were lit up like a fairground as the weather moved in. A string quartet played in the dining room, visible to the many guests but muted. In the living room, three servers stood behind Becky's mahogany table, one carving crowns of well-aged mutton flown in from Keens Steakhouse in New

York, another at work on game birds piled high, the third over a whole wild salmon. Everybody who was anybody milled about in the conservatory with champagne flutes. Security was heavy. A couple of sleek young men in black – headphones, earpieces, expressionless faces – made no attempt to look discreet. They were part of the celebration, a presence that heightened the importance of the event as well as the guests' excitement and sense of privilege.

The security had nothing to do with Becky; she didn't need it any more. Nobody was worried about the new mayor of Springfield either, nor even about the governor of the State of Illinois. The three people here that other people might want to kill were international royalty: Christina Haggarty, CEO of the newly formed GalleasUCAI and Director of the newly formed IPWAC – maybe a woman in form but, like Elizabeth I, every inch a king – and her two vassals, Francis and Sebastian Slad, Joint Chairmen of the Boards of both organizations.

In addition to their usual brief, the security officers were to listen for signs of dissent. Becky had withdrawn the Coalition's suit against UCAI. She'd had no choice: publicly owned utilities were now against the law. Even so, there was a lot of anger about the idea of a corporate-driven regulatory agency with the power to enforce privatization. Some members of her Coalition of Concerned Citizens had joined with Greenpeace and various other environmental groups to form an international opposition.

No such people had been invited this evening. The two security officers wandering through the guests caught only grumbling on the subject:

'. . . water prices *doubled* in the single month of December . . .'

'. . . pipes on Washington Boulevard broken for *weeks* . . .'

'. . . the stench of sewage *again* . . .'

Mostly though, gossip concentrated on the new baby and Becky's vibrant health: not even a hand at the elbow now, a gait as steady as it ever had been. The only talk with guts to it concentrated on the uneasy regrouping of opinion about the baby's father. David Marion had fathered a male heir for the Freyls. That changed everything. Becky's tongue was no longer acid on the subject of her grandson-in-law, which left the elite of the west side alone with a puzzled, defeated resentment. But it would pass. Shifts of power in the town were common. Shifts of allegiance went with them. Meantime, there was Becky's flowing champagne, toasts to the newborn, plates of mutton and salmon, black ties and glittering jewellery.

Towards midnight God made a second contribution. He eased the storm so fireworks could begin across the Freyl lawns in isolated flashes of light that exploded into a criss-cross of fire fountains with perfect spheres floating above. A canopy outside protected David and Helen from the cold while they watched.

'It's your baby they're celebrating,' Helen said to him, leaning into the warmth of his arms.

'No it isn't.'

'Ours then.'

'He doesn't even look like me.'

'Oh, David darling, fortunately *nobody* looks like you.'

David's face had arrived at an Elephant Man stage, but it would heal. Faces do. Helen was uncomfortably aware that she rather liked him as a gargoyle off a church. There's something vulnerable about a gargoyle. 'You didn't do *any* of this to protect me and Grandma, did you?' she said, not irritated, only amused.

He shrugged. 'Too complicated.' Not really true. The deal David had brokered was blindingly simple: turn Jimmy over to Christina with sufficient evidence against UCAI for her to force the Slads to their knees and wrest control of IPWAC for herself. The choice she'd presented them with was stark. Somebody had to take the fall for Springfield Fever. The only two candidates were UCAI and Jimmy Zemanski. David's reward? Removal of the UCAI contract on his life. If he told Helen about that, it would scare her, and she wasn't altogether rational when she got scared.

But she wasn't so easily put off either. 'Come on, David, damn you. Answer me. Did you do *any* of this for Grandma and me?'

'Some of it.'

'And the rest?'

'I don't like being pushed around.'

Helen removed her gloves and found the postcard she'd been carrying with her since she'd uncovered it in Aloysia Gonzaga's house: a Mississippi sidewheeler and the single word 'Remember?' where the address should be. The fireworks burst into chrysanthemums and peonies, croisettes, pearls, spinners, swirls. In the light they gave, she showed it to him.

'I figure you were just about twenty when you wrote this,' she said.

He took it from her, looked it over, nodded. 'How'd I miss it?'

'She kept it in a math book. Nobody looks in math books. Except me. Jesus, though, I searched that damned place – up, down, inside out – for *any* trace of a laptop, iPad, cell phone. I was certain there'd be something about you on one of them.'

'Possible.'

'You took them?'

He nodded again. 'She wasn't a good person.'

'You only kill bad people?'

'I try to discriminate.' He glanced at the card once more, frowned, looked down at her. 'It's a limitation in a Freyl, isn't it?'

'Killing only bad people?' She stroked his arm. 'I imagine it's a limitation you're stuck with.'

A final rocket opened out into a gold shell and disintegrated into stars that drifted to the ice-covered ground below.

'You don't think . . .' David began, then paused. 'I'm not sure a man as rich as me should have limitations. You think maybe you could teach me to overcome them?'

Helen studied the lopsided cheeks – the eyes were almost back to the eyes she'd known – then laughed delightedly. 'Now that is *really* going to be fun.'

They went back inside as the storm built up again, the party ended and the guests went out to their cars to brave their way home through the ice.

Acknowledgements

A book with a disease as a central character calls for medical expertise that I just don't have, and my first thanks go to Dr Tim Manser and Dr Tony Maggs; between them they built me a bug to fit my symptoms and provided many fascinating medical and microbiological details along the way. A good number of sociological ones too. For the same reasons, I want to thank my niece Tanya Syfers, who has a wonderful eye for detail.

I needed help in other techniques too. My cousin Eleanor Barrett, ex-prosecutor — who read the manuscript in more versions than anybody could have wanted to — made many excellent suggestions on the law. So did my correspondent Ellen Shaffer, who came through my sister Judy Brady; both of them shed truly scary lights into some of the dark corners of international profit-making. As for city government, my dear friend Sylvia Sutherland, five-term mayor of Peterborough, Ontario, did what she could to give me some idea what goes on there. And thanks also to Kasimierz Debek and Piotr Buzdygan, who were endlessly patient in working out ways to construct a canal using labourers instead of machines.

I owe so much to my superb editor Suzanne Baboneau that I can't quite tie it down. I also owe a very great deal to my persevering agent John Saddler. As to my son Alexander Masters and his partner Flora Dennis: how can I ever thank them? They read, suggested, discussed, analysed, supported, encouraged throughout, even spent a gloriously drunken Christmas working on pages with me.

But no list of thanks could be complete without a nod to the South Hams District Council, whose relentless attacks gave me practical lessons in how to hate and whose name fits so neatly as a 'facility' in the singularly unpleasant US penal system. Nor can any list be complete without a final thankyou to Nigel Butt, who rescued me from their clutches.

**Two stunning biographical novels from
the award-winning author Joan Brady.
Available exclusively in ebook.**

Theory of War

Costa/Whitbread Book of the Year Award 1993.
Forced into slavery as a child, Jonathan Carrick escapes to
a new life but within him lies the need for revenge against
George Stokes, the son of his former master.

Mallory Carrick, confined to a wheelchair, seeks to find
out the truth about her grandfather's history.

Haunting, elegant and passionate, *Theory of War* is a novel
about how the past lives on through following generations.
It follows one woman's journey to discover what her
grandfather might have experienced and how
his suffering still haunts his descendants.

Ebook ISBN 978-1-84983-953-2

The Unmaking of a Dancer

Shedding light on the raw, fiercely competitive
and often vicious world of ballet: this is the truth
behind the fiction of *Black Swan*.

Ballet was the first thing Brady was good at, and lessons
and performances kept her away from her unpredictable
father and formidable mother. But nobody can stay away
for good, and when she finally made it into the New York
City Ballet, her mother delivered a career-destroying blow.
And yet with the help of the love of her life, Dexter
Masters, she found another way of living and
the chance for a family of her own.

Ebook ISBN 978-1-84983-954-9

Joan Brady
Bleedout

'Dangerously deceptive and steeped in shocking betrayal . . . a masterclass in suspense' Val McDermid

Hugh Freyl is the most respected lawyer in Springfield, Illinois. That he is blind only enhances his reputation: justice should be blind. And yet late one night, in the library of his law firm, he is savagely beaten to death.

There is just one obvious suspect: David Marion, a convicted killer from the wrong side of the tracks. Hugh himself secured David's release from a brutal maximum security penitentiary. David has never seemed grateful.

But how much – or how little – does it take to make a man kill . . . ?

Paperback ISBN 978-1-41650-209-8
Ebook ISBN 978-1-84983-951-8

Joan Brady
Venom

Betrayal is the deadliest poison of all . . .

Recently released from prison, David Marion didn't expect
to find a hitman at his door. Warned that a powerful secret
organisation is after him, David goes underground and
off the radar – waiting for the perfect moment
to wreak revenge.

Mourning the recent death of her lover, physicist
Helen Freyl has just accepted the offer of a research post
at a giant pharmaceutical company. She joins a team close
to finding a cure for radiation poisoning, which will not
only save lives but make millions for the company. But
when a colleague dies in mysterious circumstances, Helen
starts to doubt her employers' motives. And when
she realises that her own life is in danger, too,
she knows she has to act fast . . .

Venom brings David and Helen together as they fight
for their lives against a backdrop of industrial espionage,
corporate greed and human tragedy in this exhilarating and
fast-paced follow-up to Joan Brady's bestselling *Bleedout*.

Paperback ISBN 978-1-41650-210-4
Ebook ISBN 978-1-84983-952-5